THE VALKYRIE'S CALLING

HALF-BLOOD RISING BOOK 2

LUCY ROY

To Agents GB and JB

Jotunheim
Lindoroth
Feld River
Lake Robron
Madrya
Greyonne
Caelora
Kildin
Selnor River
Iston
Palace
Bay Of Brystone
Watoria
Iladel
Aldridge Academy
Allanor
Rimar River
Saith
Port of Iladel
Olthanas
Errest
Gefhorn River
Edhil
Edhilian Desert

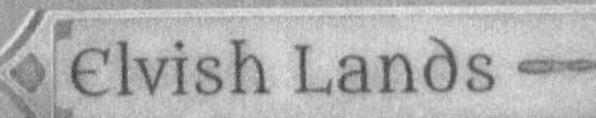

Elvish Lands →

Dystone
Teid
Port of
Caldel
Caldel
Aren
Vindarria
Leford

Moors
Summer Court
Andradath
Morhalo
Forg
of
Age

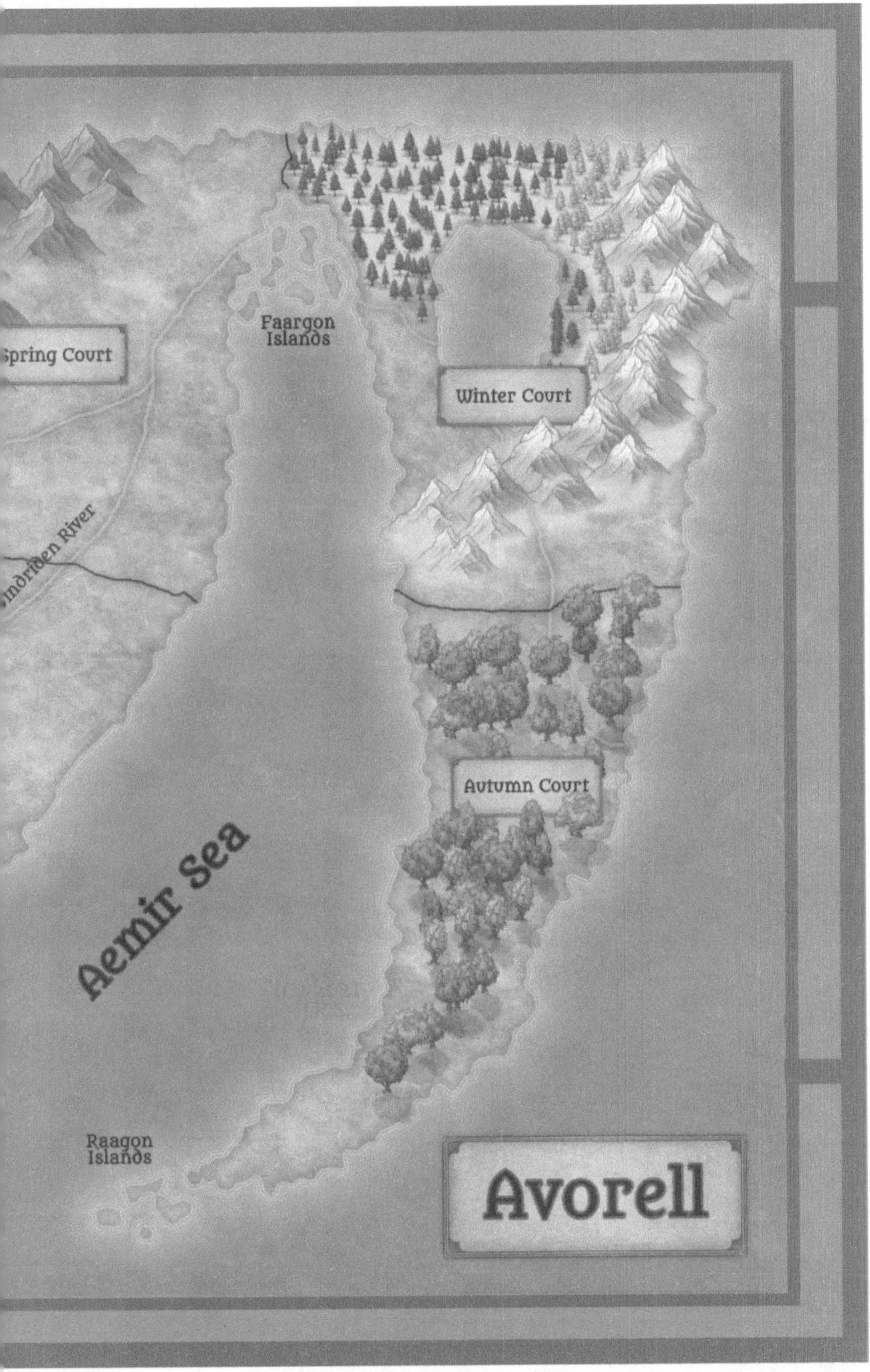

Spring Court
Faargon Islands
Winter Court
Aemir Sea
Autumn Court
Raagon Islands
Avorell

PRONUNCIATION GUIDE

Freya – Fray-uh
Aerelius – Air-el-yus
Grevillea – Gruh-vil-ya
Lazarus - Laz-uh-rus
Collin – Col-lin
Byrric – Bir-ric
Salazar – Sal-uh-zar
Ordona – Or-doh-na
Myria – Meer-ya
Dystone – Dis-tone
Jotunheim – Yot-un-hime
Lindoroth – Lin-duh-roth
Haegin - Hay-gin
Naedan - Nay-din
Nalaea - Nuh-lay-uh
Ruehnar - Roo-nar
Ratatoskr - Ra-ta-tos-ker

1

LEA

There was a time in Lea Calliwell's life when she would've sworn to do anything for her family. It had always been easy to say she would lie for them if it meant keeping them safe, debase herself or die for them, even, because that's what family does.

Now, as she stared up at Lessia Edrin and Willem Ristner, the two royals who'd so swiftly usurped the thrones of Lindoroth, her hand clinging tightly to Jonas,' she couldn't help but wonder if that sentiment had been a bit too broad, a bit too naïve in thinking.

Lessia's elbow rested on the arm of the throne she was perched upon—Ordona's throne—as she eyed Lea and Jonas. The knights who were scattered about the room sat silent as they waited for her to speak. Finally, she tapped a long, pale finger on her chin and pursed her lips.

"Alright, Jonas. Let's say I buy this," she gestured toward Lea, "and allow her to live. Let's say I buy that you two are now... lovers. How are we to believe she won't turn on us at the first chance? This was her uncle's palace, after all. We *are* responsible for the deaths of a good number of her family members." She arched a perfect brow at Lea. "Including her father."

Lea swallowed but held her chin high as she met Lessia's piercing stare. "A cruel man, Empress. The main reason I insisted upon attending Aldridge was to get away from my home in Edhil." The words were like ash on her tongue, thick and bitter as she forced them past her lips. She set her mouth in a thin line and took a deep breath. "I can assure you, when Lord Edrin informed me of his death, I was not disappointed."

The corners of Lessia's perfectly red mouth twitched. "Interesting."

"And quite convenient," Willem drawled. "The cousin of the *former* prince of Lindoroth is happy with the outcome of tonight's events?"

Jaw tight, Lea shifted her gaze to the human king who'd taken up residence on Salazar Harridan's throne and made herself the picture of disdain. "I did not say I was *happy*, Your Majesty. My uncle was quite beloved, as is my aunt, and I love my mother dearly." She squeezed Jonas' hand and smiled up at him before looking back at Lessia. "But Lord Edrin has shown me a different side of the Jotnar people in recent weeks. He's told me things about your lands, Empress, that go against everything I've ever been told."

"And what *have* you been told, dear?" Lessia asked, leaning forward. Her eyes danced, as though this were a game and she was waiting for Lea to step into some trap.

"That you are a cruel and unforgiving people. That your rule is one of fear, not respect, and you only managed to stay in power after your husband died because you killed all who attempted to oppose you." Lea looked around the room at the dozens of Jotnar and human knights that milled about. "Yet your people are happy, according to Lord Edrin. I wouldn't expect that to be the case if people were living in fear of their ruler all the time."

"And this..." Lessia inclined her head toward their conjoined hands. "Why wasn't I informed of this sooner, Jonas? You seemed quite happy at the wedding, certainly, yet this is the first I'm hearing of any type of relationship?"

"It didn't seem pertinent," he replied. "You've never required me to report what I did during my spare time on previous trips and I saw no need."

"Even though this girl was so clearly unhappy here?" Willem asked. "It would've been nice to know of a potential ally before this."

"Had I known what you both intended, perhaps I would've seen a better use for this relationship," Jonas said through gritted teeth. "As it stands, she and I both think she could go a long way in solidifying your new rule, at least in the southern realm."

"I'm surprised you even took up with her in the first place," Willem commented. "The palace staff haven't been enough for you?"

Jonas sent the human king a bland look. "Do I strike you as the type to be amused by servants, human?"

Willem's face purpled, then his furious glare shifted to Lea. Something in his eyes nearly had Lea scrambling to hide behind Jonas, but she forced herself to meet them.

"Well, as tempting as this idea is, you'll have to wait," Willem told Jonas. His gaze dragged across Lea's body. "We have more important things to address, and I think there are a few here who might also like to make a case for her."

Lea froze, and Jonas' hand tensed in hers.

The look of pure disgust Jonas threw at Willem made it quite clear what he thought of the human king. "I don't recall asking your permission. What's mine is certainly not yours."

"You are not in charge here," Willem said calmly.

Jonas bared his teeth in a grin so cruel and so unlike the male she'd gotten to know, that Lea would've feared for the king if she wasn't so eager for his demise.

"Unfortunately, nephew, Willem is correct," Lessia said tiredly when Jonas took a menacing step forward. "I've had no sleep, and as it's now dawn, I won't discuss divvying spoils until I've had a few hours rest."

"I haven't asked to claim her as spoils," Jonas said evenly. "She is not my belonging. I've brought her to you as a potential ally."

"Indeed," Lessia said with a nod. "And while your stories are quite convincing, I'm not quite ready to allow the niece of Salazar Harridan loose in my palace without proper consideration first."

Lea forced back tears as she realized just how bad a turn this had taken.

"Yes, how are we to know she hasn't simply whored herself out to you in order to get a foot into our court?" Willem added, his gaze not leaving Lea. "You may not be the best judge of character in this instance. Someone else may need to bring her in hand, first."

"She will remain with me," Jonas growled. "If you so much as touch her—"

Lessia made a sound of disgust. "Enough. You can sort that all out later." She tilted her head in a small, predatory motion as she eyed Lea. "Not to worry, sweet thing. I find your story to be...tempting, and until Jonas' request has been granted or denied, you'll be kept perfectly safe."

Before Lea had a chance to look at Jonas for any measure of comfort, Lessia flicked a slender hand toward one of her guards. He was half-draug, by the looks of it, and smelled of death, with yellow teeth that flashed behind his bile-brown lips. Gnarled hands gripped her curly hair at the roots as he jerked her toward the door.

"Jonas!" she screamed. "Stop them!"

"Walk, witch!" the guard snapped.

"Lessia, this is unnecessary!" Jonas shouted. "Where are you taking her?"

With a scream, Lea rounded on the guard who'd grabbed her, shoved him to the floor, and ran toward the exit, knowing it was useless but needing to try all the same.

This had gone wrong, so horribly wrong.

She made it nearly halfway to the door before she was tackled to the ground by two human knights. When she lashed out with her magic, calling forward the thorny stems of the roses that still decorated the room to aid her, one of the knights slammed her head to the ground and set her world spinning. Jonas gave a shout, and the next moment, a powdery substance hit her face and everything went black.

~

WHEN SHE STARTED to come to, the gray-blue light of evening filtered through her eyelids, drawing her out of the fogginess of her mind.

A hissing sound brought her forward a little more. It was a bit like a cat, only not.

"Grevillea!"

No. Not a sound, a voice.

Her mother's voice.

Lea's eyes flew open, and her eyelids slammed shut at the sudden onslaught of light. Her body screamed in protest as she tried to shift her position on the damp and dirty dungeon floor, and her head swam with each movement.

Perida Calliwell let out a relieved breath when Lea stirred.

Lea carefully pulled herself into a sitting position and leaned back against the wall, pressing a hand to her forehead. "How..."

"They brought you in just past dawn," Perida said quietly. "It's nearly nightfall."

Lea drew her legs up to her chest and rested her forehead on her knees as she tried to find her equilibrium. Whatever they'd tossed in her face before bringing her here was making it impossible for her to focus.

"What did they give me?" she murmured. "I can't feel my magic."

"Powdered widow venom, most likely. It's being put in our food."

Several moments of silence passed as her mother waited for Lea to speak. When Lea finally turned to look at her mother in the cell across the way, Perida, who'd been thrown in the dungeons much the same way she had, only a few hours before her, looked as though she'd been there for months. Her soft, dark hair was a knotted mess, and her pretty golden skin and ice-blue gown were caked with blood. And, though her body seemed unbroken, the hollow-eyed look she wore told Lea her spirit was anything but intact.

Lea could only assume the blood was her father's, but that wasn't a truth she was willing to face just yet. No, she would tuck that away until she was in the proper setting for screaming out her grief. She would save that anger and sadness, bottle it up tight, and let it out the moment she had the chance on those who truly deserved it. Not now. Not when she couldn't properly grieve that loss, not when she couldn't watch her father be put to rest. As it was, whatever they'd used to knock her unconscious was making it hard enough to grab hold of the fact that her father was dead, that she'd never see him, nor her uncle, again. Dwelling on the wretched things so far outside her control would only make things worse.

"Where did they catch you?" Perida asked quietly.

"In the caves." Lea averted her eyes. "Jonas Edrin brought me back." She wasn't ready to tell her mother about the plan she and Jonas had come up with in the caves; a plan that had seemed nearly foolproof at the time, at least to her admittedly-inexperienced mind, that now seemed foolhardy at best.

They'd deemed the plan they'd made with Byrric—for Jonas to claim her as spoils—as imprudent, considering the circumstances. She needed to be able to act as a spy, and the length of time it would take for her to convincingly develop fealty to her captors was not conducive to helping Freya and Aerelius get their kingdom back.

So, they would pretend to be in love and she would pretend to be someone she was not.

She would spin the tale of a cruel father and an enabling mother. She would convince them how jealous she'd been of Aer, who'd had such an easy life in the palace with loving parents. And, most importantly, she would allow them to believe Jonas had convinced her that everything she knew of the Jotnar people, who were, in fact, cruel and unforgiving, was based on falsehoods and lies told by her parents.

Disgusting lies, all of them, but if she wanted to become privy to valuable information in a timely manner, they were a necessary evil.

"And the others?" Perida's eyes were vaguely hopeful. "Who else got away?"

Lea averted her eyes. "I'm not certain, Mother."

Perida slumped back against the wall morosely. "They killed your father."

Lea's hands curled into fists, her nails biting into her palms as she tried to halt the flood of tears that pressed behind her eyes.

Now is not the time, she reminded herself again.

"I know," Lea whispered, turning to pull herself closer to the prison bars. Her mother was no more than five feet away, but being trapped in this cell, where she couldn't even reach out to touch her hand in comfort, made the distance seem miles wide. "I'm so sorry, Mother. I wish I had been there."

Perida gave her a soft, pained smile. "No, Grevillea, you don't."

Lea stared at her, wondering how much she should tell her, or if it would be safer to just keep everything to herself.

"Have they harmed you?" Perida asked.

Lea shook her head. "No, Lessia said—" She clamped her mouth shut, but realization dawned on Perida's face.

"He—he's going to claim you as spoils, isn't he?" Perida rose to her knees and gripped her cell bars as something akin to hope lit in her eyes. "Is that what he said? Lea, do you know what that *means?*"

"He's not claiming—"

"It means no one can harm you until Lessia makes her decision," Perida pressed on, her words quiet and hurried. "And when she does, she will allow him to keep you with him, and he'd be a fool not to. The moment you get out of here, the moment he takes you to his room, you fight like hell, do you hear me? I don't care how you do it. You fight like mad and *get out.*"

Lea blinked. "Mother, I won't leave you here."

Perida let out a strangled laugh. "Oh, you most certainly will! If you get the chance, you leave and you *do not come back*, do you hear me? Don't spare me or anyone else here a second thought. I mean it, Lea. Promise me!"

But I came back for you.

Lea shook the thought off. It didn't matter what her mother said—she wasn't going to leave this palace without her.

"Alright, Mother. I promise."

❧

Despite the discomfort of the filthy pile of straw that acted as bedding, Lea managed to doze off now and then. Each stretch of sleep was fitful, fraught with nightmares and bursts of angry color. The cruel faces that haunted her, despite her waking knowledge that she was alive and not being tortured, brought on no small amount of fear.

It was two days before Lessia came to question her on the whereabouts and plans of Freya and Aerelius, who'd disappeared into the forest to head west toward Freya's home city of Watoria. It wasn't as vicious as Lea had expected of an interrogation with someone as feared as Lessia; the worst abuses being a few hard cuffs to the ear. Lea wasn't sure if Lessia decided she was lying or simply ignorant of her wayward monarchs' plans, but either way, Lea's relationship with Jonas seemed to keep Lessia from harming her too extensively.

On the fifth day, Lea had all but given up hope of Jonas coming for her.

By the seventh, as she looked down at the crude wooden tray on her lap that held a slice of moldy bread tainted with powdered widow venom, she'd decided she had made a terrible mistake in returning. Jonas either wasn't coming for her or...

No. She wouldn't think of any alternative.

She looked across the corridor to where her mother sat, staring down at her own meager meal, her face slack with grief, and sighed.

"He should've come for you by now," Perida said, setting aside her own tray. "I wonder why he hasn't?"

"I'm sure he will, soon enough."

She tried to be reassuring to keep Perida from losing even more hope, but she couldn't help but acknowledge just how little was left to cling to.

2

———

FREYA

Freya peered into the cave near the banks of the Selnor River that carved a path between Caelora and Allanor. Beads of frozen rain stung her cheeks and clung to her hair, the cold of which made the dry interior of the cave seem all the more welcoming. She conjured up a ball of light, then sent it drifting into the dim interior, illuminating the walls that stretched back several dozen feet.

She let out a quiet whistle, signaling to Aer.

He turned away from Florian and the others, then squinted into the trees, looking for her. When he caught sight, he tightened his cloak around his shoulders and made his way toward her.

"Our home for the evening?" he asked, eyeing the cave dubiously.

"There's no scent of anything living inside," she said. "It seems deep enough to house everyone, and getting out of this weather would be a good thing for all of us."

"Alright, I'll let the others know." He gave her a soft kiss on her temple, and she leaned into him, lacing her fingers through his.

"We should get a hunting party set up as well," she said. "It's been nearly a day since we've eaten anything substantial."

"I've already told Collin to organize it," Aer replied. He cast a glance over his shoulder, then stepped into the cave and drew her against his chest. "How are you doing?" he asked quietly. "I can feel your exhaustion."

She wrapped her arms around his waist and heaved a sigh. "I should be asking you that," she murmured. They'd hardly spoken of his father's death, or even had a chance to, since fleeing the palace a week ago. Their only goal had been to keep pushing their party of nearly thirty west toward the city of Watoria. There, they hoped to find word from her father, who'd promised to meet them, and a home base at the former home of her grandparents, Jora and Selinda Enri-eth, a manor to the south of the city that had been in her family for centuries. It remained heavily cloaked with Selinda's magic—long-lasting spells that only allowed entry to those given express permis-sion by Selinda's family—and would give them someplace safe to lay the rest of their plans. Their trek, a journey which would've taken, at most, four days by boat, was taking nearly thrice that on foot due to the circuitous route they'd been forced to take. Despite the glamours she and Florian had been weaving to obscure the appearances of their group, she and Aer felt a direct path to Watoria would be fool-ish, and Florian and their guards had agreed. So, they kept pace along the border between Caelora and Allanor, following the Selnor as it wended southwest, stopping each night as near a village as they would dare.

"I've got you," Aer replied after a moment, his words tense as he tightened his arms around her. "That's more than enough for now."

BY THE TIME they finished making camp an hour later, Freya wanted to do little more than collapse on the floor of the cave and fall asleep. The mounting exhaustion brought on by their exposure to the elements and the stress she bore due to the absence of her father, not to mention the burden she felt over the losses on her wedding night, had been wearing her down day-by-day. It wasn't something she cared to discuss with any of the others, whose losses had been just as great, if not more so. That she'd been draining her magic each day helping Florian wield an invisibility glamour over their party only made that exhaustion worse. She'd been hiding it quite well, in her opinion, but she'd noticed Florian eyeing her more than usual the last few days. When he'd offered to take on more of the share of magic-wielding so she could take a break that morning, she'd refused, but she was self-aware enough to know that that was more out of pride than a true belief that she didn't need a reprieve. The last thing she wanted was for anyone—her husband, in particular—to worry that she was struggling.

As she leaned against the cave wall and accepted the canteen of water that Aer had forced into her hand, she tried to ignore the twin looks of annoyance he and Florian had been casting her way.

"Your Majesty, I must insist on taking the larger share of this burden," Florian said, coming up to her. The tall, wiry warlock rarely held his tongue when he spoke to her or Aer and did little to hide his annoyance at her obstinance now. He knew far more than she did when it came to magic use, something she both appreciated and loathed at times. As he was currently trying to convince her to lessen her contributions to the well-being of her people, this was one of those times that leaned more toward loathsome.

She waved off his request and ignored her husband's glare. "It's fine, Lord Florian, truly."

"We still have three more days of travel, if we're lucky. I've been doing this far longer and don't tire nearly as quickly," he pressed.

Taking a sip from her canteen, she purposely ignored the unstated "as you" that was attached to the end of that sentence. "If I wanted to be scolded, Lord Florian, I would've insisted Byrric accompany us on this journey."

Florian sent her a level look, then glanced at Aer, who shook his head.

Before he could push further, Freya's aunt, Ana, appeared at her side, back from a scouting mission with Naedan and Amara, the hawk shifters that Byrric had assigned to act as scouts and messengers.

"Any news?" Freya asked, eager for the distraction.

"Some," Ana replied. "It's clear Lessia and Willem's knights know we're heading west, so we can only assume that they're expecting us to go to Watoria or perhaps Iston."

"How do you know?" Aer asked. They'd seen more than a few patrols the past week, some seemingly on the lookout for them, others rounding up any stragglers who may have escaped the towns and villages that dotted the countryside that had been attacked by the human and Jotnar knights. Now and then they'd witnessed a few prisoners being carted off, and as much as it pained her and Aer to stand by and not offer help, she knew they had little choice. Lindoroth needed their king and queen, and the only way they could ensure that end would be to get to Watoria undetected. The information they'd gleaned so far had been that Willem and Lessia were holed up in the palace in Iladel and had sent representatives to each capital, along with a small battalion of soldiers, to take control of the cities.

"There are more Jotnar and human patrols concentrated along the Selnor, and their numbers are increasing westward," Ana explained. "It would be my suggestion to veer away from the river, stick to the deeper forests for the rest of our journey. Let them split their troops between the north and south banks of the river."

Florian nodded. "Yes, that makes sense. Perhaps we'll detour south a bit before continuing west."

"If the patrols are expecting us in Watoria, Lessia and Willem must be as well," Freya murmured.

"Meaning, whoever they put there is likely one of their strongest and most trusted." Aer rubbed a hand across his brow. "Did you see any sign of Lindorothian soldiers?" Most notably absent on their journey had been knights from Lindoroth's five armies. Freya and Aer assumed they'd been directed toward the capitals, but when it became clear just how far-reaching Lessia's and Willem's attack had been, that assumption gave way to the knowledge that Lindoroth was likely on the verge of being completely overrun.

Ana shook her head, her expression grim. "None. My hope is that they're concentrated near the cities. But we'll learn more as we get closer. Lessia and Willem's plans might not be spread throughout all of their troops, but those who are closer to the city will know more. They wouldn't have placed a human there, at least not alone, no matter how skilled."

"Unlikely," Florian agreed. "Willem would've pushed for it, but Lessia is no fool."

"Debatable," Freya muttered.

Ana sent her a look before continuing. "I was hoping we'd receive word from Byrric by now, but it doesn't seem that'll be happening before we arrive. I overheard one of the Jotnar knights say Olthanas still seems salvageable, so I'm assuming that's where he's gone."

Freya's eyes automatically drifted to Myria Bryton, who was helping Isadora and a fox shifter named Amber sort out sleeping arrangements. Olthanas was the capital of Saith, Myria's home realm and the place her father, Emric Bryton, had governed for more than seventy years. Myria had been subdued this past week, her sharp tongue far more still than usual after the death of her father. Freya assumed she was holding in her grief just as much as everyone else, but she could only imagine how Myria felt, being unable to get to her family's seat and knowing her mother and brother were still held prisoner. The only thing that gave Freya cause to hope was that Olthanas was only considered salvageable to their enemies, which boded well for the rest of Saith and whatever Lindorothian soldiers had managed to make their way there.

As she watched Myria, who'd put on a brave face, despite it all, she could only pray that bit of news would give her some reason to hope, too.

"Freya?"

Freya turned her attention back to her aunt, who was looking at her with wide-eyed concern. "Yes?"

"I said that we'll need to sort out our plans tomorrow for our arrival in Watoria. I think it might make more sense for me to leave for Iston sooner rather than later, especially if we're going to detour south."

"How long will it take you to fly there from here?" Aer asked.

"Two days if I don't stop, three if I break for a few hours to rest. I'd prefer to wait another day or two to see if we get word from Byrric first, but I'd rather not delay too much longer. The Valkyrie need to be fully briefed and ready to launch an attack if needed."

"I'm sure we'll hear from him soon," Aer said.

His words were of little comfort to Freya, who knew her father's silence meant that he was either physically unable to send her a messenger or too occupied with enemy forces to take the time to.

"I have no doubts," Ana said. "My brother is nothing if not thorough, so if we haven't heard from him by now, it's because his focus is solely on the task before him." She gave Freya a pat on the arm. "Try not to worry, dear. We'll see him soon enough, and this isn't his first battle. In the meantime, rest. Give your magic a break for a day or two so you're at full strength when we reach Watoria."

Freya gave her a tight smile, then watched as her aunt and Florian walked away.

With a sigh, Freya cracked her neck and rolled her shoulders, still unable to shake her lingering discomfort, then sat down on the floor of the cave. Someone had gotten a fire going, and an air-user named Derrick had spread the heat throughout the space, giving the hard stone floor a soothing layer of warmth against the cold that had sunk into her bones.

"Freya," Aer said quietly, sliding down to sit beside her. He looked at her, annoyance clear in his eyes. "You should've told me it was your magic that was exhausting you, instead of letting me think it was just the travel."

She looked at him, searching his chocolate-brown eyes, and frowned. "Would you ask someone else to work harder just because you were feeling a bit peaky?"

Aer's brows lifted, but his answer was immediate. "If that someone was several centuries my senior and held far stronger magic than mine? Yes, without question. Just because you're the queen doesn't mean you have to exhaust yourself getting us to Watoria. It means quite the opposite, actually. Cast your glamours every day if you like, but there's no need to carry more of the burden than necessary."

Before she could reply, Collin appeared beside them, looking nearly as weary as Freya felt. "We managed to find a doe and a brace of rabbits. The doe should give us enough for tonight and a bit left for breakfast tomorrow." He glanced at Aer, then addressed Freya. "I saw a patch of witchbloom a few miles back, so I'm going to add some to your dinner. It will help with the fatigue."

She arched a brow. "For Florian as well, then."

"Florian doesn't need it," Aer told her the moment Collin walked away shaking his head. "You're being stubborn."

"My stubbornness is one of the many reasons you love me," she pointed out.

"Not when it's detrimental to your health." He huffed out a breath. "Please, Freya."

She heard the pain in his voice and could feel how much he hated asking her to limit herself. And yes, maybe she was being stubborn, but she couldn't help the feeling that she was—not for the first time —failing her people. To concede to her husband and Florian felt as though she were admitting defeat, admitting that she fell short in some way, even though the reasonable part of her mind told her that was patently false.

She met Aer's eyes and softened some when she saw the worry there. The gravity of it gave her pause as the weight of his own emotions mingled with hers. He'd lost his father, and his mother had been taken to an unknown location, someplace she'd only return from once they'd managed to eliminate the threats to their kingdom and their lives. Right now, they were nearly all the other had left. He'd forced a brave face this past week for their companions, but the pain was clear as day, both on his face and in the bond that ran between them.

Selfish. She was being selfish.

"I'm sorry," she whispered, taking his hand and lacing their fingers together.

"You can take care of yourself, Freya. I know that. But you need to know when to quit, when to accept help." He lifted her hand to his lips and kissed her knuckles, then brushed his thumb over the ruby ring that encircled her ring finger, a smaller, more delicate version of the one he wore. "You have nothing to prove to anyone, and needing to share a load like this doesn't make you deficient in any way. You and Florian might be the best here at casting glamours, but even the best of us need to pause from time to time."

She wrapped her hands around his and laid a kiss to his palm. "You're right. The last thing you need is to worry about me. If it will make you feel better, I'll take a break tomorrow."

"I think that would be for the best," he replied. "We all need to have our strength up when we near Watoria, and the last thing I want is a Valkyrie half-blood at diminished capacity." He grinned when she squawked out a protest and punched his side.

"I will throttle you, Aerelius Harridan! Don't test me."

"Ah, there she is," he murmured, putting an arm around her shoulders and kissing her temple. "What do you say, Valkyrie? Do you suppose with your waning strength, I'll be able to take down more Jotnar than you?"

"Why make a bet you know you can't win?"

He shrugged. "Under normal circumstances, that might be the case." He clicked his tongue and appraised her weary state. "Now, though... I wonder."

She rolled her eyes. "As much as I love you, I often find myself hating you."

"Impossible." He motioned for Rodrick, one of his guards, to come over before adding, "I'm going to make sure everyone is sorted. Go make up with Florian, will you?"

She smiled as he turned to speak with Rodrick. Then, tiredly, she looked around the cave, at the filthy faces of her companions, their clothing so sodden no mix of elemental magics could offer relief, and prayed they'd make it through the final days of their journey unscathed.

3

FREYA

It was well after sunset by the time everyone was settled in for the night, and a fire was crackling near the mouth of the cave. Once the guards were set and a watch scheduled, Florian and Freya combined their earth and air magic to barricade the entrance, obscuring them from passersby and ensuring no one came or left without their knowledge. Everyone took spots relatively near the fire as the game that had been caught were roasted and portions were handed out. Freya, Aer, Collin, Laz, and Myria sat toward the back of the cave, separating themselves a bit from the rest of the group but staying close enough to be present for the others.

Freya had just finished her food when Rini, the tiny palace pixie who'd taken a liking to her during her time at Aldridge, appeared at her side and clicked her tongue. Freya had been overjoyed when she saw that the pixie had been able to sneak out of the palace, only learning belatedly that Tyna had remained behind to tend to Lea, who, along with Jonas, was working out a plan to free the prisoners who'd been taken in the attack.

"Your Majesty, you must get some rest," Rini crooned, her brow furrowing as she flitted toward Freya and plucked a leaf from her hair. "Come, I've prepared a bed for you both—"

"In a bit," Freya told her, gently disentangling her hair from the pixie's small hands. "What news do you have?"

"Has there been any word from Tyna?" Aer asked.

Rini nodded, her shining lips set in a thin line. "This morning. I worry over her concerns regarding Lord Edrin and Lady Calliwell."

Freya and Aer exchanged a worried look. The most recent news Rini had gotten from her sister had been troubling. By Tyna's account, Lea had been thrown into the dungeons within minutes of returning to the palace with Jonas, despite their insistence that she was on their side. Meanwhile, Jonas looked to be going about his normal business, meeting frequently with Lessia and Willem to discuss plans to solidify their conquest of Lindoroth.

The only information Tyna had given of the other goings-on in the palace was that the other prisoners were alive, including Lazarus' mother, Collin's parents, Aer's aunt and cousins, Lea's mother, and Myria's mother. But, sadly, their circumstances in the dungeons were quite dire. Aside from that, Tyna had only seen Lea once, and that had been just a brief glimpse as Lea was being dragged from the throne room to the dungeons by a Jotnar guard.

"Both were sent back with a part to play," Aer said, sounding as though he needed to remind himself just as much as Freya did. "Unsavory as it is, we should all assume they're playing those parts as planned. If nothing else, the blood bond Jonas swore will keep her safe."

Freya nodded, although she was becoming increasingly unsure that was the case. She struggled not to picture Lea sitting in the cold and damp dungeons with the other prisoners, receiving nothing but meager portions of stale bread and gritty water. The gods only knew how much longer Lessia and Willem would see fit to keep any of the prisoners alive. Blood-bond or no, without Jonas' immediate protection, Lea would be the perfect target for the Jotnar and Dystonians, and all manner of horrid things done at their hands.

She shuddered at the thought.

"What about Iladel?" Collin asked. "Has Tyna managed to get out of the palace and into the capital yet?"

Rini bobbed nervously in the air beside Freya. "According to Tyna, there's a bit of a stalemate at the indoor market, which is where the citizens who managed to escape have barricaded themselves. All entrances have been successfully blocked by a group of witches and warlocks, and Lessia and Willem haven't sent more than a handful of Jotnar troops to attempt to infiltrate."

Myria frowned. "That hardly makes sense."

Aer shook his head. "No, it makes perfect sense. Iladel is one city, and they've already taken the throne. The dissent will be easy enough to squash once morale has weakened more, and if the citizens have barricaded themselves, that means they have limited supplies."

"Which also means they're of little threat to Lessia's and Willem's cause," Collin said with a nod. "They're not worth expending the energy of the knights."

Freya sighed. "What else?"

"Caelora's capital is not doing well," Rini replied, sending a sympathetic look at Laz. "It appears Kildin was hit first when the Jotnar invaded from the north, then again the next day when the humans came in from the sea. The last report Tyna heard was that the Caelorian and Royal Armies were struggling to hold the city."

Laz's jaw clenched as he took the hand Collin offered in comfort. "How bad has it gotten?"

Rini sighed. "I'm unsure, my lord. I'm certain we'll know more when I speak to her next."

"Word from the Commander would go a long way in easing our minds," Collin said, giving Laz a sympathetic look.

Freya leaned back against the wall. She looked at Laz and tried to give him a comforting smile. "It'll be alright, Laz."

He shook his head. "You can't know that."

"We can do our best to ensure it's the truth," Aer told him. "Our hands may be tied while we're here, but once we get to Watoria, we should have more to work with."

"What about Saith?" Myria asked Rini. "Have you heard anything from the capital?"

"At last report, circumstances were still tenuous in Olthanas," Rini replied. "I'm sorry, I wish I had more," she added when she saw Myria's disappointment. "For all of you."

"You're doing more than we could've asked," Freya told her.

Rini's silver eyes inspected Freya's face and hair as she fluttered closer. "Come, Your Majesty, let me tend to you," she said pleadingly. The braided chignon Rini had put in Freya's hair that morning had taken on bits of forest throughout the day, and several stray locks had escaped, tickling Freya's neck. "You look quite dreadful."

Freya gave her a wry smile. "I'll be going to bed soon, Rini. Toying with my hair would be pointless."

With a small harrumph, the pixie vanished.

"It soothes her to have a task," Aer said quietly, lifting his arm for Freya to slide closer.

"I know." Freya tucked herself under his arm. "I just struggle with focusing on hairstyles when we're trekking through the wilderness."

"We all have things that help us through difficult times," Aer said. "It's important to remember that when dealing with a pixie who's spent her life beautifying the females of the court. Fighting, hunting, being on your guard—those things are second nature to you, but for the rest of us..."

Freya looked down at her hands and tapped her thumbs together absently. "You're right, I'm sorry. I'm just so focused on the next few hours that I can't think about much else."

He kissed her temple, then rested his head against hers. "It's alright. Let's just try to get some sleep, alright?"

Freya looked at their friends, each face drawn and distressed.

"Yes," she agreed. "We all should."

Collin met her eyes. "We only have a couple of days to go. Once we get to your grandparents' estate, we'll be able to regroup and find out more."

Closing her eyes, Freya rested her head against Aer's shoulder. "I certainly hope so."

THE FOLLOWING EVENING, they came across the first camp of prisoners they'd seen in their travels. Freya was surprised they hadn't come across one sooner. It was far smaller than she'd expected. The number of citizens they'd seen being dragged off by patrols so far would've indicated that they were being held somewhere, but there'd been no evidence of such a place until now.

From their perch on the edge of a large depression in the earth, Freya, Aer, Collin, and Florian could just make out a group of Jotnar and human soldiers clustered around a fire. The wooden carts, each bearing an iron cage full of prisoners, were arranged in a curve around the fire behind the group of soldiers, who were mostly Jotnar with a few humans. Freya couldn't make out the prisoners' faces and they were too far away to identify by scent, but she could only assume they were all Linds who'd been taken after Lessia's coup had spread west.

Collin looked at Freya, confusion clear on his face. "Do they think themselves so invincible that they don't need to cloak their location?"

"That's certainly how it would seem," Florian replied.

Frowning, Freya glanced back toward the camp. "Or their master is far more fearsome than anyone out here might be."

Florian motioned for them to retreat, and the four slunk away from the crumbling edge, then made their way back to the small camp they'd set up for the night. Despite the undeniable effects of the witchbloom, Freya had grudgingly handed over her portion of the glamouring to Florian in order to rest up for a confrontation that would inevitably come when they reached Watoria.

"So, what should we do?" Freya asked.

"Nothing," Florian said brusquely. "We cannot risk exposing our location and we don't have the resources to take on that many more travelers."

"He's right," Collin said, seeming to take note of the look of an impending argument that had bloomed on Freya's face.

She shared a look with Aer, whose eyes held the same frustrated look she saw in Collin's. Shaking her head, she looked away, hating that there were people in danger, hungry, cold, and in pain, less than a half-mile away and there was nothing she could do to help them.

"Alright," she finally said. Without waiting for a response, she stalked off toward the shelter she and Aer planned to use for the night.

She relaxed a little when Aer fell into step beside her and took her hand.

"I'm sorry," he said quietly as they approached the small lean-to of branches Rini had helped set up for them. It wasn't much, but it would give them a small bit of privacy. A few other shelters had been set up for the larger groups, but she and Aer preferred to have their own space when they could manage it.

"They aren't wrong, so there's nothing to be sorry for," she said, resigned to the truth of those words. With a sigh, she rolled her shoulders, still unable to shake her lingering discomfort. "It doesn't lessen my aggravation that there's not a damn thing we can do to help those people."

Aer frowned at her movements. "You haven't stretched your wings since our wedding night. In the morning, you should try to get a quick flight in."

Although she had a strong desire to do just that, Freya shook her head. She'd never gone so long without releasing her wings and, until now, she'd also never had a need to keep them so concealed. The feeling of confinement had begun to shift toward claustrophobic.

"I've thought about it, but I don't want to risk being seen. Even with a cloaking spell, if there's a Jotnar patrol out there with magic strong enough to feel through mine, we'd be done for."

"An invisibility glamour—"

"—requires far more magic than simply changing my appearance," she snapped. "And if I'm to rest my magic, it doesn't make sense to expend extra energy just so I can stretch. That's not an option right now."

Hurt and a touch of aggravation flashed across his face. "I'm just trying to help," he said flatly. Shaking his head, he fixed his eyes on a point past her shoulder. "You're hurting yourself and taking it out on me, Freya. I don't appreciate it."

They stood silently for a moment as she stared up at him, waiting for him to look back at her.

"I'm sorry," she whispered. Hard eyes met hers as she stepped closer. "I just feel like I'm—"

"Failing? Welcome to the club. We've been crowned barely a week and already our kingdom has fallen."

Freya closed her eyes and leaned against his chest, not knowing what else to say. Ever since they'd left their parents and friends, she'd struggled to find the right words to express how sorry she was for the loss of his father's life and of his mother's constant, soothing presence. Freya felt their absence, along with that of her own father's, like a blow. But that didn't hold a candle to the feelings he was doing a very good job of hiding from everyone else.

After a moment, he wrapped his arms around her and kissed the top of her head. Tightening her arms around his waist, she tried hard not to cry.

"You're not doing this alone," he whispered, his breath soft against her hair. "I know you're used to being on your own, but that's not the case anymore. You need to let people help you."

"Once we get to my family's home and we're under the protection of my grandmother's magic, I'll do a few laps around the property." She lifted her face to his and smiled. "I promise."

"I'll hold you to that." He tilted her chin up and laid a soft kiss on her lips, then let his hand slip down to link his fingers through hers. "Come, let's get some sleep. Tomorrow will be a long day."

4

LEA

Lea had just managed to drag herself out of a particularly vile dream on the evening of her eighth day in the dungeon when a door clanged open and heavy footsteps sounded in the corridor. Groggily, she sat up and had only caught on to her mother's warning hiss when she saw the familiar white-leather-clad legs of Jonas.

She shoved her knotted curls out of her face and glared up at him. "Finally come to pay a visit, then?"

His lips twitched in amusement. Wordlessly, he jingled a ring of keys, the sound painful as it teased at freedom, then slid one into the lock of her cell. She exchanged a quick glance with her mother before scooting back a few feet, her hands curling into fists in the dirty straw on the floor.

Jonas crooked his fingers. "Lessia has deemed it acceptable to release you, so it's time to go."

"It's about time," Lea muttered as she pulled herself to her feet, wincing. The chill of the dungeon had caused her muscles to cramp, and standing was proving to be a painful feat. She stepped out of her cell, sending Jonas a scathing look as she passed him.

"Please, my lord, don't hurt her!" Perida sobbed, gripping the bars of her cell. "She's all I have left! *Please*."

"It will be alright, Mother." Lea gave her mother a small smile. "I promise, it will be alright."

Perida stared up at Jonas beseechingly. "Lord Edrin, I beg you. Don't harm my daughter."

He smirked, and Perida let out a small, shocked whimper when she saw Lea slip her hand into his.

Lea wrapped her other hand around one of the bars of her mother's cell. "I will do what I can to get you released," she whispered. "But you must be patient."

"Come," Jonas snapped. "We have things to tend to."

Without giving her a chance to say a proper goodbye to her mother, he tugged Lea down the dimly lit dungeon hall, then up the stairs to the darkened palace yard, where the only entrance to the dungeons existed.

"Keep your head up," he murmured as they made their way toward the palace entrance. "Don't let any of them think you've been cowed by a week in the dungeon."

She didn't say a word as she followed him through the echoing palace halls, seething at the fact that he'd taken so long to come for her. Having their story questioned was bad enough; being thrown in the dungeon was worse, but understandable, at least from Lessia's perspective.

But for Jonas to take more than a *week* to free her from the dungeons...?

She huffed and sent him an irritated glare.

Jonas either didn't notice or pretended not to.

Two guards were stationed outside Jonas' door, both tall, slim, and donning the dark gray uniforms of the Jotnar royal guard. Jonas strode past them, giving them a muttered command to "take a walk," before slamming the heavy doors behind us.

He flicked the lock shut, then released Lea and took several steps back.

"Lea—"

She slapped him. Hard.

Eyes wide, he rubbed at his cheek.

"Do you have *any* idea how *disgusting* those cells are? What kind of food—if you can even call it that!—your prisoners are fed?"

"I tried—"

"Not hard enough, apparently!" She adjusted her dress and tucked her hair behind her ears, doing her best to look a bit more dignified than she felt.

There was the scuff of a boot in the hall, followed by a snicker and a vile comment from one of the guards.

"I told you to take a walk!" Jonas roared.

"Apologies, my lord," the guard mumbled. Fading footsteps quickly followed. Jonas narrowed his eyes, then dropped a silencing spell over the room.

"I wanted to get my mother out of there," Lea hissed. "Not watch her rot for an entire week, unable to do anything but cry and eat moldy bread!"

"As I said—"

"You tried." She put her hands on her hips. "Tried what, exactly? You're the Empress' nephew! Do you need permission from anyone but her to get what you saw as rightfully yours?"

"There has been a good deal going on here, and convincing Lessia that we're... involved was not an easy feat." He scratched his chin. "I'm still not sure she believes it. There was also a good deal of back-and-forth regarding the divvying of the 'trophies' of their coup, which Willem continues to insist you are. It took a good bit of time to get it through his head that I had no intentions of letting you slip away. Not to mention, I needed to ensure this room was secure, which took far longer than I anticipated." He rubbed the reddening spot on his cheek again. "I can't believe you hit me."

"Secure?" Lea looked around, suddenly wary as she stuck on that one bit of information. "There are passages connected to this room?"

He nodded. "Two, as well as nearly a dozen spy holes, which is presumably why Salazar chose this room for my quarters. Bringing you here without first ensuring all means of eavesdropping were blocked was not an option, and to cast a silencing spell over this room regularly from the start would raise suspicions. As Lessia requested my presence for more hours out of the day than I cared for, I didn't have much time to thoroughly examine the room." He shook his head. "There were spy holes in the ceiling, Lea, and Willem, along with half of his men, were hoping to catch themselves a pretty Lindorothian female to take to their beds. I'm sorry, but I had to be certain you'd be safe once here."

Lea's stomach went sour at the thought of one of Willem or his men taking her instead of Jonas. In the brief moments she'd been in the throne room after she had arrived, the humans had caused feelings of disgust nearly as deep as the Jotnar. Willem, in particular, made her skin crawl.

"I don't understand," Lea said slowly. "If you insisted our relationship began prior to Lessia and Willem's attack, why would he feel entitled to me?"

Jonas ran a hand through his pale blond hair and huffed out a breath. "I don't know, but for the time being, you will not leave this room. Is that clear?"

"So I'm a prisoner, then?" She scoffed. "Why not just leave me in the dungeon?"

"You're not a prisoner, not by any stretch, and Lessia has acknowledged that openly. But Willem is proving to be a bit more shrewd than I first believed him to be. I don't trust him."

Lea closed her eyes and leaned against the wall, suddenly overcome with exhaustion. While in the dungeon, the only thing that had kept the grief over the loss of her father and uncle at bay was the knowledge that she'd soon be out and hopefully working toward exacting revenge. But when three days turned into four, then four into five, she slowly began to lose hope that their plan would work. She'd truly become concerned that Lessia had discovered Jonas' deceit and had executed him. Or worse, that his deceit had been so thorough she'd allowed herself to be led right into a trap.

To be quite honest, she still wasn't sure that hadn't been the case. She lifted her eyes to his, suddenly wary of what he might expect of her now. What she saw when she looked at him was a bit of sadness mixed with aggravation. Whether that was with her or their circumstances, she couldn't be sure.

"How did you finally manage to convince Lessia to release me?" she asked quietly.

Jonas' jaw tensed, then relaxed. "I managed to convince her you would be fully amenable to switching sides, so to speak, and that there might be potential for getting the people of Errest to follow you. I assured them that was by no means guaranteed, but even the possibility of it helps you," he said when he saw her dubious look. "Now it's just a matter of sticking to our plan."

Lea exhaled quietly.

"I had one of the maids prepare a bath," he said quietly. "And Dina managed to salvage some of your clothing, although I wasn't able to retrieve the clothes Freya gave you in the caves."

She waved a hand tiredly. "I don't think pants would be appropriate, considering the circumstances."

Jonas opened his mouth, then let it fall closed in a tight smile. "Get yourself cleaned up, then we'll talk a bit more."

With a nod, Lea pushed herself away from the wall and walked toward the bathing room on the other side of the room. Jonas reached out to touch her arm as she walked past, but she shrugged him off, not wanting him to see how uncertain of him she still was.

She waited until she'd closed and locked the door before finally allowing her hands to shake. Clenching her fists, she slid to the floor and let her head come to rest on her knees. Then, slowly, she started to pick through her scattered thoughts.

Byrric trusted Jonas, and while Freya and Aer still didn't seem on board with allying with Jonas, they trusted Byrric, so Lea did, too. When they gave Lea and Jonas approval to go through with their plan to infiltrate Lessia and Willem's court, Lea assumed she would be safe. She'd become doubly sure once Jonas swore in blood not to harm her or anyone who shared blood with Aerelius.

Now, having spent more than a week in the dungeons, she begged to differ, although it was yet to be seen whether Jonas' account was true.

But... if what Jonas said *was* true, and he really *had* managed to convince Lessia that he and Lea cared for one another, then perhaps this plan wasn't as crazy as she'd started to think.

Heaving a sigh, she stood, then began to strip out of her dress, the same one she'd worn to Freya and Aer's wedding. What had once been a beautiful shade of red was now the color of mud. The silk-and-lace garment had been ripped and dirtied beyond repair, a thing that saddened her a good deal. The laces on the back had frayed and loosened, so it was an easy task to untie herself.

As she stepped out of the garment, she caught a glimpse of her reflection in the mirror above the washbasin, and the sight brought her up short. Her black curls were a frayed, frizzed mess, with the filth of the dungeons plastering portions to her cheeks. Her skin, a warm brown on a typical day, had taken on a grayish hue, which told her the poison that had tainted her food in the dungeon had done more than just suppress her own magic. It, along with the meager nutrition, had sapped her strength. All that looked back at her now was a hollow-eyed shell.

Gingerly, she picked up a washcloth that lay folded beside the basin and began scrubbing away most of the dirt and grime from her skin. Once the bulk of the filth was gone, she eased herself into the warm bath that had been prepared for her. The steaming water smelled sweet and felt soft, its heat a balm against the cold from the dungeon that still chilled her bones. After a few moments, she felt a bit of magic creep back into her body. It was faint, but the water seemed to be touched by some sort of spell—likely from Dina, the water witch who'd served Freya during her time at the palace.

She tried not to picture her mother wasting away in her cell while Lea soaked in hot water filled with rose petals and scented oil, nor did she dwell on the horrid thoughts that must be racing through Perida's head after watching her only child willingly walk off with an assumed-enemy. Her mother was smart—she knew Lea's best chance at escape was to allow Jonas to claim her as his, so if that's what she believed was happening, then Lea would allow her what small comfort that might offer.

She slid down and let her hair sink beneath the surface of the water, combing her fingers through the curls to loosen them. As the water eased her tense muscles and settled her mind, she thought of what her next steps should be. She could trust Jonas' intentions and see their plan through, hopefully glean some worthwhile information that would help strengthen their chances of taking back Lindoroth. Or she could take the first opportunity to flee, make her way to the Northern Road and follow the Selnor River across Lindoroth to find Freya, Aer, and the others. A trip that long on her own would be difficult, especially with minimal supplies, but it was possible.

Her confidence in their plan when she'd made the choice to stay had nearly shattered after her reception in the throne room, and it was becoming clear that admitting defeat and slipping away might be the better, albeit less desirable, of her two options.

"Oh, my lady!"

Lea startled, sloshing water over the edges of the tub as she moved to cover herself.

"What—*Tyna?*" Lea sagged with relief at the sight of the glittering silver pixie who'd attended her these past months. "Gods above, you scared me!"

Tyna fluttered over to the edge of the tub and sat, and Lea took a good look at her. The small female held the same silver gleam she always did, but there was something tarnished about it, as though it had dulled a bit. Her hair, normally twisted into an elaborate coronet, hung loose, and her iridescent wings drooped at her back when she sat down. The shimmer that normally surrounded her like a cloud of gossamer had all but vanished.

"Apologies, my lady," Tyna said, letting her feet sink into the water. She waved a hand, and the water that had become murky with the lingering dirt from Lea's skin was instantly clear as crystal. "I wanted to come see you in the dungeons, but Lord Edrin assured me you would be here soon enough."

"He did?" Lea sat up a bit straighter. "You've been speaking with him?"

Tyna nodded quickly. "A bit, my lady. The empress has had spies on him since you both returned. It's clear her trust in him has diminished a good deal, especially since you came back with him so willingly."

"How do you know?"

"I'm quite small and have ways of making myself unseen," she replied haughtily. "Has he caught you up on the goings-on of late?"

Lea shook her head. "I've only just been brought from the dungeons."

Tyna's silver brows puckered. "Well, there's been quite a bit happening, and I've been conversing with Rini when I can."

"Conversing? She hasn't stayed behind?"

"Oh, no, my lady! She left with Their Majesties. She and I thought it best I remain behind with you, so I'll be sure to update her shortly."

Lea let out a quiet sigh of relief. While the pixie might not be her closest friend, her familiar presence, not to mention her ability to travel from one place to another in the blink of an eye, gave her a small bit of comfort. "When did you speak to her last? What of Freya and my cousins?"

"I spoke with her a few days ago. Rini's last update was that they were halfway to the Enrieth family's manor outside Watoria, although she wasn't clear on where that was, exactly. They should arrive in three days' time." Tyna gestured for Lea to sit forward so she could tend to her hair. "Come, my lady, let's get you properly cleaned up."

After Tyna spent copious amounts of time combing the rest of the grime and tangles from Lea's hair and smoothing sweet-smelling oils over her skin, she twisted her hair into a long braid and helped her dress in a warm wool nightgown and matching robe.

Lea smoothed a hand over the soft fabric and frowned. "I expected silk... or something..."

Tyna smiled her understanding. "Lord Edrin wanted me to ensure your comfort on your first night out of the dungeons."

Lea's mouth tightened. "But not after?"

Tyna gave her a pitying look. "I can't say, my lady. He seemed to have your comfort in mind when he chose your wardrobe. You aren't his prisoner, so you'll have some freedoms, but it is quite typical for Jotnar males to dress their females. Whether Lessia will insist he do so with you is anyone's guess."

"'Dress me,'" Lea scoffed, tightening the belt on her robe with a scowl. "I suppose we'll see, then."

Tyna winced, a tiny, pointed tooth digging sharply into her lip as she fluttered closer. "A bit of advice, my lady?"

Lea sighed. "Of course."

"Choose your battles wisely. Your attire may seem important now, but you must remember—"

"That I'm here to play a part?" Lea finished. She sat down on the edge of the tub and pressed her fingers against her forehead. "Yes, I'm aware."

Tyna swooped down beside her and sat on the lip of the tub, then patted a tiny hand on Lea's thigh. "It will be alright, my lady. Lord Edrin is waiting to discuss how you both will handle things in the coming weeks, but just know...I do not plan to leave you."

Lea smiled wanly. "What do you think of..." she inclined her head toward the door to the bedroom where Jonas was waiting for her.

Tyna followed her gaze and her jaw tightened. "I trust him... for now, but there are many reasons why I plan to stay by your side, my lady."

5

———

FREYA

The former home of Jora and Selinda Enrieth and the place Freya had spent the bulk of her early years was just to the south of Watoria, about four miles into the woods on the western edge of the ravine that encircled most of the city. The road that came northwest from Errest ran along the large crevice for several miles to the east, while the long road from Olthanas stretched along the southeastern edge of the property, effectively sandwiching Freya's family home between two of the only means of entry to Watoria. Not only would the area be heavily patrolled, it would also be heavily travelled by Lessia's and Willem's soldiers, who they'd seen scouring the countryside in greater numbers since they'd encountered the camp of prisoners a few days earlier. Sometimes it seemed they were looking for something—presumably her and Aer—and other times they were driving more carts of Lindorothian prisoners to some destination Freya was unaware of.

They made camp on the final night of their journey in a thick copse of towering pines. Between them and the manor lay two more miles of forest. Based on the scouting Amara and Naedan had done, the woods were crawling with Jotnar and human knights. Whether they knew of the existence of Freya's family home was uncertain, but it became clear as they neared the convergence where all roads toward the city dovetailed into one, the need for stealth grew and Freya's hopes of crossing onto her family's lands unseen diminished. For now, the assumption they were working with was that the Jotnar and humans fully expected her, Aer, and a cadre of soldiers at their backs bearing down on Watoria intent on wresting it from the hands of whoever Lessia and Willem had sent in to take over.

After everyone had been fed, Freya, Aer, Ana, Florian, Reginald, and a handful of others sat down to discuss their plan of attack for the final leg of their journey. A map lay in the middle of their circle showing Watoria and the surrounding forest.

"We're outnumbered," Ana said briskly. "We've got barely thirty, many of whom have no experience in battle of any sort, and we counted nearly four dozen patrols between here and there, almost all Jotnar."

"Probably more," Freya added. "There are plenty of hiding places in these woods. It would've been easy to miss a few others, and far more of them have the ability to glamour than we do."

Amara, one of the hawk shifters, tapped her finger on a spot several miles to the southeast of Enrieth Manor where the forest was particularly dense and the ravine narrowed to barely a crevice. "This is the most sheltered section of the forest between here and your family home and the nearest point where we can cross the ravine on foot," she said. "We'll have the best chance of slipping across your property line with minimal detection here."

"It will also be the most heavily patrolled," Aer said, shaking his head.

"Agreed," Ana added. "Crossing at a place of convenience wouldn't be wise."

"They can't see the property, though," Reginald pointed out. "They don't even know it exists."

Florian looked at the human and shook his head. "No, Jotnar have powers far different from those of the Linds. They may not be able to see through Selinda's enchantments, but there's a slim chance they'll know *something* is there. If they see that our aim is to get to that *something*, they'll know it carries great significance."

"So you leave none alive," Isadora said. At Ana's surprised look and Florian's arched brow, her eyes widened. "I mean... I know little of battle, Lord Florian, but as they are the enemy, wouldn't that be the most prudent method of dealing with them?"

Florian nodded slowly. "Yes, I suppose it is."

Shifting forward, Freya eyed the map, then looked at the others. "I agree with Amara. Our best chance is a direct shot. My grandmother's enchantments protecting the property extend nearly to the roads on either side. Once we get over the ravine, it's barely a mile until we reach the property line, then we'll be obscured from sight for the rest of the journey. We'll get rid of any patrols and bring the bodies south toward the Saithian border. It won't be a stretch for anyone who finds them to assume there was a skirmish with Saithian soldiers."

Florian gave her a steady look. "Then I would implore you to rest for the night, because a direct shot would mean glamouring everyone, including the shifters, if we want to ensure maximum loss of life for our enemy."

"I don't think glamouring the shifters will be necessary," Freya told him. She glanced up at her guard, Rissen. "What are your thoughts?"

He shook his head. "We don't have many magic-wielders with us, and you two are the only ones who can effectively cast invisibility glamours for the amount of time we'd need them. I don't find it worthwhile to spread your magic so thin when it can be wielded defensively against our enemies. Naedan and Amara will have plenty of coverage in the branches. Amber as well," he added, referring to the fox shifter that accompanied them. "The rest of us can rely on our senses to guide us through."

"We were able to slip through the woods unseen easily enough when we were scouting," Laz said when he saw Freya's hesitation.

"Wolves are native to this part of Lindoroth," Freya said, nodding. "Seeing one here or there wouldn't be considered odd, but there are six of you. Considering things are the way they are, a pack of wolves would certainly raise suspicions."

"Then we spread out as much as possible," Collin said. "To the north and southeast of the manor. It's the most logical plan and will expose fewer weaknesses than if we spread the magic of two over nearly thirty people."

Aer nodded. "Alright. Naedan, Amara, do one last sweep over the forest. Amber, you take the forest floor and stick to the trees as much as possible. Once we have more information, we'll finalize our plans on how to proceed."

Amber, the small fox shifter, gave a quick nod, then she and the two hawks shifted and took off into the darkening woods. After dismissing the rest, Ana turned to Freya and Aer, her brow slightly furrowed.

"A word, Your Majesties?"

Freya gave her a chastising look but nodded.

"I'd like to fly ahead to Iston," Ana said. "The charm Florian gave me will keep me concealed long enough to get to the sea, and from there it's hardly more than a day's flight to Iston."

"Why?" Aer asked. "It seems it would make more sense to remain here with us."

"I'm not sure how much the Istonians know about our current situation, as they typically keep to themselves. I spoke to a few old acquaintances when I was there to ensure allegiances for the new king and queen, but now that I've got something concrete to approach them with, I'd prefer to brief them as soon as possible."

Freya shook her head. "We should go together. Wait until we get Watoria in hand, until we've heard from Byrric."

"If they were any other people I would agree, but you know how the people of Iston are," Ana replied. "If we show up at their gates with a full battalion behind us, which we presumably will once we're done here, they'll immediately go on the offense."

Aer and Freya exchanged a look.

"Alright," Freya said with a nod. "What will your plan be?"

"My mother, for one," Ana replied. "Assuming she's there. She's been gone the last two months."

Freya didn't miss the bitter tone Ana's voice carried. It had been more than a decade since Freya had seen her father's mother, partly because Freya's trips to Iston consisted of two visits when she was a girl and partly because Vara Balthana spent most of her time traveling, rarely staying in Iston for more than a few months at a time.

"And if she isn't?" Freya asked.

Ana shrugged. "I have a few other acquaintances I can tap, but I'll need to go about getting her back to Lindoroth as soon as possible, which could take time. I'll try to do a fly-over of your grandparents' home," she said to Freya. "If anything seems amiss, I'll fly back."

"Do what you think is best," Aer told her. "Just be careful."

Ana gave him a sharp nod before looking at Freya. "You do the same?"

Freya's answering smile was tight. "Aren't I always?"

Ana snorted, then gave Freya a warm hug before slipping on the ring Florian had given her to conceal her presence. A moment later, Freya felt the brush of air as her aunt spread her wings and lifted off, disappearing into the night.

THEY CROSSED the road from Saith without being detected the following morning and came to a stop in the woods on the eastern edge of the ravine to make the final leg of their journey. Once they crossed the ravine, they would be within striking distance of Enrieth manor, but the forest was riddled with patrols, meaning this part would be their most treacherous.

The eerie silence of the forest that faced west toward the edge of the Enrieth lands set Freya's nerves on edge. No birds sang, there was no crunch of animals among the trees, and no breeze rustled the leaves. Jotnar magic, heavy and viscous, pressed against the cloak of magic Freya and Florian had laid over the small cluster of trees they'd taken cover in. There were no enemy patrols in sight, but considering the ravine had narrowed to only ten feet across, they could only assume the enemy was simply lying in wait.

Freya cast her eyes upward, watching as Amara and Naedan flew above, black silhouettes against the gray sky, swooping and circling lazily about as though hunting for prey. Her own wings tingled beneath her skin, itching to be let free after more than a week of disuse. The promise of a free sky to fly in above her grandparents' land beckoned her forward, and it was only logic, the cloaking spell she and Florian had cast around their small group, and their careful planning that kept her feet planted firmly to the ground.

Letting her gaze fall back to her surroundings, she looked around, searching for any sign of pursuit. She, Aer, Reginald, and Isadora walked silently behind Florian as Laz and Collin prowled the forest in front of them, sniffing out any tracks that might indicate nearby enemies. Every now and then their tails would brush, as though reminding each other they were still there. The rest of the shifters had spread out a half-mile to the north, but Laz and Collin had insisted on staying close. Reginald and Isadora, the only two who held no supernatural abilities, stood beside them.

"What is the likelihood their knights will see through your shielding?" Reginald asked Florian.

"Nil."

"I must say I disagree," Isadora whispered to Freya. "You and Lord Florian are strong, but I fear Jotnar magic might trump yours."

Freya averted her eyes to avoid laughing at the poisoned look Florian sent the human queen.

Aer gave Isadora a curious look. "Could you have seen through it when you still had your powers?"

She shrugged and stared ahead. "It's hard to say because it's been some time since I had any magic to wield." Her face turned thoughtful, as though she was trying to remember what her own magic had felt like before Lessia leached it away. "Lessia only ever had the strongest warlocks in her employ, no matter the rank, so it's safe to assume these knights are old and come from long lines of strong magic."

Freya couldn't help but feel a bit of contempt at the way Isadora spoke of the strength of Jotnar magic.

"It's no matter," Reginald said quietly, sliding his longsword from the sheath at his hip. "It's not far to the property line. If we run—"

"*You* may run, human," Florian interrupted. "*We* cannot leave any alive to report on our whereabouts. One sentry returning to whoever holds Watoria is all it will take to have these woods swarming with Jotnar and human alike. Selinda's magic is strong, but it is not infallible."

"Let's just hope that whatever luck has gotten us this far without detection holds out a bit longer," Freya murmured.

Her head jerked upward when Naedan called out a warning, then dove for the trees on the other side of the ravine, Amara on his tail. Freya watched grimly as an arrow sailed past, missing both but confirming that whoever was patrolling this area knew they were there.

"That's our cue," Aer said quietly. He looked at Freya. "Wings out, my love. Something tells me you may need to fly."

Grinning, she let her wings flare wide, relishing the freedom of movement as she gave them a slow flap. The moment the cold forest air hit her feathers, she felt a bit of her strength return. She sent Aer a grin. "If circumstances weren't so dire, I'd think you intended to offer me as bait."

"Only you would think I would use my queen as a means of drawing enemy fire."

"I'm certain Her Majesty could easily outfly their arrows if it came down to it," Florian said absently as he scanned the forest around them.

"You'd offer up your queen?" Reginald whispered, aghast.

When Florian didn't respond, Reginald looked at Aer in horror.

"My spymaster would never suggest such a thing." Aer tilted his head toward Freya. "I don't think I can say the same for my wife."

"Only as long as Byrric isn't around," she said, smiling. "He'd poison me with my own feathers for even—"

Crack!

The sound of a snapping twig caused Laz and Collin to halt in their tracks, their noses low to the ground as their eyes roamed over their surroundings.

"They're close," Freya breathed, the smile fading from her lips.

With a flick of his wrist, Florian sent out a small ripple of magic. "Ah, that's better," he murmured, smiling grimly at the handful of knights who he'd just relieved of their glamours.

They had the typical gnarled looks of Jotnar soldiers, tall and lanky with faces that seemed twisted in permanent scowls, but Freya could feel their power creeping along the forest floor. It didn't seem any had noticed that Florian had obliterated their shields, but Freya knew it was only a matter of time.

"Remember, keep them on this side," Florian cautioned. "We need to drive them south."

Collin and Laz growled out a warning and Florian widened his stance in front of Aer and Freya. Aer's spirit magic swirled pearlescent around his forearms and palms, and Freya slid two feathers from her wings, wincing slightly at the sharp pain as two immediately began to regrow in their place.

Freya cast a glance over her shoulder at Reginald and inclined her head at Isadora. "Stay back and keep her safe."

Reginald nodded grimly and tightened his grip on his blade. Isadora took a small step behind him, a look of resignation on her face. It had been ten years since Isadora had been in possession of her own magic, and while Freya was uncertain how old Isadora actually was, she could only assume backing down from a fight due to lack of power wasn't something Isadora had gotten used to. Jotnar females prided themselves on strength of both body and magic, both of which, once taken, would be difficult to regain.

Suddenly, Freya heard the yowl of a lioness in the distance followed by a wolf yelping in pain. Recognition flashed across the faces of the knights as they took in Freya's wings and the power that dripped from Aer and Florian's fingers, but their shock lasted only a moment before they launched their attack.

Florian flicked a hand, then spun his finger, calling whip-thin roots up from the ground, wrapping around the arms and ankles of two the knights before spearing them through and cutting off their shouts.

Collin and Laz sprung forward, taking two down by their necks and landing in a flurry of fur and snapping teeth. Freya took flight after four took aim at her and Aer. She flew above them as Aer sent out a heavy burst of spirit magic, instantly diverting their intentions away from harm. Giving the knights no time to recover, Freya did a quick lap around them, slicing the neck of each with her feathers. The feel of the wind and thrill of being in the air again instantly began to revitalize her, and the magic that had begun to feel stagnant awoke.

She conjured up a handful of daggers from the air and tossed them at another cluster of incoming knights, taking them down just as they would've converged on Laz and Collin below. The sounds of fighting from the north increased as almost all of the shifters who'd come with them drove the Jotnar patrols south, further away from Watoria, to where Freya and the others would be waiting. Florian dispatched the last two of the group that had attacked them just as Freya landed on the ground beside him, and they all ran toward the battle a half-mile to the south.

Aer, Laz, Florian, and Collin continued to fight beside her, fending off the Jotnar coming from other directions as Reginald protected Isadora. Freya spun, kicked, punched, and sliced as one after another came at her. Each movement, each hit, each flex of muscle was a balm to her frustrations and anger of the past week.

The other shifters appeared, fighting against the Jotnar and a handful of human knights as they aimed to close in on Freya and Aer. More came from the trees, dropping down all around them and popping into existence as the glamours hiding them evaporated.

There are too many, Freya thought as she sliced the metallic tip of her feather through the neck of a human who'd attacked from her side.

She tossed the body aside, and as magic and growls flew around her, a burly, broad-shouldered Jotnar bore down on her, singling her out above the rest.

Freya gripped her feather tighter, then flung three magical daggers straight at her attacker.

He deflected them with a single blow.

"Noble effort from the Valkyrie queen," the Jotnar soldier said with a sneer. He twirled his knife and took aim. "It's a shame—"

She silenced him with a flick of her wrist, cutting off his air and piercing his throat with her feather. Hardly a second of satisfaction passed before three others took notice of her and began to converge. Feigning bravado, she widened her stance and beckoned them forward. She knew it was an idiotic move, but she needed to keep them focused on her so the others could handle their own fights.

Just as they lunged for her, streaks of black, gray, and russet tore through the trees, aiming for the enemy knights. Freya stumbled back into a tree as the wolves joined the melee. A Jotnar who'd taken aim at Aer was dragged to the ground by one, while the soldiers who'd turned their attention toward Freya were taken down by two others. The late arrivals mixed with Freya's party, using magic and claws to shred into the Jotnar soldiers.

Minutes later, the woods were silent once again and the air was clear of enemy magic. The only sounds were the heavy panting of wolves, the gurgle of blood, and the crunch of pine needles and oak leaves underfoot as the newcomers cautiously approached.

Freya's heart pounded as she took in the destruction around them, reaching blindly for Aer's hand when she felt him take his place beside her.

The largest wolf, black as midnight with wide, gold eyes, lumbered up to Freya and butted her shoulder with his snout.

"Freya—" Aer said as he tightened his grip.

She held up her other hand and let out a relieved laugh as the wolf shifted into her old friend and former commanding officer.

"Freya Balthana," Ashton Carinald said with a grin. "Aren't you a sight?"

6

———

FREYA

There was little time for reunions as Ashton and Aer began to bark out orders to scour the woods for any surviving enemy knights and to dispose of the bodies as far south as they could. The other marshals—twenty-six in total—who'd accompanied Ashton helped Freya's party lug the wounded across the border of Enrieth lands. As soon as they crossed through the rippling magic that protected the property, Freya breathed a sigh of relief and hoped Haegin, the earth-wielding groundskeeper Byrric had continued to employ, was at least somewhat prepared for their arrival.

When they broke from the forest onto the rising green that held the main house, a sprawling stone structure fit with turrets and wide, arched windows, and multi-level gardens bursting with flora, Freya's relief increased. She hadn't visited since before her grandmother died, which was nearly ten years ago. It was the place she'd grown up in before Byrric had moved her into Watoria, and no matter how much she'd loved the house she and Ana had lived in, this would always be her home.

Haegin seemed to have been expecting them, because they were halfway across the lawn when the lumbering old male came out to meet them. He was tall with a ruddy face, a broad nose, and soft, wide brown eyes.

"Ah, Your Majesty!" he called. "Have you got wounded?"

"We do," Freya replied. "Is the infirmary stocked?"

"Yes, yes, take them in," he said, stepping aside as those carrying the injured rushed past.

Freya watched as Myria, Amber, Naedan, Rissen, and three marshals were carried inside by Rodrick, Perinald, and four other marshals. Once they'd passed, Aer came to stand beside her and put a hand on her shoulder.

"Cecilia and the rest are disposing of the bodies and doing another sweep for stragglers." His eyes ran over her face and a slight furrow formed on his brow as he took in the blood drying on her neck. "Are you alright?"

She nodded, then looked up at him. "I am, considering. No injuries. You?"

"Likewise." He inclined his head toward where the rest of the marshals were approaching. "I suppose there are introductions to be made?"

"Yes," she agreed. She couldn't help but smile as she took in the people she'd worked with for so long. "Let's make sure everyone inside is tended to first, then we'll handle that."

"So long as someone here can wield a needle and thread, your soldiers will be fixed up," Haegin said.

"Not to worry, Your Majesties, I'll take care of them," Florian said. He snapped his fingers at one of the marshals and motioned for him to follow. The marshal balked at the command but kept quiet at Ashton's silencing nod before following Florian into the house.

When they'd passed, Haegin gave Freya a sympathetic smile. "It's wonderful to see you, Freya, dear. I only wish it were under better circumstances."

"That makes two of us," she said, reaching out to give the warlock a hug. "But it's good to be home."

∽

ONCE THE WOUNDED HAD BEEN TENDED to and Florian had done all he could to hasten their healing, everyone gathered in the large dining room at the rear of the house to catch up.

After the marshals were introduced to the rest of the group, Freya and Aer filled them and Haegin in on the status of Iladel and the rest of Lindoroth they'd seen during their travels.

"We didn't get near any of the larger towns," Aer said. "The patrols we encountered closer to Watoria looked to be gathering up prisoners and taking them away."

"We saw very few of our own people along the way," Freya added. "I don't know if it's because most are captive or if they're all hiding. I would've expected to come across more who were fleeing, though."

Ashton folded his arms and shook his head. "No, they're likely captive. If the other towns, at least the larger ones, are in a state like Watoria, the city limits were probably sealed."

"Magically?" Florian asked.

Ashton gave a sharp nod.

"How did you find us, anyway?" Aer asked.

"Ana came yesterday. She stayed only long enough to rest for a few hours before departing for Iston. She told us you would reach Watoria by today and that we needed to get to you as soon as possible to give you cover for the rest of the trip. We've been patrolling as discreetly as possible, but Gideon felt Lord Florian's cloaking spell the moment you neared the property. We knew you were there, but I couldn't detect your scent at all. The best we could do was follow the push of his magic."

Myria, who'd insisted on staying in her lioness form to help her wounded leg heal faster, let out a low hiss, conveying her annoyance at the lack of backup.

Ashton arched a brow at her, then looked at Freya in question.

"We're just thankful you all found us when you did," she said, shooting a silencing look at Myria. "I'm afraid things would've turned out much worse if you hadn't."

"Yes," Aer agreed. "Now, what can you tell us about what's happened in Watoria?"

Ashton blew out a breath and shook his head. "Ten days ago, approximately five hundred human troops were found marching toward the city. Our own army laid waste to them, of course, but while their focus was on the humans, one thousand of Lessia Edrin's soldiers seized Watoria from the north while another battalion of humans came from the east, taking out a very large portion of our knights along the way. By the time the Allanorian knights that remained were able to get closer to Watoria, it had been sealed off and was surrounded by enemy soldiers."

Ashton waved a hand, indicating the house before continuing. "Byrric told me long ago to use this as a safe house should anything ever warrant doing such, so I and the other marshals who managed to get out of the city came here. Then, a few days ago, Byrric arrived in the dead of night to tell us what happened at your wedding. He told us he'd gone to Kildin immediately after leaving Iladel and found Caelora's capital overrun, its army crippled, so he shifted his focus to the outer capitals."

"Kildin is overrun?" Laz asked quietly, his voice pained. Freya sensed he knew it would eventually come to that, but knowing your home would be lost and hearing that it had actually come to pass were two different things entirely.

Ashton gave him a sharp nod. "Yes, my lord. Unfortunately, Byrric's report does not bode well for Caelora's citizens, Kildin's, in particular, as it seems to have been taken before Iladel and is now held by a human male and a Jotnar female. Due to its proximity to Iladel, remaining behind instead of rallying the outer regions would've been a mistake."

"A mistake?" Laz's eyes widened. "To protect—"

"Laz," Collin said quietly.

Aer frowned at Ashton. "Did Commander Balthana leave forces behind in Kildin at least?"

Ashton nodded. "Roughly five hundred of the Royal Army's knights stayed to back up the Caelorian army, but their main purpose is to aid the outer villages and towns should the Jotnar or humans attack there. Byrric left five hundred additional troops to supplement the Allanorians here, who are currently blocked from entering Watoria by two thousand human knights. He also sent his lieutenant commander to Errest to assess the situation there. Byrric's plan was to go from here straight to Olthanas to offer assistance, should they need it, but the Royal Army took a large hit when Lessia and Willem invaded."

Freya's heart twisted a little at the pained look Laz wore as he listened to Ashton describe the current state of their land. She knew Byrric wouldn't have left Laz's home behind if he didn't believe the prospect of more aid could be found farther west, but knowing that Laz's people might be suffering a similar fate as those in Iladel was troubling.

"My father said he'd spoken to the marshals already," she said to Ashton, wanting to divert the discussion to their immediate circumstances. Kildin would be saved, but based on its proximity to Iladel and the fact that it was nearly two weeks' travel in the direction they'd just come, it would be foolish to go there now. "He said he spoke to you before our wedding, weeks ago."

"With all of the sitting governors hundreds of miles from their houses for your wedding," Gideon, Ashton's second-in-command, said, "Commander Balthana told us to be on the lookout in case anyone chose to utilize their absence to their advantage. Out of an abundance of caution, we started ensuring the city's guards and marshals were prepared. That's not unusual for any royal wedding, though."

Ashton nodded in agreement. "That was about four weeks ago. He told us to come here, should something happen, and await further instruction from either him or you. He had nothing definitive to tell us, but he had a concern that something 'didn't feel right,' so if you arrived seeking assistance, we needed to be ready."

"Byrric's assumptions are rarely wrong," Aer murmured, his mouth turned down in anger as his eyes slid to Freya. "Why wouldn't he tell us this beforehand?"

Freya dragged a hand through her hair and let out a frustrated growl. "Why let us go through with a damn *wedding*—"

"A failsafe, Your Majesties," Florian said patiently. "To reign, you must be wed. If, the gods forbid, there was an attack and the reigning king and queen fell, you both needed to be prepared to take your crowns at a moment's notice. Commander Balthana may not have known what, if anything, was coming, but his gut told him enough to lay preparations, just to be safe. And for the record, I agreed, as did your parents," he added, looking at Aer.

"Byrric said we may need your assistance," Collin said to Ashton. "What did he mean by that?"

"Ideally? Stabilizing Watoria," Ashton replied. "After seeing the state of Kildin, he knew Lessia would be sending someone to take the governor's seat and with it, the city."

"He expects us to do that without the support of an army?" Aer asked, aghast. "You said the Allanorians can't get to the city!"

Freya huffed out a laugh. "Yes, of course. 'Retake the city with a handful of marshals and palace guards and a boxed-out army that can't get within a mile of the city.' That certainly sounds like my father."

"I'd say it's more likely he'd hoped for us to collectively assess the circumstances once you arrived and come up with some sort of plan for a smaller operation, one that doesn't require a large military force," Ashton replied, annoyance beginning to show in his tone. "You know your commander better than I, but even I find it unlikely he'd want or expect a few dozen soldiers and civilians to attempt to take on two armies, head-on."

"More explicit instructions still would've been appreciated," Freya muttered.

"Did Byrric give you any numbers regarding losses?" Florian asked. "Soldiers, civilians, and so forth?"

Ashton sent a look at Freya and Aer, then met Florian's eyes. "Byrric estimated we'd lost approximately one-quarter of Lindoroth's forces by the time he arrived here. That was three days ago. The rest are being spread throughout the kingdom."

Freya's frustration with her father evaporated as she let that news sink in. When they'd left Iladel, they thought the attack had just been on that city and would spread from there. As they'd traveled west, it became clear the attack was more far-reaching than that. Now, as Ashton confirmed the fears that had begun to grow within her, she realized just how hard her kingdom had been hit.

For the next few minutes, she listened intently as Ashton described the events of the past two weeks. The marshals had done as Byrric asked, shoring up their defenses, checking weapon stocks and food stores inside and outside the walls, reinforcing the city gates and so forth. When Byrric returned a few days earlier and found the city surrounded, he'd come to Enrieth manor and found the remaining marshals had done as he'd directed and taken up residence there with Haegin. He'd instructed them to do what they could with the Allanorian troops, but to remain sequestered at the manor as much as possible in order to maintain secrecy until Freya and Aer arrived.

Ashton's voice caught when he spoke of the last few days.

"Watoria..." Ashton shook his head, then met Freya's eyes. "It's bad."

Freya tensed as she took in his expression. "How bad?"

"The brother of Lessia's late husband, a Lord Fredrick Edrin, came in not half a day after the commander left. He's taken over the governor's manor and has been systematically executing anyone he feels won't swear allegiance to him as their new governor." He swallowed hard. "Which is most of Allanor, it seems, including the human woman he arrived with. The central square has become home to a guillotine that is put to use at least once per day."

"He's executing the citizens?" Freya whispered.

"Why did he kill the human he came with?" Aer asked.

"*Humans,*" Ashton corrected. "Another woman arrived two days ago and he put her head on a pike beside the first within hours. From what we've been able to deduce, the captain of his guard is a vicious bastard that has a tight hold on his ear, and Frederick is quite impressionable. The assumption is that he doesn't feel the need to feign regard for human life this far from where his leaders are."

"Who were the humans he sent?" Reginald asked, dread settling on his face.

Ashton's eyes darted between Reginald, Isadora at his side, and Freya before responding. "I'm unsure, my lord. Both were executed within a day of arriving."

Isadora ran a comforting hand up Reginald's arm, her eyes full of pity as she took in his expression. "We knew Willem would use his own people to achieve his ends," she said quietly. "This should come as no surprise."

Reginald gave a quick, jerky nod. "Yes, of course. How do the other citizens of Allanor fare?"

Ashton's expression turned grave. "He's been bringing them in by the wagon-full. We attempted to call in reinforcements from the surrounding regions, but the enemy came in droves, seemingly out of thin air. We'd hardly formed a plan of attack when they first appeared over the ravine and at the harbor. Human and Jotnar knights, draugs, huldra. The city was overrun within an hour. We protected it as best we could, but once it became clear the city couldn't be saved, at least not by us, most of us retreated here."

"You just *fled*?" Myria exclaimed, outraged as she shifted out of her lioness form. Her blonde hair had come out of its braid and hung in a tangled mass at her shoulders, but her eyes still sparked with fury. "You're tasked with protecting the city!"

Ashton sent her a flat look. "There are forty-two marshals left, my lady, out of more than two hundred. Twenty-six of them are here; the rest remained in the city with their families. I made the call to retreat because we were vastly outnumbered and overwhelmed. Staying in the city would've done nothing, Ana would likely be dead, and you all would now be going in blind."

It took all of Freya's strength not to slump into a chair. Sensing her distress, Aer squeezed her shoulder.

"Have we gotten any word on the status of the other capitals?" Aer asked, still wearing a mild look of shock.

"A messenger from Olthanas arrived a few days after the Commander left," Ashton told him. "He said a human male and Jotnar female now hold the governing seat of Saith. Byrric and the bulk of the Saithian army were in the process of ousting them and had been quite successful so far. We hope to hear from Byrric any day now."

Myria's outrage peaked again, this time mingling with disgust as she flicked a glare at Reginald. "I don't suppose *you* know who your wretched brother might have sent to take over *my* family seat?"

"Likely one of his allies in Caldel," Reginald replied, arms folded. "Knowing Willem, he wouldn't trust anyone outside his own circle to hold a seat as far from Iladel as Olthanas is." He looked back at Ashton. "Have there been any other humans in this region?"

"The humans assisted the Jotnar in breaching Watoria, but their encampments are outside the city. Frederick doesn't seem to want them inside the city walls, and as far as we can tell, the Jotnar have little use for them. They took the city and have been having their fun ever since," he said bitterly.

"Reinforcements, then?" Freya asked.

"That's what it appears," Gideon said. "Another marshal and I snuck down to their camps a few nights back and it sounds as though they're just waiting to be put to use."

"That seems a bit odd," Isadora commented.

"How so?" Freya asked.

Isadora looked at Freya. "Willem is no fool. He wouldn't send his men here to simply wait around."

"It seems that's exactly what he's done, Your Majesty," Ashton said.

Isadora blushed and looked up at Reginald. "Lady Edrin will do, Officer."

Freya saw Ashton's lips tighten as he gave Isadora a sharp nod.

"Perhaps we should all get some rest, reconvene a bit later," Freya said, sensing Ashton's irritation with the number of people in the room. "We'll regroup in the morning."

"Lord Florian, Lord Ristner, if you wouldn't mind hanging back?" Aer said. "The rest of you, there's food available in the kitchen, and if anyone needs further healing, Haegin will be able to assist you."

Once everyone had filed out, Ashton turned to Freya and Aer and smiled grimly. "Now, tell me about Iladel."

7

———

LEA

Jonas kept Lea under lock and key in his chambers for the first two days out of the dungeon. Lea wanted to protest, but common sense told her she was better off waiting for Jonas to do whatever it was he was doing to better ensure her safety before wandering around the palace on her own.

While Jonas was out performing whatever his daily duties were, Lea spent the hours doing her best to suss out the secret entrances and spy holes in his chambers he'd spoken of on her first night. All had been sealed up, according to him, but she wanted to see for herself. Tyna appeared twice to assist her with the higher places, indicating three spy holes in the ceiling, one of which was directly above the canopied bed.

When Lea questioned the purpose of spying from a vantage point where there'd be nothing to see but heavy fabric, Tyna informed her that the four-poster bed had only held a canopy for the last five days.

"Considering you are to be in a... relationship with Lord Edrin, he had the canopy installed," Tyna explained. "He wasn't certain who knew of the spy holes in this room, but it would look quite suspicious for you to be sharing a bed without... sharing it." Her cheeks flushed.

"Ah." Lea nodded. She and Jonas *had* been sharing his bed, but both had kept to their own sides, a thing that would, indeed, arouse a good deal of suspicion if someone caught sight of them from above. Even though the canopy consisted of a simple piece of fabric, it gave Lea a bit of solace when she lay down at night, knowing no one could see her while she slept.

Learning that Jonas had the forethought to install it ahead of time also helped ease some of her concerns about him, although the question of her trust in him still lingered.

On her third day of freedom, Jonas informed Lea that she would be dining with him, Willem, and Lessia that evening in the palace's main dining room. While the thought of leaving the room she'd been stuck in was tempting—and seeing as Tyna had a good deal of information to share about the passageways that were hidden throughout the palace—the implications that such a dinner carried left a pit of dread in her stomach.

"You'll need to show a certain level of subservience," Jonas explained. "Jotnar females are respected and are typically allowed their independence, but as you are not Jotnar, it would be... unseemly if I gave you the same latitudes I might one of my own kind. If Lessia or Willem become overly suspicious or think you're not adapting to our ways adequately, you're more likely to be handed off to someone they feel will have a firmer hand, and our main goal right now is for you to stay with me."

She inhaled slowly, then nodded as she set her fork down on the small window-side table where they'd just finished eating lunch. "Yes, I know. I only wish... Sometimes I wonder if this was a good idea or if we were foolish to rush into things."

Jonas set his napkin aside then leaned forward and took her hands between his, not noticing or ignoring the way she tensed at his touch. "If the commander of Salazar's Royal Army hadn't given his approval, I might agree with that sentiment. Byrric has faith in us, and because of that, so do Aerelius and Freya."

"Wherever they are," she murmured, slumping back in her seat and letting her hands slip from his. Tyna hadn't received word from Rini since the day after Lea had been released from the dungeons, and even then it was only briefly. Freya, Aer, Laz, Collin, and the rest had avoided detection so far and were hoping to cross the border to Freya's homeland within three days. Lea hoped to hear word today as to whether or not they had reached their destination, but as the hours stretched on, her concerns only increased.

"It's still early in the day," Jonas said soothingly. "Earlier on the other side of the continent. It's unlikely we'll hear anything for several more hours, possibly not even until tomorrow."

"Do you suppose they'll have to fight?" Lea asked quietly. Whether it was due to her lack of knowledge of its location or to limit the amount of information she shared at court, Rini hadn't told them the precise location of Freya's family manor. At first, Lea wanted to press, find out exactly where her friends and cousins had fled to, but both Jonas and Tyna stopped her, citing the less knowledge they had of the location of Lindoroth's monarchs, the better.

Jonas leaned back in his chair and folded his arms. "That all depends on where they cross into Watoria and how successful they are at maintaining their cover. With Freya and Florian with them, my guess is their chances of slipping in undetected are good, although that says little about their ability to stay hidden."

"I wish I was with them," she whispered. "I know what I'm doing here will help them. At least, I hope it will. But it doesn't change the fact that I wish we were all together."

"I understand, Lea. I promise, I do. I can't even begin to presume how you must feel, being told to feign attraction to a male you hardly know." He rubbed a hand across his forehead and sighed. "Let's finish going over how you'll behave at dinner this evening."

Lea rolled her shoulders and took another breath. "Okay. Tell me what to do."

～

THE INSTRUCTIONS JONAS had given her made sense. She would allow him to touch her, although she'd been very clear as to how and where. He'd promised to keep things within the realm of proper, considering their true relationship, which hardly bordered on friendship. Her main goal tonight was to show her contentment with him, to demonstrate to Lessia and Willem how happy she was to finally be out of the dungeon and back in her lover's arms. A small step, but hopefully one in the right direction.

But Lessia was sly, and while Lea knew little of Willem, she could only assume he wasn't lacking in intelligence, either. No, they wouldn't be easily fooled.

When they entered the dining room, still adorned in the gold accents the Harridan's were so fond of, Lea saw that the table had been set for five. Three of the seats were already occupied by Lessia, Willem, and a raven-haired female who sat at Willem's side. The two empty seats meant for her and Jonas were opposite Willem and the female, with Lessia at the head.

"Ah, Jonas, Lady Calliwell," Lessia said as they approached, her red lips curving into a smile. Her crown, a spidery thing made of sleek, black metal, sat atop her perfectly smooth hair. "So kind of you to join us." Her eyes narrowed a bit as she took in Lea at Jonas' side, the fitted charcoal gown Tyna had chosen that was so typical of Jotnar fashion.

"Lady Calliwell, I'd like you to meet my cousin, Lady Effina Veldin," Jonas said.

Lea gave her a shy smile. "It's lovely to meet you, Lady Veldin," she said.

The smile Effina offered back lacked both sincerity and any semblance of kindness.

Jonas brushed a thumb across Lea's cheek and angled his head toward a table on the side of the room. "Get us some wine?"

She itched to tell him to have a servant get it but knew this was one small way she could show Lessia and Willem that she wanted to care for her lover. So, she smiled up at him. "Of course. Go sit, I'll bring it right over."

As she made her way over to the table where a carafe of wine had been left out, she made a quick note of the guards in the room and committed their placement and numbers to memory. Then, she picked up the carafe and began to pour, keeping her ears peeled for the conversation she knew was about to begin.

"Has there been any news from the west?" Jonas asked as he slid into his seat.

"Nothing as of yet," Lessia said airily. "It's only a matter of time, though."

"It's been more than a week," Jonas pointed out. "Kildin is well in-hand. Should I pull some knights from there and send them toward Watoria?"

Quietly, Lea returned to her seat, setting a goblet of wine down at Jonas' place, then Jonas motioned for a servant to fill her plate.

"Anything in particular, my lord?" the servant asked, a male Lea recognized as one of the palace servants. His face was carefully expressionless, and if she wasn't mistaken, it seemed he was struggling not to meet her eyes.

"A bit of what we're having is quite alright," Jonas replied. "She is our guest, after all."

"Yes, my lord." The servant leaned forward and began spooning food from the various serving dishes on the table onto Lea's plate.

Jonas waited until Lea began cutting into her food before addressing Lessia. "Well? Should I send some of our knights west?"

Lessia pursed her lips and drummed her long, pale fingers against the table. "Perhaps. Although we can only assume Freya and Aerelius have reached their destination, whatever that may be." She angled her head to the side and gave Lea a coy smile. "I don't suppose you know where they're going, do you?"

Lea swallowed the small sip of wine she'd just taken and gave Lessia a bashful smile. "I just assumed they were going to travel straight for Watoria. That was Freya's home for so long, after all."

"Yes, that's what I've been told," Lessia said. "Have you any idea *where* in Watoria they might try to go? I can assure you, the city is locked down. They will not get in, and I would venture to guess they know that."

Lea shook her head. "I'm sorry, Empress. I heard very little of their plans when we were in the caves. We weren't there very long."

Lessia made a considering hum, but before she could say more, Jonas spoke.

"So has this become official?" Jonas gestured toward Willem and Effina. "Are you to wed?"

Lea shoved a large bite of chicken in her mouth to conceal her shock.

Effina preened at Willem and took his hand. "We are. In three days' time."

Ignoring her, Willem stared directly at Lea. "Don't bother hiding your thoughts, pretty girl. Say what's on your mind."

Lea swallowed her bite of food quickly. "My—Your Majesty?"

"Speak, girl!" Lessia snapped, causing Lea to jump.

"Apologies, Empress, Your Majesty. I was just surprised—"

"That I might cast aside that opportunistic whore who thought fleeing with my brother was a better option than ruling at my side?" Willem dabbed his mouth with a napkin and leaned back in his high-back chair. "I'll have you know that once I found out Isadora was a Jotnar spy, I thought we'd be a great match, perfectly poised to take over Lindoroth together." His eyes slid to Jonas, then back to Lea and his lip curled. "Clearly that was not the case."

"I—Jotnar?" Lea didn't have to feign her surprise at that bit of information.

"It's quite shameful," Effina said with a sniff. "Even Salazar's royal warlock didn't know the sweet human queen was none other than Jonas' sister, working with the humans. Some spymaster that Lord Florian is."

Lessia leaned forward and rested her chin in her hand, a challenge in her gaze as she looked at Lea. "Well? What are your thoughts on that, dear?"

Lea's lips parted, then closed as she carefully weighed her response. If chosen carefully, her words could go a long way in improving her position with Lessia. If chosen poorly, she could seem overeager, if not outright suspicious in her desire to please.

"I suppose... well, I would say congratulations are in order."

A perfectly groomed black brow winged up. "Oh?"

Lea cleared her throat and twisted her hands in her lap, quelling the myriad questions that ran through her mind as she held Lessia's gaze. "While I may be a bit unhappy with the outcome, I can't ignore the great level of intelligence and cunning it must have taken to achieve such results. To join forces with the human monarchy in such a way as to hide it from your closest neighbors... well, forgive me, but it's quite impressive."

"Yes," Willem said, his tone condescending. "My father may have been a fool to miss the Empress' deceptions but it was quite simple, once I married her, to see that Isadora was far from the human woman I had been betrothed to years before."

"You overheard a conversation between me and my sister," Jonas drawled. "It was hardly high-class espionage."

Willem scowled at him, then turned back to Lea. "So you admit you are unhappy here?" he asked, his tone both teasing and dangerous.

"No," Lea said firmly. "I am unhappy that so much blood was shed, especially at such a joyous occasion as a wedding. As for the rest..." She smiled up at Jonas, doing her best to appear happily enamored, before looking back at Lessia and Willem. "I am not unhappy with the rest."

Willem held her eyes, his cold gaze narrowing slightly before he looked at Jonas. "Impressive. I'd almost go so far as to say you should take this one as your wife, seeing as how loyal she's become."

Lea nearly choked on her wine.

"Oh, as though Jonas has ever had a hard time training a lover!" Effina said with a laugh.

Jonas hardly spared her a glance before going back to his meat.

"Frederick is planning on taking a Lind bride, after all," Effina continued, eyeing Lea consideringly. "And she *is* quite pretty."

Jonas gave a non-committal grunt. "What of the humans you sent Frederick after he took over Watoria?" he asked.

Lessia laughed and waved a hand dismissively. "Oh, those were doomed to fail."

"Yes, I believe I chose poorly on both accounts," Willem admitted with a sigh. "I can only hope he finds a suitable replacement."

Lea nearly frowned at the odd statement but forced her face to remain neutral.

"Has he had any luck quelling unrest to the south of Watoria?" Jonas asked.

"Byrric and the Saithian commander have been keeping us busy in the southwestern regions," Willem said. "Edhil and Olthanas are likely lost for now."

Lea's heart leapt at that news. Jonas' reports over the past two days had been scarce, especially as news related to her home realm. To hear that Edhil hadn't yet fallen gave her a heart a much-needed jolt of hope.

"We'll get it back," Effina said, patting Willem's hand. "Try not to worry, darling."

"Yes, our armies combined are no match," Lessia agreed. "Those Edhilian mines will be ours."

Willem sent Lea a chilling look. "Perhaps stringing up the bodies of their former governing family at the gates would sway them."

A lump rose in Lea's throat, but she kept her eyes locked on his. "I believe you underestimate the will of the Edhilian people, Your Majesty." She tensed when Jonas touched her ankle with his boot.

"Oh, leave the girl alone, Willem," Lessia said, waving a hand in annoyance. "It's not your job to threaten her or convince her of anything." She smiled sweetly at Jonas. "That's what my darling nephew is for, isn't it?"

8

LEA

Lea spent the walk back to Jonas' chambers lost in thought as she went over all she'd learned at dinner. Nothing was terribly incriminating—the most shocking thing was that Willem was to wed the Empress' cousin. Other parts, such as this Frederick fellow who'd taken Watoria or Kildin's siege, were of interest, but also likely to be easily deduced, assuming Freya and Aer were managing a good watch of Watoria.

She couldn't get the image Willem painted of her parents' bodies strung up outside the gates of Errest out of her head, though. No matter how much she tried to commit every other bit of conversation to memory, the image of her mother's and father's bloated bodies piked at the city entrance kept flashing through her mind, a reminder as to just how lightly she must tread.

Jonas shut the door quietly when they returned, then dropped a silencing spell over the room.

"So? How did I do?" Lea asked once the room was secured.

Jonas sighed and removed his jacket, then draped it over the back of a chair. He seemed to be struggling to meet her eyes. "Wonderfully."

"Do you think Lessia will actually believe I'm happy here?"

He closed his eyes and collected himself before looking at her. "I think she will believe that I have trained you well enough that being unhappy wouldn't even be an option, which is all she needs."

Lea thought back to Effina's comment about the other lovers Jonas had 'trained.' She desperately wanted to ask about his past, but on the same token, felt it was best she simply didn't know. They did things differently in Jotunheim and that was something she would have to pretend to understand in her time here. With few exceptions, females there were often subservient to an extreme. That Lessia had managed to hold on to the throne after Crispin died was a testament to her ferocity and viciousness. Knowing that, Lea felt it was categorically better she *not* delve into Jonas' romantic history. Not if she was to convincingly pretend to be falling in love with him.

Jonas walked over to the table and poured them each a goblet of dark red wine, then sat down in one of the chairs beside the window. He gestured for Lea to take her wine and sit, so she did. They sat in silence for a few moments, and Lea took a moment to study him. He was handsome in an unconventional way, with white-blond hair, light gray eyes, and a striking face. He didn't appear physically strong, as his body was long and lean, but Lea knew his strength was in no way lacking.

Something about him didn't lead her right into trusting him, though, at least not yet. She hoped that would change in time because she truly believed he was different than the rest of his family, but it was hard to imagine living in this pit of vipers and being able to put her trust in anyone.

As she swirled her wine in her goblet, she wondered what he saw when he looked at her.

She took a careful sip of wine. "Do you really think Willem has cast Isadora aside so easily?" The shock at finding out Isadora was Jonas' sister and a Jotnar spy still lingered. She knew Isadora had fled with Reginald, but with the chaos that ensued in the caves after the coup, she hadn't bothered to ask questions regarding the human queen. It was easy to see they'd cared for one another, making it even easier to deduce why she was fleeing with him, but there had been no indication that she was anyone other than a human woman.

Jonas tapped a finger on the gleaming tabletop as he pondered his answer. "I'm not sure," he finally said, letting his hand flatten. "Effina will grant him children blessed with Jotnar magic, which will strengthen his lineage far more than children with Isadora, and, regardless of her status, Isadora still fled with his brother. Any male would be insulted at a shun like that, regardless of how beneficial she might be to his purposes. In time, it's possible he'll change his views, attempt to get her back, although I think his pride will prevent that from happening."

"Wouldn't children with Isadora have given him half-Jotnar offspring?"

Jonas shook his head. "Lessia had leached away all of her magic, so the lineage would be in name only. Isadora was meant to be a spy, a foot in the door to Dystone, but never anything more."

"Did Isadora truly love him? The man seems insufferable and she seemed so... sweet." *An act,* she reminded herself. All she had seen of Isadora had been an act. The sweet, soft-featured queen was a Jotnar spy, not a meek human who'd been forced into marriage with a horrible man. It was all a charade, just like the one Lea was putting on now.

"I don't believe so, no. Despite what you may have seen, my sister is smart. While Willem certainly has good characteristics, she knew better than to fall for a man who would so easily turn his back on his people."

He smiled softly. "I miss her. Before this visit, it had been years since I'd seen her. She'd been such a light in my life, and then she was just... gone."

Lea's heart twisted as she tried to imagine how Isadora's absence must've felt for him. Jonas was young for a Jotnar, hardly thirty, but it seemed clear he loved his sister dearly.

"What was she like? Before Lessia sent her away?"

"Vibrant." He sighed. "Her name was Dania when she was born. She bore a striking resemblance to the real Isadora. Uncanny, really.

Once Lessia heard of Willem's betrothal to the human Isadora, she began to shift Dania away from the female she was to the female you met just a few weeks ago. Her vibrance dimmed when Lessia began to take away her magic, and the glamour Lessia used to alter her appearance was so thorough..." He cleared his throat. "Before that, though, she was my best friend. We were fairly close in age, so when she was taken away, it was like losing a part of myself."

"I'm so sorry," Lea whispered. "She sounds lovely."

"Hopefully once all of this is over you'll get to meet her. The *real* her."

Lea frowned. "What happened to the real Isadora? The one she replaced?"

Jonas stared down at his hands, idly twirling his goblet from side to side. "Lessia brought her to Jotunheim for a time, but what use was a twelve-year-old human girl to someone like my aunt? She fell ill a few years after the switch, some kind of human disease that we didn't have in Jotunheim. Lessia didn't see fit to have our healers tend to her, so after a month of suffering, she died." A small muscle twitched in his jaw as some memory flashed across his face. "I tried to help her, but so few Jotnar have true healing magic, and those who do only healed with Lessia's permission. I thought if I could help her, I could have a small part of my sister back. Foolish, I know."

"I don't think so," Lea replied, putting a hand over his, stilling his movements. "I think it makes sense, if I'm being honest."

He gave her a rueful smile. "I suppose it does, in a way. I couldn't help my sister, but I wanted to at least help that human girl. After she died, I didn't see any need to stay in Jotunheim permanently, so I requested the job as emissary, seeing it as the only way I'd be able to keep an eye on my sister."

"And Willem," Lea added. "It allowed you to keep an eye on him as well." Though she'd never had a sibling, she could only assume if hers was sent to a foreign land with the intent of deception, she'd want to keep close tabs on both them and whoever it was they were sent to spy on.

Jonas gave her an odd look. "Yes, I suppose that's true, although the nature of my job, in general, allows me to monitor those I consider allies or enemies, so that was never a true consideration. And, magic or no, Isadora was quite capable of holding her own."

"Do you enjoy being an emissary?" she asked. "I've always wondered what that might be like." Her tooth dug into her lip. "Freya told me of Reginald's travels and I wondered if yours were similar. Have you gone as far to the east as he claims to have gone?"

"To the elves?" Jonas chuckled and topped off his goblet. "No, Avorell is not yet a place I've attempted to tap into. Perhaps after a few more decades." He grimaced, looking slightly apprehensive. "Or centuries."

"You fear them?" The thought amused her more than she expected. While the elves—powerful creatures from the eastern lands of Avorell, a place few ever ventured due to unfamiliarity, fear, and distance—were rumored to be odd, even hostile to outsiders, it was a bit surprising that the emissary from a land such as Jotunheim would be hesitant to make contact.

"Fear?" He scoffed. "No, I don't fear them. Lessia has been making mention of attempting to form a relationship with them to aid in her current endeavors, even, but I simply feel there are more important things to deal with here at home than a people who live on the other side of the world."

Like the hostile takeover of a foreign nation?

Lea chose to keep that thought to herself as she turned the rest of his response over in her mind. His logic made sense, to an extent, but the fact that Lessia was actively trying to pursue a relationship with a race long-assumed to be disinterested in the rest of the world struck her as more than a little interesting. Lessia had spent years cultivating her relationship with Willem's father, Christopher, and later, Willem, as they formed their plans to take over Lindoroth. It seemed logical that it would take a good deal longer to solidify their joint rule. Those years of instability would make it imprudent to try to build a relationship from scratch with far-off lands when so many more beneficial ones would need to be made within their own lands.

The only reason Lea could think of as to why Lessia might

attempt such a detour would be if she wasn't planning on a joint rule at all.

"What I don't understand," Lea said slowly, "is why Lessia and Willem wouldn't marry. Wouldn't that make more sense than handing her cousin off to him?"

"Lessia has been fairly tight-lipped with me on that aspect of all of this," Jonas began, "but my assumption is she wants a Jotnar tied to the human crown. This is the start of a new empire, three kingdoms in one, so my aunt is unlikely to leave Lindoroth anytime soon." He took another sip of his wine. "And, as she is nearly seven hundred years old, she's out of her child-rearing years. Not that she would never consider bearing a half-human child, anyway. Effina is still quite young and doesn't hold the same reservations, so this will give Jotunheim a legitimate heir to the human throne. When Lessia offered her to Willem as a prize for a job well done, they both happily took the offer."

Lea frowned as she tried to reason that out in her mind. The logic was there, she supposed, from a conqueror's perspective. For a good while, Willem would likely be unwilling to leave their newly-conquered lands, either. Having a queen who could act as his surrogate in Dystone would make sense. Seeing as Isadora was no longer an option, Effina was a logical second choice.

But even as the thought formed, she decided it still didn't make sense. If all went as Jonas said and Effina bore Willem a son, it would just be a matter of her killing Willem, taking his portion of this new empire for herself, and holding it until her son came of age.

Willem couldn't possibly be that obtuse, she thought.

"But what about the Jotunheim throne?" she asked. "If Lessia can't have children, how will she have an heir to take over?"

"I am Lessia's heir," Jonas said. "As with Effina, she expects me to carry on that lineage. Her brother is currently acting as steward in Jotunheim, but as I actually share blood with our late emperor and her husband, Crispin, I'm considered a legitimate successor in the eyes of our laws once she passes."

Lea scoffed. "Couldn't she simply have the laws rewritten? Name whoever she'd like?"

Jonas shook his head. "She won't touch Jotnar traditions. No one will. They're too long-held."

Lea picked up her goblet, swirled the contents a bit, then took a sip as she thought over the mess Jonas had just laid before her. Willem's idiocy. Lessia's obvious duplicity. And the mere thought that Lessia might try to reach out to the elves was simply ludicrous.

As though he'd read her mind, Jonas sighed. "I suppose it would benefit us all if Lessia did turn her eye to the east, wouldn't it? Attempting to contact the elves would certainly draw a bit of attention away from us."

"Indeed, it would," Lea agreed. She finished off the last of her wine, then stood. "I think I'd like to take a bath and get some rest," she said.

"Of course. I'll call Dina—"

"No need, my lord." Tyna, small and glittering, appeared in the air beside Lea. "I'm happy to take care of Lady Calliwell."

Jonas gave her a sharp nod. "I've got a few things to address, anyway. I'll be back soon."

A SHORT WHILE LATER, Tyna had filled the tub with steaming, sweet-scented water and was working the pins from Lea's hair.

It was several minutes before she finally spoke.

"How was dinner, my lady?"

Lea closed her eyes and leaned back against the edge of the tub, letting Tyna and the water do their work. "Disconcerting. Even a bit horrifying, perhaps."

Tyna tsked as she fluttered to Lea's other side to begin combing through her locks. "The more days pass, the more I wish you hadn't come back, my lady."

Lea made a small, noncommittal noise. "Tyna, do you know anything of the elves?"

"Oh, yes, my lady. Strange creatures they are."

Frowning, Lea turned her head to look at her. "You've met some, then?"

Tyna's thin, silver brows puckered. "We pixies have been around for a long time, my lady. We know all the creatures of the world."

"Are they evil?"

"Not evil, necessarily, but they can be quite cunning. Conniving, even." She finished combing Lea's hair and began to work amber-scented soap through. "They can't lie, so they've adapted quite impressive ways of spinning the truth."

"Do you think they'd ever join with Lessia in this war?"

"The only reason a country would join another in a war would be if they wanted something from said nation. They say Avorell is so large it stretches halfway around the world and is filled with riches unimaginable, so I don't think they need bother with acquiring outside territories, nor do they have need of our goods or allegiances. The elves aren't so vast in numbers that they need more lands, so why bother going through the hassle of trying to acquire them?"

Lea turned to give Tyna a dubious look but didn't voice her disagreement, even though the thought of a race being so content that they'd never bother conquering other lands seemed a stretch. Despite how much she loved her late uncle, she knew even Salazar wouldn't have been opposed to the idea of conquest. He certainly wouldn't be as duplicitous as Lessia and Willem, but it was what rulers did—expanded their kingdoms, their empires, either by force or treaty.

She sat quietly as Tyna finished tending to her and waited patiently as she braided her hair and rubbed her skin with oil.

When she was done, Lea dressed in a long, silk nightgown and wool robe and smiled at the pixie, who seemed to genuinely care about Lea's well-being and made no secret of her thoughts on Lea's mission. "I know you wish I hadn't come back, Tyna, and sometimes I think it would've been better if I'd left with the others. But this is something I have to do. If I had doubts before, dinner this evening erased them all. Especially now that I know Lessia is considering attempting an elvish alliance."

Tyna was quiet for a moment, then bowed her head. "I understand, my lady. Please don't take my wishes as a desire to leave. I have no intention of abandoning you. As long as you are in Iladel, I will be, as well."

Lea let out a small sigh of relief. "I appreciate that more than you know."

9
———

FREYA

Haegin brought food into the dining room, insisting Freya and the others eat while they talk. After waiting for all the guests to be fed, Freya, Aer, Reginald, Isadora, and Florian relayed the events of the wedding to the marshals, with Florian, Isadora, and Reginald filling in the gaps from the reception during the time after Freya and Aer had gone back to their room that night.

Freya and Aer had heard Florian retell the events before, had sat and dissected them several times since they'd left Iladel, but hearing his cold, simple way of telling the story still brought a tightness to Freya's belly that made it hard for her to focus on his words. The thought of the mothers of Laz, Lea, Myria, and Collin wasting away in the dungeons, their thoughts consumed with the images of their husbands and children being murdered, was something that would haunt her for a long time, and the knowledge of that pain, something she could do nothing to alleviate, caused her to cling to the fury that had ignited inside her. She knew she would need that fury when it came time to face Lessia and Willem again.

After they'd finished telling their tale, Ashton looked back to Freya. "Were many left behind?"

"Too many," Freya said quietly. She didn't know how many in the palace hadn't been able to flee, but she knew the number was far higher than she'd hoped. "Only a few dozen of us were able to get out, but the wedding had hundreds of guests, most of whom were staying at the palace. And the staff..." She ran a hand through her hair, hissing when her fingers snagged in the tangled pink-and-brown locks, then let her arm fall to her side and looked up at Aer, feeling an overwhelming urgency to *fix* something. "We have to help them. The thought of the number of guests that had been tossed into the dungeons or worse..."

She squeezed her eyes shut, trying to shut out the images of what "worse" could actually be. Lessia and Willem weren't the type to show mercy with those who had no solid ties to the governing houses or royal family. The relatives, children, and spouses of those houses could and would be used as leverage to gain allegiance, to convince many high-ranking Linds to join their cause and bring their territories with them.

As for the rest... she could only assume they'd become collateral damage.

Aer laced his fingers through hers and kissed the top of her head. "We will, Valkyrie. Don't worry," he murmured.

"Are your staff well-trained?" Ashton asked, then held up a hand when Aer gave him a sharp look. "What I mean is, are they capable of being seen and not heard?"

"Of course," Aer replied. "My father wouldn't have had it any other way."

Ashton nodded. "If Lessia and Willem are at all like this Frederick seems to be, they'll only execute those who outwardly oppose them. I've never seen it myself, but from what I understand, your palace is tricky to navigate with no knowledge of its layout. Intuition helps very little, am I correct?" When Aer nodded, Ashton continued. "Then if you're lucky, they'll attempt to use some of the staff to learn the palace's secrets. Those who oppose them won't be spared, I can promise, but those who keep their heads down may get through this with their lives, at least for now."

Freya thought of Dina, Oscar, Syndar, Maghda, the palace pixies, and all of the other staff who'd been left behind. While she hoped they might've been spared, the thought of them disclosing the inner workings of the palace, mainly its passage system, was disconcerting. The number of staff who knew of the passages was small, as far as she knew, but all it took was one person who valued their life more than the secrets of their dead king and queen to reveal them.

"So you think they might be spared?" she asked.

Ashton shrugged. "It's possible, for now. Frederick killed the governor's staff who fought back, but it appears those who surrendered went unscathed."

"That's something, at least," Aer muttered.

"It's unfortunate we can't say the same for the governors' wives and children," Reginald added with a sigh.

"Except Lea," Isadora pointed out. "You sent her with my brother. I can assure you all that she's in good hands."

Ashton cast a look at Freya and Aer, then nodded. "Of course."

"It's unlikely her mother can say the same," Florian said.

A flush bloomed on Isadora's pale cheeks. "I only—my point is, we should see Lea's safety, singular as it is, as a good thing. Perhaps she'll be able to make some inroads. Willem can be quite easily influenced, after all, and she's such a pretty thing."

Reginald nodded his agreement, causing Freya's stomach to turn. "If he sees Lea as an asset of any sort, he'll almost certainly make sure she remains unharmed by his men."

"Unless Willem is content to move in on a female who belongs to another male, I doubt that would happen," Aer said. "For a number of reasons, Jonas and Lea opted not to have him claim her as spoils and instead have her portrayed as his lover. I may not know him well, but I think it's safe to say, if he plans to continue playing that game, he won't be quick to share with a human."

"That's if Lessia allows her to stay with Jonas," Reginald countered. "It's entirely possible she's hesitant to trust Jonas now that he's returned with a Lindorothian female, so if Willem feels *he* could do a better job of getting her to convert the people of Edhil—"

"That's highly unlikely," Isadora said, shaking her head. "Willem is strategic. Trying to take Lea for himself would be done out of spite, and nothing more, and I can assure you Lessia knows that."

"And it's the best we can hope for," Freya said when Reginald looked like he was going to argue. "Lea is smart, Lord Ristner. Smart enough to outmaneuver your brother, certainly."

"And a damn good actress," Aer added.

"Then I'd say we're quite fortunate," Ashton said. "I'm assuming you'll have means of contacting your friend to keep an eye on things in Iladel?"

Freya nodded. "Yes, we've worked something out."

Florian frowned at Ashton. "Have you heard anything about who's holding Jotunheim in Lessia's stead? She wouldn't have left Madrya unattended."

"Based on what we managed to catch wind of in the city, her brother Daniel is there now with three thousand Jotnar troops guarding the capital," Ashton explained. "He's much like her—strong, vicious, cruel, and will defend her throne like his own."

"So no hope of getting to her that way, then?" Aer asked.

Ashton shook his head. "No, I would say that's firmly out of the question."

"Right." Aer sighed and dragged a hand through his hair, causing the brown locks to stand on end. His eyes looked tired, despite the early hour. "Let's take the afternoon and night to heal and rest, then we'll regroup in the morning. I have a feeling rest will be in short supply in the coming weeks, especially once Lord Edrin gets wind we're here."

"Does everyone have accommodations?" Freya asked Ashton.

He nodded. "Haegin set most of us up in the cellar at my request." When he saw her frown, he continued. "We're rotating patrols every few hours. The cellar has an outside entrance that makes it easy to rotate out without disturbing the rest of the house."

She gave him a dubious look. "Are you comfortable down there?"

He flashed her a grin. "After the barracks at the marshal station? Yes, the feather mattresses and hot stones Haegin leaves at the wood stove to warm our beds are quite welcome. The coffee he leaves on the burner at all hours is quite wonderful as well."

She huffed out a laugh and shook her head. "Alright. Just let me or Haegin know if you need anything else."

"Will do, Your Majesty."

FREYA HARDLY HAD time to appreciate her warm bath or the clean, welcoming state Haegin had left her old room in before she and Aer collapsed on the down-filled mattress and fell asleep. She'd expected her dreams to be fraught with darkness; nightmares that would cause her to toss and turn, yet she slept soundly, waking when the sun shone through her window to Aer stroking her arm, a small smile on his lips.

"I haven't seen you sleep so peacefully since our wedding night," he said quietly.

"I suppose sleeping on the forest floor tends to take a bit of the 'peace' out of sleeping." She rolled to her side and snuggled against his chest. "I didn't expect to sleep so well, actually," she admitted. "I thought..." She squeezed her eyes shut and pressed her palms to his chest, then exhaled. "I don't know what I thought."

"You're home," he said. "Despite everything, I'd hoped that would bring you a small bit of comfort." He gave her hair a small tug when she went to speak. "And don't say 'Iladel is my home.' You know what I mean."

She laughed. "Yes, I know what you mean. I only wish you could feel that same comfort."

"I have you," he said simply. "You're my home now."

Pulling back, she frowned. "Do you think I don't feel the same?"

"Of course I do." He touched his hand to his heart. "I feel it every day, right here. It doesn't change the fact that this is a place of solace for you, just as Iladel is for me."

"And we left it behind," she whispered. Tears threatened to fall as she took in what he was feeling, a small press through their bond that she felt when emotions were running high. "I'm so sorry."

He touched a finger to her chin and tilted her face toward his. "Freya, do not for *one* second think I regret the decision to leave. We would've been of little help there. Useless, even. We'd be dead or locked in a cell, not here, in a position to help save a city and gather more forces."

She rolled onto her back and stared up at the smooth, white ceiling. "I know. I just wish there was a way we could be in two places at once, preferably without a near-definitive risk of death."

"Sadly, that's magic we're both lacking."

There was a knock at the door, and Freya frowned.

"They couldn't even let us get out of bed first?" she muttered.

Aer chuckled. "Come in!" he called.

Laz and Collin came in, both looking as refreshed after a night in a warm bed as Freya felt. Laz still carried a bit of the hollow look he had worn when he'd left the dining room last night; a clear sadness at the loss of his father and now his home. Collin, despite the loss of his uncle and having no knowledge of where his own parents were, seemed to be using those losses as fuel, diving into planning and scouting throughout their journey from Iladel, gladly taking up patrols and working out shift schedules with the guards.

"Good, you're both up," Collin said. "Haegin is showing Amber around the kitchens, so breakfast will be up soon."

"Oh, thank the gods," Freya said, sitting up to lean against the mahogany headboard. The thought of a hot breakfast, especially one of Haegin's, instantly set her stomach rumbling. When Aer laughed at the sound, she scowled and hit him with a pillow.

Laz sat down on the end of the bed and gave them a tight smile. "Did you two sleep well?"

"Yes, thankfully," Freya said. "And you?"

"Like a babe," he replied. "If I didn't know better I'd think your grandmother's cloaking spells kept out any bad dreams and fitful sleep as well."

"I wouldn't have put it past her," Freya said with a smile.

"The marshals have just come back from night patrol," Collin said, leaning against one of the tall bedposts. "I thought it best we wait for you both to arrive before hearing their reports."

"Tell everyone we'll be down shortly," Aer said.

Collin nodded. "Before we go, there was something we wanted to talk to you about privately." He cast a glance toward the door, then sat down next to Laz and waited while Freya dropped a silencing spell over the room before continuing. "Including the marshals, we have nearly sixty people here. I think you both should get on the same page regarding who's in charge of what and how patrols should be scheduled." He gave Freya an apologetic look. "Officer Carinald seems well-intentioned, but—"

"He also seems to be a bossy bastard," Laz finished, smirking.

Freya laughed. "That's because he is. Don't worry about Ash. I don't know anyone who respects chain of command more than him."

Laz let out a startled curse as Rini appeared at the foot of the bed in a flurry of silver and pixie dust. Ignoring him, she addressed Freya, her wings fluttering like mad, her eyes wide, chest heaving.

"Your Majesty, I've just heard from Tyna! She's spoken to Lea!"

Freya exhaled a sigh of relief.

"When?" Aer demanded. "Tell us everything."

"It's good news, at least it seems to be," Rini said. "She's alive and well. Or as well as to be expected."

"How so?" Aer asked, squeezing Freya's hand when she slid it into his. Freya smiled when she saw Laz exhale with relief as Collin squeezed his shoulder comfortingly.

"Jonas was finally able to get her out of the dungeons," Rini began, her words flying rapidly from her lips. "It took some time, but as of now, it does *not* appear he has deceived us. Although, of course, that remains to be seen. He brought Lea to his room after sealing up all means of spying, which he allowed Tyna to help with." Her silvery eyes flicked to Freya, then Aer. "I conveyed Your Majesties' concerns regarding his allegiance and she plans to regularly ensure the spy holes they found remain sealed."

"Lea remains wary, though?" Laz asked. "She doesn't trust him?"

Rini shook her head. "And rightly so, if you ask me," she said, a bit of her normal haughtiness peeking through. "The poor thing was stuck in those rotten dungeons for a week!" She clicked her tongue and shook her head. "His reasoning *is* sound, I suppose, and our hope is that he's being truthful. Regardless, she's out and plans to seek a means of escape should she need one."

"Has Tyna shown her where the passages and spy holes are in Jonas' chambers?" Aer asked. "There are quite a few."

"A bit, although Lord Edrin initiated the search for them the moment they returned to the palace. He's plugged all of the holes up that he could find, with Tyna's help. She plans to show Lea where they all are as soon as possible, although she doesn't want to raise Lord Edrin's suspicions. If he's being deceitful, he won't want Lea finding her way out of there easily." She bit her lip. "And there's more. She's already had one dinner with Willem and Lessia. From what Tyna can tell, that will now be a regular occurrence."

"That sounds positively dreadful," Aer murmured.

"Suspicious, more like," Laz muttered.

"Has Lea witnessed anything worth noting?" Collin asked.

"Well, for one, Willem seems to have moved on from Isadora," she said, perching on top of the bedpost. "He plans to take Effina Veldin for a wife."

They were all silent for a moment before Freya choked out a laugh. "The same Effina that attempted to seduce my husband at our wedding?"

"The very same," Rini confirmed. "Quite the opportunist, that one. According to Jonas, Willem plans to take her back to Dystone and Lessia will hold this continent with a human or Lind consort. Lea and Tyna both believe Willem wants to imbue his bloodline with Jotnar magic, and Effina presumably assumes she'll be able to bring Dystone under Jotnar control." She sniffed. "She'll probably kill him, first chance."

Laz laughed in disbelief. "Wait. Lessia Edrin, taking a human husband? And Willem *believes* that?"

"He doesn't hold nearly the amount of dominance in the palace as he'd like others to believe, but he also doesn't seem to be a fool. Tyna finds it unlikely he believes her, but it's worthwhile to go along with their plans, regardless."

"That's something, at least," Collin said.

Rini shrugged. "Regardless of Lessia's true intentions, it appears their plan is to place human and Jotnar pairings in each of the capitals, although that doesn't seem to be working out all that well here in Watoria. The word is that Frederick Edrin is looking to take a Lind for a wife. He has a strong dislike for humans."

"Interesting," Aer murmured. "That could be why we saw so many Lindorothian females being rounded up. Was there anything else?"

"Well, there was one thing..." Rini did a nervous flutter toward the bedside table and picked up a comb. Freya tried to hide her grimace as Rini drifted over and started combing through Freya's hair, starting at the ends and slowly working her way up. "Tyna said Jonas mentioned Lessia attempting to reach out to our friends in the east."

"The east?" Aer frowned and shared a look with Laz and Collin. "The Dystonians are already here."

Rini shook her head, her jaw tight. "No. Avorell."

Laz let out a disbelieving laugh. "Lessia thinks she's got enough clout to call the *elves* to her side? It's been how many centuries since any have ventured out of Avorell? Six?"

Rini shrugged and shifted to Freya's other side, focusing intently on a particular tangle in the brown and pink locks. "A bit less, and it's anyone's guess as to whether or not they'd responded." She huffed in annoyance when she came to a particularly large knot. "It's unlikely, of course, but when was the last time our emissaries heard from them?"

Aer leaned back against the headboard and his brow furrowed. "I'm not sure. Decades?"

"Did either of your parents mention speaking with the elvish leaders?" Freya asked quietly. The elves had maintained their distance from the Linds and Jotnar for so long that stories now told of them were passed on as legend, holding bits of truth but were mostly fabrications, or at least that was what Freya had always assumed. Her mother and grandmother had told her tales of the elves when she was a child, of light and dark beings with unfathomable power, tales that she was certain had been exaggerated to quell her frequent misbehavior.

"No," Aer said. "The last time Father sent an emissary to discuss trade with them was long before I was born, and he returned with hardly more than a 'no, thank you' from their rulers."

Freya drummed her fingers on her arm. "You know, I recall Reginald mentioning visits to Avorell. Perhaps he'd have some insight as to why Lessia thinks they'd be open to discussing an alliance."

Laz's brow shot up. "Visits? As in, more than one?"

"So he claimed. He only mentioned it in passing, though, so I'm not sure to what extent he may or may not have formed a relationship."

"Is it possible he went to speak with them on Willem's behalf?" Collin asked. "If Lessia *does* think it's worth reaching out to the elves, that could be why."

Freya thought for a moment, trying to recall the conversation she'd had with Reginald nearly two weeks back. "No, I didn't get that impression, but it was also the only conversation I'd had with him at the time. I believe he enjoys travel for pleasure, not politics. He said it was 'an interesting land,' but didn't get into detail."

"Since it seems we have more than a few bad actors in this play, we can't rule anything out," Laz said with a shake of his head. "Considering how easy it was for his brother to deceive so many people, I wouldn't put it past Reginald to be much different."

"Perhaps," Aer said. "Regardless, we should talk with him, feel him out a bit. He may reveal something, even if he doesn't intend to."

"And Lea?" Collin asked. "If it seems there is any true threat of more forces entering our shores, *especially* the elves, we should start working to get her out of there now."

"We never should've sent her back," Freya murmured. "We allowed her to walk right into a pit of snakes."

"She's strong and she knows how to play a role," Laz said reassuringly. "Maybe you shouldn't have sent her, but if anyone can do what our cousin is doing, it's her."

"He's right," Aer said, although his expression seemed less certain than his words. "She's in a better position now, and she's already gotten us useful information. We need to trust that she's doing her best to take advantage of her circumstances, especially if Lessia's intentions prove fruitful."

Freya nodded, but she couldn't help but find their assurances underwhelming. Lea was as fierce as she was feisty, but regardless of her mettle, she was surrounded by a palace full of people who wanted her dead. Freya hadn't known her friend long, but she could only pray that she knew how to play her role well.

10

FREYA

The remainder of the morning was spent getting debriefed by Ashton's marshals and the palace guards on the rounds from the night before. Now that the marshals had the advantage of two hawk shifters, surveilling their enemies had become a bit easier. Naedan and Amara had done a fly-over of the forest and of the city, basing their route off of the areas Ashton and Freya had indicated were of greatest importance. The forest had been quiet, so they felt it was safe to assume they had managed to take out all of the Jotnar and humans they'd encountered in the woods the previous day.

The rest of Naedan and Amara's reports were just as troubling to Freya as those of the marshals', and she struggled not to let her emotions show as she listened. Not only had the town square become home to a guillotine, the heads of those who were executed were now set on pikes along the nearby avenues, lining the streets where citizens had formerly done their shopping and dining. Half of the residential areas in the South and West Wards had been burned to cinders, and businesses in the East and North Wards were overrun.

Freya faced the window, staring out over the grounds as she listened intently to the macabre picture they painted. She needed to collect herself before contributing to the discussion, both for her own sake and that of the people she was supposed to be leading, so she was thankful when Aer took the lead once they'd finished speaking.

"Where are their patrols heaviest?" he asked.

"Along the bay," Naedan replied. "I found it odd, but—"

Freya cursed and shook her head. "Godsdamned draugs."

"Draugs?" Aer asked, confused.

She turned to face the room. "When I patrolled, it was always a safe bet I could find a draug or two slipping in through the docks at least once a week. I never questioned why they would come to Watoria instead of cities or towns in Caelora that are closer to their own lands."

"They were seeking our weak points," Ashton murmured, shaking his head.

"But I always caught them," Freya said quietly, staring past the others toward the door. The memory of a night months ago, the night before she left for Iladel, flashed through her mind. "*Almost* always, anyway." She sighed. "Perhaps we can use that to our advantage, use it as a way to take out some of their forces without actually entering the city."

"It's certainly worth considering," Ashton said with a nod.

"Alright, so what does that tell us?" Aer asked. "If Lessia was using the draugs to suss out Watoria's weak points, we have to assume she was doing something similar in the other capitals, or Kildin, at the very least."

"Kildin is hardly an easy area to sneak into," Laz countered. "Watoria has the bay, but my city is surrounded by fifty-foot walls."

"Walls have weaknesses," Ashton said simply. "As do guards. If Kildin was overrun so easily, we must assume that Lessia had prior knowledge of how best to do that. Brute force wouldn't have been an option, correct?"

Laz clenched his jaw and shook his head. "No, it would not. But I can assure you, the marshals who protect our city—"

"Are just as fallible as we are," Ashton said.

Seeing Laz's temper rising, Freya cut in. "We can determine how they got into Kildin when we make our way back east. It will do us no good to speculate now. Right now we need to settle things in the west, then push the enemy back east."

Ashton looked at Freya. "Did the Commander or King Salazar mention disturbances similar to those we dealt with anywhere else?"

"Nothing that seemed out of the ordinary," Freya replied. "Draugs are never seen further south than Watoria. The occasional huldra makes its way down to Olthanas now and then, but Edhil is too far south for them to bother with." She gave Aer a questioning look. "Did your father ever say anything to you?"

"Only that more knights were sent to Caelora's northern border." He inclined his head toward Laz. "Governor Cailen was concentrating more of his foot soldiers there."

"There was something else that struck us as a bit strange," Amara said. "All of the soldiers we saw, all of the guards, they were all Jotnar."

"That confirms they haven't let humans into the city with them," Freya said with a nod. "It makes sense, in a way."

"The Jotnar hardly trust each other," Aer said, "so being this far from their ruler, they won't bother pretending to trust foreign soldiers."

"Well, I'd like to do my own fly-over sooner rather than later," Freya said. She sent Florian a sharp look when he opened his mouth to protest. "I was a marshal long before I was a queen, Lord Florian."

"But you are no longer a marshal, Your Majesty. Going into the city without the backing of an army would be foolish at best."

"He's right," Ashton said. "They expect us to be in the area. Whether they know we've got a base as solid as this is anyone's guess, but at the very least, they know the marshals who fled are still in the vicinity. If you were spotted and followed, it could be catastrophic."

Freya looked at Aer, hoping he'd agree with her but knowing he held the same stance as the others. "Alright," she said with a sigh. "But I'd like it on the record that I don't like it."

"Noted," Florian said. "Now, was there anything else?"

Once they'd finished going back over Naedan and Amara's reports and had heard from the marshals who'd patrolled the forest nearby, Collin and Gideon spent another hour detailing a schedule that included shifts of both Watorians and Iladelians that covered the area immediately surrounding the manor. Flights into Watoria would be limited until they'd formulated some semblance of a plan, but regular aerial patrols of the forest and the shoreline were set for twice per day. For the time being, they didn't intend to inform the Allanorian soldiers who were encamped outside Watoria of their presence, knowing the fewer people who were aware of their existence, the better.

After roles were handed out and everyone began to disperse, Ashton called out to Aer and Freya to stay behind. As they waited for the others to shuffle out, another marshal stood at Ashton's side. He was tall and lanky, with light brown hair and dark eyes. Freya recognized him immediately and grinned.

"King Aerelius, I'd like to introduce you to Steffen, our resident wielder of spirit," Ashton said. "Considering your similar magics, I wanted to introduce you personally."

Steffen gave Aer a short bow. "Your Majesty, it is an honor to meet you."

"Likewise." Aer gave him a curious look. "Is there something I can do for you?"

"I was hoping we might be able to discuss a few things regarding strategy, perhaps how our combined powers could be put to use as one." He flashed a quick smile at Freya. "It's been some time since I had someone to work with, and I believe Her Majesty can attest to my skill."

Freya laughed. "Steffen was one of my trainers when I first joined up with the marshals. He quite gleefully helped me get my ass kicked on more than one occasion."

Aer gave her an amused look. "You admit to someone kicking your ass? More than once?"

"To be fair, *I* didn't do the, ah, kicking," Steffen said. "I merely..."

"Facilitated it?" Freya bit her lip to keep from laughing. "It's alright, Steffen. Aer has been known to give me a run now and then."

"All of the marshals who made it out, save Steffen and Jenna, are shifters," Ashton said. "And while the bulk of your party are shifters as well, you've arrived with a good number of magic-wielders. As His Majesty is the only other spirit user with us, I thought they might join forces, so to speak. See how their powers might complement one another. I'm not sure where your skills lie, Your Majesty," he said, looking at Aer, "but Steffen is quite skilled at weaponizing his power."

Aer gave Steffen a curious look. "How so?"

"A simple matter of training it to take physical form," Steffen replied. "It sounds more complex than it is."

Freya looked at Aer in question, hoping he saw the same opportunity she did. Steffen had been a good teacher to her, so there was no question that he'd do just as well with Aer. She knew Aer felt his training had been lacking when it came to defensive and offensive spirit magic, although he wasn't without skill. His ability to shift emotions toward deeply positive, even pleasurable, made it fairly simple to distract an opponent long enough to take them down physically, and his physical combat skills were some of the best Freya had ever encountered. The more creative aspects of being a wielder of spirit were beyond the scope of what Ordona could have offered him, though. As magical powers didn't fully emerge until the teen years, Aer hadn't had the opportunities of lifelong training that Freya had.

"Alright," Aer said with a nod. "Let's talk."

FREYA AND ASHTON left Aer and Steffen to talk and did a walk around the property. Now that Freya's exhaustion was somewhat quelled and her magic didn't feel quite so poised to burst, she wanted to take a bit of time to see her old home, see that it was intact and unscathed by the recent incursion, while also assessing the property line and its potential weaknesses through the eyes of a trained adult.

It had been nearly seven years since she'd spent any significant amount of time at her family's manor after Byrric moved her into Watoria, but it was just as she remembered. The main building and its two guest cottages had been built by her grandfather's father some eight centuries back. The windows that faced east and west were tall and wide, with each of the ten bedrooms boasting a balcony that gave the occupants a grand view of the sunrises and sunsets. Though the gray stone of the exterior had become smooth with age over the centuries, it did nothing to diminish the manor's splendor.

"So, Freya Harridan, Queen of Lindoroth," Ashton mused as they made their way down the front walk. He smirked. "I have to say, I'm surprised you didn't insist on keeping your birth name."

"Oh, I considered it," Freya told him. "For a variety of reasons, I chose not to let that be the hill I died on."

He chuckled. "Are you enjoying your new role?"

She sighed. "Every moment so far has been fraught with people itching for my death, so I can't say things have been ideal. Aer and I are a good team, though," she said, smiling. "Once this is over... I think we'll be able to do good things for Lindoroth."

She thought of all the times she and Ashton had gone on patrol together, all the training he'd put her through, and the quieter time they'd spent together when they weren't working. Guilt pricked at her heart as she considered what a shock this all must be to him.

"I'm sorry I never told you what my family had planned for me," she said. "It was just—"

He held up a hand, stopping her. "I understand. As much as I would love to say the marshals wouldn't have treated you any differently if we'd known you were going to be Queen, I know that's a lie."

"No, I know. I'm just sorry I didn't tell *you*. We were...close and—"

"Freya, stop," he said, putting a hand on her arm. He waited until she'd stopped walking and turned to face him. "Was I a bit perturbed when I found out I'd unknowingly shared a few kisses with the future queen? That someone I was close with hadn't been fully honest with me? Yes, and I don't think you can blame me." He put his hands on her shoulders and crouched down to meet her eyes. "But I also don't blame *you*."

She frowned. "You don't?"

He laughed. "Gods above, Freya! You were one of the best

marshals we had in ages. Do you think we would've had you out on the streets alone if we'd known? You and Byrric were smart to keep it quiet."

She searched his face for any sign that he wasn't being forthright. "Do you mean that?"

He squeezed her shoulder and started walking again. "Absolutely. And you wear it well, if you don't mind me saying so. Your authority," he added when she looked at him quizzically. "Not that you ever had a problem telling others what to do."

"So says the bossiest marshal to have ever held office in Watoria," she teased, then instantly regretted her words. The marshals of Lindoroth were strong and well-trained, but they were small forces compared to what they were faced with, especially now. They were tasked with keeping order within a city, but fending off a foreign invasion was another thing entirely. She could only imagine the horrors they'd faced when Lessia and Willem's armies descended on Watoria, watching their loved ones and fellow officers be slaughtered.

"How are your officers doing after the attack on the city?" she asked quietly.

"As well as is to be expected, I suppose," he said quietly. "There's been no word of any of their families, which is worrisome."

Freya swallowed back her sadness at that. While some marshals were young like she'd been, most were much older, climbing the ladder toward becoming soldiers in the Allanorian or Lindorothian army. Many had started families of their own decades ago, had wives or husbands or children, even grandchildren. All, as far as she knew, had extended families who still lived in the city.

"Haegin certainly did well maintaining this place, didn't he?" Ashton commented.

"Thank the gods for that," Freya murmured, acknowledging that the subject of the marshals' losses was closed for now. She added checking on the marshals' families to her list of priorities for when she finally did her first patrol into Watoria. A risk, to be sure, but a necessary one. "When you arrived, did anyone test the strength of Selinda's spells?"

Ashton nodded. "Gideon and Steffen both did. They're still holding strong, although with so many living occupants now you may need to reinforce them a bit."

"Florian and I will strengthen any weakening magic, if necessary. He's more than adept," she added when she saw the dubious look on Ashton's face.

"I'm certain he is. I just think it would be wiser to limit the amount of people who have access to the magic that protects this property, that's all."

"Unfortunately, that isn't a luxury available to us at the moment, so we'll have to make do. I trust Florian. He's been with the Harridan family for centuries."

Ashton chose not to push the subject, so they walked in silence for a few minutes while Freya took note of their surroundings. The property hadn't changed much over the years, the gardens still bearing Haegin's talented touch, the lawn perfectly manicured, windows gleaming, and fountains softly burbling water from the cold underground springs. The sky was heavily overcast, the pinch of the cold air telling Freya snow would likely be upon them in the coming days.

She paused when they came up to the woodshed, a large stone structure that sat along the forest on the eastern side of the house. When she peeked inside, she was satisfied to see it had been stocked to the brim with split firewood, more than enough to heat the house for several weeks.

"I think I'm going to do a quick flight around the property," Freya said once they'd finished their walk. "I need to stretch my wings and I'd like to see how the wards feel from above. Can you go reassess the stores in the root cellars now that we know how many mouths we have to feed? Collin and Laz can help consolidate that with what little we have left from our travels. Medical supplies as well."

His lips twitched as he nodded. "It's good to have you back, Freya."

She stared out over her family's land, then nodded. "It's good to be back. I only wish the circumstances weren't so horrid."

"As do I." He took a few steps back when she let out her wings to give her space to take off. "I'll go check on our stores."

With a nod of farewell, she took to the air.

The Enrieth property extended about a mile out from the house in all directions, so while it wasn't a long run, it gave her plenty of time and space to work her wings. The small bit of flying she'd done the day before had helped relieve a bit of the tension that had built up, but this was what she'd truly needed.

She looped around, crisscrossing the grounds and taking note of game trails that cut through the trees in the surrounding forest before heading toward the outermost edges, where her grandmother had set her wards. Invisible as they were, Freya had to reach out with her own power to feel where they were placed to avoid flying clear through them. When she felt the earthy taste of Selinda's magic, she slowed, back-flapping slightly as she squinted, trying to see the shield that surrounded the property. It was there, but only visible because she knew exactly what her grandmother's magic felt like. She flew higher, carefully running her fingers along the wall as she went, feeling for weak spots and seeking an endpoint, if one existed.

When she reached the apex of the magical dome that enshrouded the property, she infused some of her air magic into it, strengthening it some. Then she paused, flapping her wings slowly as she turned and looked out over the forest toward the city. Her heart ached and anger spiked through her when she saw the plumes of smoke, tall and black, rising from multiple points around the city. Looking further out, she took in the encampments of soldiers that surrounded the city on three sides, with the Bay of Brystone on the fourth, largely obscured by the smoke that billowed across the city. Beyond that, the Brystonian Sea stretched off into the horizon. Rows of tents, smoke from campfires, and soldiers spread from the outside of the ravine, blocking the path of any who would try to cross and eliciting painfully strong feelings of hate and sadness from Freya.

Searching further on the horizon, she could just make out the encampments of Allanorian soldiers, too far to be of any use to them.

Closing her eyes in frustration, she turned away to continue her assessment.

It took nearly two hours for her to complete her inspection. By the time she touched down on the front lawn, it was past midday, and Aer and Florian were waiting for her at the front portico.

"How did your discussion with Steffen go?" she asked Aer as she retracted her wings.

"Good, I think," he replied. "Depending on how things go while we're here, I may consider offering him a position at court, if you think it to be a good idea."

"If you can convince him to leave Watoria behind, I think it would be a wonderful idea," she said. "He's been with the marshals for nearly sixty years."

Aer shrugged. "I suppose we'll see, then."

"Were there any problems with the warding, Your Majesty?" Florian asked.

"I didn't feel any weak spots, but I'd like you to take a trip around the property and feel its connection to the ground, make sure it's well-seated, shore it up a bit if possible."

Florian nodded absently, then cast a glance past her into the yard. As his dark eyes ran over the grounds, Freya gave Aer a questioning look.

"Give him a moment," Aer whispered.

Freya watched as Florian continued to stare into the distance, his eyes darting here and there. A few moments later, he looked back at Freya.

"There's a spot toward the southeast that I'd like to address more closely, but all else seems well."

Her eyebrows shot up, causing Florian to chuckle, a rare sound coming from the warlock.

"Earth magic is tethered to the *earth*, Your Majesty. I simply follow its trail."

She pursed her lips, torn between annoyed and impressed. "I suppose I could have saved myself a bit of time had I come to you first, then."

"No, it's better to assess these things yourself, and infusing it with air was a good plan. If it's alright with you both, I'd like to place some of my own wards down to strengthen your grandmother's. Hers are strong, but as she is no longer here to refuel them, I'd feel better if my own magic was in place."

"Of course," Aer said with a nod. "Can either of us help?"

"Possibly," he replied. "Selinda was an earth witch, but her spells indicate she had a good grasp on all of the elements which is why her wards are so effective. It was common in the Cantor line," he added when he saw Freya's surprised expression. "They would claim the power most prevalent, but Cantor witches were sought after for a reason, Your Majesty. Most of the females boasted small amounts of additional elemental magics."

"Byrric never told me that," she said quietly. "I wonder why?"

Florian shrugged. "Your magic is quite similar to hers, although it's lacking the depth. You can touch each of the elements, draw on them some, but air and fire are the strongest." He shifted his gaze to Aer. "Adding your spirit magic into the wards could help strengthen the areas that cause the observer to be diverted."

Aer held out a hand, gesturing down the steps to the front walk. "Lead the way." He gave Freya a kiss on the cheek before following the warlock away from the house.

Freya watched them walk off, her arms folded as annoyance pricked at her. She'd yet to come upon a situation where power—either magical or physical—was needed and she wasn't able to contribute. It was silly, she knew that, but the feeling of uselessness rankled a bit, nevertheless.

Shaking off that thought, she turned and walked inside.

11

FREYA

Freya took a bit of time to explore her childhood home before making her way to the kitchen to find lunch. Walking the halls now, running her hands along the smooth banisters of the curved staircase, listening as her boots thudded softly along the gleaming oak floors, brought back every fond memory she had of her time there as a girl.

After her mother was killed and Freya and Ana moved into the city, Freya had little reason to return to the manor she'd shared with her grandparents, as they'd both died when she was still fairly young. Byrric used it from time to time when he stayed in Watoria for more than a day, but since she came of age and as Selinda and Jora's heir, the land now, technically, belonged to her. She'd always assumed she and Aer would use it as a second home, a place to visit in the summer months, or just when they needed to get away from the hectic world of Iladel.

There had never been a time when she imagined this home would be used as a refuge during war.

She paused in the doorway of the room that her parents had once occupied and leaned a shoulder against the doorjamb, taking it in. She'd never been one to run to her mother and father after a bad dream, but she had vivid memories of waking them on birthday mornings, bouncing across the thick mattress to drag them from bed, tugging at the beard Byrric had long-since shaved. Back then, when he was still given leave to return to Watoria regularly, those mornings were more frequent. As she grew and began to understand his absence more, that became time spent with her mother, who'd greatly lessened her role within the army after she'd had Freya.

Freya often wondered if her mother regretted that or resented Byrric for leaving her and Freya behind, but knowing what she knew now, that her marriage to Aer had been in talks since before they were born, she could only assume her parents were in agreement about giving her as simple a life as they could, at least until that simplicity was no longer possible.

"Has it been long since you've been back?"

Freya jumped at the sound of Myria's voice behind her, then turned to face her.

"It has," she said. She forced a tight smile as she dragged herself back to the present from her ruminations. Myria looked thoroughly refreshed in a pale blue dress, her hair loose around her shoulders. "Did you sleep well?"

Myria leaned against the wall outside the bedroom she'd been assigned, her hands clasped behind her back. "I did. I didn't expect to."

"Grandmother's spells," Freya told her. "I don't know the full intricacies, but I'm fairly certain they protect more than just the physical health of the people inside."

"Thank the gods for that," Myria murmured.

Freya inclined her head toward Myria's dress. "I see Haegin dug out some of my mother's old clothes?"

Wrinkling her nose, Myria looked down at the pretty blue fabric. "Yes, he did. Your mother had a lovely wardrobe. I managed to snag a few pieces before Isadora came sniffing about." With a look of consternation, she looking toward the stairs. "It seems I've missed breakfast."

"You're in time for lunch, though," Freya said, giving her best attempt at a real smile. "I'm just about to head down myself if you'd like to join me."

Myria nodded, and the pair walked in silence through the house, Myria seeming lost in thought as Freya struggled to find something to talk about. She and Myria had started their time at Aldridge at odds, later growing to grudgingly respect one another as skills and true personalities were revealed. There had never been a time when Freya thought they might be friends, and even now, she wasn't sure.

"How are you doing?" Freya asked quietly, wincing at how idiotic her question sounded.

"My father is dead and my home has been overtaken by mongrels," Myria said tiredly. "How do you think I'm doing?"

The lack of venom in her tone worried Freya. Any words of comfort Freya might offer would likely be seen as pointless platitudes, useless things that would do nothing to ease the pain of Myria's grief. Not wanting to upset her further, Freya gestured toward the stairs.

"Come on," she said quietly. "Let's go find something to eat."

When they reached the kitchen, Haegin was sliding a long-handled peel that held a large loaf of bread out of the oven, while Amber stirred a tall pot of stew. Haegin gave them both a quick nod of acknowledgment before delivering the bread to the table. The steam that rose from it immediately set Freya's stomach grumbling.

"Hungry, Your Majesty?" Haegin asked when she touched a hand to her stomach.

"Quite. What are you making?"

"Haegin has been showing me how to make your grandmother's venison stew," Amber said as she tilted up on her toes to peek into the large pot. "I hope we've managed it to your liking."

Freya smiled. "If Haegin has become your teacher, I have no doubts. Is that what we'll be having for dinner tonight?"

"It is," Haegin said, setting down a cutting board with a basket of rolls, a wedge of hard cheese, a tub of butter, and a knife in front of Freya and Myria on the long table. "Give me just a moment and I'll have lunch for you both."

Freya sat down on the narrow bench seat and gestured for Myria to join her.

Myria picked up a roll and began pulling small pieces off. "Have you gone out to patrol yet?"

"I have," Freya said. "Only to check the property, though. Florian and Aer are triple checking the wards, but it seems we're safe here for now."

Myria nodded slowly and took a bite of bread. Freya studied her for a moment, recalling the girl who'd been so hostile to her upon her arrival at Aldridge. That person seemed eons apart from the one who sat before her now, staring absently down at the cutting board, her face pinched with sadness and anger.

"Is there anything you need?" Freya asked her.

"I'm not quite sure you're in a position to give me what I need, but thank you," Myria replied politely.

Freya's jaw clenched as she tried not to let Myria's words hit their mark. All she'd been focused on since they'd left was ensuring retribution for those who'd lost people in the palace massacre. Myria, Laz, Collin, Aer, Lea, and all the rest who had lost so much. For the fathers and uncles, and the mothers, cousins, and siblings who were still in chains.

She would imagine Myria felt Freya had lost comparably little, considering Freya's father still lived, and the grief from her mother's death had long-diminished. Freya couldn't say she disagreed, even though the ache at missing her father seemed to grow each day.

Footsteps sounded at the doorway, and when Freya turned, Reginald, Collin, and Laz were entering the room.

Freya smiled and quickly swallowed her mouthful of cheese. "Here for a late lunch as well?"

"Indeed," Reginald said. "I ran into Lazarus and Collin in the hall and they invited me to join them."

Laz sent Freya a pointed look as he dropped down on the bench beside her. Reginald and Collin sat down across from them.

Laz took a few pieces for himself before sliding the plate of cheese toward Collin, then looked at Freya. "How was your survey of the property?"

"Good," Freya replied. "The wards are being reinforced now." She frowned at Reginald. "Where is Isadora?"

"Still resting," he said, smiling his thanks to Haegin, who set another board with rolls and cheese on the table. "The journey seems to have taken a lot out of her."

"Well, of course," Myria replied. "The poor thing surely hasn't had to do any form of physical activity in years." Despite the pity in her words, it was easy to detect the disdain Myria still felt for Isadora. Though the human queen was considered an ally, Isadora was still strongly connected to both the Jotnar and human royal families. Freya could certainly understand Myria's reticence when it came to both Isadora and Reginald, although she wished she'd tone it down just a bit.

"She'll come round soon enough," Reginald said, smiling softly. "Isadora is more resilient than she looks, I assure you."

Myria flashed him a hard smile, then stuffed a piece of bread in her mouth.

"So, Prince Ristner," Freya said, needing to distract him from Myria's attitude, "the other day, Lazarus and I were talking about places we'd like to travel, and you came to mind." She smiled brightly and propped her elbow on the table, resting her chin on her fist. "Didn't you once tell me you visited the elvish lands once?"

He nodded. "Indeed. A few times, actually. They were short visits, but enjoyable."

Myria looked at him sharply. "They let you into Avorell? Why would they do such a thing?"

He gave her a confused look. "Because I had no ill intent nor did I wish to discuss trade with them."

"They allowed you onto their lands under the guise of friendship?" Freya asked dubiously.

Myria shook her head and muttered something under her breath, then went back to her food.

"They did," Reginald confirmed. "And it wasn't a guise; it was the truth."

Freya looked at Collin, then nodded her approval when she saw the question in his eyes.

"Do they seem the type to ally with the likes of your brother or Lessia?" Collin asked Reginald.

Reginald chuckled. "Highly unlikely. They want little and less to do with those outside their shores. They want for nothing, neither lands nor goods. Why do you ask?"

Freya smiled. "Call it... political curiosity."

Myria picked up a slice of apple from the bowl of fruit that Haegin had just put down and eyed it contemplatively. "Did Willem enjoy a friendship with them as well?"

Freya sent her a look of caution.

Reginald looked around at the four of them. "He did not. In fact, to the best of my knowledge he was entirely unaware that I'd even met Nalaea and Ruehnar. Avorell's monarchs," he added when he saw Myria's confused look. "I only ever told Willem that they seemed wholly uninterested in a trade relationship. Again I ask, why?"

"I think Her Majesty's initial answer was sufficient, don't you?" Myria asked airily. "There are many lands in this world and the only thing between us and them is your kind."

"Well, I can assure you that the likelihood of the elves venturing from their homeland to help nations with which they hold no ties is nearly nil," Reginald said.

"In other words, magnanimity isn't their strong suit?" Laz asked.

"No, not at all." Reginald gave Freya a curious look. "If I didn't know better, I'd think you'd received news from Iladel."

Freya smiled easily. "Nothing of note. We're only talking strategy. There are many allies out there that Lessia and Willem will likely consider reaching out to, and you are the only person I know who's interacted with that nation specifically. Apologies if we seemed intrusive."

"That's completely understandable, Your Majesty. Those are questions you should be asking, certainly." He looked as though he wanted to question her further but was cut off when Amber set a bowl of sliced chicken down in the center of the table with a heavy thud.

"Lunch is served," she said brightly, giving Freya a look. "Let me know if there's anything else you need."

"So, do we believe him?" Laz asked Freya when they left the kitchens a short while later.

Freya gnawed at her lip as she thought over their conversation with Reginald. He'd seemed sincere, but despite that, his family ties gave Freya enough pause to question whether that sincerity was real or not. If there was anything Freya had learned over these past two weeks, it was that even the most unassuming person could be a convincing liar.

"We need more information," she said. "None of us know him well enough to know what kind of liar he is—"

"Are *any* of you going to tell me what's going on?" Myria asked, exasperated. "For the gods' sakes, you've been babbling on about bloody *elves* like they're actually relevant in our world. Why?"

"Lord Ristner spoke to me about his travels to Avorell and I was simply curious as to whether or not he'd formed a relationship strong enough to convince them to join Dystone in a war," Freya explained. "Strategy, as I said."

Myria gave them both a dubious look. "Well, I, for one, think we should look to the threats that are a bit closer to home. I know our current focus is Watoria, but when will we begin to look to other areas?"

"Once we hear from Byrric," Collin told her.

"I know it isn't what you want to hear," Freya said when she saw Myria's disappointment. "But right now we should assume that we've heard nothing because he's focused on saving your city."

Myria's jaw tensed as she stared at Freya. "You truly believe he can save it?"

Freya smiled reassuringly. "I do."

"Because you know him so well?"

"Myria," Collin admonished.

Freya bit back the retort that came to her and took a deep breath before responding. Myria's barbs were a defense mechanism; she knew that. She also knew Myria had a strong respect for Byrric, so her words were more aimed at striking a nerve than challenging Freya's logic.

"Byrric has earned his reputation," Freya said evenly. "And Salazar made him commander of the Royal Army for a reason. Now isn't the time to doubt him."

Myria came to a stop at the bottom of the main staircase. "I certainly hope you're right. I'm going to go lay down for a while. Let me know when it's time for dinner."

Freya and Collin watched her flounce up the stairs, both wearing identical looks of bemusement.

Laz let out a quiet chuckle and shook his head. "Which one of you is Queen again?"

Freya huffed out a laugh. "That her demeanor hasn't diminished entirely gives me a bit of hope for the future, to be honest."

Collin glanced up the stairs, then down the hall that led off the foyer. "Have you any thoughts on how best to go about gathering information from inside the city?"

Freya shook her head, then began to walk toward the front door, gesturing for them to follow. When they got outside and began to walk down the wide stone steps, she glanced at Collin. "We haven't come up with anything yet. You?"

"Infiltration of some sort would be ideal, but I'm not quite sure how to manage a thing like that."

"Especially with the Allanorian soldiers unable to get any closer," Laz added.

"Exactly the problem," Freya said with a sigh. "It's incredibly frustrating being so close but having no real means of recourse."

"Has anyone been sent to speak with the Allanorian soldiers?" Collin asked.

"Not yet," Freya replied. "Even sending one of the hawks out that way will risk raising alarms, and we need to keep our arrival a secret as long as we can. There are more than one thousand enemy troops between us and our own, which is far riskier to fly over than a simple patrol in the city."

"What will you do, then?" Laz asked.

"Ashton and I are going to look over the maps of the city and try to find a few points of entry that the Jotnar may not have discovered yet. There aren't many, but I think at this point our priority should be attempting to get aid to the people who are still inside, hopefully getting as many out as we can."

"Perhaps they'll be able to mount an offensive attack?" Collin suggested.

"Assuming Frederick Edrin hasn't pillaged all the weapons from homes, that's certainly a possibility. The Watorians are strong, but the Jotnar have the advantage of numbers."

"Do you think Reginald is being truthful about Dystone's relationship with Avorell?" Laz asked.

"I honestly don't know," she said with a sigh. "He *did* steal his brother's wife, after all. That seems to speak to his stance."

Collin wrinkled his nose. "I suppose."

Laz gave him a curious look. "You don't believe him?"

"I think it's unwise to trust anyone here," Collin replied. He gave Freya an apologetic look. "Not even your marshals. I'm sorry."

"I trust them," she told him. "But I respect your choice not to. If I were in your shoes, I wouldn't, either." Movement toward the end of the drive caught her eye, and she smiled when she saw Aer and Florian coming toward them. "Come, let's go listen to Aer brag about how helpful he's been."

12

———

LEA

Willem and Effina's wedding was held three days after Lea's release in the palace garden. The sprawling, walled space was lovely, even in winter, with flowers still in bloom, thanks to Ordona's lingering earth magic. Lessia hadn't deigned to employ an air user for the day, however, so the bitter chill in the air made what was already an awkward event even more uncomfortable.

The ceremony was held near a quiet fountain at the center of the garden. It was the same fountain Lea, Aer, and the others had sat by after a night of dinner with their families just a few months earlier. On that night, the melodic voices of the pixies had drifted across the water as they lounged about on the giant lily pads, smacking down the cinderfish that tried to nip at them. The night had been warm, one of the last of the season that didn't require at least a light cloak for comfort, and it was the first time the five friends had been able to spend time together outside the confines of school.

Today, it appeared the pixies who had once cast their pretty lights throughout the space had fled the palace grounds entirely, leaving the poisonous cinderfish to poke their wide mouths above the surface unhindered to whatever insects or smaller fish they could find.

A handful of courtesans from Dystone and Jotunheim, along with Willem's younger sister, Rosie, were the only guests in attendance.

As she stood silently at Jonas' side while Willem and Effina wed, Lea couldn't help but feel as though that memory and this place would now be tarnished irrevocably.

Lessia presided over the nuptials, as was typical of Jotnar unions. Willem hadn't brought a human officiant, nor did he seem put off by adopting Effina's customs, so the ceremony went smoothly. The absence of the mating bond, a gods-blessed magic that tied two people together more than spoken vows ever could, seemed odd to Lea, as it was always the main focus of Lindorothian weddings.

Something told her the gods wouldn't grant that kind of bond to two creatures such as Willem and Effina, even if they'd cared enough to try.

When the ceremony was over, the union sealed with a less-than chaste kiss, the small group moved back into the palace for dinner.

Rosie Ristner, the youngest of the Ristner siblings, fell toward the back of the procession beside Lea, who walked arm-in-arm with Jonas.

"Princess," Jonas said with a short nod.

"My lord," Rosie replied. She gave Lea a small smile, its hesitance matching her youth. Lea recalled her age to be about sixteen, only three years younger than herself, but everything from her appearance to her demeanor seemed childish.

"Lady Calliwell, how are you faring now that you've been given a bit of freedom?" Rosie asked.

Lea cast a quick glance at Jonas before answering, wary of the girl's sudden interest. When he nodded, she smiled brightly at Rosie. "Quite well, Princess, thank you."

Rosie looped her arm through Lea's free one, earning herself a glare from Jonas, then patted Lea's hand. "That's good to hear. You seem like *such* a lovely girl, and I do hope in time we might be friends."

Lea wanted to laugh at the absurd statement, but instead gave the girl a tentative smile. "Your words are a great kindness, Princess."

Biting her lip for effect, she looked up at Jonas, her eyes questioning. "Jonas?"

Jonas considered Rosie for a moment, then smiled down at Lea. "Yes, I suppose that would be a good thing. I'm absent a bit too often as it is, so perhaps the princess would be able to occupy you while I'm away. I know how stuffy that room has gotten."

"Yes," Lea agreed. "A new companion would be nice."

"Lovely!" Rosie said, squeezing Lea's hand. "I'll come fetch you soon, then. Perhaps you can show me around a bit? I'm sure you know all of this palace's secrets," she added slyly.

A brazen and quite obvious request, but not one Lea was about to shoot down, so she gave Rosie another smile. "There's quite a lot to see here."

They continued to talk as they walked to the dining room, the conversation largely led by Rosie. Lea learned that the young woman was betrothed to a human lord in the southern Dystone province of Leford who she hoped would join her in Lindoroth once the dust settled, though as of now, her plans were to return home within the next month or two. Apparently, she'd spent a good deal of time in Leford over the last few years getting to know her future husband and, much to Lea's annoyance, enjoyed comparing the similarities of the southernmost region of Dystone to Lea's home in Edhil.

"This is just so lovely, don't you think?" Rosie asked as they took their seats at the dining room table. "It's such an improvement over that horrible gold!"

Lea looked around the dining room, noticing with dismay that all of the golden decor that the Harridans were so fond of had been removed, replaced with tones of silver and gray. Her heart ached at the thought of her family being erased so fully from this place. Even the garish gold—it *was* garish, after all—had been a soothing reminder that this whole ordeal wasn't yet finished, that there was still work to be done to ensure things got back to normal as quickly as possible.

Her anger grew as she let her eyes roam across the room. Charcoal-colored velvet panels hung at the windows where gold brocade had once dominated. In place of the golden lanterns hung ornate, wrought iron fixtures, and dull pewter now replaced the gold flatware that had been in her family for so long. The wide mantel, so often decorated with elaborate floral arrangements created by Ordona, sat bare, the fire in the hearth the only sign of life.

She seethed as she took it all in, wanting nothing more than to tear down the curtains and toss them into the flames, smash the candelabras against the marble floor, and shove the silver napkins down Lessia and Willem's throats until they choked on the fine fabric.

Instead, she gave Rosie a tight smile. "Yes, it's quite lovely. Gold has never been a favorite of mine."

Once everyone was settled in, Jonas stood and raised his goblet of wine. "To Willem and Effina. May your rule be long and your offspring, strong."

"Here, here!" Lessia said, looking at Willem and Effina with a smooth smile. "Cheers to the start of a new empire."

Lea took a small sip of her wine. Willem and Effina appeared genuinely happy, whispering softly while everyone else made conversation. Jonas quickly became occupied with one of Willem's cousins, and Rosie seemed content to prattle on about the things she hoped to see and do in Iladel, as if a war wasn't currently ravaging the country.

Doing her best to not appear obvious, Lea settled in to watch the interactions of the others as she kept one ear on Rosie's chatter.

As was her fashion, the Empress sat quietly, sipping her wine and observing the others. Lea thought they were a bit similar in that respect. In a room full of people who you couldn't fully put your trust in, watching them when they were at their most candid was one of the best ways to glean information about them.

When Lessia's eyes began to drift toward Lea's side of the table, Lea shifted her attention to the newlyweds. She thought back to her conversation with Jonas regarding heirs and lines of succession, and still struggled to believe that Willem thought he would truly come out of this with his crown—or his head. Yes, Effina was lovely to look upon, and she would give Willem magic-wielding children, but in that scenario, Willem was little more than a stud used for breeding.

Jonas' arm snaked around her shoulders, startling her. He pulled her closer, until his lips were at her ear. "You're staring," he said. "If I didn't know better I'd think you were jealous."

She swallowed hard and did her best to look chagrined.

"Look at me," he murmured.

Obeying, she tilted her head toward his and met his eyes, forcing adoration. "Yes?"

"Would you like me to take you out of here?" he asked.

She bit her lip, pretending to hide a smile, and cast a quick glance past him to where Lessia was watching them with amusement. "No, that's unnecessary."

He touched a finger to her chin. "Are you certain?"

"Yes. Forgive me, but I believe it would be rude to leave such a joyous occasion. We're here to celebrate Their Majesties." She leaned a bit closer and lowered her voice to a breathy whisper, one she knew Lessia would hear, even if Willem couldn't. "We can have our time together later."

Jonas chuckled and brushed his thumb across her jaw before letting his hand fall back to the table.

Willem laughed. "We may not need to string up the governor's body outside the gates of Errest after all." He shifted his gaze to Lea. "What say you, Lady Calliwell? Do you think your people might listen to you now that you're getting to know their monarchs' usurpers so well?" His face took on a slight sneer. "Do you think you might be able to sway them? Convince them to set down their arms peacefully?"

Lea tried to force as much chagrin into her answering smile. "As I said, Your Majesty, I think you underestimate the will of my people. They won't look to me unless they believe I have their best interests at heart. In this case, I don't believe what you're suggesting is something they'd ever see as truth, at least not so soon after... everything."

"Hmm." Lessia angled her head and eyed Lea, her heavy silence speaking volumes about the level of control she held in the room. "Perhaps their late governor's daughter marrying a Jotnar lord would do a bit more to convince them."

"Not to mention it wouldn't require the transport of rotting bodies," Effina said, her tiny nose scrunching in disgust.

Lea's heart stuttered and all the breath seemed to flee her lungs, but she forced a laugh. "Perhaps, in time," was the best answer she could force out.

No, Lea thought. *I'll never do it.*

"And you both would make such lovely children, don't you think, Jonas?" Lessia asked. She sent Jonas a challenging look, and in that moment, with that one piercing stare, Lea knew that Lessia was far more suspicious of her and Jonas than Jonas had let on.

Jonas gave Lea a small smile, then looked back to his aunt. "Whatever you say, Empress."

IT WAS all Lea could do to hold herself together for the rest of the meal. Little else was said that garnered her interest or could draw her mind away from Lessia's suggestions, both involving her father's body and a potential marriage to Jonas. Neither of those options would sway the Edhilian people; if anything it would cause them to fight harder, but Lea knew it was worthless to attempt to convince Lessia or Willem of that.

Jonas shut the door to his room quietly when they returned, then, seeming to sense her need to speak freely, cast his silencing spell.

"*Marriage?*" she hissed, rounding on him. "They expect me to *marry you?*"

He blinked, taken aback, then cleared his throat. "Perhaps, but it wouldn't be as bad as you're imagining, Lea."

She let out a slightly hysterical laugh. "Oh no? Please, *my lord,* tell me. How is marrying someone against my will not a bad thing?"

He touched her arm and gestured for her to sit on the divan at the foot of the bed. Once she'd settled, he pulled up a chair and sat down across from her. "Jotnar marriages are not as complex as Lindorothian ones. While the annulment of marriages is rare in my land, it is still quite a simple process."

"Oh." Lea relaxed a bit at that. Though she balked at the idea of saying vows with every intention of breaking them, doing that was a far easier future to live with than having to go through the process of nullifying a mating bond. She'd never heard of it being done and could only imagine it would be an incredibly painful process to untangle the magic that wound two souls together.

That's even assuming that the officiant who performed the bond was willing to undo it. *And* that the gods would grant such a thing in the first place, which was highly unlikely.

"Do you think it will come to that?" she asked quietly. "Marriage?"

He sighed and leaned back in his chair. "I can't say. Lessia's whims are often fleeting, so she may see it as a good idea today, but by tomorrow, it could be all but forgotten."

"That says nothing of Willem's thoughts on the matter," she said bitterly. She thought back to the king's words, his insinuations about her, her people, and her bourgeoning relationship with Jonas. She had seen his expression of interest and glee when Lessia had mentioned marriage. While Jonas was an attractive male and one Lea would normally see herself drawn into a relationship with, her distrust of him still hung in the back of her mind. Jonas had been treating her well, and he had sworn a blood oath to keep her safe, but oaths could be broken. Lessia was a powerful witch, one Lea was certain could break that oath if he requested it.

Although that would involve admitting to its existence in the first place, which Lea wasn't entirely sold on him doing, not unless he was partial to the pain of Lessia's wrath.

"Willem's thoughts are of little import," Jonas countered. "Despite what he may think, Lessia is in charge. She might allow him his slivers of power, provide him with a pretty Jotnar bride, but his commands carry little weight in this palace."

Lea huffed. "Someone ought to tell him that."

13

FREYA

Over the next few days, patrols to and from Watoria came and went throughout each day with reports of the human and Jotnar's movements, both within and outside of Watoria. Frederick Edrin appeared content to remain sequestered in the governor's manor near the city's town hall while his knights patrolled the streets, keeping all residents on lockdown. There was the occasional raid, but as much as Freya wanted to storm the city gates and oust them all, Aer and Florian reminded her repeatedly that doing so would equate to a suicide mission.

Gaining knowledge about Frederick became a prime concern, although how to go about that was problematic. The town hall and governor's residence were in the center of the city, which would be easily accessible, so long as one could fly invisibly. Florian and Freya had made charms for just such an occasion in order to keep Naedan and Amara from being seen during their patrols, but so far, their trips had yielded little in the way of intel regarding the sitting governor.

Aside from being the empress's brother-in-law, Frederick had spent little time in the military, and much of his childhood had been spent torturing small creatures, if what Amara had overheard in the manor's courtyard was to be believed. He had ten guards, the commander of which was often seen whispering in his ear. Lindorothian females were being brought in daily for his inspection, proving true the suspicions that he planned to take one for a wife. Those he felt could please him were thrown in the cellar for later use. Those he felt were unworthy of his attention were handed off to his guards to do with as they pleased. Those he or the captain of his guard deemed particularly displeasing were executed in the main square.

When Frederick wasn't dealing with the prisoners, he was sending his guards out to pillage the homes and businesses of the city, taking anything of value and killing those who'd been foolish enough to remain behind hoping to keep their property safe while remaining hidden from those who were robbing them.

"Is it possible he's worse than Lessia?" Aer asked as he, Freya, Florian, and Reginald listened to the hawks' most recent report. "It's as though he sees this as a means of entertainment."

"Nothing about him speaks of experience, I can tell you that much," Naedan muttered.

"Yes, the commander of his guard seems to be the one in charge," Amara added.

"What does that tell us, then?" Freya asked.

"If he's adhering to the word of his commander?" Reginald asked. "It tells us we should not take Frederick's seeming lack-of-care as truth. He may not care how things here play out, or he may just want anyone spying on him to think that."

Florian gave him an appraising look, then nodded. "I agree. Whether Frederick Edrin is lazy or playing at such doesn't matter. What do we know of the rest of his guard?"

"Nothing remarkable from what we can tell," Amara said. "They seem more skilled than most of the soldiers, but that's to be expected. We'll continue to do our sweeps, though. I'd like to put my feet on the ground in the city and speak with some citizens, if possible."

"Have you seen many?" Freya asked. Ashton's last report had given no information on where the citizens who'd remained behind had been hiding.

Naedan shook his head. "Not yet, no."

"Before your next patrol, we'll give you a few more areas worth checking," Ashton said.

Amara nodded. "Alright. Tomorrow at noon, then."

Freya flicked a glance toward the setting sun and sighed. "Hopefully we'll be able to learn something that will help us get a leg up."

Ashton shook his head. "I wouldn't plan on it."

THE FOLLOWING EVENING, despite being briefed on the lesser-known areas of Watoria and the best ways of sneaking into the city near the shore, Naedan and Amara had nothing more to report regarding the whereabouts of the citizens who'd remained behind. Freya and Aer sent a message to Byrric in Saith with one of the wolves, hoping they might get an answer from him soon regarding his plans or even a suggested course of action. She didn't allow herself much hope they would receive a response, considering he was currently in the midst of trying to save a city, but permitted herself a small sliver.

Very small.

Rini's most recent report from Tyna had done nothing to improve anyone's spirits, either. They were all gathered in the dining room to hear her latest news, and her nervous flutters were far more manic than usual.

"Willem and Effina's wedding was... less than savory," Rini said, nervously biting her lip.

"Willem and Effina were married?" Isadora said, her eyes wide with shock.

"Does he know you've defected along with his brother?" Ashton asked.

"I don't know," Isadora replied, frowning. "I—I assumed he believed I was kidnapped or killed, but it doesn't seem he cares much, either way."

"According to Lea, Willem considers you an 'opportunistic whore,' so it's safe to say he's aware of your status," Rini said loftily.

Ashton coughed, and Myria smirked as Isadora's face turned scarlet.

"Even still, it's a bit surprising he wrote you off so quickly," Aer said. "Humans have laws against marrying more than one person, don't they?"

Isadora gave him a small nod as she seemed to recover from her embarrassment. "Yes, which is why there's no other explanation for him remarrying so quickly."

Myria snorted. "Willem doesn't seem the cuckolding type, so I would imagine running off with his brother would be motivation enough."

Reginald barked out a laugh. "No, he'd execute me and take her back to Dystone, feign forgiveness, then lock her away and bring her out for appearances only."

Rini did a quick loop at Freya's side. "Well, you're clearly better off," she told Isadora.

Isadora smiled weakly. "Thank you, Rini. You're right. It's just a bit of a shock, that's all."

"Is there anything else?" Ashton asked, eying Rini's movements warily.

"Well, Rosie Ristner has attempted to befriend Lea, and it seems as though Lea has accepted her advances."

"Rosie?" Reginald laughed. "She's hardly a threat, I can assure you."

Isadora gave him a small smile, then looked to Freya and Aer. "He's right, Your Majesties. Rosie is... sweet."

"We once thought the same of you, and look how that turned out," Myria said flatly.

Isadora flushed scarlet. "I beg your pardon?"

"Myria," Freya murmured, resisting the urge to swat Rini away. "Enough."

Myria sent Freya a haughty look, and had circumstances not been so dire, Freya might've laughed.

"Is there any reason you can think of that we should be concerned about a burgeoning relationship with Rosie?" Laz asked Reginald, moving the conversation in a better direction. "Perhaps this is a good thing."

"Unlikely, my lord," Rini said with a shake of her head before Reginald could respond. "According to Tyna, Rosie looks up to Willem in a way that borders on worship. Anything Lea says will assuredly be reported right back to him." Flustered, she pulled a small comb from the pouch at her waist, and Freya winced when she aimed for her hair.

"It's true," Reginald said. "Rosie adores Willem, but she's by no means sly enough to trick Lea into giving her legitimate information. Whether Willem will trust the information Rosie retrieves from Lea is another thing entirely."

"I would assume Lessia is still a bit hesitant to trust Jonas, considering the amount of time he's spent with you all in Lindoroth," Isadora added. "Returning to the palace with Lea, getting her to go along with his ruse..." She clicked her tongue and shook her head. "Lea is in a good position if she can convince Rosie she truly... feels for Jonas. Forming a relationship with someone aside from him could be a good thing."

Laz grimaced, then nodded. "Any inroads can help, I suppose."

"If nothing else, it will expose Lea to more parts of the palace than if she only sticks to Jonas' side," Freya said.

"Agreed." Aer turned to Rini. "Were you able to assess the situation in the city?"

Rini started separating out the locks of pink from the brown in Freya's hair. "Yes, Your Majesty. The citizens of Iladel are still sequestered in the market. Willem's troops are the only ones surrounding the market itself. Lessia has pulled all the Jotnar back to surround the city, should they escape."

Doing her best to ignore the anxious pixie, Freya looked to Isadora and Reginald. "Are you both certain Willem's troops are fully loyal to him? Is there any chance at all they might be swayed by the plight of the Iladelians?"

Isadora shook her head grimly. "To those who didn't know him well, he was a kind ruler, so they won't betray him."

"And your marriage, if you don't mind me asking?" Florian asked. "Was he kind to you?"

Isadora's face turned grave. "Everyone thought he was a wonderful man, but he was... not a good husband. He did a good job of concealing his cruelty."

Jonas had told Freya as much months ago when they conversed for the first time, but Freya never saw it as her place to find out what that had entailed.

Rini completed the braid in Freya's hair and tucked away her comb, then let out a satisfied breath. "There has also been talk of using Lea's captivity to bring Perida on board with Lessia and Willem's plans. They believe it will help bolster their cause with the Edhilians and give them a leg up on taking the city."

"How?" Aer asked. "Lea will never convince her mother to do such a thing, and even if she did, she and Perida could shout their allegiance from the rooftops, but their people will never fall for it."

Rini shrugged. "I agree, Your Majesty, but Lessia and Willem either don't know that or think their powers of persuasion are strong enough to win out."

"Is Lea doing an adequate job of convincing them she's fond of Jonas, at least?" Freya asked.

Rini bobbed her head from side to side. "It's tough to say. Conversations at meals tend to be a bit more restricted when Lea is present, but Lea's still able to glean quite a bit from what she hears. Her ability to act convincingly is quite good, so we're certain that, in time, Lessia, at the very least, will attempt to draw her in."

Aer made a disgusted face at that and sighed. "That's something. If she can get on Lessia's good side, that would be a benefit, certainly."

"Remind her to be wary, though," Isadora cautioned. "It's quite possible Lessia is becoming amenable to Lea, but Lea could be with her for centuries and still never gain a sufficient amount of trust."

"Lea's smart," Aer said quietly. "She knows better."

Freya slid her hand in his. "We wouldn't have allowed her to return if she wasn't, Aer."

He nodded, then tightened his fingers around hers. "I know."

14

FREYA

Later, after new patrols had been sent out and Isadora, Reginald, and the others had turned in for the night, Freya, Aer, Laz, Collin, and Myria made their way to the drawing room. Haegin had set a roaring fire in the fireplace and brought them two carafes of wine, along with a plate of cheese, fruits, and meats. Freya assumed it was his own little attempt to help them feel a bit of normalcy. It was one the few times the five friends had gotten time to discuss things together with no one else around.

It did little to quell the unrest she was feeling inside, a feeling that was continuing to mount as the days passed with still no word from Byrric nor a more sufficient solution to helping the Watorians.

"I want to go into the city tomorrow," Freya said, cutting Collin off in the midst of whatever he was saying. "These raids Frederick is doing... that means there could still be a lot of people in their homes and businesses. At the very least—"

"What would you like to do, Freya?" Aer asked. "If you go in there to help them, you might save a few lives, a few homes, but at what cost?"

"We're far more likely to lose some of our own and lead Frederick and his soldiers right back here," Collin said, shaking his head.

"I know," she said with a sigh, knowing there was no sense in pointing out she was more than qualified to go in herself. "I know that, but it doesn't change the fact that I utterly *despise* being so useless!"

"Welcome to life as a monarch," Aer muttered.

"How do you think we feel?" Myria said, gesturing toward Laz. "At least you're within striking distance of your home. At least you've got a chance to save it."

"That's not fair, Myria," Laz admonished. "We'd be of no use to anyone if we left now."

"I know that," Myria snapped. "I'm simply pointing out the advantageous nature of her position here, mere miles from her own city, while you and I are days away from ours!"

"Byrric is in Olthanas," Collin reminded her. "He won't leave until he knows it's in good hands."

"Or no longer worth saving," she countered sourly.

"I'm sorry," Freya said quietly. "I know this must be difficult for you both and I wish there was something we could do to change things."

Aer reached out and took her hand, then let their joined palms come to rest on the sofa between them. "We will. Father always told me waiting is the hardest part of war. The time between battles, those moments when each side takes their collective deep breaths, tend to bring with it a feeling of uselessness."

"But it's time we need," Collin said. "We'll gather all possible information, form a plan of attack that we can hopefully execute once Byrric makes his way here, and take back the city. But there are just too few of us right now." He looked at Freya. "Even if you go in, find and rally all of the citizens remaining in the city, and launch an uprising against Frederick, we've still got an entire human army blocking the Allanorians from helping. We'd succeed for a few minutes, at best, without their help. Until we can get more reinforcements from elsewhere, we need to stay put."

"We should have gone straight to Iston," Freya said, shaking her head. "Ashton and the others could do what we're doing."

"Ashton and the other marshals don't have aerial patrols," Aer countered. "We do. Naedan and Amara have gathered far more information regarding the placement of Edrin's soldiers, not to mention the goings-on in the human camps."

Freya rubbed a hand across her brow. "I'll just feel better once I'm able to see it all for myself. I could just fly over, wear my invisibility glamour, but not touch down."

"Do you truly think you would be safe ?" Laz asked.

"Yes." She sent a look to Aer before continuing. "I've gotten quite good at going unseen over the years, and I know this city inside and out. I know it's a risk, but I'm also confident in my ability to do this."

"The costs of being seen haven't ever been so high, though, have they?" Myria said. "A few filthy draugs knowing you've found them is a mere annoyance. It's much different when the ones who are aware of your location seek not only to kill you but take over your kingdom. too."

"I just want to see it," Freya said quietly. "You would feel the same if we were this close to Olthanas."

"The price of my head is not quite so great as yours."

Freya held Myria's stare, knowing she was right and hating it all the same. Finally, she looked away and stared into the fire. She relaxed a little when Aer squeezed her hand, and she leaned into him as Collin and Laz shifted the conversation toward other, safer topics. But the tension in the room that was ever-present had yet to lift and Freya could only assume it would still linger long after this war was over.

There was a tapping at the glass door that led to the veranda, and when Freya looked up, she saw a large red-tailed hawk sitting on the stone.

"Is that Zane?" Aer asked, getting to his feet and walking quickly to open the door. He was halfway there when the bird shifted into Zane Ristheld, the tall, broad-shouldered combat instructor they'd had back at Aldridge. Aer opened the doors, and Zane stepped inside, rubbing his hands up and down his leather-sheathed arms briskly, then nodded in greeting.

"Ah, that fire is a welcome sight," he said, relief and exhaustion clear in his voice. "Nearly two full days in the air have put quite an ache in my bones."

Myria stepped forward eagerly. "Have you come from Olthanas?"

"I have." He turned toward Freya and Aer. "Your Majesties, I've brought word from Commander Balthana."

"Thank the gods," Laz said, exhaling.

"When will he be here?" Freya demanded.

"Three days' time, Your Majesty."

"Tell us everything," Myria ordered. "Now."

Zane gave Aer a questioning look. When he nodded, Zane gave his report.

"Olthanas has been saved," he told Myria. "Commander Balthana has gotten it under control and helped your knights drive out the invaders."

Myria sighed in relief, leaning against Laz gratefully when he wrapped an arm around her shoulders.

"The Commander has left behind five hundred knights of the Royal Army to assist," Zane continued, "but the Jotnar and humans who had taken the city have been executed, imprisoned, or have fled. The citizens and approximately one thousand Saithian soldiers have secured the city, and residents of outlying villages have been brought in for refuge."

"How much damage was done?" Freya asked.

"It was... significant," Zane said, giving Myria an apologetic look. "But it can all be rebuilt in time."

"I should go there," Myria said, sending a pleading look to Freya and Aer. "I should be there at my family's home, helping them."

"You will be," Freya said. "I promise, Myria. Just wait for Byrric to get here to give us more information."

"She's right," Laz said, cutting Myria off before she could protest further. He looked down at her, his eyes filled with understanding. "If I could leave for Kildin this moment, I would, but it would be foolish and we all know it." He gave Collin a tight smile when he took his free hand. "The smartest thing to do right now is wait until you've got backup to go with you."

Myria's face was hard as she worked over his words. Freya could see the truth of Laz's words penetrating Myria's resolve, but knowing Laz was right and admitting it were two different feats entirely.

"He has the city in good hands, Lady Bryton," Zane told her. "If that weren't the truth, I'd tell you."

Myria brushed a hand across her eyes and nodded, then turned and faced the fire, shutting herself off from the conversation.

"Why hasn't my father come with you?" Freya asked, turning her focus back to Zane.

"He wanted me to get word to you both as quickly as possible and it was easier for me to travel quickly and inconspicuously on my own."

"Of course," Aer said as he pulled the call bell for Haegin. "Let's get you fed and warmed, then you can tell us everything."

Ten minutes later, Haegin had brought Zane a bowl of hot stew, a loaf of warm bread, and a goblet of wine on a tray and set it on the small table near the windows. "Will there be anything else, Your Majesties?"

Freya smiled. "No, Haegin, that will be all for tonight."

With a quick bow, the caretaker left them to their business.

As he ate, Zane relayed the events of the past two weeks to the others. He'd escaped Iladel the day after the wedding and headed directly east toward Olthanas, where his family still lived, in the hopes of getting them to safety. Along the way, he encountered a battalion of Byrric's knights going in the same direction and had joined their party, stopping in a few villages and towns along the way to oust invaders. One week ago, he and the remaining knights he'd traveled with reached Olthanas only to find it in the midst of a siege.

"It was quite terrible at first," he explained. "They'd come in the night and at poorly-guarded areas, so the city was taken by surprise."

"Poorly guarded?" Myria's sharp eyes went wide. "I can assure you—"

"Sewers, Lady Bryton," Zane interrupted. "Your city has three underground sewer conduits that run from the center of the city to the shoreline. The beach is not heavily patrolled, so they were able to slip in unseen." He took another spoonful of stew. "There were about two thousand enemy soldiers from what I could tell, but they were not well-organized. It was a simple thing to sneak up on their encampments and dispatch a large number of them quite quickly."

"It seems to be the opposite here," Freya said. "The human encampments are organized, although there isn't much movement in and out. The Jotnar have completely locked down the city to all outsiders."

Zane considered that for a moment before responding. "That's smart, from a strategic standpoint. Two foreign armies with as little in common as the humans and Jotnar are unlikely to mesh well."

"Especially when this is their first venture into battle together," Collin added.

Zane nodded. "Although, considering the vast differences in strength, I think it's safe to assume the Jotnar have little to no intention of including the humans in any meaningful way in this new kingdom they hope to build."

"Agreed," Aer said. "So how do we use that to our advantage?"

Zane drained the last bits of his soup and set the bowl down. "Keep thinking like that, to start. Byrric will want to hit the ground running once he arrives, so we'll need to have every potential advantage ready."

"We've been sending out aerial patrols daily to monitor the human army and the governor's manor," Freya told him. "Ground patrols have been rotating out three times a day."

Zane nodded. "Good. Keep that up until Byrric arrives. He'll have some of his knights with him, so they'll need as much cover as possible when they arrive."

"We'll increase patrols to the south of the property starting tomorrow, then," Aer said. "For now, though, you should get some rest. It's been a long journey."

As if on cue, Haegin appeared in the doorway. "Come, Lord

Ristheld. I've got the guest house prepared for Byrric and his officers, so there is a bed already made up for you."

Zane heaved out a contented sigh and set his napkin down on his tray. "Rest would be much-welcomed." He looked at Freya. "Try not to worry too much. Byrric will be here soon and then you'll be on your way to taking your city back."

She smiled and said goodnight, but no matter how hard she tried, she found no relief in his words.

15

LEA

Lea spent the next several days increasing her attempts to prove her admiration and gratitude toward Jonas, as well as toward Willem and Lessia. She anticipated Jonas' needs at meals, bit her lip like a simpering fool, and gave bashful smiles when he nodded his thanks to her for pouring his wine. She sat tall, her head held high without even an ounce of hesitation toward her enemies. After hearing Rini's report regarding Isadora and Reginald's opinions of Rosie, she began working a bit harder to cultivate a relationship with the girl. Lea didn't expect much to come of it as far as pertinent information went, but at the very least, she hoped it would demonstrate her desire to become a more permanent part of Jonas' life.

While she worked to accomplish those feats, Jonas continued to make it clear throughout the palace that she was off-limits to any males who might see her as open for perusal, despite what insinuations Willem might make to the contrary. He ensured they all knew she was a lady of Lindoroth who had chosen to side with those who'd taken her kingdom. She saw that the Jotnar and humans might have better plans for her lands than their predecessors, that they may have done Lindorothians a service in ousting the Harridans, and she should be accepted as an ally.

The thoughts made her sick, but she did her best to make it look as though Jonas' initial story of her disagreement with her aunt and uncle's rule was the truth.

She'd been there two weeks when she was surprised by a knock at the door. Jonas had left a short while earlier to attend to some matters with Lessia, leaving Lea to spend the afternoon behind the locked doors of his room. Though she was becoming more accepted in the palace, it was only slightly so; meaning, walks on her own or with anyone other than him were not yet an option she nor Jonas considered safe. Her stroll through the palace with Rosie had been postponed, as Willem had given his sister other duties, but she had come by to have tea with Lea twice now. Her youth and the depth of her brother's power made her bubbly and proud, a mixture that annoyed Lea to no end, but Lea appreciated the company, nonetheless.

Jonas had done what he could to find solitary means of entertainment for Lea, bringing her books from Freya's chambers and a sketchbook and charcoals on the off-chance she decided to teach herself to draw, but still, boredom became a problem as her fear of being harmed by others in the palace decreased.

Despite her lessened concerns, however, the fear didn't disappear entirely, which was why she called forward her magic before opening the door.

She felt even more sure of her power when she found Willem on the other side.

"Ah, Lady Calliwell," he said, his hands clasped behind his back, lips tilted in a smile. "How are you today?"

"I'm well, and you?" She closed her fist, drawing her magic just beneath her fingertips. "I was just about to pour some tea. Would you like some?"

"I was actually hoping you might join me for a walk." He looked past her, his shrewd, blue eyes taking in the room, before giving her a smooth smile. "I would imagine it's been some time since you've walked the gardens?"

A flutter of excitement bloomed in her belly at the idea of being surrounded by so much nature, away from the hard stone and wood of the palace, materials that had once held the earthly magic that flowed inside her but now only bore tired remnants of what had once made them part of the world. True, she could feel the magic in the wood that had been towering oak, stone that had been mountains, glass that had once been coral and shellfish, but now it was no more than an echo.

The thought of being among living things, trees and flowers that still grew and vines that wrapped around trellises, made it hard for her to conceal how excited the prospect made her, but she held it in, biting her lip as she searched Willem's face.

"I don't know that Lord Edrin would approve," she said quietly.

"And if I needed Lord Edrin's approval, that would be a problem, wouldn't it?" He stepped aside and gestured with his arm for her to come out into the hall, then gave her an expectant look. "You want to be a lady of Jotunheim, do you not?"

Seeing that he was giving her no choice, she nodded, then picked up a white wool cloak trimmed in gray fur from the chair near the door and wrapped it around her shoulders, taking time to give herself a moment to settle her nerves before turning back to Willem. Knowing that she had magic and Willem didn't did nothing to change the fact that the vast majority of creatures in the palace could outmaneuver her magically with little effort if she attempted to harm or simply defend herself against him.

Regardless, she allowed her magical advantage to give her some comfort as she followed him through the halls of the palace toward the stone archway that led to the gardens.

"Lord Edrin has done a good job with you," Willem commented when they stepped onto the stone garden path.

"I'm sorry?"

"Now that he no longer has to feign attraction to your kind, I assumed your attraction to him would've vanished by now." He smirked. "I expected you to be back in the dungeons within a week, to be honest."

She angled her head curiously, though his insinuation that Jonas had been faking his friendly demeanor all this time was not lost on her. "What do you see now?"

"Pragmatism and intelligence, although I haven't quite figured out what you'll do with them. You could be of good use to me in time."

Lea stared at him, perplexed. "I'm not sure how to take that."

"As a compliment, of course!" They rounded a corner that led toward a long, low fountain. "I've acknowledged both your intelligence and your ability to take me by surprise, not to mention my consideration in forming a... friendship with you. The correct response, then, would be—"

"Thank you, of course," she said quickly, ducking her head. "I only meant... well I hope you don't question my feelings toward Lord Edrin?"

"Of course I question it, silly girl! Only a fool wouldn't." He held up a hand when she went to speak. "Please don't mistake me, Lady Calliwell. I think you have potential, a good chance at coming around to our side of things, but I know little of you or your ability to act convincingly. It's entirely possible—probable, even—that you're pulling the wool over our eyes." He gave her a sly smirk. "Or trying to, at least."

Her heart began to pound. "I can assure you, my ability to act is far inferior to yours." She bit her lip again. "I apologize if that's overstepping a bit, I only meant—"

"It's no matter." He stopped, then turned to face her. "Considering our reversals of fortune, there's little you can say that I might take offense to." His eyes ran over her face, and she had to force herself to remain pleasantly neutral so he wouldn't see how much his perusal revolted her.

When he stepped forward and gently brushed a loose curl behind her ear, his own shift in expression told her he knew exactly what she thought of him. His hand slid down, then he brushed a thumb against the hollow of her throat and sent her a level gaze. "And if you did manage to offend me, it would be a simple matter to punish you adequately, wouldn't you say?"

She tensed at the pressure on her neck and forced herself not to step back, lest she lessen the distance between her and the hedge behind her and show him just how much he was scaring her. "While I may agree with that statement, Lord Edrin will not be happy if you attempt to use me in the way you're implying," she said, surprised at how steady her voice was. "Nor will I."

"If I thought I could do a better job of convincing you to cooperate than Lord Edrin, no one would deign to stop me." He squeezed tighter, the sharp points of his ring digging into her skin, cutting off her air and sending spots dancing across her vision. "Not even—"

Her power came, unbidden, at her distress, and Willem's words cut off with a snap when a branch from a nearby tree whipped across his cheek. He stumbled back, his hand slipping from her neck as she took a step away, gasping as she rubbed a hand against her throat. More branches, along with thorny vines from the rose hedge behind her, crept along the stone pathway beside her.

Willem put a hand to his cheek and looked at his fingers, tinged red with blood. With eyes filled with fury, he advanced on her.

"You've made a grave mistake, little girl," he growled.

Branches and vines rose up at her side, stopping him in his tracks.

"I think you underestimate the amount of privilege Lord Edrin holds here." She felt a burst of strength as more whiplike branches crept forward. Willem scrambled back as they aimed toward his ankles. "If you believe you can touch another male's female, one who belongs to a lord of Jotunheim as great as him, you are sorely mistaken, *Your Majesty*." The flora surged forward, wrapping around his chest and wrists more quickly than he could react, contracting slowly. Taking a step closer, she tilted her face toward his, staring directly into his furious eyes. "You may believe you are able to take those liberties in Dystone, but you will do no such thing with me. Are we understood?"

Willem gave a sharp nod, then let out a gasp when Lea released the branches and let them snap back into place.

"Lord Edrin was told to spell your food," he hissed as he rubbed at his wrists, where two vicious red marks were forming, spotted with blood where thorns had dug in.

"Then I suppose he should increase my dose. Now, I'd like to go back to my chambers, if it's quite alright with you."

Willem rolled his shoulders and pulled himself up a bit straighter. "Not just yet, Lady Calliwell. There's still another matter—"

"Ah, there you are!"

Lea jerked her head to the side, forcing herself not to slump in relief at the sight of Jonas.

"Lord Edrin!" Willem called. "How lovely of you to join us!"

Jonas flicked Willem a cursory glance, frowned at the way he rubbed his wrists and his rumpled clothing, then looked to Lea. "You weren't in our room."

Her mouth fell open, then she looked at Willem, whose lips were twitching in a smug smile.

Her face burned as she ducked her head. "Apologies, my lord. His Majesty asked to take me for a walk and I thought it would be improper to deny him."

"Come with me. Now." He glared at Willem. "I'll deal with you later."

With that, he wrapped a hand around Lea's arm and pulled her down the garden path.

Jonas' face was set in a stony scowl the entire way back to their room. When they stepped inside, he slammed the door with a deafening thud, then dropped his hand so Lea could step back as he slumped against the wall. He closed his eyes, and Lea felt his magic wash over the room, silencing their words from the outside.

"Are you alright?" he asked. His voice shook slightly, his chest heaving as he looked at her. "Did he hurt you?"

Lea swallowed hard and shook her head, a hard, jerky motion

that set her curls bouncing. "A little." She rubbed her neck. "He...
tried, but..."

"Lea, I am so incredibly sorry. We should've discussed this possibility. Had I known..."

"I can handle a power-hungry human, Jonas," she said, insult
blooming. "I don't think even your aunt would abide by him touching
something of yours."

"You're not—" He scrubbed his hands over his face and exhaled.
"Yes, you're right. I didn't mean to question your ability to defend
yourself." He paused. "How *did* you defend yourself?"

She averted her eyes as she recalled the look on Willem's face
when she'd trapped him with the branches. "I... might have used my
magic to call forth some nearby flora for assistance."

His eyes widened. "Lea, you can't do things like that! They'll
expect me to punish—"

"He put his hands on me, Jonas," she snapped. "He tried to *choke*
me! And to be honest, I expected a bit more from you than simply
wagging your finger at him!"

"I didn't—"

"If your only rebuttal when another man touches me is 'I'll deal
with you later,' what in the gods' names is to stop him from doing it
again?"

"The last thing we needed was for me to draw *more* attention to
the situation," he said slowly. "Lessia will not allow me to ruin this
alliance over a lover."

"Alliance," she spat. "We're not here to secure alliances! If
anything, breaking them would benefit us more!"

"Dressing her accomplice down over improprieties would do the
opposite of help, Lea. If anything, it would affirm the idea that we are
not here to do her bidding!"

"Well, what would you have me do?" Lea hissed, taking several
steps forward. "I am not here to be the plaything of every male in this
palace, and that fact needs to be crystal clear to all of them! I don't
give a damn if he's the king!"

"I understand—"

"You brought me back as *your* lover, not his. The rules of your empire are quite clear in that regard. The only male here with permission to touch me is you. No one else! Lessia made Willem aware of that fact the moment you brought me here. He chose to go against that rule. Now is the time to show him you won't be cowed, not that you'll side with him over me! All that will do is give him leave to do it again!"

Chest heaving, she turned away from him, not wanting him to see the disgust she was unable to keep hidden. She knew the blood oath he'd sworn would prevent him from intentionally harming her, but foolish decisions like this could still put her in danger.

"Lea..."

She held up a hand to stay his response and faced him again. "I came back here to help my king and queen," she said evenly. "I cannot do that if I am constantly looking over my shoulder for Willem and his ilk waiting to get me alone. If you can't or won't do all within your power to prevent that from happening, I will leave tonight. Am I clear?"

Jonas' lips formed a thin line, but he nodded. "You know as well as I that you won't be able to get free of this place without my help."

Her eyebrows lifted. "Is that a threat?"

"No, it's a statement of fact." He shook his head, then took a slow breath. "They'll expect me to punish you. It's how we handle things in Jotunheim."

Lea let out a dark chuckle. "Setting aside your blood oath to keep me from harm, if you try to put your hands on me just to placate those bastards, I will remove your manhood. Are we clear?"

He blinked at the threat, then swallowed and gave a sharp nod. "Crystal."

16

───────

LEA

Despite the strength of her words earlier, Lea couldn't help the flutter of nerves that ailed her as she walked through the palace to dinner. Jonas had chosen not to continue their argument, acquiescing to her demands that he not bow to Willem's whims. She knew it was a risk, but Jonas needed to demonstrate strength, and she needed Willem to think twice before he considered coming near her again.

And for her own sake, she needed to know Lessia wouldn't insist she be punished for defending herself.

But whether Willem's attempts to harm her were valid or not, she'd learned two things today. First, Willem was more than a little suspicious of her, and likely Jonas, too. And, although his underlings were barred from coming after her, Willem could and likely would return. He was the king and Jonas was not, and as such, felt himself entitled to do what he wished with her. He would think she wouldn't risk fighting back again, lest she risk a true punishment. Or worse, risk Lessia deciding she was better off under Willem's control than Jonas'.

She *would* fight back, though, regardless of what punishment Lessia or Willem might deem appropriate. She would strangle him with rose stems, drag the thorns through his flesh, his eyes, his ears before she let him touch her, before she let him do the things he believed Jonas was doing to her every night. No, she would take death over that.

Her mind drifted back to Lessia's off-handed suggestion about marriage. A small part of her wondered if marrying Jonas would offer her the protection she needed. If she became his wife, her standing here would become a bit more stable. She could be free of the annoyance of Willem's advances and have more time to focus on her true purpose—helping her king and queen regain their thrones. If Lessia and Willem truly believed Lea could get the people of Edhil in hand, that meant she'd be able to talk to them, which would be a huge advantage. She'd also be in a better position to free her mother, which was something she wanted above all else.

Yes, perhaps marriage would be for the best.

In that moment, with that thought, Lea felt ill.

"Be careful of what you say tonight," Jonas murmured as they approached the dining room. "I will do what I can to ensure Willem knows his place, but it will be left to Lessia to decide what happens from here."

Lea couldn't help the small sneer that formed on her lips. "I trust you'll be as convincing as possible, then."

"Lessia favors me over Willem, so we should be alright."

His words brought little relief as they entered the dining room and found Willem, Effina, and Lessia already seated. When Willem took note of Lea's appearance, a look of disgust spread across his face, presumably at the absence of evidence of any type of punishment. She noted that the sleeves of his shirt were a bit long and tight around his wrists, covering the marks the vines would have left. She took a small pleasure in knowing he hadn't been tended to by one of Lessia's healers.

"Ah, Lord Edrin. So wonderful of you to join us," Willem said.

Ignoring him, Jonas gave a nod to his aunt. "Apologies, Empress. I had a few things I needed to address prior to coming."

"Of course," Lessia replied.

Ignoring Willem's perusal, Lea walked to the side table and poured wine for her and Jonas as he took a seat at the table.

Lessia eyed Lea as she settled into her seat beside Jonas. "Willem tells me your toy was quite rude to him today, yet I see no signs of punishment. Have you lost your touch?"

Jonas snorted. "Lea is not palace property. She is my lover, which means she can defend herself from the likes of him if she sees fit." He jerked his chin toward Willem. "I don't share. You'd do well to remember that, human."

A small muscle in Willem's jaw twitched as he and Jonas stared one another down. "I think you would do well to remember who you are speaking to."

"I don't know how you do things in Dystone, Willem, but when a female is spoken for, she becomes off-limits to others," Lessia said coolly. "*You* would do well to remember *that*."

Surprisingly, Lessia's words brought Lea a smidgeon of relief. She was far more terrifying than Willem, and if the man had any sense, he wouldn't defy her.

The silence that descended over the dining room as Willem's contempt at the two Jotnar grew more apparent in his expression hung awkwardly in the air. Finally, and wisely, his face broke into a smile. "I suppose there are a good number of cultural differences we'll still need to sort out." He inclined his head to Jonas in a show of acquiescence. "Apologies, Lord Edrin."

"And while undeserved, I think it would be wise for Lady Calliwell to better know her place here," Lessia said. "Lady Calliwell, I believe you owe King Willem an apology."

Lea's head jerked up, her eyes wide with indignation when they met Lessia's. Before she could speak, Jonas held up a hand.

"The only apology owed here is Willem's to me, which has been given and received." He arched a brow in challenge at Willem. "And if this happens again, the punishment will be far worse than a few scratches, isn't that right, Empress?"

"Indeed," Lessia murmured. She gave Willem a sweet smile. "I'd say the matter is now closed, wouldn't you?"

Willem's eyes were poisonous when he looked at Lea. "I suppose it is."

~

Have you lost your touch?

Lessia's words replayed themselves throughout dinner and long after Lea's head hit her pillow. Jonas had been nothing but kind to her, ensuring she was comfortable and as safe as was possible. There was only so much he could do in front of Lessia and Willem, of course, but she couldn't deny he'd been doing all he could to minimize the amount of direct conversation she was forced into with either of them.

Reconciling the person who, based on Lessia's statement, was skilled at punishing lovers with the person who'd treated Lea as well as Jonas had over the past two weeks, her time in the dungeons notwithstanding, was proving to be quite a mental leap.

Just ask him, a voice in her head told her. *The worst that could happen is he reaffirms what you're already assuming.*

She rolled onto her back and stared up at the gold-and-red tapestry that stretched across the four posts of the bed, a reminder that he was doing his best to shield her from the dangers lurking all around them. Pressing a hand to her forehead, she let out a quiet breath, then closed her eyes. There was a truth she needed to confront, one that she didn't want to but knew it was imperative if she was to continue on with this mission. If she wanted to save her kingdom, she had to ask herself, and answer honestly, whether or not it mattered.

If he was cruel to lovers in the past, did it have any bearing on what they hoped to accomplish now?

Possibly.

It might deter her from becoming romantically involved with him and it might change her opinion of him as a person, but not necessarily as an ally. It certainly didn't change her course of action as it stood before her. It didn't change the fact that he was blood-bound to protect her.

The blankets rustled beside her, and when she turned her head, she saw Jonas staring back at her.

"What's wrong?" His voice was thick with sleep. "Can't you sleep?"

"Not tonight," she murmured, turning her head away. He was on the other side of the bed, nearly three feet away, so she hoped he couldn't see the concern on her face in the dim light.

Silence hung between them for a moment before he spoke. "Ask your questions, Lea."

Yes, ask him, the voice said.

"What did Lessia mean when she asked if you'd lost your touch?" She spoke more softly than she'd intended and she hated the weakness it likely conveyed, so she turned and looked him in the eye.

He drew in a slow breath and nodded. "I expected you to ask about that." He tucked his arm under his pillow, his eyes looking a bit more alert than they had a moment ago. "I've never punished anyone who was not deserving, Lea. You must understand, though, that as the empress' nephew, as *Lessia's* nephew, in particular, certain things are expected of me."

"Like cruelty?"

His jaw tensed and he seemed to wrestle with his response before delivering it. "I am not a cruel person and I think you know that."

"I'm not accusing you of being cruel, Jonas," she whispered. "But you must understand how a statement like that must make me feel, how it must make me question... things."

"I do," he said. "But there are bigger things at stake here than concerns about my past behavior. Your focus now needs to be on helping Freya and Aerelius, on helping your people and mine come out of this as unscathed as possible."

Lea sighed. "Yes, I know. It just seems as though each day, more and more is piled into my head, taking up space that I can't afford to spare."

"I can appreciate that, but my past is a thing none of us can control. Do your best to push it out of your mind, along with any implications you feel it may have on your ability to do this."

A bit easier said than done, she thought. His past, the proprietary way he looked at her when they were in mixed company, his family, and the way in which the Jotnar lived their lives made it impossible to comprehend, in her fear-addled state, a high-ranking male having such progressive opinions about the world.

She couldn't say any of that to him, of course. It would only lead to a longer back-and-forth than she cared to delve into, one that would most assuredly not end in reassurance on her part.

She also didn't point out that he'd completely avoided answering her questions.

17

——————

FREYA

The day Byrric was set to arrive in Watoria, the hawks didn't return from their morning patrol.

Freya paced back and forth on the balcony in her chambers throughout the afternoon, casting her eyes toward the city with every other step in the hopes of catching a glimpse of Naedan and Amara returning. The sun had begun its descent toward the horizon, casting a vibrant orange glow along the sea that Freya would've appreciated for its beauty if it didn't signal the many hours it had been since Naedan and Amara were supposed to return.

Finally, she called for Florian and Ashton to meet with her and Aer in her chambers.

"They've been gone too long," she said once they'd arrived.

"What do you propose we do?" Ashton asked.

"We can't be without our aerial patrols," she said, then paused, facing the city. "If they haven't returned by dusk, I'm going to do a sweep of the city myself."

"Your Majesty, I must object," Florian said. "It's far too risky. If you were seen—"

"I've spent years training not to be seen," she shot back, her tone brooking no argument. "And I've done a damn good job of it, if I do say so myself."

"We could send Zane," Aer suggested. "He's just as capable."

Freya gave him a pained look. "Zane can go with me as backup, and I'll have Ash place a few marshals in the woods outside the city to escort me home if need be. Two sets of eyes will work more quickly, anyway."

Aer looked at Ashton and raised his eyebrows in question.

"Gideon, Marcus, Steffen, and I will go as backup," Ashton said after a poisoned look from Freya. "They're stealthy, quick, and with Steffen's magic, we'll be able to hold back any pursuit should the need arise."

Aer folded his arms and looked back at Freya. She saw the resolve in his eyes before he voiced his thoughts.

"I'm going, too."

"You don't trust me to—"

"You know damn well that's not the case. You're my wife and my queen. If you think I'm going to send you out there without me, you're sorely mistaken. I can handle myself just as well as you, and I'll be able to supplement Steffen's magic with my own."

The two stared at each other for a few moments, neither willing to yield, until finally, Freya held up both of her hands in defeat.

"Alright." She huffed out a sigh. "We leave at dusk."

WHEN THE HAWKS still hadn't returned after sunset, Freya and Zane left Aer and the marshals at the Enrieth property line, roughly a mile from the city walls, and started their search. The plan was to fly ahead to Watoria while the others headed to the edge of the forest closer to shore.

Just before Freya and Zane flew through the warding around the manor, she slipped on an invisibility glamour, leaving them with the appearance of a lone hawk soaring above the forest. Now that she was only concealing herself, her use of magic was back to feeling effortless. It was simple as breathing, something she was thankful for as she soared over the trees toward the city. They spotted a few human patrols here and there in the woods along the way, but hardly any Jotnar.

They either think we're not coming, or they've hidden themselves more efficiently, she thought as she scanned the forest. She hoped it was the first, but strongly suspected the Jotnar were using glamours of their own.

Naedan and Amara had been sent to scout through the South and East Wards to attempt to seek out any citizens who might have managed to go undetected within the city with the aim of leading them out in small numbers through a portion of the wall near the bay. That seemed to be the best starting point, so Freya aimed for the southern portion of the residential areas, while Zane shifted west.

A large portion of both areas had been burned out or looted, but based on Naedan and Amara's previous sweep, it seemed a lot of the residents who'd gotten out of their neighborhoods had managed to regroup in other less-crowded and less-visible areas of the city, away from soldiers who continued to walk the streets and torment the citizens. Under the older docks and bridges and the old, rotted out barns on the outer edges of the city would be the ideal places, as they were well-hidden enough that outsiders would have a hard time finding them, even if they thought to look. Freya had every intention of visiting them as soon as she could to confirm her thoughts, but that wasn't something she could afford to do tonight.

Even as the thought of seeing her former citizens gave Freya some hope, her heart sank when she neared her old neighborhood and came up on the street she'd lived on less than a year ago.

Nothing remained but ash and a bit of smoke here and there where hot spots hadn't yet been extinguished. The house she'd shared with Ana was indistinguishable from the burnt-out mess of cinders and crumbled wood around it.

She did a full loop around the neighborhoods, flying a bit low so she could get a better sense if anyone was in the area. Finding no trace of Naedan or Amara anywhere, she reconsidered her options.

After some deliberation, she took aim for the governor's residence near the central square. She wasn't entirely sure what she expected to find, but she hoped she might be able to locate some clue as to the hawks' whereabouts. If they were missing, they were either dead or captured. She felt the latter was more likely, considering there were very few people hawks would be scouting for. Two hawks scouting for the missing king and queen would be invaluable as sources of information, if Frederick had methods strong enough to extract it. If they were anywhere in the city and still alive, this was most certainly where they'd be.

Zane appeared to her right and let out a soft call when they sailed over the square and saw the carnage Frederick Edrin had allowed his guard to leave behind. The guillotine Ashton and Gideon had described sat blood-stained and silent over a pool of dried blood on the stone beneath. The heads of the victims had been piked, the ends of the long weapons that held them standing upright along the streets, replacing the pretty pixie lights that had always softly illuminated the area. Now, as the waning light cast long shadows over the city, the square sat in darkness, as every pixie that had once lived nearby and set the streets aglow had either fled or had been killed.

Zane came to rest on the roof of a building across the street from the governor's manor, an ornate, three-story house, then let out a call for Freya to join him. She ignored him, tightened her glamour, then flew to the roof of the manor, landing near a chimney on a section of roof that overlooked the building's central courtyard.

She waited silently, the minutes ticking by as the darkening sky continued to turn the city gray. More time passed as the stars began to wink on in the sky, and she had just about given up on any hopes of gathering information when the sound of voices from below reached her ears. Closing her eyes, she focused on listening as intently as she could to the people speaking. She dare not sneak any closer and risk a fall or being scented, so she trained her ears as best she could on the muffled conversation below. As far as she could tell, there were two speakers, both male, and one's voice held far more authority than the other.

"...know where they went...to be...king and queen."

"...given... information...Willem..."

"Lessia... changed mind..."

She angled her head toward the edge of the roof, trying to make sense of what little she was hearing. Someone was giving Willem information, but who? After the last report from Rini, Freya knew Willem had his eye on Lea, for whatever reason, but Lea certainly wouldn't give him any information worth having. The other option, of course, was Rosie, who Reginald and Isadora had assured her would be relaying each conversation she had with Lea back to her brother.

Suddenly, the voices went silent. Alarm bells rang out in Freya's head just as Zane let out a loud call from across the way. She leapt to her feet and had just taken to the air when a vise-like grip grabbed hold of her ankle. Zane swooped forward, narrowly missing her attacker as she slammed into the hard clay shingles, sending shards of broken clay everywhere. Wings, wide and black, flared in front of her. Her attacker released their hold on her to knock Zane from the air and down to the street below. She lunged forward, spreading her wings to dive down for him, when a hand wrapped in her hair and pulled her back down.

Wincing at the pain in her shoulder and the bits of clay digging into her palms, she looked up at her attacker.

Shit, she thought. *Shit, shit, shit!*

A Valkyrie, easily twice her width and two heads taller, and who could *clearly* see right through her glamours, stood before her, a vicious leer twisting his lips. Clad in black leathers, metal-plated armor covered his chest, shoulders, and forearms. He was handsome, and the touch of gray at his temples made him look to be a few centuries old. The only other soldier she'd seen so fearsome had been her father, whose mere presence spoke of impending ass-kickings.

This one... he was a predator. A violent, uncompromising predator.

"Ah, little Valkyrie." His voice was low and dark as he stepped closer. "I thought I might be seeing you soon."

She recognized the voice instantly as the authoritative one she'd just heard speaking in the governor's courtyard below.

Not giving herself a moment to bother with her normal banter, she slipped on her glamour and leapt to her feet. The Valkyrie was taken by enough surprise to give her time to take off, but within seconds he was on her tail. She swooped and dove, her mind running over all the things she'd learned and all the evasive maneuvers she'd practiced over and over with Byrric and Ana and the marshals.

Yet no matter how many sharp turns and vertical leaps or dives into dark alleys she took, he remained there, inches behind her. As they came to the western edge of the city, she closed her wings and let herself freefall, then flipped around and flew underneath him, shooting in the opposite direction in an attempt to buy herself more time.

But it wasn't enough. She felt the air push in on her back as he moved to overtake her.

"I know exactly who you are, girl!" he sang. "I know your sire, I know who trained you!"

And then he was on her, his talons tearing into her wing and sending her into a spin. She bit back her scream of pain as the injury registered, barely remembering to throw out her air magic to stop herself from crashing to the ground just inches before she hit. She didn't bother wasting magic on keeping herself invisible when she leapt up to run; it was clear he could see right through it. So she used her only advantage—superior knowledge of the city and all of its hiding spots.

She retracted her wings, the right limb barking in protest as the movement compressed the injury, then turned and fled down a narrow alley. With his size, there was no way he'd be able to maneuver easily between the walls of the buildings there, so she pumped her legs as hard as her body would allow.

She'd reached the end of the alley when the Valkyrie landed in front of her with a heavy thud, his wings tucked tightly against his back as she skidded to a stop in front of him.

"Who are you?" she demanded, her breath coming in heavy pants. Her wings snapped from her back and she pulled them in tight between her shoulder blades, slipping a feather from the edge. The injured one burned something awful, but her healing would kick in soon and she could fight well enough without taking flight. "What do you want?"

"I believe you were the one spying on me, were you not?" His lip curled in disgust, showing nothing but ugliness. "The Valkyrie queen, returned to her city. I surely can't say I'm surprised." His dark eyes flicked downward, and his cruel smile turned taunting when he saw the feather she gripped there. "Careful, there. You've just bitten off far more than you can chew."

She forced her mouth into a crooked smile. "Are you certain of that?"

"Cocky, just like that bastard father of yours." With a growl, he lunged, his face finding purchase on the cobblestone as she took to the skies in a vertical leap that set her injured wing screaming. When he found her in the air, he wrapped a hand around her bicep and pulled her toward him. Panic shot through her as she realized what he was doing.

He wasn't trying to kill her—he was trying to capture her.

"Not a chance in hell," she muttered, wrenching herself from his grip and shooting off toward the bay. Putting all her strength and magic behind her speed, she darted between the tall masts of the fishing boats, hoping his bulk would force him to slow down. When it didn't, panic began to sink in more heavily and she frantically looked around for something—*anything*—that could help.

Her eyes snagged on a net piled haphazardly on the deck below. Casting up a prayer to any god that cared to listen, she swooped down, the sudden change in her altitude giving her precious seconds as the Valkyrie changed direction. Freya snagged the net in both hands, then shot upward, kicking hard when he tried to grab her leg. Grinning, she flew farther over the bay, away from the boats.

"You'll tire eventually!" he sang.

"Not a chance!" she shot back. Then, with all her might, she darted upward, flung open the heavy net, and felt a grim satisfaction when his size made it impossible to avoid flying directly into it. With his wings trapped and hindered, he roared, falling to the darkened water, where Freya could only hope a hungry Kraken was waiting for something fresh to eat.

With a hiss of pain, she turned direction and took off for the woods. She wanted to fly straight back to the manor, but her injured wing wouldn't let her get more than a quarter-mile into the forest before she half glided, half fell to the ground, where, blessedly, Aer and the others were waiting for her. At the sight of her, Steffen, along with Gideon and Marcus, still in wolf form, put their backs to their monarchs and took up defensive positions.

"What happened?" Aer demanded, dragging her by her arms further into the trees. "Where's Zane?"

Freya struggled to her feet as he released her, then bent at the waist and rested her hands on her knees as she worked to control her breathing. "He fell, but I think he's alright." *Please be alright.*

"Fell where?"

"At the governor's manor." She rolled her shoulder, then winced at the pain. "He—"

Steffen let out a bird call, the faint hoot of a horned owl. Seconds later, the sounds of patrols crashing through the forest were behind them, closing in swiftly.

"I can't cast a glamour," she whispered hoarsely. "My magic—it's all going to my wing. We have to run."

Aer gave her a hard, wide-eyed look, then glanced at Steffen and nodded. The pair threw a joint bolt of magic toward their pursuers, causing them to falter, then they took off, Freya and Aer at the head while the marshals and Florian took up the rear. They were less than two miles from the boundaries of her lands, so if they could just make it there, they'd be under the protection of Selinda's magic.

He could see through your spells, a voice in her head reminded her. She shook it off, told herself if that Valkyrie could see through her grandmother's spells, they would've been dead a dozen times over by now.

Their pursuers closed in, the sounds of their movements only a few hundred yards back.

Steffen turned and sent another wave of power, followed quickly by one from Aer. Freya couldn't see who was chasing them, but she could only assume they were Jotnar. Humans would have been no match for the spirit magic Aer and Steffen were throwing their way. She felt Florian's cloaking spell slip over her, but she could tell he was struggling to maintain his own speed while cloaking them all in the dark.

Freya gritted her teeth and forced her legs to move faster, ignoring the pain in her wing and the fury she felt at being nearly helpless. She smothered a growl of pain, then retracted her wings, knowing she would regret it later when she had to flex them to heal. A moment later, she felt Florian's magic slide off of her, the glamour that had concealed her vanishing.

An arrow whizzed past her ear, and she stumbled to the ground, rolling behind a large tree just as a second arrow flew by. Aer slid to the ground beside her and reached for her hand as she cast a glance over her shoulder. The property line was hardly five hundred feet away, but if they gave up their position now, their pursuers would see exactly where they faded out of view. The spell protected the manor and diverted passersby around it, but nothing could prevent the sight of another being disappearing in midair.

The sound of pursuit stopped and the forest went silent.

Freya closed her eyes and trained her ears and nose on the woods around them, seeking any sign that their companions were alright. Steffen's even breathing sounded from fifty feet away, while Gideon's scent reached her from behind a boulder nearby. Ashton and Florian were about two hundred feet in front of them.

Marcus was the only one she couldn't detect, which, in her mind, only meant one thing.

Focusing her senses, she inhaled deeply, seeking out unfamiliar scents or tinges of magic.

She looked up at Aer, then opened and closed both fists five times, signaling their pursuers were only about fifty feet back. Aer's jaw tightened as he brought his magic forward. He pressed his hands flat against the earth and let his fingers sink into the layer of pine needles that covered the ground, then closed his eyes. The faint glow of spirit magic shone beneath the needles, hardly visible to Freya and likely invisible entirely to anyone further off. When she felt it brush past her, she wrapped her hand around his forearm, giving as much of her own strength as she was able.

"It won't do more than hold them off," he breathed. "As soon as I let go, they'll get their sense back and be right on us."

Freya slumped back against the tree and closed her eyes. "Can you feel Steffen?"

Aer nodded. "We're confusing the Jotnar, but they're pushing back." He opened his eyes and gave her an expectant look. "Any brilliant ideas, Valkyrie?"

"Perhaps they'll get bored with waiting," she suggested lightly. She looked at the ground where she could still see the faint glow of magic. "That's quite a trick you've got, Highness."

"Steffen and I toyed around a bit this afternoon. Under other circumstances I'd say it's nice to get to put our ideas into practice so soon." He slid a look at her and she nearly winced at the frustration she saw there. "Care to explain how a trip over the residential neighborhoods turned into you and Zane getting attacked at the governor's residence?"

"Berate me all you want later," she murmured. "For now, we need to figure out how to get back." She turned her head toward the direction they'd just come. "There are more coming."

"Yes, I can feel them," Aer muttered.

"Running would be our best option. If we can get closer to Florian, he'll be able to cloak us all," she said, then cursed. "We shouldn't have split up like we did."

"No, even for Florian, running at a full sprint while cloaking all of us would've been a feat." He looked down at his magic, then at her. "It seems we have a choice to make."

Freya banged the back of her head softly in frustration against the tree they were hiding behind.

"I have one," she whispered. "You won't like it, though."

"Unsurprising."

She flared out her wings and took a shaky breath as the pain hit, then raised up into a crouched position. "Stay here and keep working your magic," she said. "Keep it tight, though, or else they'll be able to sense us."

Aer stared at her with clear conflict in his expression. She knew he wanted to stop her, to be the one to step out in front of their enemy, but she knew he *also* knew that he was of best use here, unseen, where he could work his own form of defense that would be more likely to keep her safe.

She gripped his shirt and leaned closer. "I know you don't like this, but it's the only plan we've got. As soon as I step out, count to ten, then pull back your magic. Count to twenty, then bring up the rear with Steffen."

He shook his head and laughed. "You'll be the death of me one of these days, Freya."

With a grin, she kissed him, hard and full of emotion, then leapt to her feet and stepped back into the open. She took a small, measured breath, then broke into a sprint. Seconds later, she felt Aer's magic slip past her, under her feet.

They were on her in an instant, but this time, she had her magic at the ready. Her air daggers flew, taking out three in one shot, then Gideon came up from behind and took out two more. She continued to run at a brutal pace away from the manor, the amount of pounding feet at her back increasing with every step.

"Twenty," she breathed, then stopped short, spun, and lashed out at the five Jotnar who'd found her. Aer and Steffen's magic slammed into them, and had circumstances not been so dire, their struggles against it, sharp jerks and grunts, would have been comical. Her own magic was beginning to weaken as so much of it was diverted toward healing, so she focused on her physical defense as much as possible. Gideon launched himself at two, taking down one with his claws, the other with teeth, while Freya let two air daggers fly as she ran full-sprint at the Jotnar in front of her. Aer's magic tightened around her attacker's neck, shimmering and blue, a beacon telling Freya exactly where to aim. She sliced a feather across one's throat, then the next, and then finally, they were all down. The woods went silent, and as Aer approached her, her shaking began to start.

There was a heavy thump at her side. She pulled her dagger from her hip and spun, breathless, hand poised to strike, when a heavy fist wrapped around her wrist.

"What in the names of *all* the gods do you think you're doing?"

She let out a quiet, uncharacteristic whimper at the sight of Byrric standing before her, then all fight went out of her and she slumped to the ground. Aer was at her side instantly, and she retracted her wings as he lifted her into his arms.

"We need to get her back to the house," he told Byrric. He shook his head sharply. "Ask questions later. She's hurt."

Byrric's teeth ground together as he looked at them both, then shot a glance behind him. "Put her down."

Aer frowned. "What—"

Wordlessly, Byrric jerked Freya from Aer's arms, got a grip around her waist, then looped his other arm around Aer's waist and lifted them both off the ground.

"We're too far to run safely," he muttered as he spread his wings wide and took flight, wincing against the weight of them both. "I've already got my knights scouring the woods. When we get back, you two have a lot of explaining to do."

18

FREYA

It took every ounce of Freya's willpower not to put up a fuss once they gathered in the dining room and Florian tended to her wounded wing. Had it just been him, she might not have worried so much. As it was, she sat on the end of the dining room table with every one of their companions present, and she couldn't bring herself to show any more weakness tonight. Ashton, Laz, and Collin all stood stone-faced across from her, Aer stood quietly at her side, seething but doing a damn good job of not showing it, while the others waited to hear the rest of her report.

Naedan and Amara sat at the end of the table, having returned not an hour after Freya and Zane left. They'd been delayed when they were forced to hide with a handful of citizens they were helping flee from a group of Frederick's soldiers. Zane, who was nursing a bruised shoulder sat beside them. He'd been left, knocked out from the Valkyrie's hit, in a dark alley and had luckily gone unnoticed by other patrols.

Fortunately, they'd managed to help the Watorians they'd been hiding with escape. All things considered, Freya saw that as a win, small as it might've been.

"When you made the decision to spy on Frederick Edrin directly, what was your initial plan?" Byrric asked, after being apprised of the events of the night. His voice was calm, but his expression was full of far more expletives than he would ever utter to his queen in mixed company, daughter or no.

Freya hissed when Florian dabbed at a long cut on the ridge of her wing with one of his ointments. She'd thought there had only been one injury, but as it turned out, the Valkyrie had sliced her wing in five places, nearly breaking the ridge and pulling out four of her primary feathers, which took the longest to regenerate. It had been adrenaline, alone, that had allowed her to fly as far as she did when she got away.

"When we couldn't find any sign of Naedan and Amara, my initial thought was that they'd been killed, but that didn't make sense," Freya began. "If two hawk shifters had been caught scouting, whoever caught them would know who they were scouting for or would at least have a damn good idea."

"The most logical assumption from there was that they'd been captured," Zane added, clearly seeing where her explanation was headed. "We had no intention of going in without backup, but we did need to ensure their location before attempting to organize such a mission."

Freya sagged a bit in relief when Zane backed her up so thoroughly. The more they talked, the more she realized just how stupid she'd been. Zane had nearly been killed; the only thing that kept him alive was that she was the more attractive prize. No other patrols seemed to have been alerted, so when he came to, he flew back to the manor and alerted the others.

Byrric inclined his head toward the two shifters and gave Freya a grim smile. "Fortunately for you both, that type of mission was unnecessary."

Zane nodded his agreement. "Quite fortunate indeed, Commander."

Byrric shifted his stony gaze back to Freya. "What did you overhear?"

"I heard two males discussing someone providing Willem with

information, then a bit about Lessia and a changed mind, although I couldn't quite make out the context nor most of what was said," she answered.

"Someone is giving Willem information?" Isadora asked, her voice taking on a sharp edge. "Are you certain that's what they said?"

"I'm not sure," Freya said, meeting Isadora's eyes. "I'd say it's more likely they were discussing his attempts to get Lea to provide him with information, which has yet to happen."

Isadora sent a fearful look at Reginald, who reached out a took her hand in comfort.

"What else?" Byrric asked.

Freya gave her father a level, pointed look. "Yes, I nearly forgot to mention... the male who attacked me was a Valkyrie. His was one of the two voices I heard speaking in the courtyard earlier and seemed far more authoritative than the other. My assumption is *he's* the captain of the guard who had such a tight hold on Frederick Edrin's ear."

Byrric's eyes flashed, but if he was shocked at her words, he contained it beautifully as whispers floated around the room.

"How did we not know this?" Aer asked, his eyes shifting toward the marshals and palace guards who'd been patrolling. "How did you miss a Valkyrie potentially being one of Frederick Edrin's guards?"

"Aer," Freya chastised as embarrassment flooded Naedan and Amara's faces.

"Describe him," Byrric demanded.

Freya sighed. "Tall, black hair, black wings with a few white feathers strewn about, easily three times my size, and angry. Wore a good deal of armor, so the fact that he was able to catch me must've been a feat."

"And speaks volumes about his strength and abilities in its absence," Byrric snapped, his temper finally showing.

"Regardless, the last I saw, he was plummeting to a watery death, hopefully on his way to feeding one of the Kraken for the evening."

"His death is hardly certain," Byrric said, shutting down Freya's smirk.

Before she could respond, Byrric turned toward Reginald, who stood beside Ashton nearby. "Officer Carinald, Prince Ristner, convene with my knights and give each other a full update. We need to discuss our next steps immediately. The Valkyrie will be injured and it will take time for him to recover from his fall, but he'll undoubtedly have more patrols alerted within the hour. I want heavier, glamoured patrols and a two-mile perimeter around the property from now until we're done here. Steffen, get Haegin and begin extending Selinda's cloaking spell as far out as you can. Lord Florian will be there to assist you once he's done tending to Her Majesty's wounds. This property needs to be locked down tighter than a fortress, am I clear? Everyone else, out!"

Freya blinked in surprise at his sudden dismissal.

Once the door shut, leaving her alone with her father, Aer, and Florian, Byrric faced her. "I taught you better than this, Freya."

"You taught me to protect my own, which is what I was trying to do," she replied.

"As a marshal, perhaps, but not as the godsdamned queen!" He pounded a fist on the table, causing the heavy candelabra in the center to rattle, then jabbed a finger at her. "The fact that you went to Watoria with hardly any backup was stupid at best! You put yourself at risk, not to mention everyone in this house! Now you're injured, Marcus will be lucky if he gets to keep his leg, and our enemy knows that the missing king and queen of this entire godsdamned kingdom are here at their doorstep!"

"I thought Naedan and Amara had been killed or compromised! I cloaked myself and was on the roof; there is no way I could've known—"

"I raised you to be smart and confident, Freya, not naïve and arrogant," Byrric snapped. "You will never know everything about your enemy and to think so is the epitome of irresponsible!"

"As much as I may agree with you, Commander, calling your queen arrogant, naïve, and stupid is quite unbecoming of an officer, regardless of your relation," Aer said. "Freya and I were in agreement and we consulted with Officer Carinald and Lord Florian before finalizing any plans."

Byrric sent him a withering look. "With all due respect, I'm not talking to my queen right now, Your Majesty, I am talking to my daughter, who very nearly left you a widower tonight, in case you hadn't noticed."

"What, exactly, did you expect us to do?" Aer rested his arms on the back of Freya's chair. "We've been sitting on our hands for a week waiting to hear from you. There are nearly sixty people here, and that includes the two dozen marshals who managed to survive Frederick's siege. When our only means of aerial patrol went missing, we had a decision to make. Despite Freya's shift once she was in the city, I still believe it was the right plan, initially."

"I was opposed at first, Byrric," Florian said. "But we needed more reconnaissance. This was the best way to get it."

"Perhaps your initial plan was sound," Byrric said slowly. "But a problem clearly arose when the person charged with executing said plan changed paths in the midst of it!"

"Enough!" Freya shouted, holding up her hand. "We can discuss my idiocy later. There's a larger issue we need to address."

"Aside from nearly leading our enemies right to us?" her father spat.

She narrowed her eyes at him. "Sarcasm doesn't become you either, Commander."

"This Valkyrie," Aer said, clearly attempting to steer the conversation back onto safer ground, "who is he?"

A muscle worked furiously in Byrric's jaw as he stared between his king and queen, clearly torn between further berating his daughter or acknowledging what had just become an unforeseen threat.

She arched a brow. "Well? He certainly had a lot to say about you."

Florian huffed. "Unsurprising, wouldn't you say, Byrric?"

Byrric grunted. "What did he say?"

Frowning, Freya relayed her fight with the Valkyrie. When she was done, Byrric ran a hand over his face and turned away. She shared a confused look with Aer.

"Who is he?" she asked. When her father didn't answer, she shoved Florian's hand away from tending to her wing and stood. "He nearly killed me, Father, and it was quite clear he enjoyed it in large part because I'm your daughter. So, again, who is he?"

"Answer the question, Commander," Aer said tiredly after her father didn't answer right away.

Byrric looked at the ceiling and shook his head. "His name is Reykr Traust. I knew him in Iston as a boy."

When he didn't elaborate, Freya rolled her eyes. "And...?"

"We have a complicated history, Freya. Suffice it to say, you should do all you can to avoid him."

"Byrric," Florian said quietly as he guided Freya back to her seat and began to rub a rough brown substance across one of her cuts. "Keeping secrets helps no one, not in this case."

Freya gritted her teeth and waited, wanting very badly to push her father but knowing his stubbornness was only rivaled by her own.

"Alright." Byrric folded his arms and met her eyes. "We were rivals, of a sort. The only two male Valkyrie our age. We were born a few months apart, and at that point, all the other males were decades old, at least." He sighed. "When we were twelve, Jora and Selinda Enrieth came to meet with my parents. My mother introduced me to them, let them see my skill and all I'd learned thus far. What I didn't know was that they were on the hunt for a proper suitor for their daughter, your mother, Freya, and they thought a male Valkyrie would be a good match, considering the strength of the Cantor line of witches."

"You mean, you'd be most likely to help bear a half-blood as offspring?" Freya asked.

He nodded. "I was far stronger than him, even as a child, and my bloodline more pure—completely unbroken by magic-wielders. The agreement to betroth your mother and me was made a few months later. Reykr's family was... less-than pleased."

"Well, he seems to be doing well for himself now," Freya commented. "Why the bad blood?"

"Reykr met Cina when they were children while he and his family were summering in Allanor. They spent a good deal of time together and he developed an affection for her. His parents attempted to use that as a means of convincing Jora and Selinda to break the betrothal with me and choose him, instead. They refused, and a bit of a feud has existed between Reykr and me ever since."

Aer balked. "A bit of a feud? He tried to kill my wife!"

"He attacked her because she was attempting to spy on his leader," Byrric said calmly. "You would've done the same."

"He was in love with her, wasn't he?" Freya asked quietly. "He loved Mother. That's why he hates you so much."

"And she, him, at least in her own way," Byrric admitted. "Cina and I met a few months before we were to wed and bonded well, but it took some time for that bond to develop into love."

Freya rested her forearms on the table and rubbed her fingers against her temples, hissing when the movement caused her injured wing to smart. "Are you telling me he took such pleasure in fighting me because he was spurned by his lover? Is that truly what you're telling me right now?"

"She's Cina's daughter, though," Aer said. "I can understand wanting to hurt you, but it seems an odd thing to do to the offspring of the female he professed to love."

"He sees Freya's existence as the single reason Jora and Selinda didn't choose him." Florian set down his last bottle of ointment. "The likelihood of her creation was the deciding factor between your father and Traust as a suitor for their daughter. If they hadn't cared so much about ensuring a half-blood offspring, it's quite possible they would've chosen him."

"You make me sound like a well-bred pup," Freya muttered, surprised at how much the statement drew offense.

"Aren't you?" Florian raised a curved white eyebrow. "Wasn't your own betrothal a product of the same reasoning?"

"Lord Florian!" Aer snapped.

"Apologies, Your Majesty, but I only speak the truth. The only difference is that no one could ever question the bond between the two of you."

Byrric shot a scathing look at Florian before continuing his story. "Which is exactly what Reykr wanted to do to Cina and me. When her parents refused to call off the betrothal and after the mating bond had been sealed, he went to the governor of Caelora, which has jurisdiction over Iston, and attempted to have it nullified by accusing Selinda of wielding her magic in such a way that she was able to force the mating bond between us. There was no basis for truth to his accusations and ultimately served to bring Cina and I closer together."

"Is it safe to assume he didn't see it that way?" Aer asked dryly.

"To put it mildly. He continued to push until the other Valkyrie got so fed up with him, he was exiled from Iston. That was about one hundred years ago."

"Which begs the question, were there any who didn't get fed up?" Freya asked. "Were there any Istonians who believed his claims and might've sided with him?"

Byrric shook his head. "It's unlikely. Iston is small and that kind of talk would have gotten around quickly."

"We just sent Ana there to gather reinforcements, so we need to get word to her and your mother, regardless," Aer said. "Anything is possible, and if he might still have allies there, we need to know."

"I'll send Naedan," Byrric said. "If he flies directly there, he should make it in a day, two at most. For now, I'd say we should all get some rest." He looked at Aer, then Florian. "If you two wouldn't mind giving me a moment alone with my daughter?"

"Of course," Aer said. He leaned down and kissed the top of Freya's head, then nodded at Byrric. "Goodnight, Commander."

Florian put all of his ointments and tinctures on a small tray, along with a handful of bloody rags that he'd used to clean up Freya's wings. "Try to wait a bit longer before retracting your wings, Your Majesty. The ointment needs time to soak in, but you should be fine within a half-hour."

Freya gave him a tight smile. "Thank you, Lord Florian. I'm not sure what we'd do without you."

"Lose the occasional limb, most likely." He picked up his tray and nodded at Byrric, then followed Aer out of the room.

Freya stared at the closed door, unsure what, if anything, she should say to her father. In all their years, they'd never really spoken of his ties to Iston, outside his connection to his mother, Vara, and his father, who'd died long before Freya was born. Once he'd married Cina, nearly three centuries earlier, and Salazar had appointed him head of the Allanorian army, he'd left Iston behind for good. He'd never shared much with Freya about his childhood aside from the training regimens he'd passed down to her from his own parents. It often seemed to Freya that his life only began when he and Cina married.

"Florian's bedside manner leaves much to be desired," Byrric commented, letting his own wings slip back into his shoulders.

Freya huffed out a breath through her nose. "Indeed." She met her father's eyes. "This Traust fellow... is he going to be as much of a problem as I think?"

He dropped down in the chair Florian had just vacated and rested his forearms on the table, then stared down at his hands. "Presumably. I lost track of him decades ago. When I didn't hear anything about him for so long, I assumed he was dead. I never bothered to have Florian look into his whereabouts because I thought he was no longer an issue."

Freya pursed her lips. "Byrric Balthana, making assumptions? Isn't that a quality far beneath you?"

His lips twitched. "One might think. It seems his disappearance was actually a relocation to Jotunheim. I'm sure Crispin and Lessia welcomed him with open arms." He looked at Freya, his eyes running over her face, and she saw that the look of annoyance he'd worn moments ago had shifted toward concern. "Are you alright?"

"Peachy." She rolled her shoulder, testing Florian's healing skills. "Florian seems to have quite the knack with healing potions."

"He was your Toxins professor, Freya. His skills *do* extend past just poisoning his students." Byrric frowned. "I wasn't speaking of your shoulder, though."

Freya tapped her thumbs lightly on the table and stared straight ahead, knowing what her father was asking and hating that she had to admit how she was truly feeling. "He was terrible," she whispered. "Everything, everyone I've ever fought has been fueled by greed of some sort. This was so different. It was... personal."

"Hatred and vengeance will do that to a male," Byrric said. "I meant what I said, Freya. Do not take him on alone if you come across him again." He held up a hand when she opened her mouth. "I am not telling you to stand down entirely if you were to encounter him again, and certainly not if you have reinforcements. I only want you to make sure you're smart about engaging with him. If it comes down to a one-on-one, you run, do you understand?"

She searched his face, expecting to see fatherly admonition there, but instead, she found fear.

She smiled softly. "Aren't you supposed to be fearless?"

"Only if I were a fool. Now, I'm not going to chastise you any further. I'll leave that bit to your husband because I'm sure he's got a few choice words for you when you go to him." He stood, and Freya followed suit. He paused for a moment as he looked down at her, then sighed and pulled her into a gentle hug, being careful not to jar her injured wing. "Don't you ever, *ever*, scare me like that again. Do you understand?"

Too shocked at her father's uncharacteristic show of emotion to respond, Freya wrapped her arms around him and nodded.

19

FREYA

Aer was standing in front of the balcony doors when Freya returned to their room a short while later. Even with his back turned, she could see the tension coiled within him.

She dropped her jacket on the divan at the foot of the bed and approached him, wrapping her arms around his waist and resting her forehead against his back. "I'm sorry," she whispered.

He tensed, then relaxed as he let out a deep breath and placed his hands over hers. "Do you have any idea what it felt like to see you come back to me injured, hardly able to fly?" His voice was painfully controlled as he turned to face her.

She pressed her lips together and held back the retort that formed on her tongue. Her instinct was to tell him not to treat her like a fool, but logic told her he was right; she *had* been foolish. She should've listened when Zane called for her to leave, but instead, she'd gone her own way. She'd acted rashly, and she should have waited until she had more backup.

"I couldn't leave them behind," she said. "Naedan and Amara were missing and I had what I felt were valid concerns regarding their and our safety."

"So you bring them to me," he replied. "To Ashton, to Florian.

Gods above, Freya, when will you get it through your head that you aren't on your own anymore?" He rubbed a hand over his face, then let his arms drop to his sides. "We're in the middle of a goddamn war and we had a plan for a reason! Going off script like that is not an option."

"I know." She linked her fingers through his, calming them both. "I know. I just didn't see the sense in leaving the city when it seemed such a high likelihood that they were in trouble. If they'd been captured—"

"I just got you back, Freya." He met her eyes, and the intensity she saw there set her off-kilter. "Six years, I've been waiting for you to come back. I refuse to lose you again."

She reached up and cupped his cheek, then smiled as she drew his face toward hers. "That will never happen."

He took the offered kiss with an urgency that revealed just how afraid he'd been for her. She shuddered when he ran his hand up the curve of her wing, brushing the injured ridge.

"How does it feel?" he asked quietly.

"Better now." She smiled up at him.

"Liar," he murmured. "You forget I can feel your pain, my love."

"Then I suppose you ought to do something to ease it, shouldn't you?"

His mouth curved against hers. "What shall it be, then? A bit of chicken soup brought up from the kitchens?" He lifted her off the ground and began to walk toward the bed. "Perhaps a foot massage?"

Freya wrapped her legs around his hips and touched a kiss to his neck. "Haegin *is* quite skilled when it comes to home remedies. His soup might be just what I need."

"Is that so?"

"It is."

She retracted her wings when they reached the bed, ignoring the dull ache the motion caused, and let him kiss her, hard and deep. As his lips ran over hers, she could feel his body relax. He ran his hand up her back and into her hair, dragging his fingers through the length of it. The fear she'd felt pulsing through him just a short while ago began to ease as he tightened his hold on her. He laid her on the bed and stared down at her, allowing himself to see that she was there in front of him and safe.

When he settled himself on top of her, caging her body between his arms, he brushed his lips against hers.

"I love you, Freya," he whispered. "Tell me what you need and I'll do it."

She knew what he was asking, knew he would never proceed unless she gave him permission.

She leaned up and put her mouth to his ear. "I need you," she whispered. "All of you."

He grinned, a lopsided smile that would've had most girls melting. Instead, it was a challenge.

She gave him an expectant look. "Do you plan to make your queen tell you a second time?"

His smile shifted and she felt the first wave of his power wash over her, pure pleasure and ecstasy. A tingle ran down her spine, and she felt it spread toward where her wings lay, hidden beneath the surface.

Leaning down, he touched a kiss to her jaw, then whispered against her skin. "Now what?"

A shaky breath escaped as she tried to think past the feelings that were replacing the pain she still felt at her back. "Undress me."

He kissed a path to her waist, then he took his time unlacing her pants. Impatience had her slipping her shirt over her head, but she'd barely managed the movement when he put a hand on her stomach and gently guided her back down.

Raw lust mingled with her own desire as another push of his power nearly brought tears to her eyes. As he slowly slid her pants down her hips, it took all her strength not to reverse their positions so she could take control.

That wasn't what she'd asked for, though. It wasn't what she needed. It wasn't what *he* needed.

Slowly, he worked her to a frenzy, using his magic and his mouth to pull his name from her lips. The pain in her back and wings she'd felt when he laid her down ebbed with each touch of his power. She recalled the first day they fought in class, the way his power had fogged her mind and made her want his hands on her. Having that, feeling that power and those hands, had every ounce of pain fleeing her body.

By the time his mouth found hers again, she was aching to feel his body pressed against her. The clothing he still wore was a painful barrier between them, one he removed almost as quickly as the thought crossed her mind.

He rolled to his back, gripping her waist as he moved, settling her on top of him.

"Let out your wings," he whispered.

She smiled curiously as she adjusted to the change in position. "Why?"

"I want to try something." When she hesitated, he smiled and ran his hands up her thighs, then curved his fingers around her hips. "Do you trust me?"

She leaned down and brushed her lips across his. "Always," she murmured as she let her wings out. She hissed at the pain that lanced across the ridge, but it was instantly replaced with pleasure as Aer's power brushed over it.

When she felt their bodies connect, felt his power course over and through her, bringing her nothing but pure joy, she knew the pain she'd felt from her injuries would be gone when he was done with her. Something within her began to stitch itself back together, and whether that was physical or magical, she wasn't sure. She let him take control, set the pace so he could care for her, a thing she knew he needed.

A thing she realized she needed as well.

Later, when they lay wrapped in each other's arms, bathed in the glow of the fire, Aer began twirling strands of her hair through his fingers. "Do you feel better?"

"Very, very much," she murmured, her words muffled against his chest. "I didn't know you could heal with your magic."

He ran his fingers slowly up and down her back, tracing a path along her spine. "I wasn't sure I could. My mother encouraged me to try, but until now, I've never had the chance to put that theory to practical use."

Freya smiled when she felt his own amusement. "Are you tired now?"

"No," he murmured. "Quite the opposite, actually."

Frowning, she rested her chin on his chest and looked at him. "How so?"

"It's hard to describe, but it's as though I felt how my healing affected you, which affected me. Does that make sense?"

She smirked. "I'd say we can thank the mating bond for that."

"It's definitely something I could get used to," he said, grinning.

She searched his face, pleased to see that his smile was relaxed, all earlier signs of tension gone. Smiling softly, she touched a finger to his lip, then laughed when he nipped playfully.

With a sigh, she propped her chin on her fist. "I'm sorry for how badly I scared you tonight. If roles had been reversed, I'd have gone mad with worry."

He touched her chin. "Let's make this the first and last time either of us has to feel that way needlessly, alright?"

"After tonight, I can say I wholeheartedly agree."

Aer shifted so he was facing her. "Have I ever told you how much I love watching you fight?"

"You seemed quite angry at that pastime not too long ago."

He shook his head. "I was angry that you put yourself at unnecessary risk. Watching you fight in the forest... you get this look of determination on your face, a sort of furrow right here," he said, touching the center of her forehead. "It's quite fascinating."

"I wish I'd felt that determination fighting Traust." Freya averted her eyes. "He was so strong, Aer. I've never felt anything like it."

His body tensed a fraction before he responded. "Now you'll be prepared if you meet him again. And if that time comes, Freya, you will tear him to bits." His eyes bored into hers, chocolate mixed with mint, conveying just how certain he was of that fact.

"You truly believe that?"

"With every fiber of my being. Know it, believe it, and believe in yourself. You've never faced someone like him before, but that doesn't mean you can't handle him. Especially with Byrric at your side."

She was quiet for a moment as she considered all that lay before them. Yes, she would likely encounter Traust again, but even without that annoyance, a war was still bearing down on them. "It will be strange, you know? Fighting alongside my father. I honestly never expected that to happen."

"I'm sure he didn't, either," Aer said with a laugh. "But the two of you combined will be able to take Traust down without a thought, believe me."

"I hope so," she said with a sigh. "I've never questioned myself until now, and it's quite unsettling."

"Not to worry, my love. You've got centuries to regain your prior level of perfection."

She gave him a look of mock outrage. "Are you saying my current level of perfection is sub-par?"

He chuckled softly and touched his lips to her hair. "Nothing about you is sub-par, Valkyrie. Not a damn thing."

20

———

LEA

Rosie Ristner was, in a word, tiresome, and her insistence that she and Lea become the best of friends was downright draining.

Even for sixteen, she seemed young, painfully naïve, and all-too excited about this new kingdom her brother had acquired. Lea might've thought she was feigning her innocence, but the way she talked with Lea about Lindoroth's takeover, as though Lea wasn't one of the victims of Willem's schemes, made it seem as though she was simply obtuse.

Lea did her best to push aside her insult when Rosie came by for visits, though, in the hopes Rosie's words would, at some point, prove of use.

And, tiring as she may be, Lea could benefit both from Rosie's companionship and the bit of normalcy her incessant chatter provided. Loneliness had begun to take hold of Lea, and Rosie's presence helped break the routine of boredom that had become Lea's new normal.

Their conversations often circled back to Rosie's impending wedding to Lord Benjamin Whitmore, the only son of one of Dystone's most wealthy landowners. Benjamin was twenty-five, and as the eldest male heir, had been under pressure since birth to ensure he found a proper young wife to continue his family line. Rosie didn't seem put off by their age difference, despite nine years being quite significant in a human lifespan, nor did she seem to care that both her brother and Benjamin's father were content to view her as a means of producing heirs and little more.

"I'm quite excited to have children, you know?" Rosie smiled, her pert nose crinkling a bit. She'd arrived an hour earlier for tea and had been showing no signs of departing anytime soon. "I know I'm still young, but children are just such a blessing, don't you agree?"

Lea gave her a tight smile. "They truly are."

"Benjamin has already said he doesn't want to rush me, but I know he wants a whole brood of children. Lots of boys, of course, but I *do* hope we end up with at least one little girl. All those *dresses!*" She smiled brightly. "What do you think, Lady Calliwell? If you and Lord Edrin do marry, how many children would you like to give him?"

Lea choked a bit on the sip of tea she'd just taken, then coughed as she set her cup down. "I—the topic of offspring has yet to be broached." She studied the girl's face, trying to determine if Rosie was being cruel or simply stupid.

"Oh, certainly! I only meant, well, surely you've always dreamt of children? And you and Lord Edrin make *such* a handsome couple."

Stupid, then.

"Our lives are very long, Princess," Lea said slowly. "And our ability to procreate is not nearly as swift as yours. To have one child is a feat in and of itself, so dreaming of multiple offspring is a bit of a fool's errand."

"Why is that?" Rosie looked at her curiously and took a bite of a biscuit. "I would think having all that time would make you more prolific."

Lea narrowed her eyes. "Are you truly asking about the fertility of my species, Princess?"

"I'm so sorry, Lady Calliwell. Is that improper? It's all just so fascinating to me!"

Lea sighed. "The long and short of it is, longer lifespans mean longer cycles in females. A human female has the ability to attempt pregnancy monthly. For Linds and Jotnar, that time can come as often as once a year or as little as once every five. Even still, it's common for a century or more to pass before a female becomes with child."

Rosie's eyes widened and she touched a hand to her stomach. "You only cycle every few *years*? Goodness, how fortunate!"

Definitely stupid.

"Yes, I suppose I can see why you might consider that lucky," Lea said with a nod.

"Mm. I just hope I'm able to give Benjamin a son quickly. Once I return and we move to Caldel, he'll be so busy that I worry it will take away from our time to try." She grinned conspiratorially.

Lea pursed her lips, debating whether she should tell Rosie her future husband would likely take her when and where he wanted, whether it was convenient for her or not. She kept that thought to herself, though, when she caught on to the other half of Rosie's sentence.

"Caldel? You'll be moving to the capital? I thought Lord Whitmore was set to take over his father's lands?"

"Oh, no! Benjamin's younger brother will take that on. He and his wife are already established in Leford with two sons, so it makes more sense for us to take on Willem's duties in Caldel."

"Ah." Lea nodded as though she knew exactly what Rosie was talking about. "Yes, I suppose that makes sense."

"Caldel is a lovely city, though. A wonderful place to raise a family, so I can't really say I'm disappointed." Rosie wrinkled her nose again. "Although, I was looking forward to living in the south. Leford's weather is so pleasant all year long. Open windows, warm breezes, breakfasts on the veranda..." She sighed. "But it's good work we'll be doing, so I'm willing to make that sacrifice, I suppose."

Lea smiled. "Any sacrifice for the sake of your family is worth it."

Rosie grinned. "Too, true, Lady Calliwell. Too true."

~

After Rosie left, Lea waited for Jonas to return, pacing the room. Now and then, she cast her eyes furtively toward the panel beside the fireplace that opened into the tunnel system. Ever since she'd become aware of the entrances to the tunnel that ran behind Jonas' room, Lea had been contemplating when she might do an exploration.

Each time, almost as soon as the idea struck, she shot it down. She didn't have Aer's ability to feel whether other creatures were nearby or Freya's shifter senses that let her smell or hear far-off intruders. Going into the tunnels now, unprepared and unaware of where they led, would be foolish, suicidal, even. If she were caught, there would be two logical conclusions as to why she was there: to spy or to escape. Both of which were punishable by another stay in the dungeons at best, death at worst.

When Jonas finally returned nearly two hours after Rosie left, it took all she had not to leap at him. Her desire to question him about what Rosie had said aside, she was dreadfully bored and in dire need of another person to talk to.

"What's wrong?" he asked when he saw her face. He shrugged out of his white jacket and tossed it on the bed. "You seem perplexed."

"Rosie was here earlier," she began. "She mentioned that she and her fiancé would be moving to Caldel, to the palace, once they're married, to take over Willem's duties there. What did she mean by that?"

Jonas paused, his hand hovering over a pitcher of water, and frowned. "I have no idea. What exactly did she say?"

Lea repeated Rosie's words and then asked,. "Is Willem not planning on returning to Dystone?"

Jonas sat down on the divan beside her, still looking a bit confused. "I'm not sure. The last plans I heard were that he and Effina were to travel back and rule Dystone, and I was to continue my role as emissary. You're certain she said they'd be taking on Willem's duties and not assisting him?"

"Yes!" She rubbed a hand across her forehead, losing patience. The thought of Lessia remaining in Lindoroth was bad enough; the thought of Willem opting to stay indefinitely as well was more than a little upsetting. Not only was he a horrid person, his remaining presence meant there wouldn't be a time in the near future when Lindoroth would only be left with one of its usurpers present instead of both.

"The only thing I can assume is that he's planning on putting Benjamin Whitmore on the throne as steward, but I'm not sure why Willem wouldn't impart that honor on one of his other brothers," Jonas said.

"They have their own lands to run, and this would still keep a Ristner in the capital," Lea said. "And Rosie worships Willem. While she may be naïve in many ways, I don't believe she'd let anything untoward happen during Willem's absence without reporting it to him directly."

Jonas drummed his fingers on his knees for a moment, then nodded. "You may be right. If nothing else, the possibility is worth mulling over, certainly." He smiled. "Keep up the chats with Rosie. I know she may be tiring, but she seems the type to let more information spill than she realizes."

Lea made a face. "And here I thought all my time would be spent attempting to avoid the lewd stares of your guards."

"There'll be plenty of that, I'm sure," Jonas said with a sigh. "Although, the interest Willem seems to have taken in you may discourage that a bit."

Lea noted the reluctance in his words, as though he were just as unhappy to voice that concern aloud as she was to think it. Willem's attention toward her—both positive and negative—was troubling, and she wasn't quite sure how to handle it. He seemed to always be present when she was around and had stopped in twice when she was visiting with Rosie, making her begin to question the human girl's motives for spending time with her. Part of it, she knew, was that Lea was close to her in age, although it was clear she didn't see just how little that meant. Lea's life had been spent learning to fight and wield her magic, helping her parents lead their people, and pushing herself to hopefully become a leader later in life. Rosie had been raised to be docile and pretty, to obey the men in her life, and create heirs for her husband.

Lea felt bad for her in a way. Rosie had never been given permission or even the opportunity to think for herself or make her own choices, a thing Lea had little patience for, even if she knew it wasn't Rosie's doing that made her that way.

In another life and under different circumstances, she might be tempted to take the girl under her wing, show her the importance of independence and strength.

As it was, though, Lea would be content to watch Rosie's world burn, along with her hellish brother.

21

———

FREYA

The newfound benefits to Aer's magic made for a solid night of sleep for Freya, despite the revelations from her father about Reykr Traust and her mother. She knew her parents both had lives before they'd gotten married, of course, but she never considered either had involved romantic relationships. She'd shared a few kisses of her own before returning to Watoria, but that was admittedly out of a desire to improve her own skill before returning to Aer. A true romantic relationship was never something she sought.

But if what Byrric said was true, and Traust and Cina had cared that deeply for one another, she knew Traust wasn't going to let up on them any time soon, regardless of how Cina ultimately came to feel for Byrric. Freya couldn't imagine him being any worse than Lessia or Willem, but he was a complication, nonetheless.

Byrric, Ashton, Reginald, and Florian were in the dining room when Freya and Aer entered. She tried to ignore the way all four of them gave her a once-over, assessing her condition without the insult of asking how she was feeling.

"Any news?" Aer asked as they sat.

"We managed to catch and kill all but one of the knights that were after you last night," Ashton said. "Steffen fogged the memory of one and dropped him further to the east, so hopefully that will keep Traust from coming through this area of the forest, if that was his intention. If there were any who escaped, Steffen had no sense of them, so it appears there were none left to report back to Edrin."

Freya let out a relieved breath. "Good. That's good."

"Steffen can alter memories?" Reginald asked.

"Not quite," Freya said. "He can cause someone's memory to be muddled, so if the knight wakes up in the eastern forest, he'll assume that's where he was chasing us. Ideally, he'll report that location to Traust."

Reginald nodded absently. "That's a useful trick."

"What else?" Aer asked.

"We received word from Ana early this morning," Byrric said. "A messenger arrived just before dawn and left shortly after I informed her of Traust's presence here."

Freya's eyes widened, though she was relieved the Valkyrie would know quickly to be on the lookout for any who might sympathize with Traust. "Has something happened?"

"Ana says there are rumors of a Jotnar battalion moving south toward the northern border of central Caelora from Jotunheim. The Istonians were unsure of the validity of the rumors, so they sent out two scouts two days ago to confirm, which they did."

Momentarily stunned, Freya rubbed a hand across her brow and looked at Aer, who looked equally as concerned. "What does this mean, then?"

"I've sent Officer Ristheld out to meet with the commander of the Allanorian battalion that's camped in the Outlands," Byrric replied. "Last we spoke, Commander Alstad planned to send a team north to see what, if any, movement was happening near the Jotunheim border."

"How long ago was that?" Freya asked.

"I heard from him three days ago. I didn't indicate when I would be in the area, just that I would be in contact once I was. This news from Iston seems to confirm what he heard."

"How long would it take that many soldiers to get here on foot?" Reginald asked.

"They were about two days north of the Jotunheim border," Florian said. "So nine, perhaps ten days, depending on where and how frequently they stop,"

"Send some knights north," Aer said. "Perhaps it will draw some of the humans blocking Watoria away from the city to support the Jotnar coming this way."

Byrric nodded. "Yes, that's what we were just discussing. Ana said it would take several days to get to where the Jotnar are to head them off, so they think it's best if we pull soldiers from here to stop them from coming any further south while the Valkyrie attempt to come in from the north. I'm assuming Traust and Edrin will see it for what it is, assuming they're aware of what Lessia's soldiers are doing, but drawing their attention even briefly could help us get into the city. Whether they pull knights from Watoria to follow ours north will hinge on whether they think it worthwhile to take out a battalion while leaving a city with fewer protections."

"They're your army, Commander," Florian said to Byrric. "Former and current. Odds are, Traust will encourage Edrin to wipe them out simply to spite you. "

"Have we confirmed Traust is part of Frederick Edrin's guards?" Aer asked.

"We have," Byrric said, his voice grave. "Zane flew out last night to see if he could confirm those suspicions, which he did."

When he didn't elaborate, Freya looked at him, Florian, and Ashton. "What is it?"

"According to Officer Ristheld, Traust seems to have left a *message* for your father," Florian said. "For you, too, I suppose."

Freya's blood went cold. "What kind of message?"

"The bodies of the marshals," Ashton said, his voice strained. "Most of those who were unable to flee the city. He spread them across the central square, on the steps of the town hall—"

"How do you know it was him?" Freya interrupted, not needing that image painted more vividly than it already was.

"Zane saw him," Byrric said quietly. "Watching from a window when he flew over. Based on the expression on his face, Zane felt Traust had been expecting one of us to fly in to check on things, confirm his involvement, even."

They sat quietly for a few moments, and Freya tried very hard not to let her emotions get the best of her as she considered this new development.

"I find it highly amusing your love life has suddenly begun causing us such a significant amount of grief," Freya said, forcing a wry grin in an attempt to clear the heavy tension in the air. "Here I thought that duty belonged solely to me."

"There's always room for improvement," Byrric said dryly.

"Going north is what you feel is best?" Ashton asked her father after a moment.

Byrric nodded curtly. "I think it's our best chance of getting into the city. Watoria is at a disadvantage in terms of defenses due to its proximity to the shoreline—"

"Yes, it's a shame someone didn't mention that before," Freya muttered.

Byrric gave her a disparaging look. "Which made it easier for Lessia and Willem's soldiers to infiltrate."

"Freya is the only marshal who patrolled the docks as often or as well as she did," Ashton said. "The rest of the marshals tended to keep to the city."

"Meaning what?" Aer asked.

"Meaning I know the harbor, docks, and shoreline the best," Freya said.

"Better than marshals who'd been at their jobs for several decades?" Aer asked.

Byrric chuckled.

She arched her brow at her husband. "I can fly, my love. There hasn't been an avian marshal in decades."

"We're mostly wolves, a few witches and warlocks," Ashton explained. "She was the first of us to be able to provide aerial patrols in quite some time."

"Again, I ask, what does this mean? I won't send my queen to infiltrate a city held by invaders," Aer said.

"Agreed," Byrric replied. He shot Freya a warning look when she went to argue. "Is this something you would encourage Ordona to do?"

Freya's mouth snapped shut. "It's different."

"No, it's not," Aer replied. "My mother could level the likes of Traust with her magic, but that doesn't mean intentionally putting her in a situation where she'd have little to no reinforcements against him would have been wise."

"Like we did with Lea?"

"That's not fair and you know it."

Freya let out a breath, rubbing a hand over the back of her neck, and thought back to her promise to Aer the night before to not give each other unnecessary cause to worry. "You're right, I'm sorry."

"Her Majesty is in a good position to help lay out a plan, should we choose to go into the city, though," Florian said.

"Which brings us back to *how* to get into the city," Aer said with a sigh.

"Getting in won't be an issue if we can get Edrin's soldiers distracted," Freya said. "It's the lack of additional forces that concerns me."

"We'll wait to see what Zane has to say once he's talked to Commander Alstad," Byrric said. "I want to know more about the movements of the enemy troops blocking the city before I make a final decision. Unless the king or queen has other objections?"

"As your experience far outranks ours, we'll defer to your judgment on this, Commander," Aer said. "In the meantime, let's send Amara and Naedan into the city while Zane is speaking with Commander Alstad. I want to know the second Frederick and Traust hear about outside movement."

"Consider it done," Byrric said, standing. Freya noticed his eyes weren't quite as sharp as they normally were.

"Have you slept at all, Commander?" she asked, genuine concern lacing her tone.

"Not for nearly two days, so I'm going to get a few hours in now while I can," he said, scrubbing a hand over his face. "Wake me if you hear anything."

"Will do."

AFTER THEY FINISHED THEIR MEETING, Freya took some time to walk the grounds to give herself a bit of time to think without the incessant chatter that seemed to fill the house at all hours. The cold air bit at her face as she traversed the lawns and made her way through the different levels of the gardens, all perfectly maintained. They didn't hold a candle to the palace gardens in terms of size, but they were still impressive and beautiful in a way the palace's never could be.

She smiled as she emerged onto the rear lawn of the property where her parents had set up a target against a tree long ago, back when Freya was still learning proper throwing and archery skills. It was a place she'd bonded with them both. Cina, as she taught Freya to use her magic to streamline her throws, Byrric, as he taught her his own methods of accuracy that required little more than muscle and a good eye.

The knives she had with her today hadn't been used in years, but the Caelorian steel still held the same gleam today as they did back then. They were flat and smooth, a solid piece of steel with a blade forged precisely for cutting straight through whatever happened to be in its path. They'd been her mother's and had sat idle in a chest at the foot of her parents' bed since Byrric had moved Freya into the city. She'd found them a few days earlier when on the hunt for a cloak for Isadora and had been surprised to discover Byrric hadn't taken them with him when he left. Surprised, but glad, as Freya was currently in need of some training to clear her head, and her favorite set of knives was still in a chest in the palace under her bed.

She unbuckled her wool cloak from around her shoulders and set it on a large rock that marked a line thirty feet from the target, then slid two knives from the sheath on her waist. The target, no more than a bullseye carved into a piece of pine nailed to an oak tree, had faded over the years, but its lines were still clear enough. She flexed her gloved fingers, loosed a breath, then gripped the edge of the first blade and threw.

Nearly an hour later, she was sweating and her shoulders were beginning to ache, but she felt as though she'd released some of the pent-up energy that had been building over the past week. Normally she would've gone out for a flight or joined the marshals and knights on patrol, but being sequestered to the manor's grounds made both of those things difficult. She understood the logic and, as discussed in the conversation earlier this morning, she would've insisted on the same measures had Ordona been with them. But it was hard not to be frustrated at her consistent lack of use. Going into Watoria hadn't been the best idea, she saw that now, but it had at least made her feel as though she was *doing* something. It had given her a task.

She'd just finished removing all six blades from the target when she heard a quick bark behind her. She glanced back toward the direction of the house and smiled when she saw Laz and Collin trotting toward her in their wolf forms. Laz's fur was a soft gray, while Collin's coat was russet streaked with charcoal; the perfect complements to one another.

"Out for a walk?" she asked as they shifted onto two legs.

"We thought we'd take a lap around the property," Collin said, leaning against the boulder her cloak was draped across.

"And we had an idea," Laz said.

"Lazarus had an idea," Collin corrected. "But it's a good one. A risky one," he qualified, "but it's worth considering."

Freya looked at them, expectant. "Alright. What's this brilliant idea of yours?"

Laz blew out a slow breath, then gave a sharp nod, as though convincing himself his idea was worth hearing. "What are your thoughts on reaching out to the elves?"

She huffed out a laugh and shook her head. "I have none. The elves don't involve themselves in outside affairs."

"Lessia seems to think it's worth attempting, or at least that's what

Jonas has led Lea to believe," Collin pointed out. "Why shouldn't we?"

Freya eyed them both, scrutinizing. "Where did this idea come from?"

Collin folded his arms. "We're short on allies. The Lindorothian army has been culled significantly and we both know attempting to contact any of the Jotnar rebels is hardly an option with a host of soldiers aimed straight at us."

"Have you discussed this with Aer?" she asked.

"We only just thought of it this morning," Laz replied. "We intended to find you both once we got back to the house. The Commander, as well."

Freya stared down the lane at the target, tapping the flat of her blade against her palm. As far as ideas went, it was ludicrous, at least to her mind. But Collin had a penchant for military strategy. It had always been an interest of his, and Laz was well-versed in history, both of Lindoroth's and that of the rest of the world, so it was no surprise to her that the two had fallen into a discussion such as this.

She looked at Laz. "What makes you think it's worthwhile?"

"The elves weren't always so reclusive," he explained. "They used to be quite the global people, actually, traveling all over and dipping their hands in here and there. They had a falling out with the humans and their relationship with the Linds fell by the wayside after that. Perhaps with the right phrasing, the right incentive, we can draw them back into the world."

"What kind of 'falling out'?"

"About two millennia back, a human queen was kidnapped by an elf prince," Laz told her. "According to stories, they were soulmates, bound by magic, so the elves went to war to keep her."

"Why?" Freya asked.

"You're mated," Laz said. "It's not a natural bond, of course, but imagine what would happen if someone took Aer from you."

Her mouth went dry at the thought, and panic, unreasonable at it was, had her heart quickening.

Laz's eyes flickered with an apology before he continued. "When the human armies attacked Avorell, the elves annihilated them, of course, but instead of returning to the world, the elves shut their borders permanently."

"That seems excessive," Freya commented.

"Be that as it may, *we* are not the ones they had a falling-out with," Collin said. He shrugged. "I know nothing of the elf monarchs currently, but if they are anything like every other race that exists, they almost certainly abide by the wishes of their ancestors."

"Meaning the new monarchs may dislike the humans just as much as their old ones?"

"It's more likely the current monarchs were around when the human queen was taken," Laz told her. "They might've been young, but they very well could have lived through that war."

Her eyes widened. "How long do they live?"

He smiled. "A very long time."

"This idea seems to be based on a fair number of assumptions with little to back them up," she observed after a moment. "But... you have valid points." She nodded. "Alright, let's talk it over with Aer, see —" She turned at the sound of footsteps behind her and saw her father approaching, looking a bit more haggard than usual.

She grinned. "Here to take me on?" she asked as he came to a stop beside Laz.

He laughed. "Not everything has to be a competition, Freya." His eyes drifted between the three of them, suspicious. "Dare I ask?"

Collin chuckled smoothly. "We were just leaving, actually. Freya's in a knife-tossing mood and we're getting hungry." He lifted his brows at Freya. "We'll see you inside."

After they walked off, she gave Byrric an expectant look, then held out one of the knives. He considered it for a moment before taking it.

"One round," he said, pointing the knife at her. "No do-overs."

She pressed her lips together to hide her smile, then nodded. "Of course, Commander. Whatever you say."

Holding the tip of her knife, she aimed and threw, grinning in satisfaction when it hit the center of the target. Byrric slid her a look as she stepped away from the line, aimed, threw, then chuckled when his knife knocked hers to the ground.

"Show off," she muttered. "Let's fly, instead. I want to test out my wing."

"Aerelius was able to heal you, then?" Byrric asked.

She paused in the middle of sheathing her knives and looked at him in surprise. "How did you know he was able to?"

"I wasn't certain," he replied as he flared out his wide, gray wings. "Ordona was hoping he might be able to learn, though, at least with you. It's a matter of redirecting that positive energy toward repair of a physical ailment as opposed to an emotional one. It's tricky, if what other spirit users have said is true, and I'm assuming it worked so well because you're bonded by blood."

Freya nodded slowly. "Yes, I suppose that makes sense." She let out her wings and gave the injured one a testing flap and was happy to find the pain from the night before had all but vanished. "It aches a little, but a bit of exercise will do it some good."

He gave her a nod, then shot into the air, gliding a bit as he caught the breeze a few dozen feet up.

She rolled her eyes as she fastened the sheath of knives to the back of her waistband and leapt into flight. "That's cheating!" she called as she closed in.

"I wasn't aware we were racing!" he shouted back. With a heavy flap, he took off toward the western edge of the property, leaving her to catch up.

Her wing throbbed slightly as it fought the current, but as the cold air rushed through her feathers, it acted as a balm. She followed Byrric as he crisscrossed the grounds, then pulled up behind him as he hugged the shields that surrounded the property. He fell back, allowing her to fly beside him and run her magic over her grand-mother's wards.

"Florian and Aer did a good job shoring them up," he commented.

"They did," she agreed.

She turned her attention to the city in the distance, back-flapping slowly as she hovered, wondering what was going on in the governor's manor, whether Traust was informing Frederick Edrin of his past with Byrric. There was really no strategical benefit to their shared past, but where vengeance was a motivating factor, facts didn't matter. He would use the fire his anger lit under him to motivate himself and his soldiers, spurring them on with the energy of his own fury.

"We should head back." Byrric gestured toward the end of the drive and began his descent.

She took one last look at her city, then followed him to the ground.

When they landed, they started to walk toward the house, and Freya glanced up at him.

"Why didn't you ever tell me about how things began with you and Mother?"

"It was nearly two centuries ago, Freya. Cina and I had moved on from her past with Traust fairly quickly once the mating bond was completed."

"So it was only the mating bond that changed her feelings for him?"

Byrric sent her a look, the insult plain on his face. "No, of course not. It helped, certainly, but she and I had bonded a good deal in the months leading up to our wedding. At that point, she'd been long-absent from Traust, so we had the freedom to get to know one another without his presence lingering in the background." He sighed. "To be quite honest, aside from when we heard he'd been banished, we didn't discuss him much."

"How did Mother react to his banishment?"

He chuckled. "She said she'd expected it and hoped he would someday find the happiness he'd been seeking with her."

"Even after he treated you and my grandparents the way he did?"

"She was caring and compassionate, Freya, but not oblivious. He'd never been cruel to her, which told her he had goodness in him, but she knew he was not truly a good person. She simply wanted him to find the life he'd hoped to have with her."

"He never wanted that, though," Freya murmured. "I suppose I can understand why she felt sorry for him."

"You should always try to see the goodness in people, Freya," Byrric said, patting her on the back. "Even if seems impossible."

She appreciated the sentiment and felt, for the most part, her father was right. It was hard to look at someone like Traust, who'd wanted to kill her simply because of who her father was, and see goodness. He didn't care that she was Cina's daughter, nor did he see that as a reason to spare her life. At the same time, she knew his rationale was almost certainly based on true feelings, extreme or unreasonable as they may have been.

It didn't change how she felt about him overall, and it certainly didn't change his purpose, which was, presumably, to kill her and her father. If a charge of regicide didn't deter him from his goals, it was unlikely any lingering feelings he might hold toward her mother would, either.

"Have you given any more thought to how we'll approach any incoming assault?" she asked.

Byrric sighed. "We need allies. Our armies are stretched thin. The plan we have for now is a good one, but it will only stretch us further."

"What about the Jotnar separatists that have been causing Caelora so many issues?"

He nodded. "We've considered that. It's an option, certainly, but they're more eager for reform in their own country than fighting a war in ours."

"Even if it means assistance in achieving their goals once Lessia is ousted entirely?"

"If we could guarantee she won't come out of this with her head, we could easily convince them. As it is, we're currently losing. Lessia and Willem's forces combined are twice ours, and they had the element of surprise on their side. A five-pronged attack..." He huffed out a breath. "It was brilliant and gives us little room to round up the Jotnar who might be willing to stand with us."

Freya bit her lip as she ran over all of the information they'd gathered, both from patrols in Watoria and from Iladel. It seemed each day brought something that hindered any efforts they might put forth to retake what they'd lost. That one of Lindoroth's capitals had been salvaged was a benefit, but the soldiers who were left in Saith were hardly in a position to be pulled away to assist others.

"I'm going to go get some lunch," she said. "Come find me if anything changes?"

His eyes narrowed slightly, then he nodded. "Of course.

A SHORT WHILE LATER, Freya, Aer, Collin, Laz, Byrric, and Florian had gathered in the sitting room in Freya's chambers. She'd considered the drawing room, but her private quarters held the promise of more privacy than the main areas of the house.

"We think we should reach out to the elves," Freya said, not bothering to mince words.

Florian gave her an amused look and Byrric blinked.

"Freya, the elves—"

"Don't leave their shores," Freya said. "Yes, I know. But they used to. It's been a long time, but it's not as if they've never come to the aid of Lindoroth before."

"Or the humans," Byrric countered. "They were once allies of all who lived in this land, human and Lind alike."

"Until the humans fell out of favor with them," Collin said.

"Two thousand years ago," Byrric said, shaking his head.

"So if we contact them, we either risk them wanting to settle a score with humans or potentially reconciling with them," Aer said. "Is that what we're saying?"

Freya looked at Florian, who wore an expression she couldn't quite decipher. It sat somewhere between amused and resigned.

His dark eyes held her gaze for a moment before he looked at Aer and nodded.

"There's no harm in trying, although considering there's already been some talk of Willem and Lessia reaching out to them, there's certainly no guarantee." He flicked a glance at Byrric, then looked back down at Freya. "But I've got a few contacts in Avorell I can attempt to reach out to."

"Do it," Freya said.

Aer nodded. "I agree. Everyone within our own land is too busy fighting. We need more allies. If they're open to an alliance, perhaps we can win them over before Willem and Lessia do."

Florian gave him a sharp nod. "Of course, Your Majesties. Give me a day or two, I'll see what I can do."

"A day or two? That's all?" Freya asked, then frowned when Byrric gave a small shake of his head.

"Do what you need to do," Aer said. "The sooner we know, the better."

22

———————

FREYA

It was two days before Zane returned with word from Commander Alstad, and the news he brought confirmed what they already knew.

Zane stepped toward the table and set a small, square stone on top of the map, slightly to the north of the Jotunheim border. "They're a bit further north than we thought and they're moving somewhat slower, but there's a battalion of approximately seven hundred Jotnar heading south from Madrya as we speak. I'd give them a week, at most, before they cross into Allanor, and another two before they reach Watoria."

Freya sighed and clenched her jaw, then looked at Byrric. "Alright, nine days, then. What will our knights do in the meantime?"

Byrric set a handful of stones between the markers that pinpointed the Lindorothian knights and those coming south. "In a few days, our knights will go north and meet the Jotnar. We aren't getting through the blockade around Watoria, so I think it might be more prudent to broaden our approach. Instead of focusing on one city, important as it may be, we should turn our eyes outward and hope our original plan of drawing enemy troops away from Watoria will give us an opening. The sooner we retake Watoria, the sooner we can make for Kildin and Iladel."

"If we can force them to come at us from the south while we go after their soldiers in the north, it will be easier to slip into Watoria," Zane finished, looking at Freya. "Your knowledge of the city combined with the other marshals will be incredibly helpful in that respect."

She nodded as she thought over the possibilities for infiltrating the city. It would be tricky, but if enough of the soldiers under Frederick's command shifted their attention away from the city to take on the Lindorothian knights, it could be possible. She'd told Aer getting into the city wouldn't be a problem—she knew it better than anyone, and therefore, knew where all of the cracks and crevices within the walls were, where the blind spots on the docks were. After her experience with Reykr Traust, though, she had begun to feel much less confident in that.

But it was *her* city. If anyone could get in unseen, it was her.

And yet... draugs had been doing reconnaissance for Lessia for years. The more she thought about it, the more she realized they likely knew much more about how to get in and out than she'd once realized.

LATER, after they had finished dinner, she told Aer she wanted to go for a walk to clear her head. So much had happened over the last two weeks, and now, with this new information, her mind felt overwhelmed to the point of exhaustion. So, she made her way toward the border of the property, comforting herself with the strength of the wards and the knowledge that they were safe, at least for now.

She went still when she reached the western edge of the property, then looked toward the forest beyond the wards. As she stared into the darkened trees, the hair on the back of her neck prickled and she was hit with a faint feeling of unease.

Someone or something was out there, and she had the unsettling feeling they were looking right at her.

She began walking again, this time more slowly as she watched the trees for movement. The moon was absent tonight, so even with her keen eyesight, it was difficult to see through the cloak of blackness the night had draped over the forest. The reasonable nature of her mind that told her to return to the house warred with the part that itched to investigate.

Carefully, she pressed a hand to the magic that protected the property and reached out with her own, brushing it through the trees and underbrush, seeking out anything living.

All she found was stillness within the dark.

With a small frown, she let her hand drop. She stared into the woods for another moment, then, acquiescing to the logical part of her mind, turned and began walking back toward the house.

Her steps were a bit quicker than normal, but she told herself it was because she wanted to be out of the cold and in front of the fire she knew Haegin would have built in her room.

"It's just the forest," she muttered to herself. "Nothing to be—"

"Talking to yourself?"

She jumped at the sound of a voice, only realizing once her blade was in her hand that it was Ashton who had spoken.

"Gods above, Ash! I nearly killed you!"

His brow furrowed as he took in her startled state. "Is something wrong?"

She huffed out a small breath and shook her head. "No, just a bit jumpy, that's all." She sheathed her blade. "Are you coming back from your watch?"

He nodded. "Yes, we're changing out the guard now." As he said it, a few of Byrric's soldiers came out of the darkness toward the house. Ashton glanced in the direction she'd come. "Patrolling on your own?"

She tightened the leather strap that fastened her braid and nodded. "I needed a walk. Have you got anything to report?"

"No, nothing." His expression of concern deepened. "Freya, what is it?"

"Nothing. It's just very... still out there and that tends to unnerve me." She flicked a glance at the house that rose up behind him. "I'm going to head in and warm up. Are you coming?"

"No, I've got to go check in with Byrric."

"Alright. I'll make sure Haegin leaves some tea on for you all once you come in."

He flashed her a smile, although he still didn't seem convinced she was alright. "That'll be much appreciated, thank you."

After giving him her goodbye, she turned and strode toward the house, eager to be back in the light and away from the shadows that seemed to be lingering about.

FREYA FELL ASLEEP QUICKLY ENOUGH, but when she awoke the following morning, she found her unease from the previous night still lingered. It was a tickle beneath her shoulders; a twinge had her wanting to take flight over the property and suss out whatever it was that was causing her to feel so jumpy.

"Care to tell me what's bothering you?" Aer asked as he fastened his leather doublet over a white tunic. "You've had that look on your face since last night."

She glanced up at him as she strapped her sheath to her hip. "It's probably nothing, but I had an odd feeling when I walked the grounds last night, as though I was being watched. Ashton said they didn't see anyone in the woods, but I can't seem to shake it."

He walked toward her and cupped her face in his hands, then gave her a soft kiss. "You know Byrric's soldiers would have found someone if they were out there. If it will make you feel better, though, we can take a look now that it's daylight."

"Okay." She didn't want to admit how ill at ease she still felt, not when she saw the worry in his eyes. "Will you come with me after breakfast?"

"Of course." He touched his lips to the top of her head and brushed a hand down her hair. "Come on, let's see if the night has brought any news. Then we'll go hunt your phantoms."

Smiling, she took his hand and they made their way downstairs.

"It's silly, I know," she said as they approached the dining room. "I just—"

"Freya."

Aer's voice brought her up short when they reached the open door to the dining room.

"What—"

She followed his stare, then froze when she realized the phantom they planned to hunt had already arrived.

Aer's hand tightened in hers at the sight of the tall, wiry elf. Black leather covered nearly every inch of his light brown skin, and his hair was a short, snowy white. Eyes that were blue-gray swirls of molten metal flicked in their direction, giving a quick, assessing glance before shifting back to Byrric, who stood before him, jaw tense and arms folded. Florian stood nearby, leaning casually against the windowsill.

"Your Majesties," Byrric said, not breaking eye contact with their visitor. "I'd like you to meet Lord Artin Silmar, emissary to King Ruehnar and Queen Nalaea of Avorell."

Silmar turned to face them, then gave a short nod in greeting. "We received word from Andreus that you requested a meeting with my king and queen." His voice was laced with a heavy accent, his words filled with soft, rolling sounds that spoke of royalty and commanded attention.

"It's good to meet you, Lord Silmar," Aer said. "Did you only just arrive?"

"Last night," was his response, confirming, in Freya's mind, at least, that his was the presence the night before that had left her feeling uneasy. Aer's surprised look in her direction told her he'd come to the same conclusion. "Your security is quite impressive."

"I take it you were the reason my hair was standing on end, then?" Freya asked. Aer's hand flexed in hers, a warning to watch her tone.

She smiled to soften her words. "I thought I felt a presence while out on patrol last night."

"Indeed," Silmar said, looking her up and down. "I was somewhat surprised you noticed me."

There was a noise in the hall, so Freya looked at her father and inclined her head toward the hall at her back.

"Let's bring this conversation somewhere more private, shall we?" Byrric said. "Your Majesties, perhaps your quarters?"

Freya nodded, then turned around, looking to ensure no one was there and signaled for them to follow them upstairs.

Once they were congregated in her chambers, and Freya had dropped a silencing spell over them, Silmar faced them. As subtly as she could, Freya took him in, trying not to stare at the striking blue of his eyes that seemed to shift in the light.

"King Ruehnar and Queen Nalaea have agreed to hear your case. But we must leave for our capital city immediately," Silmar said.

"Leave? Our kingdom is at war!" Freya exclaimed.

"We can't just leave," Aer agreed. "There's too much at stake here if we do."

"You can if you want our help." Silmar countered.

"You'd ask our king and queen to abandon their kingdom?" Byrric asked sharply.

Silmar eyed him curiously. "Quite the opposite, Commander. I'd ask them to risk everything for their kingdom. Isn't that what kings and queens are supposed to do?"

A silence hung over the room, and it was clear the other three in attendance were waiting for Freya or Aer to speak.

The thought of fleeing her home for a second time caused something in Freya's chest to twist, and based on the thrum she felt through her bond with Aer, he didn't feel any better about the prospect of leaving their people behind again, either.

"How long will we have to be away?" Aer asked.

Silmar shrugged. "That all depends on you. Five or six days, most likely."

"You expect us to travel to Avorell and back in the span of a week?" Freya asked. Even as she spoke the words, though, it dawned on her how incredibly odd it was for him to have shown up so soon after they'd discussed contacting his people. She didn't even know for certain exactly how far away Avorell was, but she knew it was no short distance.

A small headache began to press against her skull. She looked at Aer to see his reaction, expecting to see a confusion that matched her own. Instead, she saw understanding.

"He'll carry us through the Between," Aer said, rubbing a hand across his brow. He looked to Silmar then. "Is that right?"

Silmar nodded.

Freya's stomach roiled at the thought. She'd heard about the Between, a space *between* spaces that only elves could traverse, allowing one to step from one place to another in the blink of an eye. With little more than a thought, one could find themselves halfway across the world. She'd thought it was just part of the stories her parents had told her as a child, and the thought of getting lost in that place, unable to return, was a fear that suddenly found purchase in reality.

"I can take you within a day of the capital," Silmar said. "To the moors of the Summer Court. We'll continue on foot from there. The rules of my land don't allow for travelers from the Between to walk directly into the capital city of Andradath," he added when he saw their confused expressions.

Freya could feel Aer's hesitation pulling at her through their bond, but behind it she could feel his resolve. She looked at him and saw in his eyes the same determination she'd often seen in Ordona's, something that had been crystal clear when they'd separated on the cliffside after Lessia and Willem had taken over.

"We'll go," Aer said, not breaking eye contact with her until she nodded her agreement.

Turning, she looked at Florian. "You'll come with us, too." Whatever his connection was to the elves, she knew it would be of no use to them if he stayed half a world away while they traveled.

"I wouldn't have it any other way, Your Majesty," Florian replied.

Aer looked at Silmar. "When do we leave?"

Silmar inclined his head toward Byrric and Florian. "I can give you one hour to get your affairs in order. I assume you have a plan for the chain of succession in the absence of an heir?"

"Commander Balthana will act as steward in our stead," Aer said.

Byrric sighed, then nodded. "Salazar and I established my duties when I took command of his army. I can't say it's a role I'd hoped to take on so soon, though."

"I'm sorry to disappoint," Freya murmured with a sigh. "Alright, so, the line of succession. Let's run through this so I understand exactly what will happen once we go."

"It's not overly complex," Florian said. "The paperwork was drawn up ages ago, although it's currently sitting in a drawer in Salazar's chambers. Salazar granted Commander Balthana all of the duties and privileges he afforded himself and Ordona, so as long as you are both willing to trust Salazar's judgement in that respect, here and now, we can skip the paperwork. I've already filled the commander in on all we've learned since we left."

Freya arched a brow. "A verbal contract? That seems risky, considering." Not that going back to Iladel to retrieve the paperwork was exactly an option, either.

Florian slid his onyx blade from its sheath and held it up, the blade glinting in the afternoon sun. "Blood contract, Your Majesty."

"It's simple enough," Byrric told her. "Find some parchment, state your terms, what duties you'll allow me to take on as Steward, and I'll reaffirm my loyalty to you both."

"Okay," Freya said with a sigh. "Let's get on with it."

Aer brushed a hand down her back as he held out his palm. "Let's hope this doesn't last more than a few days, Commander."

"Agreed."

~

THEY DIDN'T BOTHER PACKING, only taking the time to change into clothing that would be more suited to the warmth Silmar assured them awaited in the Summer Court of Avorell. According to him, they would be provided everything they needed during their stay there, including clothing, and the trek from their landing point to the capital would only take longer if they had packs to carry.

They were allowed one weapon each.

Freya grumbled at that but reminded herself this was supposed to be a peaceful mission, so weapons would, hopefully, not be necessary.

Having only been told stories of elves as a child, Freya had been unsure just how much of what her parents and grandparents had read to her was fact or fantasy. Although magic was heavily present in her world, the idea of a place such as the Between seemed strange to her. As a Valkyrie, she could travel faster than most, but that was limited. She couldn't, say, traverse an ocean easily unless she knew there was a place along the way she would be able to rest. Convenient as it was and as trusting as Florian seemed of Silmar, she couldn't shake her unease.

She'd also been told the elves' pretty, metallic eyes and smooth smiles could talk a person right into dancing themselves to death, that their wine sent any who weren't elves into a lustful stupor, and that they were all too keen to cause incurable medical maladies in those they felt slighted by.

Her farewell with her father had been brief. Byrric gave her explicit instructions not to get killed, to measure each word she spoke, and not to besmirch her family names by falling into an ill-conceived bargain with an elf.

"Aren't most elvish bargains ill-conceived?" she asked as he pulled her into a hug.

He chuckled, then patted her on the back and rested his hands on her shoulders. "Not all. I trust your judgement as queen to avoid such traps. You'll do fine."

"I'm sorry about Traust," she said as they stepped apart. "If I come through this in one piece, I'll help you take him down."

"He's the last thing you need to worry about, Freya." He smiled.

"Focus on the task at hand. The time will come to deal with him, but it's worthless to spare any energy on that now."

With a final smile of farewell, she, Aer, and Florian took hands with Silmar, and Byrric stepped back to avoid being accidentally brought along for the trip.

"The trip may cause a bit of stomach upset," Silmar said, his shining eyes flicking toward Freya and Aer. "And you may want to hold your breath."

Freya opened her mouth to ask why, but before she could breathe a word, frigid air pressed in around her and everything went gray.

23

———————

LEA

There were times, to Lea's mind, that one should always assume the worst and never doubt a thing's possibility, no matter how improbable. One should never believe a thing's proper place was at the back of one's mind, because, at any moment, it could force its way forward.

That had become a mantra of sorts as the days passed. She wanted to trust Jonas, but the implications about his past haunted her mind. She wanted to believe Rosie Ristner had true intentions of friendship, but Lea could not discount the possibility that she was simply a means of information for Willem.

But most of all, she wanted to believe she could get out of this mess of her own making alive, along with her mother and the rest of the females in the dungeon, but she couldn't deny the probability that may not ever happen.

So, it was in her best interest to assume she was on her own.

She was lost in these thoughts a few days later, when a knock sounded at the door while she was in the midst of dressing for dinner, which instantly put her on alert. With the exception of Willem or Rosie, the only people who'd come to their room had been servants, and they tended to slip in and out unseen and unheard.

When Jonas answered, they found a human knight, one of Willem's personal guards, standing in the hall. "My lord," he said. "The king has asked me to inform you we will have additional company for dinner."

"Company?" Jonas stiffened. "Who has arrived?"

The human shrugged, and Lea could see the disdain he held toward Jonas flash through his eyes. "I have not been made privy to that information, my lord. I was only told to tell you to ensure your lover dresses and behaves appropriately."

"Appropriately for *whom*?" Jonas demanded.

"Again, I have not been made privy to that information. I am only passing on the message."

Not bothering to say goodbye or thank the man, Jonas closed the door and turned to Lea.

"Who—"

"Go get dressed," he snapped.

Lea's mouth opened in outrage, but she snapped it shut when she saw Jonas' warning look.

Tyna, who'd arrived a short while ago to tend to Lea's hair, scowled, then fluttered toward the bathing room. "Come, my lady. Let's finish up in here."

Lea shut the bathing room door behind her quietly, then frowned at Tyna. "What was that about?"

"It's Willem," Tyna said quietly. "I overheard him say he thought Jonas was being too soft with you. That human will certainly return to tell him how Jonas behaved after he left."

Lea closed her eyes and collected herself. "So am I to tolerate Jonas treating me poorly for the foreseeable future?"

Tyna shook her head. "No, my lady. Jotnar males tend to be a bit controlling. To behave otherwise when he knows Willem questions your place here would arouse suspicion. His main goal is to solidify his bond with you, at least outwardly, and Willem sniffing about could make that difficult." She circled a finger in the air and lifted her eyes skyward. "I've been checking the spy holes in here daily," she explained, pointing out the three spots where small holes had been drilled through the wood in the walls that Jonas had sealed up, first with wood, then with magic. Tyna, untrusting, had gone behind him and added a third layer of protection to each, using her own pixie dust, a thing that was both beautiful and powerful, although Lea didn't quite understand how it worked. "The uncertainty of new guests in the palace makes it imperative we keep this room safe, so he's doing another check of the entrances and spy holes in the main room as we speak."

"Why would new arrivals cause concern?"

Tyna motioned for Lea to face the mirror so she could get back to work on her hair. "My guess is these new arrivals are more humans, here to bolster Willem's hold and bring him a bit more even with Lessia in terms of control. Eastern Dystone has yet to send their forces, but I would imagine they'll be arriving any day now." She lowered her voice to a whisper. "Also, I've seen Willem exploring the passages a few times now, twice this past week alone. He's aware Lord Edrin has sealed off your chambers but from what I can tell has no logical argument against Lord Edrin denying himself privacy. I don't know that Willem is aware of exactly how many points of access there are to this room, but it's quite clear to me, at least, he does not trust Lord Edrin in the slightest."

Lea stared at her reflection, deep in thought, as Tyna deftly twisted her curls into an elaborate twist at the nape of her neck.

Willem hadn't bothered her for more than simple conversation since their encounter in the gardens, which she was grateful for, although she also felt it was simply a matter of time. Despite Willem's seeming distrust of her, he didn't seem keen on the idea of her wielding her magic against him again, no matter how much Jonas assured him and Lessia that he'd increased the dosage of the magic-dampening tincture that he'd been ordered to put in her food.

She'd found herself drawing on her power daily just to reassure herself that wasn't actually the case.

"I don't understand," she said. "None of them trust each other and they don't seem to care enough to even pretend they do. Why agree to ally with someone to field a coup when you don't trust the people you're supposed to be working with?"

Tyna shrugged and moved on to framing Lea's face with a few curls. "In their case, I'd say both Willem and Lessia think they're more intelligent than the other, and where seemingly-infallible intelligence is involved, trust is completely unnecessary." She lowered her voice to a whisper. "I, for one, don't believe for a single second Lessia plans to share Lindoroth with the humans. She's hardly the type to divvy lands when she could simply take them all for herself."

"And then what of Dystone?" Lea whispered back, casting her eyes furtively toward the door.

"Anyone's guess, I suppose. It's a good land with plentiful resources, so conquering that would be to Jotunheim's benefit. Ruling a land that's separated from its monarchs by an entire ocean may be more trouble than she feels it's worth, though."

"So, use them for their assistance in taking Lindoroth, a country connected to them by both land and blood, then cast them out like trash, perhaps pillage Dystone for good measure?" Lea clicked her tongue. "I understand the logic, but it's horrid, nonetheless."

"Agreed, my lady, but such is the way of war." Tyna picked up a pot of rouge and began brushing some color onto Lea's cheeks and lips. "Willem seems to think he's made inroads with the empress, but knowing what I do of her, it's highly unlikely."

"Perhaps that's why he intends to stay," Lea mused. "It's sad, in a way, if that truly is the case."

"Indeed. I've always felt bad for the humans, you know." Tyna winced at Lea's look of surprise. "Do not mistake me. I think Willem and all who follow him are wretched creatures, his ancestors, in particular." She gave a brief shudder. "But the humans suffered a great deal of indignities before and during the last war. There may be none alive today who remember just how bad it became for them, but those stories carry weight over generations."

"But they suffered at the hands of the Jotnar," Lea said slowly. "Lindoroth helped them!"

"By sending them to a foreign land to start from scratch," Tyna corrected. "It was preferable to remaining here, so near a hostile race and constantly in need of protection, but they were still forced into a new home, nonetheless."

"And now Willem thinks they'll be able to reclaim their homeland and live peacefully with their former oppressors?" Lea eyed Tyna dubiously. "I find the man rotten, but I'd never consider him that stupid."

Tyna's expression went carefully neutral as she dabbed a bit of shimmering powder to the low neckline of Lea's gown. "He may not be, but greed or a desire to right wrongs can often make people do stupid things."

Lea pursed her lips and narrowed her eyes. "I sense pointed undertones. Is there something you'd like to say, Tyna?"

Tyna's eyes flashed to Lea's in the mirror and her lips pressed into a thin line. "I think you neither greedy nor stupid, Lady Calliwell, but I do feel your being here is foolhardy, considering all that's happened since."

Lea pondered Tyna's words, shoving aside her initial offense as best she could to assess their accuracy. She'd never attempted subterfuge to this extent before and readily admitted it was harder than she'd anticipated, but she didn't necessarily think she'd been foolhardy. Her goal was to help her family, both to escape imprisonment and take back their kingdom. She'd lay down her life for those things without batting an eye if it came down to it.

Tyna wasn't wrong, though. Since Lea had arrived, she'd been put in a cell, had her magic suppressed, been interrogated by Lessia, nearly assaulted by Willem, suffered all manner of vulgar comments from the other males in the palace, forced to fake a romantic attraction to Jonas, not to mention she'd been threatened with a forced marriage to him as a means of securing Edhil's allegiance.

"I suppose I see your point," she allowed. "Although, if given the chance, I can't say I would make a different choice. Someone needs to be able to—" her eyes darted to the door, then back to Tyna, and she raised her eyebrows.

Understanding, Tyna nodded. "You should trust only yourself, my lady, I agree. When Rini and I discovered you'd separated from the others and returned here, there was no question that we would also split up. I want this kingdom back just as much as you." The determination in the tiny pixie's eyes and the conviction in her tone seemed counter to her size but spoke volumes about her mettle. She held Lea's eyes for a second, then went back to tending to her hair, her face carefully neutral. "Might I ask you something else, my lady?"

"Of course."

"Would marriage to Lord Edrin be so bad? I understand why you might be reticent, of course, but considering the lengths you've gone to already to ensure your kingdom's safety, I'm curious. Would you marry him if it came down to it?"

Lea let out a quiet breath. It was a question she'd asked herself a dozen times over since it had been brought up at Willem's wedding. Had someone asked her at Aer's wedding, on the night Jonas twirled her around the dance floor in the palace ballroom, the answer might've been yes; she could go through with this ploy and they would come out stronger on the other side. He'd seemed a good male then, someone who was caring and a joy to be around, and yes, might make a good husband once he was out from under the rule of his vile aunt.

And yet... she couldn't shake the reservations that had been building in her since he'd brought her back to the palace.

"I would struggle," Lea said slowly, choosing her words carefully. "Because I've seen the masks he so easily puts on when speaking of Lindorothians as beneath him. I know he's putting on the same show I am, but that wasn't always the case. To hear the way his cousin speaks of him, of his past, and to hear the way he speaks to me when he thinks others are eavesdropping..." She looked down at her hands, clasped loosely in her lap. "Those are not memories I'm sure I'll ever be able to rid myself of, no matter how many centuries I live."

Tyna's hands stilled briefly, and it was all Lea could do not to look at the pixie who was most certainly staring at her with shimmering eyes filled with pity. If Lea saw that, she might break, and she'd been doing a damn good job of keeping herself together. Now was not the time to lose focus, not when Lessia and Willem seemed to be inching a bit closer to accepting her presence at Jonas' side.

"I'll do what I have to for my people," she continued quietly. "If Lessia demands I marry Jonas, or I believe it will better my chances of succeeding here, I'll do it. It's possible, in time, I could come to care for him, see him as I once did."

"Oh, Lea," Tyna said softly, fluttering around so she could face Lea and touched a small hand to her chin, forcing her to meet her eyes. "Anything you do in this palace can be undone. If it comes to marriage, gods above, if it comes to a mating bond, those things can be undone."

"But not easily."

"Easier than you might think." Tyna ran her thumbs under Lea's lower lashes, wiping away the tears that had begun to pool there. "Now, set that aside for the moment so I can finish preparing you."

Appreciating Tyna's shift back to her more upbeat demeanor, Lea smiled and straightened her back. "Thank you, Tyna. I can't tell you how much I appreciate your presence here."

Tyna patted her cheek. "Likewise, my lady."

"We better finish, as I'm sure Jonas is wondering why I'm taking so—"

Suddenly, there was a burst of pixie dust and Rini appeared beside Tyna, her chest heaving with exertion.

"Rini!" Tyna scolded, startling back from Lea a bit. "You're not—"

"Their Majesties," Rini huffed, pressing a hand to her chest. "They've gone... to Avorell!"

Lea jerked forward in her seat. "They've done *what?*"

"Slow down, Rini," Tyna said. "That doesn't make any sense. Why would they do such a thing?"

"To seek aid for Lindoroth." Rini started to wring her hands. "Their Majesties don't know that I know. At least, I don't think they do. I've been hovering a good deal, and I just happened to be outside their chambers when they were speaking and I—" She bit her lip and her silvery eyes widened.

"And you *what*, Rini?" Tyna snapped.

"I might've... pushed through Her Majesty's silencing spell and listened in," Rini replied, the words tumbling out in a rush.

Tyna goggled at her sister, her shock causing her face to go slack. "You did... Rini, that goes against everything we stand for! We don't betray—"

"I know!" Rini cried, wringing her hands. "But I just knew something wasn't right and now they're *gone* and I don't know when they'll be back and *why didn't they take me with them?*"

Glittering tears began to slide down her cheeks, and Tyna huffed. She darted toward her sister and slapped her cheek, her tiny hand making a surprisingly loud crack.

"Pull yourself together!" Tyna snapped.

"They took Lord Florian with them," Rini said, her lips turning in a pout. "Why wouldn't they take *me?*"

Lea stood up and looked between the sisters. "Can we focus on what's important here, please?"

Rini straightened herself up and knuckled the tears from her eyes. "Apologies, my lady. You're right. My feelings are immaterial right now."

"That's not what I meant, Rini."

"She knows that," Tyna said with a sigh. "She's just being overdramatic." She gave her sister an expectant look. "Now, tell us everything."

"They want the elves to side with us in the war," Rini said. "An emissary from Avorell arrived not long ago and told Their Majesties that they'd been granted an audience with their king and queen to plead their case. The emissary will be taking them through the Between—"

"Through the what?" Lea asked.

"The Between," Tyna said. "A space between places. The elves are the only creatures with access to it. It can take you next door or across the world."

Lea struggled to recall the stories of the elves she'd been told as a child. After a moment, she nodded. "Flitting from one place to another in the blink of an eye. Yes, I remember now."

"It's actually quite fascinating," Tyna said. "Complex earth magic, from what I understand."

"Oh, that doesn't matter!" Rini exclaimed, waving her hands. "The emissary will take them into the Summer Court, where the elvish capital of Andradath lies. Then, they'll go about finding out what they need to do to gain the support of the Avorellian army."

"What they need to do? What do you mean?" Lea asked.

"The elves won't just grant support," Tyna explained. "If they think ours a worthy cause, they'll take it on, but a bargain must be struck first."

"What kind of bargain?" Lea asked, feeling tension start to build.

Tyna shrugged. "Who knows? They're an animalistic sort, those elves. Wrestling a pack of wolves, perhaps?"

"Don't make jokes like that!" Rini exclaimed as her eyes filled with tears again.

The three were quiet for a moment, and Lea took that time to process the news Rini had just delivered. She could understand the logic behind seeking out allies, but it seemed odd that the elves, of all creatures, would be who Freya and Aer sought out.

But maybe, having been separate from the rest of the world for so long, the elves would be willing to step back into it.

She eyed Rini again, who was sitting on the edge of the vanity, still wringing her hands, and sighed. Somehow she guessed it wouldn't be that easy.

LEA'S HEAD was filled with worry as she and Jonas made their way to the throne room. She hadn't told Jonas of Freya and Aer's departure and didn't intend to, but by the sidelong glances he kept sending her, it was clear he knew something was wrong. As she walked, all she could imagine was the type of bargains the king and queen of Avorell might try to strike. With so little knowledge to go on, wrestling with wolves seemed tame to some of the darker images that sped through her mind.

When they arrived at the throne room, her attention was drawn away from her heavy thoughts and toward the newly-decorated room instead. Every ounce of the Harridan family had been removed, transforming it into a conglomeration of Dystonian and Jotnar royal colors. The black and gold Harridan banners that had once hung had been replaced with the blood-red banner of Jotunheim that bore the black bull of House Edrin, along with House Ristner's blue and green banner with its embroidered silver whorls. Effina, Lea noticed, had been given an official place on the dais in a smaller throne beside Willem's. Its design was simple and did nothing to depict its occupant as a king's wife. Rosie stood at the foot of the dais, hands clasped in front of her.

The thrones Salazar and Ordona had made for Aer and Freya had been removed and likely burned, and the two that now remained were made of smooth, black wood; nothing like the heavy oak adorned with carvings of lynx that had been there before.

"Lord Edrin, Lady Calliwell, so nice of you to join us," Willem said, his white teeth flashing. "Dinner will be served shortly, but I wanted you both here to greet our guest first."

Lea's arm tightened in Jonas' when she saw the sly, triumphant look in Lessia's eyes.

"And who has chosen to grace us with their presence so suddenly?" Jonas asked.

Willem looked down at his nails, and though he feigned disinterest, Lea could tell he was practically bursting. Rosie, too, from the eager expression on her face.

"Prince Ettrian Tordove."

Lessia's face broke into a wide, triumphant smile, one that instantly set Lea at unease.

Lea felt Jonas' fingers flex on her arm. He recovered himself instantly and smiled at his aunt. "I must say, I'm impressed. It's been some time since we've had visitors from such a distance."

Willem narrowed his eyes at Lea and licked his lips. "I don't believe your female is aware of who we speak, Jonas. Care to enlighten her?"

There was movement behind her, causing Willem's attention to shift. Whoever stood there had him leaning back in his throne, his smugness clouding with a bit of the unease Lea had just felt.

Rosie's face filled with awe, while Lessia looked perfectly content. Victorious, even, as an unfamiliar voice spoke.

"I think I can handle that part, don't you?"

Lea and Jonas turned at the sound of the smooth voice. When Lea saw who it belonged to, a bolt of fear shot through her. It was by will alone that she kept herself from gawping like a fish.

She'd never seen an elf before, had only heard stories of them as a girl and had seen some drawings here or there in books; violent-looking creatures with sharp teeth and wicked magic. None of those captured the pure, savage grace that emanated from the male in front of her. He was tall and lean, with the palest skin, and eyes that glinted gold. His hair was black as tar and just brushed the tips of his pointed ears. His clothes spoke of royalty, a silvery gray that glittered with embroidery and diamonds.

When he smiled down at her, needle-sharp teeth flashed. His voice was fluid, accented, and frighteningly intriguing.

"Well, hello there. Aren't you a lovely little witch?"

24

LEA

ead, Lea thought as panic and fear began to cloud her mind.

In her mind's eye, she could see the ease with which Lessia would finish the destruction of Lindoroth. An elvish army, wrought with magic more powerful than she could imagine, bearing down on her kingdom...

I am, without question, going to die. There will be no marriage to anyone, no life beyond this palace. No children, no grandchildren. I will never rescue my mother, never see my people freed.

And Freya and Aer...

She had no doubts they'd just been led right into a trap.

The only thing that kept her from falling over was Jonas' firm grip on her elbow.

The elf prince looked at Jonas, his head tilted in question. "Is she defective in some way?"

Jonas gave the prince a nod of greeting. "Welcome, Prince Ettrian. Lady Calliwell functions perfectly well, I assure you. She is simply unaccustomed to company such as yours."

Ettrian shifted his golden eyes back to her. "Well? Lady Calliwell, is it? Do you not curtsy for princes?"

"Apologies, Your Highness," she murmured, dipping into a low curtsy. "It is a pleasure to make your acquaintance."

Dead. Dead, dead, and dead.

"Hmm." Ettrian strode forward. "They aren't quite so skittish in Avorell."

"You'll have to excuse her, Prince Ettrian," Lessia said as she sidled up beside Lea. "She's still getting used to the way we do things here." She brushed a finger down Lea's cheek, then her arm before offering the prince a smile. "You'd be surprised at how much she's improved these last few weeks."

Lea forced herself to keep still and not cringe away from Lessia's touch, but the feeling of revulsion that welled within her was nearly unbearable.

The prince's grin widened.

Blessedly, a servant entered the room to announce dinner, drawing Lessia and Ettrian's attention away from Lea. Rosie appeared at her side and clutched her hand in excitement.

"Isn't it just amazing?" she whispered. "My brother, a *human*, managed to bring the elves out of hiding!"

"Let's go," Jonas murmured. He led Lea down the hall to the dining room, standing a bit closer and holding her hand against his arm a bit more tightly than he normally would. Rosie trailed along beside them, and for once, Lea wasn't thoroughly irritated by her presence.

When they'd all settled at the table, Jonas addressed the prince.

"Prince Ettrian, what made you decide to leave your lands after so long?"

"One of our seers informed my father of the unrest here in Lindoroth not long before we received the empress' letter."

Lea allowed herself a small breath of relief at the confirmation that she was right to inform Freya and Aer about Lessia's potential involvement with the elves.

Ettrian tapped his goblet, signaling to a nearby servant to pour his wine. "As I have always seen value in a relationship with humans, I was curious as to what your plans were, so I informed my father I would be traveling here to see for myself."

Lea's teeth clamped down on the inside of her mouth at Lessia's look of annoyance when the prince neglected to speak of how much he valued the Jotnar. Lea could only assume their inability to lie was preventing him from being forthright, but it was also just as possible he simply enjoyed irritating her.

Willem nearly preened.

"Well, we're certainly thrilled to have you," Lessia told him. "I've long wished to form a bond with your people, so I hope this visit might be the beginning of a new friendship."

Ettrian flashed her a brief smile. "So, what is the state of this land you hope to conquer? Have the people accepted you as their monarchs?"

"In time," Lessia said smoothly. "We have the northern realms in hand, but the southern ones are a bit more... fussy."

Willem grinned at Lea. "We're hoping Lady Calliwell might be able to sway the people of Edhil to our way of thinking."

Ettrian gave her a curious look. "Such a small thing, isn't she? How might she help you?"

"Her father was the governor, and her mother is the former queen's sister. Her word holds weight with her people." Lessia smiled at Lea. "Isn't that right, dear?"

Lea nodded. "Yes, Empress."

Ettrian circled a long finger in the air. "And what do you two plan to do here once all is said and done?"

Lessia slid a look at Willem. "We plan to rule, of course."

"Three countries?" Ettrian laughed. "Might I ask how you intend to go about such a thing?"

Lessia seemed to bristle at the contempt in his words. "For now, we will remain in Iladel, with stewards in the capitals of our respective lands."

"It takes time to reorganize after a takeover, as I'm sure you can understand," Willem said. "Lands must be divided and so on."

"Hm." Ettrian picked up a piece of bread and began picking the seeds off the crust. When his disinterest registered with Lessia and Willem, Effina cleared her throat.

"Well, we're grateful to have you," she said. "It's been some time since our people have worked together and I think a reconciliation would benefit both our lands, don't you?"

Ettrian raised a brow. "Oh? How so?"

Willem and Lessia exchanged a look, then Lessia spoke. "Friendship with foreign lands is never a bad thing, is it?"

Ettrian set the bread on his dish. "I suppose you have a point. Now, let's set aside that discussion for another day. I'm quite famished."

Lessia gave him a tight smile, her annoyance poorly disguised. "Of course, Your Highness. As the first guest in this new home of ours, we defer to you."

Lea thought she might be sick.

FEAR AND DESPAIR for her king and queen, along with a bit of curiosity, kept Lea silent throughout the rest of the meal, her newfound concerns hardly giving her the energy for one-word answers when spoken to. The only thing that kept her from getting a scolding was Lessia and Willem's pure glee at the sudden, unquestionable victory that now seemed to lay before them.

Their assurance that they would win this war was hardly unfounded. Should Ettrian choose to offer his father's elvish army in support of their cause—which his presence here all but indicated he would—Lindoroth could be decimated within a week. While Linds and Jotnar had strong magic, that of the elves could destroy worlds, if stories were true.

Lea desperately hoped that was an exaggeration on the part of historians and storytellers.

"I'm getting you out of here," Jonas said when they got back to the room. His tone brooked no argument, and Lea had the suspicion he would carry her out, bound and gagged, if she even considered putting up a fuss.

"How?" She slipped off her stole and carefully hung it up in her wardrobe. "How on earth do you plan to sneak me out of here now? I think it's safe to say the passages are a poor option, and now with elves here?"

"Ettrian is the only elf who's come, at least as far as I can tell, so he might not be a factor."

"Well, I suggest you find out!" Lea dropped down on the edge of the bed. "I'm all for fleeing now, but not if it will mean an entire elvish army coming after us!"

Jonas sat down next to her and put a tentative hand on her shoulder. They sat silently for a few moments as Jonas gave her time to process their new arrival. She suspected he needed that time, as well, but had no intention of calling attention to that fact.

As she stared at the wall before her, the cherry-stained wood inlaid with pearl that had graced the walls since its construction under King Eroan, she wondered how much longer the palace would stand. If the war made its way to Iladel, the city would fall, most certainly. If those armies managed to make their way through the Aldridge mountains to the palace—a feat made much simpler now that the elves were involved—the palace could very well fall along with it.

It was also made much simpler by the fact that her king and queen now seemed to be smack in the midst of enemy territory.

She let her head drop to her hands as tears, the first she'd allowed herself to shed since she'd escaped the dungeons, slipped down her cheeks.

Jonas' arm slid around her shoulders and he pulled her into his side. She stiffened, but he held firm, waiting a moment until she decided to allow herself the comfort of being touched in a way that wasn't soaked in deceit or falsehoods. She leaned against him, resting her head on his shoulder.

"I was such a fool," she whispered as her tears fell from her cheeks and formed round, gray spots on his white jacket. "Such a damn *fool* to think I could help return Lindoroth to normalcy."

His arm tightened around her. "If you were a fool, then so was I. All I wanted was to get my sister back and make my land a better place."

Lea pulled back and wiped away her tears, feeling silly that she'd let the mask she'd tried so carefully to keep in place slip. "Where do we go from here, then?"

"Take a day to think," Jonas said after a moment. "My gut instinct is to leave immediately, before Ettrian manages to get wind of the tunnel system, but with his type of magic—" Suddenly, his eyes widened. "Lea, your earth magic! Gods above, I should've seen it before!"

She straightened her shoulders and looked at him. "What about it?"

"I think many of those passages run underground. Do you think you could use your magic to... feel your way out?"

"I never thought about that, to be honest." She thought for a moment, then nodded. "That could explain why Aunt Ordona had such a deep knowledge of their layout. How can that help us, though? Tyna said Willem has been sneaking around, so unless I can detect other living creatures within the tunnels, which I cannot, we'd still run a huge risk of being caught."

"Just think about it. Take some time tomorrow while I'm out and see if you can feel out where some of the tunnels lead. I think, if you try hard enough, you might be able to sense the change in magic if someone else is in them without even leaving this room." His eyes met hers. "I've only just realized I haven't shown you where they are. Would you like me to—"

She shook her head, although that fact hadn't slipped her mind for a second. "No. I know what to look for." She slid her eyes to the left, toward the panel beside the fireplace.

Jonas followed her gaze, then gave a small nod. "Let's get some sleep. Having Ettrian here changes things, so I'd like to be well-rested tomorrow."

"What for?"

"I want to be as alert as possible for any planning meetings I may be included in, and you and I need to come up with the best way of getting you out of here."

Lea frowned. "What about you?"

"What about me?"

"Will you leave, too?"

He shook his head. "No, my place is here. I swore to keep you safe, Lea, and the best way to do that is to ensure you are as far from here as possible. And, if my plans are to come to fruition, I need to stay."

Lea lay back on the bed and rested her hands on her stomach as she considered his words. She came back to get as much information as she could, and while she felt she'd given Freya and Aer a good deal to work with, leaving just as the elf prince arrived seemed counterintuitive for someone in her current predicament. Freya and Aer knew little of the elves, yet they'd just run off to Avorell searching for assistance from a people who now seemed unlikely to give it. Yes, they had Reginald Ristner with them in Watoria, and he'd spent a little time with the elves in the past, so it was likely he'd given them some insight into their behaviors, and whatever he said must've been enough for them to think reaching out could be useful.

But what did a few visits really say of Reginald's knowledge of the elvish ways? Worse, if the elves were here supporting his family, what did it say about his true allegiance? Their best chance of getting a leg up on their enemies was if Lea stayed and relayed every word she heard to them.

First thing the following morning, she would call for Tyna and have her send word to Byrric immediately. Lea might not be able to wrap her head around this new development or suss out what Prince Ettrian's intentions might be, but if anyone could, it would be their commander.

25

FREYA

The sound of the frozen Between continued to roar through Freya's ears even after they came to a stop on a wide, grassy moor of the Summer Court. The sudden warmth was a brutal shock compared to the cold they'd just traveled through. Freya's stomach threatened to revolt, the sudden nausea causing her to double-over.

"Yes, the first time can be a bit rough," Silmar said. "Apologies for that."

"Are you alright, Your Majesty?" Florian asked.

Freya held up a finger and covered her mouth with the back of her hand, then waved him off. A moment later, she felt Aer's hand on her back. Slowly, she took a few deep breaths, focusing her attention on the soft, emerald grass beneath her, tall enough that it nearly obscured her feet from view.

"I never thought I'd see the day my Valkyrie was weakened by something as trivial as motion sickness," he murmured.

Freya glared at him as she righted herself. "I never thought I'd be traveling in such a way before today, so you'll have to excuse me. And why aren't you vomiting right now?"

He shrugged and took a deep breath, sucking in the warm air of the elvish lands. "Vomit is unbecoming of a king, wouldn't you say?"

Freya smacked his stomach with the back of her hand. "Sometimes I hate you nearly as much as I love you." She glanced at Florian, who looked as unruffled as usual. "Are you alright, Lord Florian?"

He gave Freya a quick nod. "It is not my first trip through the Between, Your Majesty."

"Andradath is a day to the east," Silmar said. He shifted his eyes upward, gauging the sun's position. "Sundown is about six hours from now, and traveling through the night would be unwise for two such as yourselves, so we will stop at an inn for the night."

Freya arched a brow but chose not to acknowledge the affront.

"Thank you, Lord Silmar," Aer said. "It's kind of you to be our guide."

The elf gave them a sharp nod, then began his trek toward the east.

The moors of Avorell were a rolling expanse of lush green with hilltops laden with vibrant flowers. The grass swished quietly beneath their feet as they walked, kicking up fluttering insects here and there that danced on the warm wind that flowed unfettered through the open space. As the gentle breeze touched Freya's hair, it pulled a few small tendrils of pink from the braided bun Rini had insisted on that morning and set them dancing. Ahead, behind the blue haze that spoke of a long distance, Freya could see a darkened strip where the moor shifted from field to forest. It put her in mind of the grasslands of Saith, only their beauty didn't hold a candle to this.

And then...the *magic*.

Magic, unbelievably strong and vibrant, pulsed all around her, beating like a drum as it thrummed through her veins and drew a welcoming caress across her skin. She couldn't see it, but she knew if she wanted to, she could reach out and twine her fingers around it and take it for her own.

"It's beautiful here," Freya murmured to no one in particular. She'd spent so much time in recent weeks in the cold of an Allanorian winter, where sunny days were few and far between. As the sun of the Summer Court warmed her face now, she was tempted to just sit in the soft grass and soak it all in.

Aer's hand slid into hers, comforting and strong, and she could feel his appreciation for this place through their bond. "Maybe we can come back one day, once all of this is over," he said quietly.

"If you both manage to make it out of here with all your parts, I would recommend returning around this time," Silmar said. "The Summer Court's weather is always warmer than the other courts, but the heat is not so great in the winter as it is during the other seasons."

His words brought them both crashing back to reality. The loveliness of the land was suddenly supplanted by the knowledge that the difference between Lindoroth's—and their—survival and destruction lay less than a day ahead. If King Ruehnar and Queen Nalaea agreed to help them, they could be on their way in a matter of days with the force of Avorell behind them. If they didn't agree, Freya wasn't entirely sure what would happen to them, although she had a feeling it would not be as simple as just sending them home.

"Have you traveled to Lindoroth before, Lord Silmar?" Freya asked.

"Long ago," he replied. "Before your people sent the humans across the sea."

Freya shared an amused look with Aer at how little Silmar seemed interested in making conversation.

They walked in relative silence for the next few hours before finally reaching the forest. Despite the beauty of the moors, the promise of shade and relief from the relentless sun that was slowly beginning to dip toward the horizon beckoned Freya forward, and it was all she could do not to hasten her feet to get to the shaded wood sooner.

"Let's stop and rest a moment before continuing," Silmar said as they reached the edge of the forest.

Pulling out her own canteen, Freya leaned against a nearby tree and took a sip. "How far is it through the forest?"

"The village of Morhalone is a few hours from here," Silmar said.

"We will need to move quickly in order to make it by sundown. We'll stop there for the night and continue in the morning."

Freya itched to ask him to take them straight through to Andradath so they could find out soon where they stood with the elvish monarchs, but she knew this was one time her impatience could not get the best of her. A few hours in the morning wouldn't make a difference, and a meal, a good night's rest, and a bath before they finished their journey were likely good ideas.

Florian pulled out his canteen as well and took a long sip, then poured a bit of the water into his hand and splashed it across his face, the droplets of water glittering like gems against his dark skin. "It won't be wise to stop for any significant length of time here, Your Majesties."

Curious, Freya brushed her hand against the rough bark of one of the massive trees. From afar, she thought the trees looked similar to the oaks that spread across Allanor. Now, as they approached the dark shade of their canopy, she saw they were easily twice as tall as the trees she was used to, and many appeared wide enough that a person could carve one out and make a roomy shelter, if they had the inclination.

When she pressed a hand to the trunk, magic pushed back.

"This forest is old," she observed.

"Ancient," Florian told her. "It's called the Forest of Ages."

"Ages?" Aer asked.

"The oldest tree known to exist here is more than three thousand years old," Silmar said. "The youngest, nearly eight hundred."

Freya's eyes widened. "How?"

Silmar gestured around them. "I'm sure you can feel the magic that permeates this place. Once it takes hold of something, it does not relent. You would do well to remember that during your stay here."

Freya let her hand fall back to her side as she eyed the tree in front of her warily.

"Why did it take hold here?" Aer asked.

"Something happened that made the magic of this forest angry." He touched a thin finger to a leaf dangling from a branch that arced over the path. "It felt affronted, so it became protective. It grew and grew until it became what it now is. Old, immovable, inhospitable."

A chill skittered down Freya's spine and she instinctively felt for her own magic. Though she felt comforted by its presence, she couldn't deny how meager it suddenly felt in comparison to the magic that pulsed around her.

"There's no need to worry, Your Majesty," Florian said quietly. "You've come here with pure intentions."

"Andreus is correct," Silmar said. "The magic protects this land. Only those who wish no ill-intent upon it are welcome here."

"I'll assume that's why so few have been able to visit?" Freya asked.

"Indeed. Most want our goods, our magic, our land," Silmar told her. "Very few want friendship."

Freya frowned as she considered his words. They weren't here for the sole purpose of seeking friendship with the elves, although that was certainly a path they would want to venture down when all was said and done. She hoped she and Aer could convince their king and queen of that during their stay.

"My queen is interested in you," Silmar said, as if he'd heard her thoughts. "That interest is the only reason you were invited here."

Aer's hand flexed against the small of her back, but he kept whatever thoughts he had regarding Silmar's words to himself.

The Forest of Ages took nearly half the day to traverse. It was almost full-dark when they neared the border and the night creatures had begun their concert; insects, birds, and frogs, along with an ethereal sound that Freya thought might be singing, filled the air. It was hauntingly beautiful and hypnotic, a sound she knew she'd be able to sit and listen to for hours without losing interest.

"What is that singing?" she asked, unable to help herself as she tried to get a glimpse through the trees of the sound's origin. "It's lovely."

"Wights," Florian said quietly from behind them. "They've become aware of our presence."

"Wights?" Aer asked.

"Spirits. Protectors of the forest," Silmar added, his steps hastening on the path. "And the reason we will not be stopping here for the night." Leaves crunched under his feet as he wound through the trees, not bothering to ensure his companions were keeping pace.

Silmar's seeming-desire to be rid of the forest as soon as possible had Freya's back up, making her want to let out her wings, to slide a feather into her hand, just in case something found their presence offensive.

As if in answer, the haunting symphony of the wights increased in volume, and there was a quiet rustling in the brush beside them.

"Keep walking, Your Majesties," Florian said. "They are just curious."

MORHALONE SAT JUST beyond the edge of the forest and was small, consisting of an inn, a dozen or so small houses, a blacksmith, stables, and a communal well. Lanterns flickered in doorways, and a large torch lit up the area surrounding the well, making the small space easy to see in the darkness. Freya couldn't imagine more than one hundred people lived here, if she was being generous, but based on the bustling inn, it seemed to be an outpost of sorts for travelers.

Silmar led them past the smithy and toward the inn, a three-story structure that bore a tavern on the first floor and several small guest rooms on the second and third. When Silmar opened the door, they were greeted with the warmth of a fire, the soothing scent of food, and the din of the village people and travelers who'd just ended their day and were gathering for a meal or a drink.

"Lord Silmar will speak with the innkeeper," Florian told them as Silmar walked toward a long counter, behind which stood a tall, green-skinned elf who looked to be in charge. "Let's get a table."

Trying—and failing, most likely—not to appear too out of place, Freya and Aer followed him toward a table near the back. Along the way, Florian stopped a server to request food. The guttural elvish language rolled off his tongue flawlessly, and the server gave him a small smile and a quick curtsy before hurrying off to the kitchen.

"So...you've been here before?" Freya asked as they sat.

Florian nodded, then rolled his shoulders and stretched his long legs out toward the fire. "Some time ago. I met Lord Silmar on my last visit."

"Last visit?" Aer said. "How many times have you come?"

Florian let his black eyes drift over the crowded room. "Part of my duties entail making friends with those who are otherwise unfriendly. At times, it takes a few attempts before that friendship can be achieved, but connections are important."

Freya's eyes narrowed at his evasiveness, but she followed his gaze as he took in the room, letting her eyes touch on each face without lingering too long. Most of the elves held a similar appearance to Silmar—lithesome, with shining eyes and a posture that spoke of speed, even at rest. The magic she'd felt outside felt especially heavy now that they were in close quarters and she was surrounded by so many who wielded it.

"Try to relax, Valkyrie," Aer murmured. "We'll be on our way in the morning."

"I know," she said, leaning back in her seat. "I'm just a bit antsy, is all."

Silmar arrived bearing four mugs of ale and took a seat beside Florian. "They have two rooms available, so I've claimed those." He slid mugs toward Freya and Aer. "Here, drink. It will help ease your nerves."

Freya opened her mouth to say she most certainly was *not* nervous, but Aer nudged her ankle with his foot, silencing her. She kicked him back, then thanked Silmar for the ale and picked up her mug. A few moments later, the server returned with their meals, four bowls of stew that smelled like heaven, along with a loaf of soft, steaming bread sprinkled with a topping of crushed nuts and seeds.

They ate in silence for a few minutes, the lack of conversation telling Freya her companions were just as famished as she was, before Aer spoke.

"Lord Silmar, you said earlier that Queen Nalaea had an interest in my wife." He tore off a piece of bread and dipped it in his stew. "What did you mean by that? Does King Ruehnar not have the same interest?"

Silmar finished chewing and took a large gulp of ale before answering. "My queen simply wants to see what all the fuss is about, especially considering Queen Freya's heritage and how unusual her ascent to power was. Ruehnar is curious as well, but Nalaea tends to be a bit more...open about her curiosities."

Freya cocked a brow. "I find 'unusual' to be a bit of an understatement, my lord."

"Be that as it may, Queen Nalaea wants to know more about you." He flicked a look toward Aer before looking back at Freya. "I would take it as a compliment, Your Majesty. My monarchs rarely take the time to entertain requests such as yours. Should you pass muster, you will have the strongest army your lands have ever seen at your back."

"And what will we need to do to 'pass muster'?" Aer asked.

This time, Silmar's pointed look was directed at Florian, who slid his empty bowl aside and rested his forearms on the table.

"You will have to pass a test, of sorts, before the king and queen agree to offer us aid," Florian explained. "You are both strong, intelligent people who will no doubt fulfill any requirements flawlessly, which is the only reason I agreed to contact Silmar in the first place."

"And the only reason I agreed to answer," Silmar said.

"A test?" Freya asked, her meal forgotten. "What kind of test?"

The two males in front of them exchanged another look.

"That will be for the king and queen to determine," Florian responded. "It won't be an easy task, whatever it is. It could involve physical or mental combat, a test of wits, endurance, etcetera."

"Their whims are often changing," Silmar added. "Anything I tell you now could be wholly different by tomorrow."

Freya narrowed her eyes. "Is it true your kind can't lie?"

That managed to bring a small smile to his face. "If we could, I would simply lie and say we could not, don't you think?"

Florian gave Silmar a disparaging look, then sighed. "No, Your

Majesty, the elvish people cannot tell a lie, although they are quite wonderful at spinning their truths."

Silmar smirked. "A bit of advice, Your Majesties?"

"Of course," Aer replied.

"Listen with all of your senses while you are here. We are not as inhospitable as stories make us seem, but we are a protective people. Our lands and those who dwell here, both elf and otherwise, will not hesitate to do whatever it takes to keep it safe." He circled a finger in the air. "That magic you both feel, pressing in all around you?"

"What about it?" Aer asked.

"It is not a thing you want to find yourself on the wrong side of. I would encourage you not to forget that."

And just like that, Freya's lingering appetite was gone.

26

———

LEA

Prince Ettrian's arrival made for a fitful night's sleep for Lea, and based on Jonas' tossing and turning, for him as well. She lay awake for hours ruminating over what Ettrian's presence could mean for the fates of Lindoroth and her people, but all she could come up with was that it meant an unequivocal end to her home as she knew it. With the backing of an elvish army, Lessia and Willem would be unstoppable. The Linds who survived the war would fall to their knees, begging for life. The Jotnar would have free rein to begin enslaving humans again—she wasn't foolish enough to think Willem would come out Lessia's equal in the end—and they'd likely start enslaving Linds as well. Freya and Aer, trapped in Avorell, would be dead soon, if they weren't already.

And the elves...

Creatures that seemed almost nonexistent only a few weeks ago were here at her shores with the promise of aid to destroy her country.

As she went over and over that fact in her mind, the idea of hope seemed to vaporize entirely. She knew how fruitless it was to fret over things she couldn't control, so by the time morning came, she set aside her wallowing. Dwelling on the inevitabilities that lay before her would do her no good and it would certainly do nothing to help her people. Instead, she rallied her strength and committed to doing all she could to convince Lessia and Willem, once and for all, that she was on their side, and hopefully suss out Ettrian's true intentions.

She'd planned to call on Tyna as soon as Jonas left for the day, but her plans changed when Lessia paid a visit to Lea not long after breakfast. She swept into the room right after Jonas left, her long black skirts swishing softly against the marble floor. The gleam in her dark eyes immediately had Lea's back up.

"I've been meaning to pay you a visit, Lea," she said. "I wanted to compliment you on how well you've adapted since my nephew has brought you here. You seemed a bit of a spitfire when I met you at Freya and Aerelius' wedding, so I initially thought you might be a bit more... problematic." She flicked aside a drape and looked out over the gardens. "Yet that doesn't appear to be the case. You seem quite enamored of Jonas, in fact."

"Thank you, Empress," Lea said. "A 'spitfire' I may be at times, but I don't consider myself a fool. I was raised to make the best of all situations, to see the silver lining, so to speak, and Jonas has shown me that."

"Oh?" Lessia turned to face her. "How so?"

"As I said when I arrived, Jonas has shown me a different side to your people, one I believe was obscured by the prejudices I was raised with." She took a deep breath and attempted to make her next words as believable as possible. "I said previously that this conquest is not the outcome I wish to see for my people, but if I can have a small part in making this new world they'll be forced to live in just a little bit better, then that is what I will do." She smiled wistfully. "That I happened to find love along the way is just an added benefit."

Lessia's eyes flicked up and down Lea's body, assessing. "I was a bit younger than you when my parents forced Crispin on me. I suppose if I'd been your age I might've seen the benefits to that marriage sooner and saved myself a good deal of grief." She nodded slowly. "Yes, I think you'll make a good wife to Jonas. A true Lady of Jotunheim."

Lea's stomach turned to stone.

Lessia smirked. "Cat got your tongue, Lady Calliwell?"

Lea forced a cheery smile. "Not at all, Empress. It's just... the thought of marriage so soon..." She looked down at her hands before finishing. "Will—will my mother be able to attend?"

"I wouldn't have it any other way, dear." Lessia's voice was sugary. "We need witnesses your people can trust, after all!"

"Of course, Empress," Lea said quietly. "And after? Where will Jonas and I go once we're wed?"

Careful suspicion flashed in Lessia's eyes before she smiled indulgently. "A honeymoon will have to wait, sadly. My nephew has duties and you will be at his side as he fulfills them, especially those concerning your home realm." She pursed her lips. "If you are asking whether you will remain in Lindoroth, well, that all depends on how useful you prove to be."

That hadn't been what Lea was asking, and the thought hadn't even occurred to her until then. She refused to acknowledge the possibility of anything but a future in her homeland, though, so she smiled. "Of course, Empress." She hesitated a moment, debating how far she should push this line of discussion.

"What is it, girl?"

"I was only wondering... what are Jotnar weddings are like? Aside from Willem and Effina's, I've never been to one. Was theirs typical of a Jotnar union?"

Lessia laughed, smooth as silk. "Of course. Your weddings are all pomp and circumstance, theater for your guests. To my people, a marriage oath is just like any other; a promise of one thing in exchange for another. In your case, you are swearing your fealty to your lord in exchange for a chance to make this world a better place for your people."

"And you will preside? I've heard the ruler of Jotnar is always the officiant at weddings."

Lessia met her eyes with an unsettling coolness. "Normally, I would, yes. Not this time, though."

"Oh?"

"I have asked Prince Ettrian to officiate for you, and he has graciously agreed. I've no experience casting mating bonds and he's quite skilled."

Lea's eyebrows shot up and she prayed Lessia couldn't hear how hard her heart had started to pound. "Apologies, Empress, but I thought you didn't believe in mating bonds in Jotunheim?"

Lessia's red lips spread into a triumphant grin, and Lea realized the trap she'd just fallen into. "How better to send the Lindorothians a show of good faith than to adopt one of their most sacred customs?"

LEA SAW it as no coincidence that Prince Ettrian knocked at her door not five minutes after Lessia left. She was still shaking with shock and grief at Lessia's revelation, that she would not so easily slip away from a marriage with Jonas as she'd once thought. She had hardly managed to pull herself together enough to call her magic forward as she answered the door.

When she pulled it open, magic in hand, the sight of the towering male brought her up short, sending her into such a fright she nearly slammed it back in his face. Sense kicked in a breath before she made such a foolish move, so instead, she gripped the edge of the door tightly and smiled up at him.

"Lady Calliwell, good morning," he said with a small bow. "Princess Rosie informed me you've spent a good deal of time here in your life, so I was wondering if you might accompany me on a walk? It's such a large palace, and you are one of the few here who are actually familiar with it, are you not?"

Dead.

Shaking off the thought, Lea did her best to look cowed. "I would love to, Your Highness, but Lord Edrin is partial to me staying put while he's gone."

Ettrian's lips twitched, then he leaned down a bit, bringing them eye-level. The gold in his eyes shifted to the color of flames when they stared into hers. "Lying to an elf prince is unbecoming, my lady, as is the assumption your lord or empress would deny me an hour of your company to give me a tour of this place."

She held his stare for a moment before dropping her gaze. "Of course, Your Highness," she said with a small smile. Slowly, she picked up her cloak from the settee and wrapped it around her shoulders, flinching when Ettrian helped her set it in place. "Where would you like to go?"

He shrugged, his hands clasped behind his back as they started to walk down the echoing marble halls. "Where is your favorite place to go in this monstrosity? The gardens? The gallery? Library, perhaps?"

Lea tightened the fur around her shoulders and considered his question. "I've always been partial to the library, myself." Though she hated the thought of sharing it with him, she was also eager to see it once more, especially considering she might not get the chance again if Jonas was true in his intentions of getting her away from Iladel at first chance. She hadn't visited the palace much as a girl, but when she did, she and Aer would often get themselves lost in the stacks, heads buried in the storybooks of their childhood and those of their parents, and, on the occasion that Lazarus joined them, the histories of their people.

"Lead the way," Ettrian said.

Lea could feel the elf prince watching her as they walked through the palace, along with the guards and staff they passed, who most certainly wondered why she'd been allowed out to wander with the elf. The prince's presence kept their leers at bay, though, which she was more than grateful for. It was difficult not to look at him, to force him to meet her eyes as he took study of her so brazenly.

But that would be improper. That would be assertive, and that was something she simply could not be at the moment.

So instead, she allowed him his perusal as she led the way to the palace's library in the eastern wing.

The scent of parchment, leather, and burning wood hit her the moment they opened the tall, ornate doors. The fire crackling softly in the hearth, along with the tapestries along the walls and thick carpets, kept the room well-insulated, making it one of the warmest rooms in the palace. Leather sofas and chairs were arranged with small tables near the large fireplace, the firebox tall enough for someone Ettrian's height to easily walk into. Towering alcoves of books flanked a wide walkway that stretched hundreds of feet toward the back of the room, while glass cases holding the most ancient tomes formed a circle in the center, separating the sitting area from the shelves, as those books were only for display, never to be touched.

At least that was what her parents had always said.

"I came here often with my cousins when we were children," she explained as Ettrian took in the room.

"A good place to get away from royal machinations, hmm?" He strolled forward and looked into one of the display cases. "Ah, *A Brief History of the Elvish Lands*." He tapped the glass above the heavy book. "Hardly what I'd call brief, wouldn't you say?"

Lea smiled. "I suppose not."

"If I am not mistaken, it was a gift from my grandfather to King Samson, your late uncle's great-great-grandfather. Our King Devdan had a fondness for your kind, if I recall. Always giving them gifts." He clicked his tongue, then moved on to the next display.

Frowning, Lea stepped forward and looked down at the book. Being forbidden to touch them, they'd never held her interest much. There was no fun in a book that one couldn't read, so she and Aer had always turned their attention toward those that were readily accessible. This one was lovely, though, and she could easily see the elvish origins. Runes adorned the front, the raised gold embossing reflecting the light beautifully. The title had been done in shades of ochre and obsidian, with flowers painted a deep indigo dressing the edges.

"Was he also the one who carved the runes at Aldridge?" she asked, recalling the symbols of welcome and protection that graced the academic building's doors.

Ettrian looked up from his examination of another book and nodded. "Devdan was the last of the elves to hold relations with any creatures outside our lands. It's my belief he wanted to leave our mark wherever he could."

"Why is that?" she asked.

"Our kingdom had a… falling out with Lindoroth and Dystone. He attempted to rectify it, but his efforts were fruitless." He tapped a pale finger on the case he was leaning against. "Interesting stories in this one, Lady Calliwell. "Have you read it?"

"I can't say that I have."

"Pity. It's a quite thorough examination of some of our more… *unusual* customs. "

She arched a brow. "Another gift from the elves?"

He gave her a knowing smile. "We're a generous sort. Now, let's discuss your impending nuptials, shall we?"

Lea bit down on the inside of her cheek, stopping the laugh that nearly escaped. 'Impending' was exactly how she felt about her wedding with Jonas, but she didn't dare confirm that. "What is there to discuss? I've witnessed mating bonds before, I understand how the process works."

"Ah, but elvish magic is a bit different, isn't it?" He walked over to one of the broad leather chairs and sat down, then gestured toward the one beside him. "Sit."

Seeing no alternative, Lea sat down next to the prince. As the proximity to the fireplace had removed any chill that remained from the corridors, she slipped her cloak from her shoulders and draped it over the arm of the sofa. When she gave him her attention, she was surprised to find him studying her again, scrutinizing her features.

"Is there something on my face?" she asked.

Ettrian's mouth broke into a grin, one that might've been endearing if not for the two pointed fangs that flashed. "No, Lady Calliwell, there is nothing on your face. I've been trying to get a read on you since last night and I must say, it's quite difficult."

Good, she thought. "I've found it wiser to keep my thoughts in my head and off my face. I'm sure you can understand."

Ettrian pursed his lips and nodded. "Yes, I suppose I can. Care to tell me what your thoughts are on marrying a man you hardly know?" A small muscle in his jaw twitched when she stiffened.

"If that is what will save the Lindorothian people," she answered,

"I will do whatever it takes. Jonas has been kind to me, so if saving my people means marrying him, so be it."

"A martyr, then?"

"A pragmatist," she replied calmly. "I want to live, I want my mother to live, and I don't want my people to suffer. If this helps achieve any of those things, then it will be a worthwhile sacrifice in my eyes."

"You don't believe Lord Edrin wishes you harm, then?"

She let out a dark laugh. "That would depend on your definition of the word. Do I believe he intends to kill me? Physically hurt me? No, I do not. It wouldn't make sense from a political perspective," she added when he gave her a questioning look. "If the intention of marrying me is to help Lessia and Willem bring my people in line, harming me would cause a revolt. My people were taken by surprise once, Your Highness. I do not see it happening again." She shut her mouth with a snap, knowing she'd probably said too much.

Ettrian nodded slowly. "A pragmatist, and a cunning one at that. Yes, I think you'll make a fine leader of your people, Lady Calliwell. I'm quite eager to see what you'll do."

Her eyebrows shot up. "You believe I'll be allowed any sort of leadership among the Jotnar?" She huffed. "You *have* been absent long, haven't you?"

When he didn't respond, she shook her head. "Alright. What about my wedding is it we need to discuss?"

"You said you're aware of how the mating bond works?"

I'm aware the gods are unlikely to grant us one, which will ensure nothing but a certain death for me.

She nodded. "I am."

He arched a slim black brow, and she got the unsettling feeling he'd heard her unspoken words.

"Did you know, Lady Calliwell, that Jotnar magic, even your own magic, is derived from that of my people?"

She blinked in surprise. "No, I was unaware. I've always been told it comes from the elements."

"Yes, but it was the elves who gave you the power to call upon it.

We shared a bit of that magic with another race long ago, and they passed it down to future generations until, eventually, that race split into two—the Linds and the Jotnar. The Linds mixed with a shifter race, combining their power, but the Jotnar magic is still quite similar to my own, albeit far less destructive," he added with a grin.

"Why are you telling me this?"

"Because you should know that the magic of elves, the magic that creates those mating bonds, is far stronger than that to which you've become accustomed. A bond cast by an elf is nearly unbreakable." He gave her a pointed look. "So I would suggest you become certain of your choice."

As his words sunk in, her heart plummeted even further. The plans she and Jonas had made—fake an attraction, get married if Lessia insisted, and have an annulment once the world settled a bit—evaporated in front of her eyes.

A mating bond, a simple Lindorothian mating bond, could be undone. Not easily, but it was possible.

But if what Prince Ettrian said was true, and she followed through with this wedding, she would be bound to Jonas permanently.

27

—————

FREYA

Despite the hospitality of the elves in Morhalone, Freya was happy to be on their way the next morning. Though she'd slept, the straw mattress was lumpy and the noise from the tavern carried up the stairwell to their room until the early hours of the morning. When Silmar came to retrieve them, she and Aer were both bleary-eyed and exhausted but eager to move on.

The final leg of their journey to Andradath took four hours through the elvish countryside. Unlike the relentlessly warm moors and dark forest, the countryside offered a more pleasant journey, with its cool, shady roads and sun-dappled woods replete with the songs of birds, insects, and other forest things. It wasn't until they got closer to the capital that more tiny villages appeared, growing closer together until they eventually gave way to bustling towns and trading posts.

"I will have your attendants take you to your chambers when we arrive," Silmar said as they passed through what he said would be the last town before they reached Andradath. He stopped at a well pump and began to fill his canteen with water, then gestured for them to do the same. "You can freshen up and I will have them bring you clothing and whatever else you may need. Once you are presentable, you will be brought before the king and queen to state your case."

"Do you think they'll decide today whether or not to offer aid?" Freya asked.

"No, that decision will take a few days, at least," Silmar replied.

"A few days?" Freya exchanged a frustrated look with Aer, but before she could question Silmar further, Florian spoke up.

"If King Ruehnar and Queen Nalaea require you to prove your worth as an ally in some way, it will not be a simple task," he said. "Things are done differently here. You must be patient."

"Indeed," Silmar said. "Exercise patience, Queen Freya, or your lack of such will be your downfall."

Freya gritted her teeth but forced her mouth to stay shut.

"Apologies, Lord Silmar. We're just eager to be back with my people," she said as they began walking again.

He gave her an understanding smile. "I understand your need for haste, Your Majesty. Just know that you will not find your urgency to be a factor in my monarchs' decision-making."

As they came around a bend in the tree-lined road, the sight of the capital gates that loomed ahead of them instantly chased all other thoughts from Freya's mind. Their size was overwhelming, standing nearly fifty feet wide and twice as tall. Runes, similar to those that were carved on the doors to Aldridge, adorned the wood, only these were surrounded by fire-breathing dragons, towering trees, and wispy creatures that Freya could only assume were the land-wights they'd encountered in the forest. The stone wall that surrounded the city gleamed pale in the sun, and, far beyond, the white spires of the palace stood tall in the distance. The soft scent of salt water brushed against Freya's nose, a hint of ocean in the distance.

As they approached, the gates began to open, and Silmar smiled.

"Welcome to Andradath, Your Majesties."

Freya's eyes were drawn upward as they stepped through into the city, skimming along the hill before them, to the massive, glittering palace above. Houses and shops filled the streets, and elves of all shapes and sizes bustled about.

"It's amazing," she murmured. "I always thought Iladel was the most beautiful city, but this..." She took a few steps forward and gazed around, desperately wanting to let out her wings and fly so she could take in Andradath from above. She smiled at Aer and squeezed his hand. "Sorry, my love, but this doesn't hold a candle to our city."

Her expression faltered a bit when she found him staring down at her, a small smile curving his lips as he took in her expression. "It's alright, Valkyrie." He brushed a thumb across her knuckles. "As it happens, I agree." He looked at Silmar. "Shall we?"

With a nod, Silmar began walking again. He led them uphill through the city, taking them through neighborhoods and shopping districts, past smiths and grocers, until they came to the drawbridge that stretched across a wide, roaring river to the palace gatehouse.

The palace itself was constructed of a strange, pearlescent rock, almost blinding in its opulence, and the spires that rose from its various levels were tall and spindly, the topmost so high Freya was sure it must touch the clouds on overcast days.

"Where does the river go?" Aer asked as they walked across the bridge.

Freya glanced down and watched as the water thundered past beneath them, its force so great it caused the wood of the bridge to thrum.

"It's called the Windriden River, and it travels from the northern border of the Winter Court to the southern tip of the Summer Court," Silmar explained.

"Our palace only has a moat," Freya commented dryly. "This seems like it would be far more effective at keeping unwanted guests out."

"Indeed," Silmar said. "If the current doesn't kill you instantly, the creatures beneath the surface surely will. Come, I have arranged for your attendants to meet us just inside."

Freya couldn't help peeking over the edge, curious as to what those creatures might be.

Silmar led them through the gatehouse and into the sprawling palace yard, where a carpet of lush grass created latticework with stone pathways. A central walk stretched from the gatehouse door to the rose-hued steps of the palace, leading the eye to a pair of gilt-framed doors spread wide, drawing in the warm breeze.

Three tall elves—two male, one female—waited for them at the entrance.

"Lyrei, Alen, Ryul, this is King Aerelius and Queen Freya Harridan of Lindoroth," Silmar said, gesturing to each in turn. "Please escort them to their chambers and see that they have everything they need."

"Yes, Lord Silmar," they said in unison, giving Freya and Aer each a small bow.

Silmar turned to Aer and Freya. "Dinner will be served at sundown. Lyrei, Alen, and Ryul will escort you to the throne room to meet the king and queen once you've been deemed presentable."

Frowning, Freya glanced at Aer, then down at their clothes, which had taken on a fine layer of dust and bits of grass during their journey. Certainly not the kind of attire one would wear to a first meeting with a king and queen, no matter how eager Freya was to get started.

Smiling, they thanked Silmar, then followed their attendants to their rooms.

It took them nearly ten minutes to make their way through the halls, and Freya wasn't sure if the route their attendants took was intentionally circuitous or if the palace was really so vast. The floors and walls were built with the same rose-colored stone as the front steps, but the ceilings, easily fifty feet high, all boasted different brightly-colored frescoes framed by golden archways.

Ryul gave them a brief tour along the way, pointing out halls and stairways that led to the few places in the palace they would be allowed to wander freely.

"Your rooms, Your Majesties," Ryul said when, at last, they came to the white doors that led to the suite of rooms they would occupy during their stay.

Lyrei opened the door and walked through, then stepped aside as Alen gestured for Freya, Aer, and Florian to enter.

"I will have a meal sent up for you shortly," Lyrei said. "You will take dinner in your room as well."

"We won't be dining with the king and queen?" Freya asked as she stepped across the threshold into a large, circular sitting room outfitted with a fireplace, three sets of veranda doors, and matching brocade sofas and chairs.

"Not this evening," Alen said. "They wish to allow you both your rest. Tomorrow, you will discuss the reason for your visit."

Aer must have seen the protest on Freya's lips, because he touched a hand to her back and smiled at Ryul. "Thank you. It was a long journey, so the rest will be most appreciated."

Ryul gave him a smooth smile. "That is good to hear, Your Majesty."

Lyrei pointed toward the closed doors on opposite sides of the room. "The guest rooms are just through those doors. Each has an armoire with clothing for you to wear during your stay, as well as a bathing room. If you require anything else, there is a call bell beside the fireplace."

"Thank you," Florian said. "We'll manage from here."

The three elves bowed their heads to Freya and Aer, then turned and left.

"*Tomorrow?*" Freya hissed, rounding on Aer and Florian the moment the doors shut. "We won't be able to see them until *tomorrow?*" A flare of panic shot through her chest at the idea of being forced to wait any longer than necessary to get an answer from the elvish monarchs. She shoved the feeling down and looked at Florian. "They said we'd be taken to them once we were presentable!"

"Do they not understand the urgency of our visit?" Aer asked, looking at Florian. "Have they been told there are enemy forces continuing to march on Lindoroth as we speak?"

Florian nodded. "I was very explicit in my letter. They are aware, I assure you."

"Then why make us wait?" Desperation crept into Freya's voice. "Every hour we delay brings the Jotnar that much closer to Watoria."

"You forget how quickly we can be back in Lindoroth once a decision has been made," Florian said patiently. "We have nearly a week before the Jotnar get to Watoria."

"If we're lucky," Freya countered. She shucked off her vest and tossed it on the sofa. "What if reports were wrong?"

"They weren't, I assure you," Florian said.

"You know as well as I that the information was good," Aer told her. "This isn't ideal—"

"'Isn't ideal,'" she scoffed. "A bit of an understatement, I'd say. Why would they do this?"

"Their choice was undoubtedly made to elicit this reaction," Florian said calmly.

Freya gritted her teeth and took a few measured breaths, then forced as much calm into her words as possible.

"Alright. I'm going to take a bath."

Not waiting for a response, she turned and walked toward the bathing room. She heard Florian excuse himself to his own room just as she shut the door behind her.

As though it had sensed her needs, the wide bathtub, built directly into the floor of the bathing room beneath a leaded glass window that took up most of one wall, was already filled with steaming, sweet-scented water.

She kicked off her boots, then stripped out of her leather pants and tunic and shoved them to the side. As she eased herself into the water, whatever it had been infused with—herbs, magic, or both—began to ease the tension out of her.

Once she was settled, she let her eyes drift around the room until they landed on the window that rose above the tub. The glass was cut in elaborate patterns, causing strange refractions as the sunlight filtered through, and was stained with swirling designs of winged creatures dancing among flowers. As she let the water seep into her skin, her gaze traveled over the scene, staring as the grass seemed to blow on a wind that had been cut into the glass itself.

She frowned when one of the creatures appeared to turn its head and look directly at her.

"The water is going to go cold."

Freya dragged her gaze away from the window at the sound of Aer's voice in the doorway.

"Hmm?"

A small smile tilted the corners of his mouth. "You've been in here nearly an hour."

"I—" She sat up and blinked groggily. "An *hour?*"

"I thought you might've fallen asleep." Aer sat down on a stool beside the tub. "A servant brought up lunch a little while ago. Are you hungry?"

"Famished," she said. She cast one last wary glance at the window, then gestured toward the other stool, where she'd set a robe aside before climbing into the water. "Can you hand me that?"

His eyes ran over her face, concern evident as he set the robe on the ledge next to her. "Are you alright?"

"Yes. I think I'm just a bit groggy from all that travel." Leaning forward, she gathered her hair into a rope and squeezed out the excess water, then stood and let Aer help her slide the robe on. "Some food will do me good."

He smiled. "As will the well-stocked armoire that's been provided to you."

She eyed his outfit, a crisp white shirt and tan pants tucked into brown boots. "I see you already got into yours?"

"I also bathed in a reasonable amount of time, too. I didn't want to disturb you, so I used the bathing room in Florian's room while he wrote out a letter to Byrric." He kissed her forehead. "But, being the considerate husband I am, I opted to wait for you to eat."

She patted his cheek. "I knew there was a reason I agreed to this marriage."

After choosing a sleeveless dress made of several layers of gauzy, blue material, Freya followed Aer onto the veranda, where Florian was waiting at a table spread with half a dozen covered dishes.

"Apologies if I kept you waiting," she told him. "I think I might've dozed a bit."

"No need to apologize, Your Majesty." He started pulling the covers off of the dishes, revealing platters of roasted meats, vegetables, warm bread, and an assortment of fruits and cheeses, and began piling food on plates for the three of them.

"Alen informed us that we will be brought before King Ruehnar and Queen Nalaea around lunch tomorrow."

Freya picked up a scone and examined it. "That's a bit odd, don't you think?"

"That the king and queen didn't greet us upon arrival?" Aer asked. "I thought so as well."

"Or even one of the princes. There are three, right?" She looked at Florian.

"Yes, although, the last I heard, the youngest had gone off somewhere."

Freya arched a brow. "Somewhere?"

Florian shrugged. "Prince Ettrian is third in line for the throne, and by all accounts, cares little for whether or not he ever acquires it."

"A fact I'm sure the other two are quite happy with," Aer commented.

"Indeed," Florian said with a nod. "Fenian and Tavian are content with the lack of competition."

"Is fratricide not frowned upon in Avorell?" Freya asked dryly.

Florian picked up a roll and dipped it in a plate of oil and herbs. "Not particularly, no."

"Hm. Somehow, that surprises me."

"I wouldn't go saying things like that too loudly," Florian cautioned.

Freya laughed. "I may be anxious, Lord Florian, but I'm no fool."

BREAKFAST AND LUNCH had come and gone the following day, and it was nearly mid-afternoon by the time Silmar came to escort them to the throne room. At that point, Freya had almost forgotten the promise she'd made to herself to keep her emotions in check, but Aer's calming hand on her back helped reel them in a bit.

"I thought they said they would have lunch with us?" Freya hissed as the three of them made their way through the palace. "If I didn't know better, I'd think they were simply stalling."

Florian touched a finger to his lips. "I said we would be brought before them around lunch, and I believe stalling is a tactic far beneath them."

She scowled at him as Aer chuckled.

"They have held their thrones far longer than you," Florian continued. "That means—"

"We must show deference," Aer finished. He flashed the warlock a smile. "We know how it works."

Florian held his gaze for a moment, then nodded. "I wish you the best of luck, then."

The throne room in the elvish palace dwarfed that of the Lindorothian one. The opalescent walls and reddish marble floors were both made vibrant by the flickering lanterns that hung along the walls and from the candles burning in crystal chandeliers suspended from the ceilings, which were so high the tops of the chains were sheathed in shadow. A plush gold carpet extended from the entryway to the dais on the other side of the hall, where two thrones had been carved from the same stone as the rest of the palace.

The stillness of the two elves who sat upon them was so preternatural, they looked carved in stone, themselves.

"Your Majesties, may I present King Aerelius and Queen Freya Harridan of Lindoroth," Silmar said with a deep bow. When he stood, he gave Freya and Aer a sharp nod, then stepped aside to let them approach.

Neither the elf king nor queen looked a day past thirty, but they were every bit as intimidating as Freya expected, although she tried not to let that show as she moved forward. King Ruehnar had coal-black hair that flowed over his white mantle, and hooded eyes that danced a fiery bronze. His skin was a deep, golden tan, a warm color that evoked thoughts of summer and beaches.

But where Ruehnar seemed warm, his wife looked the opposite. Queen Nalaea's snowy hair fell in a cascade over her glittering gown, the shade a near-perfect match to her wintry skin and stark against narrowed, obsidian eyes.

Aer bowed as Freya dipped into a low curtsy, letting out a small breath to steady herself before standing.

"Your Majesties, thank you for inviting us into your home," Aer said.

Nalaea hardly spared him a glance as she looked Freya over.

"Queen Freya." Her voice was like honey. "Your reputation precedes you."

"As does your beauty," Ruehnar added, smirking.

Freya smiled gracefully. "I pray you've heard only good things."

"Indeed." Nalaea rested an elbow on the arm of her throne and touched a finger to her pale chin. "Quite the fighter, from what I hear." She cast a glance toward her husband. "Wouldn't you say, Rue?"

"Yes, one of those half-bloods your kind prize so much, isn't that right?"

Freya suppressed a smirk. "We're a rare breed, yes."

Nalaea's eyes ran over Freya's face, then settled near her shoulders. "May I see your wings, Queen Freya?"

Freya hesitated, surprised at such a brazen, and admittedly odd, request. Her hesitation lasted only a moment, though, before she let her wings flare out behind her, holding them wide so the full span of them could be seen.

Curiosity flashed in Nalaea's eyes as she took them in, her eyes drifting from tip to tip. "Like smoke and flowers," she murmured, leaning forward slightly. "How lovely."

"And you, King Aerelius?" Ruehnar asked, dragging his gaze from Freya. "What of your powers?"

"Mine are not so impressive as my wife's, unfortunately," Aer replied. "I only wield the power of spirit."

"Humility," Nalaea commented. "A rare quality in a male."

"Some might consider it a weakness," Ruehnar commented.

Aer's smooth smile came immediately. "Some might," he allowed. "I've always considered it a sign of strong character."

"So you don't feel your parents betrothed you to her as a way to strengthen your bloodline?" the elf king asked. Freya could see the challenge in his stare, hear it in his words, and hoped Aer wouldn't rise to the bait.

"I have no doubts," Aer replied easily. "Just as my blood will strengthen hers."

"Your marriage is strong, then?" Nalaea asked. "You consider yourselves true partners in *every* sense of the word?"

"I don't believe the gods would have granted our mating bond if that weren't the case," Aer said.

Ruehnar drummed his fingers on the arm of his throne and looked at them with shrewd eyes. "You may be correct. But—" he held up a finger, "how can we really know for sure?"

Aer and Freya exchanged a confused look.

"Isn't the gods' blessing enough?" Freya asked.

"You have the blessing of your gods, certainly, but not ours." Nalaea's lips quirked. "Ours are much more... particular."

"I see." Freya frowned.

"You are here to ask for our assistance in winning your war, correct?" Nalaea asked.

"We are," Aer said. "We're also aware of what a large request that is, which is why we were so eager to visit."

"You only come for that?" Nalaea cocked a brow. "You do not even pretend at the guise of friendship?"

A trick question, and one that could decide the fate of Lindoroth if answered incorrectly.

"We come to ask your allegiance," Freya said. "Friendship is something we would like to earn from you, certainly, and we had every intention of attempting such a thing once we took our crowns." She took a deep breath. "However, we were forced into monarchy quite suddenly after the death of our former king at the hands of people who seek to overthrow our kingdom. While we would like to build relations with you, the safety of our kingdom is paramount right now."

She felt Aer stiffen beside her, but she held the queen's gaze, focusing on the depth of her eyes and not the speculation within them. She examined Freya as though she were a new toy she was eager to play with, and it took all of Freya's strength not to look away.

Nalaea and Ruehnar were quiet for several moments, the former continuing to eye Freya as the silence weighed heavily in the cavernous room.

"Alright," Ruehnar said as Nalaea's mouth curved into a smile. "We are willing to offer our aid."

Freya's heart leapt with joy, but when she opened her mouth to thank him, Ruehnar held up a hand to cut her off.

"There are conditions, of course." Two fangs flashed as he grinned at his wife, who chuckled in return. "You must prove yourselves as worthy of our help."

"We will gladly do all in our power to prove our worth," Aer told them.

"But not *anything*?" Nalaea gave him a curious look.

Another test, Freya thought.

"Only a fool would promise such a thing," was Aer's response.

"Only a fool, indeed," Ruehnar said with a grin.

"What do you ask of us?" Freya asked.

Nalaea's eyes drifted toward the window above the throne room entrance. "The hour is getting late. Go to your room, get a good night's sleep, and we will discuss how you might prove yourself tomorrow."

The joy Freya felt moments earlier disintegrated at the thought of yet another day away from her people with nothing to show for it.

"Thank you for your time, Your Majesties," Aer said with a bow. "We look forward to speaking with you further."

"Likewise," Nalaea said. She gave Silmar a nod. "Lord Silmar will escort you back to your room. Dinner will be brought to you shortly."

Freya gave another low curtsy, then they followed Silmar back through the echoing palace halls to their room.

As they walked, she couldn't help but find her gratitude for Avorell's aid becoming overshadowed by an unsettling feeling that she and Aer might've taken on more than they could handle.

28

———

LEA

The blazing sun mocked Lea the next morning, as though trying to convince her that today would be a good one, when she knew damn well it would likely be one of the worst of her life.

A marriage.

She shuddered at the thought. The only things keeping her from running were her mother's continued imprisonment, the hope that she could still help their people from the inside, and a very specific desire not to die.

It would be a simple affair, according to Jonas. No fanfare, no big ceremony. Just them, in the throne room with Lessia, Willem, Ettrian, and Perida, who Lessia had promised could attend.

It will be worth it, she told herself as Tyna dressed her in a lovely silk-and-lace gown the shade of a winter sky. *It will be worth it when my mother and the rest are safe, when I can actually speak to the people of Edhil.*

Most importantly, Jonas would be trusted more by Lessia and Willem once they believed Lea was wholly faithful to him and his lands. He would have more information to pass to Lea, which would be more helpful to Freya and Aer.

Assuming they made it back from Avorell alive.

Now, more than ever, Lea's resolve strengthened. Her king and queen were in danger. She didn't know if anything she did could help them at this point.

In the end, even a small chance was worth it.

When Oliver, the former assistant to Queen Ordona, came to fetch her just before sunset, her stomach roiled and threatened to upend its contents. She took a few moments to steady her breathing as she wrapped a gossamer stole around her shoulders, one purely for show that offered no protection against the cold air that flowed through the corridors. She'd spent much of the night convincing herself that marrying Jonas was a good plan, especially if she wanted to continue to build relationships in the palace. Though trust was still tenuous between the two of them, she knew he would, at the very least, be kind to her.

And yet, she was still being forced into marriage.

No, not she. They.

She didn't know if Jonas held an attraction for her, but whether he did or didn't was beside the point. They were still being forced into a union that was not of their own choosing. Yes, it was for the greater good, but what would happen if there never came a time to go through with the annulment Jonas was so certain could happen? Or if the mating bond Lessia was insisting on couldn't be broken? What if Lessia and Willem succeeded in their takeover of Lindoroth and Lea had no choice but to stay married to a male she didn't love?

Each thought piled onto the next, causing the anxiousness within her to build. Her heart thundered as they walked the halls toward the throne room, and when they passed an open window that looked over the gardens, it was all she could do not to leap through it and flee for the forest.

But what good would that do? Her mother would still be in the dungeon, their people would still be fighting for their lives, and her king and queen would still be trapped in a foreign land. If she went through with this wedding, she might be able to free her mother, at the very least. Her mother, who'd been sitting in a dress soaked in her own husband's blood for weeks now.

Oliver was silent as they walked, and Lea wondered if he'd defected entirely, or if he was just doing what he could to survive. His knowledge of the palace's inner workings was most certainly valuable and of good use to Lessia. Lea knew better than to ask his purpose or even offer a hopeful smile, though.

When they reached the throne room doors, Lea's stomach lurched once more, but she straightened her spine and rolled her shoulders, then smiled at Oliver to proceed.

Lessia, seated on what had once been Salazar's throne, appeared gleeful, although she seemed to be trying very hard to conceal it. Willem's face was expressionless from where he sat beside her, Effina at his side. Jonas stood in front of them wearing an easy smile, while Prince Ettrian stood beside him. Rosie stood at the foot of the dais, hands clasped lightly in front of her.

Lea's face fell into a small frown as she tried to read Prince Ettrian's expression, but he was the picture of stoicism.

Lea felt a burst of relief when she saw Perida standing beside the elvish prince, her confusion evident. She'd been scrubbed clean of all the grime of the dungeons and dressed in a lovely gray dress for the occasion. Yet, despite the pretty dress she'd been given, the toll life in the dungeon had taken on her was evident. Jonas had said the prisoners were being fed better than they had been, but Perida's face was still gaunt, her cheekbones sharper than they should be. Her back was straight as a rod, but her shoulders were slightly rounded, as though the effort of simply existing was wearing on her.

Her heart breaking, Lea forced herself not to shed a tear at her mother's plight. Instead, she tried to convey to her mother that this was for *her*, this was for their people, for the entirety of Lindoroth. This was the only way Lea could prove to their usurpers that she would not betray them, and therefore the only way she would be allowed access to the Edhilians and better information that might help Freya and Aerelius.

It was the only way.

Once the mating bond was in place, her loyalty would be to Jonas, or at least, that's what Lessia and Willem believed. It was clear in the triumphant gleam in Lessia's eye she believed that loyalty would transfer directly from Jonas to his lands and kin, and Lea was happy to let her continue to believe that.

She could only pray Jonas still held the same intentions he once had; otherwise this bond, this eternal, unbreakable bond, might ruin her.

"Ah, Lady Calliwell." Willem gave her a small smile. "I had a question for you, one I thought it best your mother be here for."

Lea tilted her chin up and gave him her full attention. "What is your question, Your Majesty?"

"The Empress and I have brought the elder Lady Calliwell from her cell for one reason—execution." Willem's hungry eyes ran over Lea's face, seeking some hint of fear. She clenched her jaw but refused to give him more than that. He angled his head to the side. "How does that make you feel?"

"I love my mother with all of my heart, Your Majesty, as I'm sure you can understand." She gave her mother a blank look before finishing. "I would much prefer she remain among the living, if possible."

"And why would we grant such a favor?" Lessia asked. "After all, you told us she enabled your father, a wretched and abusive creature, to harm you for so long."

"That is a lie!" Perida exclaimed, turning shocked eyes on Lea. "How could you say such things?"

Lea gave her mother a bland look, hoping she could see the ruse, before shifting her attention to Lessia, Willem, and finally Jonas in turn. "You have given me a renewed perspective." She smiled ruefully. "We may have gotten off to a rocky start, which I feel should not have been unexpected, but I believe offering her the same chance could be beneficial to us all."

"Oh?" Lessia gave her a questioning look. "How so?"

Ettrian cut in, a curious glint in his eyes. "The wife and daughter of the Governor of Edhil, the aunt and cousin of the former Prince

Aerelius, himself, could certainly fare better than you two at gathering Lindorothian allies. Wouldn't you agree, Empress?"

Lessia's lips twitched in annoyance. "Alright." Her eyes went sly. "I'll grant you your request, Lady Calliwell. Your mother will live. On one condition."

"What condition would that be, Empress?" Lea asked.

"You marry my nephew, complete the mating bond here and now. You're in love, after all. I see no reason to wait." Lessia grinned, sliding her eyes toward Perida, clearly eager for her reaction. "Then your mother will be free as a bird."

Lea frowned, momentarily confused. She'd known that was why Oliver had come to fetch her, so Lessia and Willem's intentions were not news to her.

When a pained cry slipped from her mother's lips, Lea understood. Perida hadn't known. Perida hadn't known she was being brought here to watch her daughter be mated to one of their enemies. Lea could only pray her mother saw the ruse for what it was, but the expression on her face nearly crushed every ounce of resolve Lea had carried into this room.

"Empress, please!" Perida cried as she fell to her knees, her face crumpling with grief. "Please—"

Lessia snapped her fingers and a guard's hand clamped hard around Perida's mouth. It took all of Lea's strength not to lash out, but instead she sent her mother a pleading, silencing look, then smiled at the king and empress.

"Of course, Empress." She let her lips slide into a grin. "That's why I'm here, after all."

"Then why so glum?" Willem asked. "Isn't this supposed to be the happiest day of a girl's life?"

Her smile faltered a bit when she looked at him. "Just a bit nervous, is all."

"No need for nerves," Effina said. "You look lovely." She looked Lea up and down and gave her a small smile. "Quite fitting for a lady of Jotunheim."

"A thing I've told her a dozen times," Jonas said with a laugh, reaching out a hand to take Lea's. "Now, let's get on with it."

Lessia propped her chin in her hand, resting her elbow on the arm of her throne. "Explain it to me again, Prince Ettrian."

The prince gave her an indulgent smile. "Of course, Empress. It's quite simple—they will say their vows, I will call on the gods to bind their souls to one another, and once that call is answered, they will be joined as one."

Lessia narrowed her eyes. "And her loyalty?"

"Will be to her bond-mate, of course."

"And the reverse? What of my nephew?"

Ettrian arched a brow. "That devotion can extend toward the families of bonded mates, as well. If one mate is stronger than the other—if one has stronger magic than the other, that is—the bond can weigh more heavily on their side. It's quite simple to say Lord Edrin is the stronger of the pair."

"Lovely," Lessia purred, her smile widening when she looked at Lea.

Lea bit the inside of her cheek, stopping herself before acknowledging the idiocy of the prince's last statement, but she couldn't help but be impressed at how... *skillfully* he'd twisted his words.

And shocked at how easily Lessia believed him.

Diverting her eyes, Lea smiled up at Jonas, then looked at Perida, hoping her mother could see just how certain she was of her decision.

"Try not to worry, Mother. This is a choice that has been given to me, not something I've been forced into. Jonas will give me a good life."

"Yes, yes, everyone is happy but the mother-in-law," Willem said with a disgusted look at Perida. "Allowing your daughter to continue your Lindorothian traditions is a show of good faith, don't you think?" When Perida stared back at him morosely, he rolled his eyes. "On with it, elf."

A small muscle in Ettrian's jaw twitched at Willem's command, but he didn't dignify it with a response. Instead, he opened his arms, inviting Lea and Jonas to step closer.

"Since Lessia has chosen to lean toward Lindorothian traditions, we'll recite the traditional Lind vows. Are you both familiar?"

Lea nodded, but Jonas shook his head.

"Alright, then. Repeat after me," Ettrian looked at Lea first, "'I, Grevillea of Houses Waisfir and Calliwell, pledge myself to you, Jonas Edrin.'"

He continued on, Lea repeating each part of the vow after him. With each word she spoke, her insides crumbled just a bit.

When she pledged herself to Jonas, her heart ached.

When she promised to give herself to him fully in mind, body, and soul, it nearly split in two.

She didn't see the same reticence in her groom's eyes, not when he pledged himself to her, nor when he promised to be her faithful husband, confidant, and friend.

They spoke the final words together, a slight deviation from tradition that carried the same weight, nonetheless. "On this day, I give you my heart freely and take you as my mate."

Lea expected him to kiss her in the same obscene way Willem had kissed Effina at her wedding, but thankfully, it was little more than a lingering peck on the lips.

"And now for the bond?" Lessia asked, staring eagerly at the two of them.

Ettrian angled his head so she could see the irritation on his face. "These things do take time, Empress. I'm sure you understand."

He looked first at Jonas, then at Lea. "The magic of a mating bond affects everyone differently, as I'm sure you're aware. If the gods grant a pair the bond—"

"Which they will," Willem said, eyeing Lea gleefully.

"—it can feel akin to a blade through the chest, or it can be pure bliss." He looked at Jonas, who nodded, then shifted his fiery gaze to Lea. Something in it seemed pointed, although she couldn't quite put her finger on what it was.

She nodded. "I understand, Your Highness."

"Then let's begin." He pulled a dagger from his waist, the blade made of smooth, black stone; the handle, mother-of-pearl. "I'll need your palms, please, and Lord Edrin, if you'll undo your collar?"

He scored each of their palms with the blade, then, after mixing their blood, he painted the bonding mark on their collar bones, the blood an offering to the gods who would determine whether or not their union was worthy of such deep magic.

It won't be, Lea thought. She repeated the words to herself over and over, silently begging Jonas to fake a strong reaction when the gods refused them.

Ettrian extended his palms, and Lea and Jonas each placed one of their hands in his. "I call to the gods to bind them eternal," he began. "I beseech the Mother to accept this offering and grant them this favor. Allow their souls to join as one." His eyes darted between Lea and Jonas. "From this moment on, until the worlds choose to crumble, they swear fealty to their mates and no other."

Seconds later, the magic hit, far faster than Lea would have expected, and at its first touch, she nearly wept. She felt Jonas' hands tighten in hers, his grip nearly painful as the power tore through them. She gasped when it twisted around her heart, swirling and green and beautiful... and familiar.

Eyes wide, she stared at Jonas. The smile on his face seemed genuine, but a bit of confusion lingered in his eyes, as though he might be coming to the same conclusion she just had.

She forced herself to keep her eyes on his, to keep her grip on his hand, and to avoid the stares of Lessia and Willem, who were eagerly awaiting the results of Ettrian's call to the gods.

A call that had not been answered.

A fact that, she realized as she forced her eyes to remain focused on Jonas, Lessia and Willem seemed completely unaware of.

~

THERE WAS no reception for Lea and Jonas' wedding. Instead, Lessia bid them goodnight with orders to consummate their union immediately.

After watching Perida get dragged back to the dungeons without so much as a chance to say goodbye to her daughter, Lea turned to Lessia.

"I thought you said she would be freed?"

Lessia inclined her head toward the door. "Finish your duties as wife, and she will be given her chance."

Lea hesitated only a beat before giving Lessia a small smile.

"Of course, Empress." She looked up at Jonas. "Shall we?"

He grinned, a leering smile that nearly disgusted her, then took her hand and practically dragged her from the room. She forced a laugh as they left, hoping everyone would see an excited wife eager to consummate her freshly sealed mating bond with her husband.

Once they'd rounded a corner and were out of earshot of the throne room, she yanked her hand from his and stopped. "You're hurting me!" she hissed.

"Quiet." He cast a sharp look down an adjacent corridor, then suddenly, he pushed her against the wall, pinning her body with his.

"Make it look convincing," he murmured, his lips hardly a breath from hers, his fingers digging into her hips. She was about to push him away when she heard quiet footsteps approaching from the direction he'd just been looking. Without giving herself a moment to question the choice, she got a handful of his hair and dragged his mouth to hers.

Kissing Jonas was odd. Not unpleasant, necessarily, because he seemed a good kisser, so it at least made the ruse *somewhat* less horrible. But there was a mechanical feel to the way his mouth moved over hers, the way his lips parted her own, how his body pressed her into the wall, as though the two of them were trying to force oil to mix with water. There were moments of niceness, but those were dominated by the overall lack of... something.

In a way, she wasn't surprised, but she couldn't help but feel a bit of disappointment all the same. It hadn't become apparent until now that a small part of her had hoped a bond would make her stop second-guessing him, because it would cause him to be faithful only to her. He wouldn't hurt her or betray her, and she wouldn't have to worry that he was double-crossing her. They could stop pretending and form a true partnership. If that led to love or a romantic relationship, so be it, but at least she would feel more secure with him.

Instead, all she felt was resigned to the fact that nothing about this ruse would ever put her at ease. If anything, their wedding had done just the opposite. She was no more certain of him now than she had been, and now she had a whole new thing confounding her. She could only assume Ettrian hadn't performed the mating bond because he hoped to use her in some way. There was no other reason for an elf, one who had only just met her, to keep her from bonding to someone else, meaning selfishness in some way had to have been his motivation.

Lea was pulled from her thoughts when Rosie Ristner skidded to a stop beside them.

"Oh! I'm—I—I'm so sorry!"

Jonas flashed her an annoyed look as he pulled back a few inches. "Good evening, Princess."

Lea huffed, doing her best to make it perfectly clear just how much she was imposing.

"I didn't mean to—I was just on my way—" She pointed down the hall. "My room is—just down there."

"Not to worry, Princess," Lea said, smiling up at Jonas. "We were just leaving."

"I—my lady, I apologize—"

"Come, wife," Jonas muttered, taking Lea's hand and giving her arm a hard tug. "She's only here to spy for her brother. Let her go give her report."

Sending a shocked Rosie one last withering look, Jonas led Lea back to their room, her footsteps hurried as she struggled to keep up with him.

Tyna was waiting when they arrived, her wings fluttering madly as she bobbed in the air in front of the fireplace. "Come, my lady, my lord," she said, smiling. "I've prepared the bath for you."

"Perfect," Jonas murmured, taking Lea's chin in his hand. He kissed her again, more deeply this time, only pulling back when Tyna cleared her throat.

"Um... what is the bath for?" Lea whispered.

"It's Jotnar tradition for a husband to bathe his wife before consummation. We've stuck to your traditions, now it's time to stick to mine." When he saw the sour look on her face, he angled his head, and it would've seemed affectionate, had his eyes not followed the movement toward the wall beside them, as well.

Lea's heart pounded with fear and disgust.

"Of course." Slowly, she took Jonas' hand and walked to the bathroom, following in Tyna's wake.

She tensed when they stepped into the bathing room and saw the tub had been filled with steaming water tinged blue with oils and dotted with pretty purple orchids and white jasmine. Candles stood along the edges of the tub and at the washbasin, on shelves, while others floated in midair.

The walls glittered with silvery pixie dust, the powdery substance ensconcing the room from floor to ceiling, making it soft and welcoming, as though the moon had been trapped and brought inside just for them.

Tyna had turned it into a place one might want to settle in for a while. A fine room for a husband and wife to celebrate their first night of marriage.

Silently, Tyna fluttered over and dumped a clear, viscous liquid into the water and gave it a quick stir with her magic, instantly obscuring the flowers with heaps of snowy bubbles.

As soon as Jonas shut the door, he and Tyna deflated and he dragged Lea into a hug.

"We're being watched," he breathed. "Get undressed and in the tub. I'll be back in a moment."

He took a small step back, and the moment he let go, her shaking began as she saw the lack of choice that seemed to hover before them.

The door shut with a quiet *click* when he left, and she turned, wide-eyed, to Tyna, who motioned for her.

"Come, my lady, let me help you disrobe."

Lea nodded shakily and stepped forward, then Tyna immediately went to work untying her corset and removing her dress.

"I found three new spy holes in the main room today and one more in here," she said in a hushed whisper, fluttering back to let Lea settle into the steaming bath until she was neck-deep in bubbles. "It took a good deal of time to get them all sealed up, but for the sake of security, we'll keep our discussions in here for now. I did a final sweep of the room just before you returned, and Lord Edrin is ensuring no one followed you."

Jonas stepped back into the room a moment later wearing just his shirt and pants, and cast a quick glance toward the tub. When he saw that Lea was fully concealed, he let his silencing magic settle over the room, effectively sealing them off from the outside.

"The dust is not just for appearances," he explained as he knelt beside her. "It will block anyone from seeing into this room, either physically or with magic."

Revulsion rolled through Lea's middle as she thought of what that meant for the rest of his chambers. "What about the main room?" she hissed. "How are we to conceal... things?"

"Leave that to me, my lady," Tyna said firmly. "I've got something brewing that should help."

Lea lifted a brow. "Dare I ask?"

Tyna pressed her lips together and shook her head. "It's best you don't know. Either of you." Her eyes darted toward the door. "Now, stay in here for another half hour. I'll have everything set by then."

She vanished, leaving Lea and Jonas alone with the uncomfortable silence that lay between them. Lea didn't know if Jonas knew the magic that coursed through them in the throne room was nothing more than a strong dose of earth magic. She didn't know if he knew they weren't bound by more than simple marriage vows or if he felt any disappointment in that fact. Based on the look he'd given her after the ceremony and the mechanical way he'd kissed her, she suspected he did, but asking aloud was out of the question.

Jonas moved behind her, then crouched down and put his hands on her shoulders. He sighed and rested his forehead against the back of her head.

"It will be alright, Lea," he breathed, confirming her suspicions. "My promise to you still holds. Whether this bond is true or not, I will not let anyone hurt you."

She sank a bit lower into the steaming water and patted his hand. "I know."

29

———

FREYA

After Lyrei and Alen brought them dinner, Freya, Aer, and Florian took the jug of wine they'd been given out onto the balcony. The air was balmy, with a warm breeze blowing in off the sea that stretched off from the eastern shores of the Summer Court, a nice change from the cold of her homeland.

Freya had accepted the fact that they would only see Nalaea and Ruehnar at their leisure, not hers, and fretting about it was only making things harder for herself.

She wished they would get word from her father, though. Florian had sent a letter back to Watoria with Silmar to ensure Byrric that Freya and Aer were alive and in one piece, but they'd heard nothing in return. Whether Silmar was keeping a response from them or if Byrric simply hadn't had time to pen anything back, Freya wasn't sure. But the lack of response, for whatever reason, unsettled her.

Aer smiled as she sat down. "Although I have no idea what tomorrow might bring, I think this will be the last night of calm we have for a while. Take advantage of it now, Valkyrie."

Freya sighed as she looked across the city, where glittering lights were beginning to light up the space between the palace and the sea. "I feel as though I'm doing something wrong, taking a glass of wine on the Veranda in the summer weather, while our people are fighting for their lives in Lindoroth."

"Don't let yourself feel bad, Your Majesty," Florian said, pouring them each a healthy goblet-full of the sweet summer wine before taking his seat. "Take this as an opportunity to breathe a bit before heading back into battle. There is nothing we can do to speed this process along, and to do so would most certainly land us back in Lindoroth with no added help. Waiting, doing this on Nalaea and Ruehnar's terms, is the best way to help our people. We've got time."

She smiled her thanks when he handed her a goblet. "It's hard when I know what's happening back home."

Aer linked his fingers through hers and let their clasped hands dangle between their chairs. "We'll be back before you know it, with or without the help of Avorell."

"Speaking of Avorell..." Freya arched a brow at Florian. "What type of 'test' should we expect them to put us through? Aside from one of my patience," she added with a wry smile.

Florian pursed his lips and stared into his wine, his expression thoughtful. After a moment, he set his goblet down and looked at them both.

"I cannot give you specifics because I have none. All I can say is that the elves are a wily sort when it comes to their bargains. It is my belief they will help Lindoroth, but what they require in return could range from access to the mines of Errest to—" He winced, rubbed a hand across his brow, and huffed out a breath. "Suffice to say, the elves have customs and ideas that are most unlike those of Lindoroth. Do not anticipate anything that resembles simple, even if it seems so on the surface."

Aer squeezed Freya's hand. "Whatever they ask of us, we'll figure it out."

Freya smiled at him, but when she looked back at Florian and saw his solemn expression, it faded from her face.

"If you could succeed by will alone, I would have no concerns," he said. "Just be cautious in your wording once you make your bargain. Be specific in your request and be specific in clarifying theirs. They may not be able to lie, but sometimes, the truth can be just as deceiving."

"How comforting," Freya murmured.

~

Queen Nalaea sent Lyrei with a message for Freya to meet her in the entry hall after breakfast the following morning. When Aer questioned whether he was to accompany her, Lyrei simply told him the king would be calling on him soon.

As Lyrei waited by the door, Freya looked at Florian, who'd joined them at the table for breakfast. "Another test?"

"Oh, certainly," he replied. "They will want to get to know each of you individually, without the other at your side to rely on for guidance."

Freya exhaled softly, then dabbed her mouth with her napkin and stood, straightening her dress. She'd chosen a flowing purple gown that suited the warmth perfectly. The fabric, silk softer than even the finest Saithian textiles, was like feathers against her skin. She'd been a bit hesitant to don the color, not wanting to look a mess when she saw the king and queen, but she found it went quite well with her hair, actually bringing out the deep, magenta color rather than clashing with it.

"You'll be fine," Aer said. The corners of his mouth tilted up. "With the interest they've shown in you, I'm beginning to worry they'll try to steal you away from me."

Smiling, she leaned down and kissed him, then took his chin in her hand and looked into his eyes. "Never, my love."

He wrapped his hand around her wrist and kissed her palm. "Be safe."

"You, too."

With a quick farewell to Florian, she turned to follow Lyrei from the room.

As they walked, she took note of her surroundings, taking care to commit all routes to and from their room to memory now that her mind was free from the haziness of exhaustion and lack of food. The elvish palace was labyrinthine, with echoing halls splitting from one another like branches on a tree. She tried to piece together an image of what it would look like from above, but all she could imagine was a maze of white.

The queen was waiting in the palace foyer, her simple blue gown telling Freya they were unlikely to be doing official palace business during this meeting. Her white hair had been left loose, a pale cascade down her back that nearly reached her waist.

"Your Majesty," Freya said with a nod in greeting.

"Good morning, Queen Freya," Nalaea said with a smile. She clasped her hands in front of her. "How did you sleep?"

"Very well, thank you. The rooms you provided for us are lovely."

"I thought we might take a tour of the city today, if that's alright?" Nalaea turned, gesturing toward the doors that had been flung wide to let in the fresh air from outside.

Freya forced back her irritation at the queen's insistence on such a casual activity when they *should* be discussing the best way to stop her people from being hunted, and instead smiled graciously. "Of course, Your Majesty. I was hoping I would get to see Andradath while visiting. A tour would be most welcome."

"Wonderful." Nalaea turned and began walking toward the doorway, leaving Freya to follow. "And let us dispense with titles, shall we? 'Queen' this and 'Your Majesty' that." She smiled at Freya. "It gets to be a bit of a mouthful, wouldn't you agree?"

Freya grinned. "Very much, Nalaea."

When they got to the yard, two white mares stood at the foot of the steps, waiting. There were no stablehands in sight. Noticing Freya's curious look, Nalaea laughed.

"The horses of Avorell are a different sort than you're used to, I'm sure." Stepping forward, she curled her fingers in the mane of one and leapt astride in a quick, fluid motion. As she seated herself, her skirts shifted, and Freya caught a glimpse of a silver dagger strapped to her slender thigh. Pale leather boots laced to her knees, and based on their sturdy look, Freya would bet they were reinforced with some type of metal.

The absence of her own weapons and the flimsiness of her leather flats suddenly felt more obvious.

Freya angled her head and looked back at the horses. "Different in what way?"

"They refuse all tack and hold a close connection to one another, along with the magic that permeates this place," Nalaea explained. "If she accepts you, we can continue on our way."

Cautiously, Freya stepped toward the second mare, who looked nearly identical to the one Nalaea had just mounted. Crystal blue eyes met Freya's as she approached, the horse's gaze feeling both calm and patient.

"Have you ridden before?" Nalaea asked.

Freya glanced up at her and bit back a remark at the smirk on the queen's face.

"Many times, although not in a good while, and never bareback. I've always preferred to fly, to be honest. I'm sure I can manage, though." Freya ran a hand along the mare's smooth coat, pearlescent in the morning sun. "Does she have a name?"

"Alene." Nalaea patted the neck of her own mare. "And this is Beline, her mother."

"Alene," Freya murmured, letting her hand curve under the mare's jaw. "It's good to meet you."

Alene huffed out a breath and nickered softly, then gently nudged her cheek with her nose, drawing a quiet laugh from Freya's lips.

"You have her approval," Nalaea said. "Come, there is much to see." She gave Beline's sides a quick tap with her boots, and the horse turned and trotted toward the drawbridge that had been lowered for them.

"Let's hope she's right," Freya murmured. "Come on, girl, let's go for a ride." She gripped the short hair at the end of Alene's mane and pulled herself astride the mammoth horse. The mare stood motionless as Freya settled herself and adjusted to the odd feeling of riding without a saddle, before breaking into a trot after the queen.

The road that led from the palace into the city was wide and curved, dovetailing at the end into two paths. Nalaea steered them to the right, onto a slightly more narrow road that was lined with pretty white buildings.

"This takes us into the residential areas," she explained as they turned onto the shady road. "Did you see much when you first arrived?"

"Lord Silmar gave us a bit of a tour. Although, I'll admit, I was quite exhausted by the time we arrived. Seeing the city with a clear head will be nice." Freya looked around at the multi-story homes and apartments that lined the flagstone street. Vivid flowers burst from boxes on the front windows, and vines of morning glory and honeysuckle wrapped around trellises and dangled from the rooftop overhangs. The sweet scent of something hung in the air, but aside from the flowers that bloomed all around, she couldn't find a source.

Nalaea smiled. "Tell me about your cities, Freya. Are they like this?"

"A bit," Freya said. "I've always felt the Lindorothian cities each held their own warmth and most are welcoming to outsiders, but this..." She shook her head and looked around again. "Perhaps it's the magic here, but Andradath feels like it could be home, if that makes sense? It's...comfortable." She gave the queen a sheepish smile. "I'm not sure if I'm conveying my thoughts quite right."

Nalaea gave her a knowing smile. "When I first visited Andradath as a girl, I felt the same way. It pleased me a good deal when Rue chose me to be his bride."

Freya smiled. "I understand. I think I felt the same way about Iladel when my parents told me I was to marry Aer. We were very young, still are, I suppose, but he's always been one of my favorite people."

"You proved yourself to his parents early, then?"

Freya gave her a curious look. "Proved myself?"

"Ah." Nalaea smiled. "Yes, your kind arrange these things differently, correct? Betrothals?" she added when Freya looked confused.

"Yes, my parents and the former king and queen agreed on our marriage when Aer and I were children. It was discussed before we were born, from what I understand. The match was mainly based on blood and politics, but Aer and I took to each other quite well from an early age, so the match worked out better than our parents expected."

"It's certainly nice when that happens, isn't it? It was quite similar for me. Rue and I... we are very much the same. I see that in you and your king, as well."

"I like to think we strengthen one another, even without the mating bond."

"A bit of magic to hold things together never hurts, either," Nalaea remarked.

Not quite sure how to respond, Freya gave her a tight smile and said, "Yes, I suppose you're right."

They continued on in silence, winding their way through the various neighborhoods. The queen stopped to talk to a few of Andradath's citizens along the way, and the smiles she gave them were nothing short of dazzling. Though she seemed reserved and calculating toward Freya, the warmth on Nalaea's face as she spoke with her subjects didn't seem fake.

Truth can be just as deceiving.

Florian's words from the night before echoed in her mind, a reminder not to forget just how skilled these beings were at deception.

As they left the neighborhood streets and crossed a short bridge onto a road that overlooked the sea, Nalaea let her horse fall into step beside Freya's.

"The Aemir Sea. It cleaves our continent nearly in two," Nalaea explained, gesturing to the endless turquoise expanse before them. "They say two of the old gods battled one another long ago. The result was a land broken in pieces."

"What's on the other side?" Freya asked, looking out at the glittering water that stretched into the distance.

"The Winter and Autumn courts are directly to the east. Lovely lands, even if their inhabitants can be... troublesome."

"Are they not under your rule?"

"They are, but we prefer to stay to our own courts, for the most part." Nalaea smiled. "Your land is divided much like ours, is it not?"

"Lindoroth is divided into five realms, including the capital. The borders between realms are always open, however." Freya looked at the sea again, at the lands that waited just past the horizon. "What distinguishes one... group from the other?"

"Only the type of magic we prefer," Nalaea replied simply. "The eastern courts have no qualms with wielding the darkest magic we elves possess. The *western* courts tend to shy away from it."

Freya supposed that wasn't so different than the split between Lindoroth and Jotunheim, but she didn't dare say that aloud.

"Which court did you come from, if you don't mind me asking?" Freya asked.

Nalaea gave her white hair a quick tug, her obsidian eyes dancing. "Winter, of course. Here, come see our markets. They are some of the best Avorell has to offer."

Seeing the subject of Nalaea's homeland was off-limits, Freya shifted her attention to the busy marketplace they'd just entered. Carts and stalls lined the street, some offering food, others textiles, and others jewels or trinkets. The scent of food and flowers mixing with the salt air was almost overpowering, but enjoyable all the same.

Freya couldn't help but notice that the mood here seemed elevated, excited, even. Most of the market-goers hardly spared their queen a glance as they bustled to and fro, and when their eyes did reach Nalaea, their gazes were instantly drawn to the stranger at her right.

"It's a rare thing, having outsiders in our land," Nalaea explained when she saw Freya frown at a few passers-by who unashamedly held her stare. "My people may seem rude, but they are quite eager to see what you and your king are like. Tomorrow, we will have a feast in honor of you and King Aerelius. A proper welcome to Avorell."

"That will be lovely," Freya said, though her heart clenched at the idea of wasting yet another day here. "Despite our reason for visiting,

I'm excited to learn more about your people," she added, hoping the queen could see just how sincere she was.

"Is your first time away from your kingdom?"

"I traveled to Jotunheim's capital, Madrya, once as a girl, which is a week's journey north from my home in Allanor, but I was on business with my father. Our stay only lasted a few days, so I didn't see much."

A small smile graced Nalaea's lips. "I have heard of the beauties of Lindoroth. After all is said and done, I hope to visit."

"And Lindoroth will be eager to have you," Freya replied, choosing her words carefully. She looked around, taking in the people, the shops, and the glittering sea. "Your citizens seem quite excited today," she commented.

"Ah." Nalaea nodded. "Yes, there is a holiday coming up that we will be celebrating soon. Preparations started just this morning, in fact," she said, pointing toward a side street. "There is a restaurant just down here I think will give you a good taste of Avorellian cuisine." Without waiting for Freya's response, the queen turned off of the main road.

Freya stared after her, trying to ignore the pit she was beginning to feel in her gut. The hurried feel of the market, the excitement that seemed to linger like a cloud over the people bustling about, and the way Nalaea's eyes seemed to sparkle as she mentioned this holiday...

Freya gritted her teeth and tried not to show her suspicion as she followed the queen toward their destination.

"That's all she said? 'A holiday'?" Aer asked.

Freya huffed. The moment she'd gotten back to their room, she'd called for Florian so she could recount her day with the queen. "Yes, a holiday." She looked at Florian. "What holiday was she speaking of?"

A muscle feathered in his jaw as he thought. "There are no set holidays coming up that I am aware of."

"Are there any that you might *not* be aware of?" Aer asked.

"That's highly unlikely," Florian said, seeming insulted to have even been asked.

"I'm sure it's nothing, then," Aer said, although his expression didn't match the certainty of his words.

Freya shook her head. "No, the way she said it... It was as if she wanted me to know, but not ask questions." She pressed her lips together and shook her head. "I don't like it. This feeling I have..."

Aer eyed her, concerned. "Are you saying you think we should leave?"

Freya hesitated only a moment, but it was enough.

"Freya, we can't make that decision without an answer from Nalaea and Ruehnar, especially based on just a feeling," Aer said carefully. "If whatever they ask us to do turns out to be too much, then we'll leave." He took her hands. "But Freya, try not to see nefarious machinations in every elvish action. It's perfectly understandable to feel uneasy with all of this... unfamiliarity, but don't let that stress lead you to see deceit where it may not be."

Freya watched him as he spoke and could tell by the set of his jaw that he was trying to convince himself just as much as her, and that leaving was the last thing he wanted to do. It was the last thing *she* wanted to do as well, but she couldn't shake the heaviness that had been growing larger in her gut since she'd left the queen earlier.

But this *was* unfamiliar—far more than any new situation she'd been faced with. This wasn't a challenge she'd been prepared for. Rather, it was a challenge that had been thrown at her with the force of a boulder, and now all she could do was struggle to keep herself upright.

She gave him a wry smile. "You know, you're far too observant."

"If I may?" Florian asked, eyebrows raised. When Aer nodded for him to continue, he clasped his hands behind his back. "Queen Freya, as much as I trust your intuition, I would strongly advise against making a decision just yet. You will both be occupied with the monarchs between now and tomorrow's feast, but I will do what I can to gather information elsewhere. Once we have more, we can reconvene here and discuss what options we may or may not have.

Freya rubbed a hand across her brow and sighed. "Alright. I suppose we'll just have to see what dinner brings."

Florian nodded. "Lord Silmar just returned, so I'm going to take care of a few things with him," he said. "I'll be back shortly."

With a small frown, Freya watched him leave the room.

30

LEA

Lea should've known better than to think her newlywed peace would last past her first night. Whatever Tyna had done the night before had kept anyone from calling on them or attempting to reach them in any way, but they'd hardly finished breakfast when Oliver arrived with a request from the Empress for Lea to join her.

"Now that you're sworn to me by blood, she'll want to test the limits of the mating bond," Jonas explained as she dressed.

Lea nodded. She wanted desperately to speak with Jonas about the non-existent mating bond, but they hadn't dared speak of it more than their few whispered words the night before. Whether Ettrian was helping them or himself, she wasn't sure, but she knew raising her questions aloud, especially when she still felt so uncertain of everyone she came in contact with, would be foolish.

After allowing Jonas to give her a quick kiss on the cheek, she departed with Oliver.

She could feel Oliver's judgement the moment they stepped into the hall. Neither spoke, but she saw his eyes dart in her direction several times. Finally, she huffed.

"What is it, Oliver?"

He tensed. "I'm not sure what you mean, Lady Edrin."

She scoffed at the disdain that laced his words when he spoke her new title. "If you have something to say, I give you leave to do so."

Indecision warred on his face, but logic ultimately won out. "I only wanted to wish you congratulations on your nuptials, my lady. That is all."

Not so loyal to your new empress, after all, are you? Lea thought.

"Thank you, Oliver. Your words are kind."

The smile he gave in response more closely resembled a grimace than anything that held happiness.

Oliver left her at Lessia's door when Lessia bid her to enter, giving Lea little more than a brief nod in farewell.

As Effina had fallen in love with Ordona's chambers, Lessia had taken up residence in Salazar's former space. Lea had only ever visited her uncle's rooms a handful of times over the years because they'd never been a place for children to frequent. He'd always taken his most important and private meetings there because it was one of the most secure rooms in the palace, so Lea could only assume Lessia would have chosen his chambers as her own, regardless of whether Effina had begged for the former queen's pretty rooms or not.

When she walked in, she cast her eyes about, wondering where the secret entrance—or entrances—to this room might be. She didn't imagine there were many—none of the kings who'd lived in these rooms would have believed it prudent to have multiple points of entry. No, it was likely there was only one, perhaps two, other means of escape.

Recalling what Jonas suggested about her earth magic, which she still hadn't attempted, she wondered if she might be able to suss out where those doors were.

Lessia was seated in a high-backed wooden chair on the terrace that overlooked the gardens. Someone, either an air or fire-wielder, had placed a spell that kept the cold air out, making it pleasurable to enjoy the space despite the frigid temperatures.

"Lea," Lessia said, her smile broad. "Please, join me for tea."

Lea stepped forward and gingerly sat down in the seat across from Lessia. A small table sat between them with a tea tray that held a tall teapot and two cups, one of which was already filled with steaming liquid. Silently, Lessia poured Lea a cup, then picked up her own.

"Thank you, Empress," Lea said, accepting the cup with a smile.

"Before we begin, I thought you would like to know that you will no longer need to remain sequestered in your chambers. I acknowledge why Jonas insisted on it from the start, but your position here is much different now. During the day, you will be allowed out of your room to find means of entertaining yourself, if you so desire."

During the day when you can't sneak about like a bandit, Lea thought. Meaning, she'd be watched closely, wherever she went. But if she had Lessia's protection when it came to Willem or his men, that was a small comfort, at least.

"You will not have to worry about harm befalling you from Willem's guards. I know they've made you uncomfortable these past few weeks. Mine know better than to tempt fate by bothering you," she added when she saw Lea's lips part to form the question.

"That's much appreciated, Empress. I must admit it's become a bit monotonous, lovely as our chambers may be. It will be nice to get out without having to worry for my safety."

Lea shifted in her seat, causing Lessia to smirk. "So, how was your first night as a newlywed?"

Lea froze when she realized how her seeming discomfort on the hard chair had been misconstrued. Crossing one leg over the other, she smiled and took a sip. "It was quite lovely, thank you."

"That's good to hear," Lessia replied. "Jonas' reputation as a lover precedes him, so I would consider yourself lucky. You'll be the envy of all the females in Jotunheim."

Lea feigned an embarrassed smile. "That's kind of you to say, Empress." She hesitated, then decided to take her ruse a step further. "The males my father suggested had none of the qualities of your nephew. I feel blessed, truly."

Lessia studied Lea over the rim of her delicate porcelain cup, letting the silence hang over them for several seconds. Just as it would've become awkward, she set her cup down.

"I'd like to discuss Aerelius and Freya."

Take more than you give, Lea reminded herself. "Yes, I expected you might. What is it you would like to know?"

"Well, we've spoken previously, of course, and you were less-than forthcoming with information. I'm still unsure whether that was due to ignorance or stupidity, so I'd like to try again. Now that the bond is complete, we can push off the charade that you actually care about our cause."

Lea's eyes widened. "Empress, I swear—"

Lessia waved off her objection. "It's no matter now, is it? You are bound both by blood and the magic of the gods to a lord of Jotunheim, which in turn binds you to his family."

Lea cleared her throat. "Yes, of course, Empress."

"Now, where would they have gone?"

Lea struggled to hide her surprise that Lessia seemed unaware that Freya and Aer had left the kingdom.

"Watoria is their most likely destination," Lea said carefully, lacing a bit of restraint into her words. She needed Lessia to believe Freya and Aer were still in Lindoroth. "Although, based on what you and his majesty have said regarding your cousin Frederick, I'm not sure they would have made it through the city walls, so perhaps they've taken refuge outside the city?"

Lessia arched a brow. "You were fleeing with them, or at least that's what you wanted them to believe. Are you telling me you truly have *no* inkling where they would've gone if they found Watoria inaccessible?"

"Jonas found me fairly quickly," Lea replied. She swallowed hard. "I knew they were going to head west, so my assumption was they would go to Watoria."

"What about Iston?"

Lea frowned. "Iston?"

"Yes. Grevillea, Iston. Has Freya ever spoken of her time with the other Valkyrie? Her grandmother still lives there, does she not?"

"To the best of my knowledge, Freya has only visited Iston a handful of times. She hasn't been back in years. I know nothing of her grandmother, though."

"Do you think they would seek asylum there?"

"If Watoria wasn't an option, then yes, I suppose it's possible."

Lessia nodded slowly. "Alright. Who else did they flee with? Dozens escaped, but I'm assuming they didn't all go to Watoria. Who else would go with them?"

Lea gnawed at her bottom lip as she tried to formulate a response that would be both adequate and not reveal too much. "Commander Balthana—"

"The commander was occupying my forces in Saith up until just a few days ago, so if he is with her, he has not been for long."

Lea barely hid her surprise that Lessia didn't seem aware that Byrric had arrived in Watoria. It had been a good five days since Rini had told Tyna of Byrric's return, and she found it hard to believe Lessia hadn't gotten word from anyone to the west to inform her of that.

Later.

Sensing impatience in the empress' tone, Lea grappled for something to give her.

"Their guards, most likely," she said. "If the Commander helped them escape and he isn't with them, he would've only left them with trusted guards, which would be the ones they were assigned here, assuming they made it out alive. They wouldn't leave their sides."

"How many guards?"

"Freya only had two assigned to her that I know of. Aerelius had more, but Rodrick and Perinald were his shadows at school."

"The king and queen's guard each consists of eight knights, though." Lessia narrowed her eyes. "Are you telling me they only have four between them?"

Lea's mouth fell open and she struggled to recover. "No, well, yes, I think, but—"

"Stop babbling, girl!" Lessia snapped. "How many guards?"

"I don't know!" Lea shot back. "I didn't even know they were king and queen until I came back here, did I? How should I know how many blasted *guards* they were assigned once my uncle was killed?"

Lea's jaw shut with a snap and her eyes went wide when she realized how harshly she'd spoken.

"Empress, I apologize—"

"It's quite alright, dear," Lessia said after a moment as she picked up her tea. "You've suffered a good deal of loss these last few weeks, so I suppose your lack of control over your emotions is mildly understandable. I would suggest, though, that you come to terms with what you've lost and accept what you've been given sooner rather than later."

Lea took a small breath in an attempt to center herself. "Yes, Empress, I promise to do better. I would like this war to be over, though, so anything I can do to help make that happen, I will."

"Well, I'm certainly happy to hear that." Lessia drummed her fingers on the arm of her chair and looked out over the balcony toward where the sun was coming over the peaks of the mountains. "It *is* quite lovely here, isn't it?"

Much to Lea's shock, Lessia actually sounded a bit... wistful.

"It is," she replied carefully. "I have always enjoyed the beauty of Iladel."

Lessia's sharp eyes found hers. "More so than your own realm?"

Lea gave her a curious look. "Edhil will always hold a place in my heart, Empress, but I've seen nothing yet in my life that can compare to the royal lands."

"Have you ever traveled to Jotunheim?"

"No, I have never had the pleasure."

Lessia smiled warmly. "I think you'll find it does not live up to its cold and harsh reputation. It's a lovely place, truly. Jonas' home on Rodrun Lake will be an ideal place to have your family."

Rodrun Lake—a three-week journey from Errest, at least. "Yes, he said it's quite beautiful. The chilly air will certainly take some getting used to, though."

"Well, as he is my emissary, I'm certain you'll find yourself traveling back this way soon enough, and to the human lands, of course.

Cold air makes for a strong constitution, I've heard. Good for bearing children."

Lea gave her a small smile. "When—when will we leave?"

Lessia shrugged. "That is all dependent on the people of Lindoroth. The sooner they submit, the sooner you may go on with your life." She gave Lea a speculative look. "I wanted to ask you a bit more about Freya and Aerelius. Their powers, more specifically."

Lea tensed. She had no idea how much Lessia already knew about Freya and Aer's powers, nor did she know enough about either to be of much use. She knew the gist of Freya's powers, of course, since she'd been with her almost daily since the term began, but Aer's powers had been kept under wraps until his last nameday celebration the prior spring.

"I'm not quite sure how much help I'll be, Empress, but I will do my best."

Lessia nodded slowly. "Freya—she's a half-blood, correct? Equal parts shifter and witch?"

Lea nodded.

"What kind of witch?"

"She's strongest in air and fire, if I recall correctly."

"Does she have any other powers or abilities I should know about?"

Lea bit her lip, trying to recall what might already be considered common knowledge. Freya's full shifter heritage made her far stronger than a typical witch, but, rare as true half-bloods were, she didn't know whether that information was something that would've made its way to the ruler of a foreign land.

"No, Empress, none that I know of. If she has touches of any other elements, she never told me."

Lessia arched a brow. "Nothing at all? She was coveted by King Salazar since birth, was she not? Surely she must hold more than just a dash of extra power?"

Of course she does, you fool.

"I'm not aware of the circumstances surrounding the betrothal agreement between her and Aerelius. As far as being a half-blood..."

they are rare among us, and there aren't more than a few hundred Valkyrie in Lindoroth, so one that holds the full abilities of a witch is even more unique. Her grandmother came from the Cantor line of witches, and their power was quite envied."

Lessia appeared disappointed. "Are you sure that's everything?"

"To the best of my knowledge, yes."

"Alright," Lessia said with a nod. "One last thing before I let you go. Freya worked for the marshals in Watoria, correct?"

Lea nodded. "Since she was fifteen or sixteen, I believe."

"What was her relationship like with them?"

Solid, Lea wanted to say. *So solid you would never penetrate their loyalty.*

"She was only a regular marshal, as far as I know. I believe Commander Balthana had a hand in getting her the position."

Lessia lifted a brow. "Did they know her true identity?"

Lea frowned. "I'm sorry?"

"I know she's been glamouring herself to conceal her identity," Lessia said. "Did they know who she was?"

"I don't believe so, no. She wanted to maintain anonymity before her return to Iladel."

"So to them, she was just another marshal, then?" Lessia nodded slowly. "Do you believe their loyalty to be unwavering?"

Yes.

"I cannot say, Empress. She didn't speak much about her time with them, so it didn't seem they left a long-lasting impression on her. They are steadfastly loyal to Allanor, but I cannot say much of how they feel for her, personally. One would assume, though, that their loyalty would be to their ruler. If the person you have put in charge of Watoria has strength such as yours, I don't think there will be much competition for leadership." Before Lessia could look more deeply into her words, Lea smiled. "I wish I had more to tell you, Empress, truly. If I think of anything more, I'll come directly to you."

Lessia turned and stared off into the distance, seemingly lost in thought. "Be sure that you do, Lady Edrin."

31

LEA

Now that she had been granted a bit of freedom, Lea stopped at the library on her way back to her room. Jonas had brought her a few books to occupy her time while sequestered in his chambers, but he had little knowledge of her interests, so the books he'd brought weren't ones she found terribly interesting.

She could feel the eyes of the guards on her and was a bit irritated when two Jotnar guards followed her, stationing themselves against the wall opposite the library doors, but ignored them as best she could.

Freedom, indeed.

She tossed a scowl at them before stepping inside, and was happy to find the large, comfortable room empty of visitors. It had been so long since she'd had time to herself, unencumbered by guards or false husbands or the four walls of her gilded prison. She contemplated locking the door but thought better of it when she realized that might draw more attention than she wanted.

Instead, she aimed for the towering shelves of books and began searching for a few to bring back to her room.

She'd been looking for nearly three-quarters of an hour when her eyes landed on one of the books Prince Ettrian had drawn her attention to two days prior. She moved closer and looked into the case, but there was no title that she could see, only a beautifully illustrated cover. Frowning, she leaned forward to get a better look when the images caught her eye.

Setting down the small stack of books she'd gathered on a table, she moved back to the glass case and lifted the lid. She slipped a layer of earth magic over her palms to protect the delicate nature of the book and lifted the volume from the box. Gently, she sat down at one of the reading tables and ran her fingers over the leather-covered wood. Gold leaf accented by deep shades of scarlet and indigo created an elaborate design of leaves and swirls that surrounded an image of a woman standing, arms raised to the heavens. On closer inspection, Lea saw that the border that framed the cover was made up of wolves in alternating shades of indigo and gold, appearing to chase each other around the edges.

She opened the book.

Instantly, her heart sank.

"Of course it's written in bloody elvish," she sighed, closing the cover and slumping in her seat.

"I could read it to you, if you'd like."

Lea leapt to her feet, exhaling a gasp at Ettrian's sudden appearance.

"You shouldn't sneak up on people like that!" she snapped. At his amused look, she flushed. Straightening her shoulders, she smiled. "Apologies, Your Highness. You just... startled me."

"It's quite alright, Lady Calliwell," he said. He gestured toward her seat. "Please, sit."

"Lady Edrin," she corrected as she settled herself back in her seat.

"I'm sorry?"

"You called me Lady Calliwell. It's Edrin now."

A smile twitched on his lips. "Is it?"

She pressed her lips together and eyed him curiously. "Unless your elvish magic is lacking, then yes, I believe it is."

"Lacking, hmm? I assure you, my lady, that is not the case."

Her eyes flicked toward the door, then back to him.

"It's spelled," he told her, answering the question in her eyes. "Go on and ask your questions."

"Why?" She didn't bother with pretense. "Why fake the bond?"

A small crease formed in Ettrian's brow as he examined his fingernails. "Did you know, Lady Calliwell, that my grandmother was a human?"

Lea huffed, annoyed by his shift, then frowned. "Then how—"

"How am I an elvish prince?" He smirked. "To make a dreadfully long story short, my grandfather, Gregory, gave over half of his power to his wife, Helena, allowing her to become immortal. Or as near as one can be to it. Did you know we elves don't even have a lifespan? I have an uncle who is five thousand years old and a cousin who is nearly eight thousand. Could you imagine living that long?" He shook his head. "There is not enough world to see to pass that amount of time."

"That's quite lovely, but what has it got to do with—"

"Helena and Gregory met when she was a bit younger than you, back before humans consolidated their power under one king," Ettrian pressed ahead. "She was a princess of Vindarria, the eastern province of Dystone, and had just become betrothed to the human king of Teid, Horace Ristner. By all accounts, Horace was a horrid excuse for a human." He frowned. "I can't quite recall the specifics of Gregory and Helena's first meeting, only what it led to."

"Which was?"

"Gregory stole her away on her wedding night, saving her from the harm that would have most certainly befallen her had she stayed behind."

"He kidnapped her? That hardly sounds loving."

"Oh no, my lady. She fled quite willingly, I assure you."

"And this is what has endeared you to the human species? A jilted king?" Lea shook her head. "I fail to see the commonalities, Your Highness."

He cocked his head to the side. "I never said I valued my relationship with humans as a species, Lady Calliwell. I only said 'humans.'"

"Are they not the same thing?"

"Certainly not. As with any species, there are humans worth valuing and others who should be thrown to whatever monsters happen to be on hand. Helena was a human worth valuing, one who brought richness and goodness into this world, into *my* world, once she was given the power to do so."

"I don't suppose I see where you're going with this," Lea said after a moment. "What has Helena and Gregory's history got to do with me?"

"It's Helena that you put me in mind of." He drummed his fingers on the table as he studied her. "Her hand was forced when her mother was killed. She was made to take her place as Horace's betrothed. Her mother could have held her own with Horace, of that I'm certain, but Helena... she was too innocent, too sweet for a man like him. Her fierceness and strength came in time, but I know what she would have suffered had she been made to stay in that marriage." Something in his face tightened as a memory flashed behind his eyes. "I made a vow to myself long ago to prevent others from befalling a similar fate, should their circumstances warrant it. While I do not think Lord Edrin would lead you to the same doom, the same cannot be said for his brethren." A small smirk twisted his lips. "I also have a general rule against performing a mating bond when the hearts of both parties are not in agreement with their words."

Lea clenched her teeth, unsure of how to respond. If she was honest with the prince, she would be revealing more than she felt was wise. If she attempted to continue this ruse of being in love with Jonas, he would see straight through it.

They sat silently for a few moments, and whether it was because he was waiting for her to speak or simply had nothing to say, Lea wasn't sure.

"Thank you," she finally said. "Whether you did it for my benefit or yours, I appreciate what you did for Jonas and me yesterday. Regardless of who it is, if I marry someone, seal a mating bond with him, I'd prefer it be at a time of our choosing, not that of another."

Ettrian nodded slowly. "Do you think you might find yourself caring for Lord Edrin enough to do those things in the future? When all the dust from this war settles?"

Lea stared at the fire roaring in the hearth as she considered his question. She knew what her answer would be if she told him the truth—that she was unsure she'd ever stop questioning the kind of person he was, if she could never unhear the things that had been said about him, ever forget that he hadn't pushed harder than he did to free her from the dungeons. Perhaps he'd been truthful when he said he hadn't been able to press without raising suspicion, but it didn't erase the days she'd watch her mother languish in her cell, coated in the blood of those who'd been slaughtered around her, knowing that if she was ever freed from her prison, she would likely be unable to put her husband to rest.

"I would like to think so," she said after a moment.

Ettrian smirked. "Careful, Lady Calliwell. Your ability to twist your words is uncannily elvish."

THE EASE with which she spoke to Ettrian in the library dissipated as he escorted her back to her room. She could feel the inquisitive stares of the guards as they passed, their suspicious looks as she made her way through the halls with the elf prince.

Whatever his intentions here in Lindoroth, she was thankful for his presence in that moment. Wife of the Empress' nephew or not, and regardless of what Lessia said, it was unlikely she'd ever be safe walking these halls.

When they turned a corner and found Willem before them, she nearly yelped at his sudden appearance.

Willem's eyes darted between her and the prince, his face turning instantly wary before his expression slid into a smooth smile. "Ah, Prince Ettrian, Lady Edrin. How lovely to run into you both. Where might you be off to?"

"I ran into Lady Edrin in the library," Ettrian replied. "It seems some of your guards have yet to accept her as their lord's wife, so I offered to escort her back to her chambers."

Willem's jaw tightened. "Well, I suppose I'll have to have a talk with my men, then, won't I?" He gave Lea an apologetic smile. "My apologies, Lady Edrin. I'm sure they're only having a bit of trouble adjusting to a female such as yourself so easily sliding into the role of a lady of Jotunheim."

"Then I suppose they should try a little harder," she replied. "Whether or not they believe I can do anything to rebuke them, Jonas can, and it's of him they should be fearful." She tilted her chin up. "Now, I'm a bit tired, so I'll be heading back to my room for a rest."

"Of course, Lady Edrin." Willem stepped aside to let her pass. "I'll see you both at dinner."

Without another word, Lea strode past him, comforted only slightly by the quiet steps of the prince at her back.

32

FREYA

If there was one thing Freya could get used to in Avorell, or, at least, here in the Summer Court, it was the fashion. Though her typical attire was wildly out of place among the elves, the dresses made of soft, jewel-toned fabrics that seemed to be so popular were nearly as comfortable as the fleece-lined leathers she often preferred.

She felt a twinge of guilt as she dressed for dinner the following evening when she caught herself admiring her reflection. She'd never been a vain person, but the last time she'd seen herself looking so *alive* had been the night of her wedding, which felt like eons ago. The face of the female staring back at her had taken on the glow of two days of walking the city streets and touring the palace gardens with the queen, and the vibrance of her hair appeared amplified. Even the gray of her eyes, a shade she only mildly cared for, seemed a bit brighter, dotted with hints of honey-brown.

She smiled when Aer came to stand behind her.

"You look lovely." He wrapped his arms around her waist and nipped at her ear. "Good enough to eat."

Sliding a hand over the one that rested on her stomach, she

leaned back, relaxing against his solid chest. "Having elves dress me each day seems to have its perks, doesn't it?"

"They *do* have good taste," he agreed. He rested his cheek against her hair and tightened his arms around her. "Do you think we'll get our answer tonight?"

Freya turned to face him, resting a hand on his chest. "I hope so. Lovely as this place is, I feel as though we're neglecting our people waiting around for Nalaea and Ruehnar to make their decision. This game they're playing... it's infuriating."

"So, we keep doing what we're doing. Ruehnar and I have been getting along well, and it seems Nalaea has taken quite a liking to you." He brushed a lock of hair from her forehead. "And thankfully, it seems they know we're sincere."

Freya frowned. "Yes, I got that impression from Nalaea. I only wish that was enough, though, so we can get on with it. Here we are, going to a feast, while our people are trying not to get killed or captured."

"Let's see how tonight goes. Perhaps, by the time dinner is done, our sincerity will have proven to be enough and we will be that much closer to taking back our lands."

She leaned up on her toes and kissed him. "Have I ever told you how much I adore your incessant optimism?"

"Yes, but feel free to tell me again." He gave her another kiss, then turned at a knock on the door and called for them to enter.

The door opened and Silmar walked in, followed by Florian. When Freya saw the expressions on their faces, her small moment of happiness evaporated.

"Your Majesties," Silmar said with a nod. "I have received word from your commander."

Freya took a step forward, eyes wide. "What? When?"

"The Jotnar forces your knights found traveling south are halfway to Watoria," he began. "According to Commander Balthana, they will be at Watoria in five days' time, at most."

Freya's mouth went dry.

"How long ago was this?" Aer asked. "And what are the Jotnar numbers?"

"I just returned from Lindoroth a few moments ago," Silmar replied. "Commander Balthana confirmed the Jotnar numbers are at approximately seven hundred. A small enough force for your army to handle, to be sure." He met their eyes, his point made perfectly clear. "I thought you both might want to know how your people are faring in your absence."

"Five days," Freya murmured, looking up at Aer. "We've got five days. Four, really."

Aer frowned. "Have the king and queen come any closer to making a decision?"

Silmar shook his head. "No, they have not. Perhaps tomorrow."

Freya gritted her teeth but forced her tongue to remain still. "Is everything else alright at home?"

"It is, Your Majesty. Commander Balthana wanted me to tell you both to do what needs to be done here and he will handle everything there." He angled his body toward the door. "For now, the feast is about to begin."

Freya wanted to snap at him that it was ludicrous to think about feasting when her country was under siege, but, as always, Aer's calming hand on her back settled her.

Patience, he seemed to say.

She huffed out a small breath through her nose, then nodded. "Alright. Nothing good was ever solved on an empty stomach, right?"

It was all she could do not to snarl when Florian simply gave her an indulgent smile in return.

Freya had expected a feast with the king, queen, some nobility, and possibly some other high-ranking citizens. What she found instead, when she entered the ballroom, seemed more reminiscent of the wild elvish revels she'd heard about in stories.

A raucousness permeated the room, mixing with the magic in the air, the intoxicating scent of food, and wild, carefree music. The combination had a smile tugging at her lips and a silly feeling swirling in her stomach, fully supplanting the stress she'd felt only moments before.

Shaking the fog from her mind, Freya rested her hand on Aer's arm as they entered the room.

The ballroom had been dressed in gossamer panels along the perimeter, and the veranda doors were flung wide to let in the warm evening air and the perfume of the flowers that lined the palace. Beyond, Freya could see the Aemir Sea, its rippling surface a fiery orange in the sunset; the sun itself no more than a slice of red on the horizon. The aroma of hot food, of spices and meats she'd never encountered that begged to be sampled, had her stomach rumbling.

"Be wary tonight, Your Majesties," Florian murmured from his place beside Freya. He eyed the crowded room with something akin to trepidation. "Two of the princes have arrived and will be joining us."

Silmar stepped forward and whispered to the herald who stood beside the door. The herald stepped forward and called for attention. Once the room settled, he cleared his throat.

"Please welcome the monarchs of Lindoroth, King Aerelius and Queen Freya of House Harridan!"

Freya rested her hand on Aer's arm and tilted her lips into a light smile. Then, keeping her chin high, they stepped into the room.

In Lindoroth, it was typical for guests to bow or curtsy when a monarch entered the room, even a foreign one. Here, they stared at Freya and Aer with unabashed curiosity painting their features. Glittering eyes looked them over appraisingly. Fangs glinted in the candlelight as a few guests whispered to one another. And, Freya noted, something intangible, like a bubble of anticipation, similar to what she'd felt in the market, seemed to be hovering over the crowd.

Refusing to be cowed by their ogling, Freya offered a few small smiles to the guests as Silmar led them toward where the king and queen sat with two other males at a long table set for six.

As Freya and Aer approached, Freya could see that the two

strangers were a striking mix of Nalaea and Ruehnar—both had Ruehnar's black hair, Nalaea's snow-pale skin, and faces that looked carved in stone. The biggest difference was their eyes. The one to Nalaea's right had piercing gold eyes, while the other, at Ruehnar's left, had eyes that were black as pitch. When the golden-eyed one beside Nalaea caught sight of them, his gaze skimmed over Aer and stopped on Freya, brewing with curiosity.

"Ah, Your Majesties!" Ruehnar smiled jovially and held up his cup in greeting. "Come, join us! Fenian, Tavian, move over, let them sit beside us. King Aerelius, Queen Freya, meet our sons, Princes Tavian and Fenian."

A few moments later, Freya found herself seated between Nalaea and Fenian Tordove, the eldest of the elf princes and heir to the Avorell throne. She tried not to feel disconcerted at the distance between herself and Aer, who had been placed between the king and Tavian. Even Florian, who sat at a table with Silmar and a few others, was nearly twenty feet away.

An arrangement that had been done intentionally, to be sure. But why?

Fenian flashed his teeth in what she assumed was a smile, although it was hard to tell. "Queen Freya, so lovely to meet you."

"You, as well, Prince Fenian," Freya replied. "Your kingdom is lovely."

"Fenian, please." He picked up a jug that sat between them on the table. "Wine?"

She slid her glass toward him and nodded. "Yes, thank you."

After he poured, he rested his elbow on the table and propped his chin on his fist, facing her, his eyes just as curious as they'd been when she'd first approached the table. "So, tell me about yourself, Queen Freya. It's been a dreadfully long time since outsiders have come to call. You are *quite* the curiosity, I must say."

Freya sipped her wine and held his gaze. "What would you like to know?"

He waved a long, pale hand toward Nalaea. "My dear mother seems quite intrigued by you. Something about being a 'half-blood'?"

"Yes." Freya set her goblet down. "We're rare among Lindorothians, but all it means is that I have the full power of both a witch and a shifter in my blood."

"That's it?" He sent a confused look at Nalaea, who smiled beside him. "That doesn't seem very interesting at all."

Freya pressed her lips into a smile to hide her amusement.

"Her grandmother was Selinda Cantor," Nalaea murmured, her eyes scanning the crowd. "And show a bit of patience, for the gods' sakes. You've only just met her."

Before Freya could ask how Nalaea knew her grandmother—or why Fenian should be showing patience—Fenian's eyes shifted back to her.

"Do you do tricks?" he asked.

It took all she had not to laugh outright. She couldn't tell if he was trying to bait her, or if he was simply being rude. "No, Your Highness. My skills tend toward the combative sort, rather than entertainment," she replied smoothly.

Full lips turned up in a wicked grin. "Perhaps I should challenge you to a duel, then." He cupped his palm, and Freya watched as shimmering golden flames danced along his fingertips, swirling around his hand. "Do you ever play with fire, Freya?"

Freya's shoulders stiffened, but not being one to back down from a challenge, she angled her head and met his grin with one of her own, then conjured up a ball of light, adding a boost of extra flame to the small orb that balanced on her own palm. "Name the time and place, Your Highness, and I would be happy to offer a demonstration of my skills."

He laughed bawdily and closed his flaming fist around hers, extinguishing her flames with his own. "Now *that* is something I would certainly care to partake in. What do you say, Mother?"

"I say it might pay to have a female step a boot on your chest for once," Nalaea said. She looked at Freya and gestured toward Fenian. "Fenian leads Avorell's army."

"I do a damn good job of it, if I do say so myself," Fenian said, looking back at Freya. "But back to stepping a boot on my chest... I think, before you leave for your homeland, Queen Freya, you and I shall have a duel." He leaned forward and lowered his voice to a whisper. "If you win, I will let you take my army back to Lindoroth with you."

She froze as his words sunk in.

No, she thought. *It can't possibly be that simple.*

Her heart began to thunder as she realized that all the waiting, the days of Nalaea and Ruehnar stringing them along, the talk of tests and needing to prove themselves worthy of the elvish army, may very well have been pointless.

Nalaea's comment about Fenian needing to show patience suddenly made sense. Freya and Aer didn't only need to prove themselves to Nalaea and Ruehnar—they needed to prove themselves to the prince in charge of Avorell's armies as well, and it was quite clear Fenian wasn't nearly convinced they were worth helping.

She tried to rein in her fury at the thought of traveling so far from her people to simply be *toyed* with—

Something tugged in her chest, bringing her up short. The familiar touch of Aer's magic, soothing and familiar, brushed against her. He could feel her distress, she realized. She clung to it, accepted the offered tether, and took a deep breath. She wanted desperately to catch his eye, signal to him that they needed to speak privately, but something in the back of her mind told her to *wait*.

Then, not daring to hope, Freya arched a brow at Prince Fenian. "Are you attempting to strike a bargain, Fenian?"

Fenian held up three fingers. "I will give you three days to convince me that you are worthy of our great elvish army. If within that time, you have given me cause to believe in *your* cause, I will travel with you and your king to Lindoroth with my army in tow."

"I assumed that was the reason Aerelius and I were invited in the first place," she said with a frown.

A smile played on Fenian's lips as he exchanged a look with his mother. "Quite true, Queen Freya. You *are* here to prove your worth. Now," he said, picking up the jug of wine and topping off his goblet, "tell me all about yourself. What does Freya Harridan enjoy doing when she is not wielding her combative magic or attempting to lure the reclusive elves into battle?"

She took a careful sip of wine, meeting his eyes over the rim of her glass. "Prior to becoming Queen, I was a marshal in my home city of Watoria. A type of law enforcement," she added when his face took on a look of confusion.

Dark eyebrows winged up. "A huntress, then?"

"Not quite, but I suppose you could say it's similar. My job was to find and dispose of the creatures who intended my city harm."

His eyes widened in what was very clearly a feigned show of surprise. "That is just *fascinating*. Isn't that fascinating, Mother?"

"Really, Fenian, is that all it takes to impress you?" Nalaea shook her head, then muttered something in rapid elvish under her breath. Whatever it was had Fenian's face hardening briefly before he slid his easy expression back into place.

"Now I'm curious," he said. "What in the *world* convinced your father to allow you to put yourself in harm's way like that? The future queen out fighting in the streets to sate her boredom strikes me as a bit irresponsible, wouldn't you agree?"

Freya picked up her goblet and leaned back so the servants who'd just approached could serve them. "I can see why you might think that, but I can assure you that wasn't my, nor my father's, purpose. Working with the marshals and being involved in the inner workings of my city allowed me to know and understand my people in ways that many monarchs can't. I also believe, if I am going to ask my people to fight for me, I should demonstrate that I am also willing to fight for them, and not just with orders given from my throne."

"Is that why you've come here? To fight?" he asked.

"I will do what it takes to ensure the safety of my people. If that means a duel with an elvish prince, so be it."

Fenian's eyes turned challenging. "Even if that duel is to the death?"

Her heart gave a heavy thump as she took in his meaning, but she didn't let it deter her. "As I said, Your Highness, I will do what it takes."

Something like triumph filled his eyes, and the smile he gave her told her whatever she'd just said was either very, very wrong or exactly what he wanted to hear.

"Mother," he said, not taking his eyes from Freya's, "I think it's time for that announcement, don't you?"

Nalaea looked between the two of them, then nodded. "Yes, I think that would be wise. Ruehnar? Do you agree?"

"Hmm?" The king paused his conversation with Aer and leaned toward them. "What would be wise?"

"Fenian has come to a decision," Nalaea told him.

Freya gripped her goblet tighter and prayed they couldn't see how badly her hands were starting to shake. Frantically, she ran over her conversation with Fenian, attempting to dissect every word they'd spoken for hidden meaning. He'd challenged her to a duel, she had accepted. It seemed so simple, yet she could tell by the way he was staring at her, as though he was about to jump out of his skin with excitement, that something she'd said had just sealed her fate... whatever that may be.

Nalaea stood, and the music that had been playing ceased. When the party-goers quieted, she gave them a smooth smile.

"I would like to thank all of you for attending the feast in honor of our visitors, King Aerelius and Queen Freya of Lindoroth," she said. "It is not lightly or often that we take in visitors from foreign lands, but we have made an exception in their case due to the... uniqueness of their circumstances."

Freya gave a nod of thanks when Nalaea met her eyes. "It is our honor to have been offered such a privilege, Your Majesty, truly."

Turning back to the room, Nalaea continued. "There is a custom in our lands that has not been seen for some time." She smiled conspiratorially at the crowd as laughter floated across the room. "Well, not since I became queen, that is."

Freya smiled, though she didn't get the joke, and when she looked at Aer, she saw he looked just as bemused as she did.

"The Wild Hunt is something we hold close to our hearts here in Avorell, as you all know," Nalaea continued, "a time-honored tradition that offers a reprieve to prisoners who have toiled long for their crimes. Although the target is usually a female vying for the elvish crown, we've been given an opportunity to offer that reprieve far sooner than expected." She slid a glance toward Freya, then looked back at her guests. "This time, the target will be the Lindorothian queen."

It took a moment for Nalaea's words to register in Freya's mind.

The Wild Hunt had been a child's tale, told to keep young girls from sneaking out of their beds at night. It spoke of vicious monsters that chased poor souls who found themselves in the wrong place at the wrong time.

Fenian chuckled at whatever expression had taken over her face. Frantically, she looked at Aer, but just as she might've shouted her objection, she felt the full force of someone's magic hit her square in the chest. It was familiar, something she hadn't felt with such strength since her wedding night but had become like a second skin in recent weeks.

Instead of shouting, Florian's magic forced her to smile.

Instead of saying she most certainly would *not* be made a spectacle of, she said, "I only hope I can prove myself as worthy of Avorell's respect as you did, Your Majesty."

Nalaea's smile grew wicked. "Good, Queen Freya. That is so *very* good to hear."

33

FREYA

Freya was nearly out of her skin by the time dinner ended several hours later. She'd been forced to sit at the table and smile and nod as elves with scheming eyes watched each bite she took and listened to each word she said. Whatever Florian had done to her and Aer had forced her into a state of semi-compliance that, despite how much it angered her, had likely saved her life.

Silmar escorted them back to their rooms after they'd bid farewell to Nalaea, Ruehnar, and the princes. The moment the door shut behind him, Florian dropped his magic.

Instantly, Aer had slammed the warlock against the wall, his hand around his throat in a vise-grip.

"You knew," Aer spat. "You knew *exactly* what they would have her do!"

Florian's eyes darted to Freya, who stood, still stunned, behind Aer.

She drew in a soft breath through her nose, then let it out slowly. "Why use your magic on us?" she asked.

Florian shifted slightly under Aer's grip, but wisely, didn't fight him.

Aer's voice was a deadly calm when he spoke. "Answer the question."

"Now is not the time to fight," Florian said quietly. "You were both poised to do just that."

Aer kept his hand around Florian's throat for another moment before releasing him.

"How are we to trust you if you keep things like this from us?" Freya asked. "You're our spymaster—"

"Which is how I knew what they were planning," Florian interrupted. "They have chosen one of the hardest tasks imaginable for you to complete. Your reactions, reasonable as they may have been, would have demonstrated weakness to them."

"How?" Freya demanded. "How would a desire to preserve my own life demonstrate weakness? And why not tell us ahead of time?"

"Another test," Florian said patiently. "Nalaea and Ruehnar knew they would take you by surprise, and they would've known the moment you entered that ballroom if you'd already figured out their plans. Allowing you to show your shock, then rein it in, was the first step in showing your willingness to complete the Hunt. You said you would do anything. Your reaction needed to back up your words."

Freya's lip curled in annoyance. "I can't decide if that's perfectly reasonable or a rotten excuse, so for now, I'll give you the benefit of the doubt."

Aer frowned. "Nalaea—she said they haven't had a hunt since she became queen. What did she mean by that? And why won't I be able to go with her?"

"It's how the elves choose their queens," Florian explained. "A king chooses a female he wants to marry, but in order to become queen, she must earn her crown through blood. Nalaea ran the Hunt nearly five hundred years ago and won quite handily, despite the number of hunters that sought her life. As for why you won't be able to accompany her... this is a challenge for the female of a pair to complete. I can assure you, if you attempt to push that custom, we will not get what we came here for."

Aer dragged a hand through his hair and paced away, then turned back. "So now they just expect Freya to adhere to the same barbaric—"

Florian held a finger to his lips, silencing Aer. "Yes, Your Majesty, they do."

"Hold on." Freya held up a hand. "I'm going to assume the reason they use the Hunt to choose their queens is because it demonstrates strength and cunning, correct?"

"Yes," Florian said. "If a female can survive the Hunt, she has proven herself to Avorell and its people. Betrothals like yours exist, but more often, the male heir will choose a female, either based on breeding or attraction. In either case, the female still must prove herself. For lower positions—nobility and the like—the task is not so great. But to hold power over the land, one must demonstrate they are deserving of it."

Frowning, Freya nodded, then tapped a finger to her chin as she began to pace back and forth. "Perhaps this won't be so bad, then. Byrric raised me to be a fighter, even a huntress, as Prince Fenian suggested."

Florian shook his head. "Byrric prepared you for a great deal, but this is not something he ever could have readied you for."

"Who will be hunting her?" Aer asked. "Fenian suggested a duel, but I can't imagine Nalaea and Ruehnar would make him the hunter."

"No, certainly not." Florian ran a hand over his face and huffed out a breath. "There is a rule in the Avorellian judicial system, a loophole, if you will, that will allow certain prisoners to gain their freedom prior to serving out their sentences."

"Prisoners?" Freya arched a brow. "Prisoners will be hunting me?"

"Prisoners who have been locked away for centuries," Florian corrected. "Murderers, war criminals. Any vile criminal you can imagine—that is who will be hunting you. In many cases, they are serving lifelong sentences, so this will be their only chance at freedom."

"Killing me, you mean." Freya folded her arms. "Bringing my head to the king and queen will be *their* way of proving themselves."

"How many?" Aer asked. The blood had drained from his face.

"I cannot say," Florian said. "The final number will be up to Nalaea."

"Why not Ruehnar? Or both?" Freya asked.

"Nalaea has done this before," Florian explained. "It is out of respect for that experience that she determines the number."

Aer cleared his throat. "Alright. How many did Nalaea have to face?"

"Twenty-two."

Freya's eyes widened as they met Aer's, and she looked at Florian in shock. "And she killed them all?"

Florian nodded. "Over the course of two days, yes."

"No wonder Fenian was so interested in my past," Freya murmured after a moment. "Here I thought he was going to make it easy."

"A duel with an elf prince would hardly be easy, Your Majesty," Florian said.

"I just meant—" Freya huffed. "Never mind. This hunt will start the morning after next?" *Three days before the Jotnar reach Watoria.* "That's cutting things a bit close, don't you think?"

Florian nodded.

Freya looked at Aer, who looked coiled to spring, and gave him a tight smile. "Then I suppose we should prepare. Florian, tell us everything you know."

For the next few hours, Florian divulged all he knew of the Wild Hunt and the elvish customs that went along with it. Not only would the prisoners hunting Freya be desperate for their only chance at freedom, they were also very old, many having been locked away in Avorell's prison system for hundreds of years. A release, even a brief one to participate in the Hunt, meant unbinding their magic and giving them unfettered access to it for the first time in centuries. Freya would have access to her own magic, of course, along with her venomous feathers, but Florian couldn't say what other weapons she'd be allowed to use, if any.

The more they talked, the more fearful she became, and not just for herself. She had no qualms about fighting to the death—she'd done it multiple times while working for the marshals, although those creatures were all generally in the midst of committing a crime, not attempting to gain their freedom after conviction. But she feared for Aer, who she'd nearly made a widower less than a week prior during her fight with Traust and who would now have to watch her go off into the wild to fight for her life, yet again. She feared for her father, who had shown more fear in those moments after she returned from that fight than she'd ever seen in him. And fear for the people she hadn't even had a chance to begin to lead.

She knew, without a doubt, that Lindoroth could very-well find itself short a queen by the time this was over.

Freya tried very hard not to imagine that outcome.

After she closed the door behind Florian, she leaned forward and let her forehead come to rest on the smooth wood, her emotions a tumult inside her. In a way, she felt better because she had facts to work with. At the same time, she felt worse because she knew just how dire this situation had become.

Aer came up behind her and put his hands on her waist, turning her to face him. He put his finger on her chin and tilted her face up.

"You alright, Valkyrie?"

She stared into his brown eyes and smiled. "I'm fine."

Seeing the lie, he pulled her in, enveloping her in his arms, and kissed her temple. "We can leave," he said. "Find another way, defend Lindoroth with our own armies."

But he hadn't even finished his thought before Freya was shaking her head. She knew he would do it, but he wouldn't want to. He knew as well as she did that this was their only chance, and she also knew he believed in her and her ability to complete such a task.

"You wouldn't leave this opportunity behind any quicker than I would," she said. "We need this to work, Aer. We might be able to get through it with our own armies, but it's unlikely, not when troops that Lessia has apparently held in reserve are marching into Lindoroth as we speak." She swallowed hard and looked away as she bit back the words she wanted to say.

I wish my father was here. He would know what to do.

"I can do this," she whispered, meeting his eyes. "I may not want to, but I can."

Aer smiled softly. "Are you trying to convince yourself or me?"

"Both, I suppose." She frowned. "What kind of weapons do you suppose they'll give me?"

"I don't know. I wouldn't be surprised if Nalaea came to speak with you tomorrow, though. She enjoyed springing this on you tonight, but even she must see sending you into a hunting ground where your opponents have an unfair advantage would lead to a quick and easy completion. None of them will want that."

"Yes, I'm sure the spectacle of my death is one the elves would like to see dragged out as long as possible," she said wryly.

Aer brought his hands up to frame her face, his own expression solemn. "You are not going to die, Freya. I won't allow it."

She couldn't help but laugh. "Once again, I adore your unrelenting optimism. And thank you. I think most husbands would demand to go in their wife's place—"

Now it was his turn to laugh. "You would castrate me if I so much as suggested it, which would be quite unfortunate for both of us."

Relief settled over her at his words as he, once again, reaffirmed how well-suited they were for each other.

She gripped the lapels of his vest and met his eyes. "I plan to love you for centuries to come, Aerelius Harridan, not to mention give you a few children along the way." She released his vest and splayed her hands on his chest. "We can do this."

Aer slid his hands over hers and closed his eyes. When he opened them, Freya felt her own soul staring back at her. The things that flowed between them—love, respect, even reverence—were unencumbered by doubts, and when he looked at her, she saw just how deep his belief in her went.

"I know, Freya." He wrapped his arms around her and pulled her close. "I know."

～

Silmar arrived the following morning after breakfast to tell Freya, Aer, and Florian that the king and queen requested their presence in the library to discuss the terms of the hunt. When they arrived in the cavernous room, they found Nalaea and Ruehnar seated at a long, rectangular table. On it was a large map and a stack of books.

"Ah, there you are," Nalaea said, her dark eyes honing in on Freya. "Good of you to join us."

"We thought it only fair that we prepare you a bit for the trials you will be facing tomorrow," Ruehnar said. "Please, sit."

Freya and Aer did as instructed, taking seats across the table from the king and queen.

"I must say, Queen Freya, you held your own with Fenian well," Ruehnar told them. "And King Aerelius, based on your conversation with him, Tavian believes you have what it takes to... *allow* your wife to partake in the Hunt."

Freya looked at Aer in confusion. "What is he talking about?"

Aer sighed and closed his eyes, then looked at her. "Prince Tavian... he asked a lot of questions about you, our betrothal, our history together." He turned accusing eyes on Ruehnar. "I assumed he was simply making conversation."

"Assumptions are a grave mistake to make in this land," Nalaea warned. "Had you not spoken to my son so highly of your wife's abilities, Ruehnar and I might not have such faith in her chances at survival." She looked at each of them in turn. "As it turns out, we believe she is more than capable."

"If you had no intention of helping us—"

"On the contrary, King Aerelius," Ruehnar said, cutting Aer off. "We would like, very much, to help you defeat Lessia and Willem. But words alone are insufficient." He gestured toward his wife. "Nalaea had to complete the same task we are asking of your wife, and she succeeded quite well."

"I mean no disrespect, but I am not vying to be queen of Avorell," Freya said.

"But you are a queen, nonetheless, and therefore must prove yourself worthy of this land."

"As our country is currently under the control of usurpers, one might argue Freya is not, in fact, Queen," Florian said.

Freya shot him an incredulous look.

"Her claim to Lindoroth is through blood, not force," Nalaea replied. "That is what matters."

"And if Lessia or Willem had attempted to sway you?" Aer asked.

Ruehnar smirked.

"They already have," Freya murmured. "Haven't they?"

"What was your answer?" Aer asked.

"We have yet to give one," Ruehnar said. "Our other son, Ettrian, is currently in Iladel—"

Freya sat up in her seat. "What?" She looked at Aer, fearful. "Lea—"

"Your little friend is perfectly safe," Nalaea said. "Ettrian is keeping quite the close eye on her." She sighed and looked down at her long fingernails. "Some things are out of his control, unfortunately."

"What 'things'?" Aer asked.

Ruehnar chuckled. "Lessia seems to have some misconceptions when it comes to how certain aspects of Lindorothian traditions work. The mating bond, for instance. For some reason, she seems to think a match between your friend and one of the Jotnar will make their quelling of the southern regions a bit easier."

Aer seethed beside Freya as he gripped the edges of the table. "The gods would never grant such a thing," he said carefully.

Freya rested a hand on Aer's arm, then slid a hand over his, loosening his grip on the tabletop.

"He's right," Florian said, frowning. "If Lessia and Willem insisted on mating Lady Calliwell and Lord Edrin, it would have to be consensual, at the very least, in order for the gods to even consider granting it."

"Indeed," Nalaea agreed.

When she didn't elaborate, Freya gritted her teeth. "Has Lea agreed to the mating bond?"

"She has," Ruehnar said. "According to what Ettrian has gathered, she believes it is the best way to help her people. It would be quite a simple thing for an elf to break it, however, should she ask."

Silence hung over them as they realized just how much more was at stake than they realized.

"So, not only are you forcing my wife to take part in your Hunt, you're also withholding the one thing that will free my cousin from being forced to live with a bond she wants no part of?" Aer asked.

"What you ask comes with a price," Ruehnar said simply. "No one is forcing anyone to do anything."

"And what will my price be?" Aer asked. "You've got my wife and my cousin's lives in your hands. What about me?"

"Your test," Nalaea said, "will be to sit at my side while your wife is thrown into a playing field with a horde of creatures who want her dead. You will not be allowed to help, you will not be allowed to offer any form of assistance whatsoever. Your magic will be bound, if need be, but I do not see it coming to that."

"Why not throw me into the field with her so we can show our strength as partners?"

"Your strength as a partnership lies in more than just an ability to fight side-by-side," Ruehnar said. "It lies in your ability to trust one another to do what needs to be done as individuals."

"Do you not trust your wife?" the elf queen asked before Aer could respond.

"Of course I do," Aer snapped.

"Do you question her strength of character?"

"Not in the least."

"Do you question her ability to defend herself, wield a weapon, wield her own magic?"

"No!"

Nalaea smiled again. "Then I do not see a problem."

Aer sat, silently fuming as he stared at the queen. His fury pulsed off of him, mixing with frustration and an overall feeling of helplessness that Freya desperately needed to settle.

"It's alright," she said quietly, squeezing his hand. "We said we would do whatever it takes to save Lindoroth and that's what I intend to do."

"I assume a written agreement will be made?" Florian asked. "I won't allow my monarchs to go through this without your swear of allegiance."

Nalaea gave Florian a curious look. "I believe you know us better than that, Andreus. We would never make a bargain such as this without binding it."

"In writing," Florian said firmly. "And blood."

Freya looked at him and was surprised at the amount of suspicion she found in his dark eyes. She thought back over all Nalaea and Ruehnar had said, analyzing each word, but found nothing that could be twisted into a falsehood. Regardless, Florian seemed to know the ways of the elves better than she, so following his lead seemed the most prudent.

Ruehnar's lips twitched. "Of course. We will happily swear our oath of allegiance to King Aerelius and Queen Freya in blood."

Florian shifted his gaze to Nalaea expectantly.

"We will swear that oath in blood and writing," she said after a moment.

"And honor it?"

Ruehnar gritted his teeth, whether in insult or irritation, Freya wasn't sure.

"We will *swear and honor* an oath of allegiance to King Aerelius and Queen Freya. Does that satisfy you, Andreus?"

Florian inclined his head to Nalaea. "Once I hear her say it, as well."

Nalaea rolled her eyes in a very un-queenly way, repeated the words, then looked at Freya and Aer. "We will make our bargain tomorrow before the Hunt begins. Until then, shall we discuss what it is you will be facing?"

"I've given them a general idea of how the Hunt typically works," Florian said.

"Good, good," Ruehnar said, nodding slowly. "There will be a few... alterations this time, however."

"What kind of 'alterations'?" Freya asked.

Nalaea smiled. "When I partook in the Hunt, nearly seven hundred years ago, I faced twenty-two of Avorell's most hardened criminals, most from the Winter and Autumn Courts. The playing field was on the moors and was quite lovely, from what I recall."

"What will be different this time?" Freya asked.

"Out of fairness and due to your lack of preparation, we've decided you will not face as many as I did," Nalaea said. "I had nearly two years to prepare for such a feat, and while I find your skills compelling, I do not believe they lend themselves to a task such as what I was handed."

Freya gritted her teeth. "How many?"

"Ruehnar and I thought ten prisoners would suffice, seeing as you want to take our army across the world."

Freya rubbed a hand across her brow and sighed. "Alright. What else? Is it safe to assume I won't have the benefit of wide, open moors as the hunting grounds?"

"Indeed, you will not," Ruehnar replied. "Your trial will take place in the Forest of Ages. I believe you came through it on your travels here?"

Freya gave a sharp nod.

"The forest is a tricky beast, to be sure, but we felt it would better serve our purposes," Nalaea said.

"Then I won't dare question your judgement," Freya replied with a smile.

"Good," Ruehnar said, rising from the table. "Now, take the rest of the night to prepare. We will meet in the morning to formalize our bargain."

Seeing the clear dismissal, Freya, Aer, and Florian stood and left.

34

FREYA

The three of them spent the night poring over the map of the Forest of Ages Nalaea and Ruehnar had provided. It was only mildly helpful, as it was such a heavily wooded area it would likely be difficult to find landmarks, and much of it was only labeled with scrawled images that, despite his knowledge of the elvish language, were indecipherable to Florian. Freya trusted her sense of direction, though, so she did all she could to commit the map to memory.

The books were a bit more helpful. Most of what they contained were stories of past Hunts and the females who succeeded and failed during their trials. Freya focused largely on the latter, wanting to understand where others had gone wrong, but she also spent a good deal of time reading up on what those who were successful, like Nalaea, had done to succeed.

"They all have elvish magic," Freya said with a sigh, feeling defeated, and slumped back in her seat. "That's the common thread between them all. In a forest like the one of Ages, elvish magic is far more likely to protect a person than any I possess."

"Don't get discouraged by that, Your Majesty," Florian said. "You have skills that go far beyond just magic. Those are where your success will lie."

"He's right," Aer said quietly. "Your magic is almost always your secondary defense. Your mind and physical abilities will serve you far better."

"I don't know that I can think my way out of this one, Highness." She took his hand and kissed it. "I promise to do my best, though."

"My suggestion would be to pull a few feathers before the Hunt begins," Florian said. "I don't know how effective your venom will be against those hunting you, but it's best to be prepared. The forest will have close-quarters, which will make it hard to let out your wings at times. Fly if you must, but only if you have no other option."

Freya shook her head. "I don't understand. Nalaea seemed so interested in my wings. Why put me in a place that would make them so hard to use?"

"Likely to see how industrious you can be without them," Florian replied. "You should not forget that the bargain you will make tomorrow goes both ways. You may be calling on them now, but if this alliance holds, they may call on Lindoroth in the future. So, seeing a Valkyrie queen fly is one thing—seeing what she can do when her wings are clipped is another thing entirely."

Freya shuddered at the thought of such a hindrance.

Florian picked up the goblet of wine he'd poured himself and downed the contents, then stood. "I think I've done all I can here, so I'll leave you both to finish up." He slid the notes he'd taken toward Freya. "Go over these again and I'll have a few supplies prepared for you in the morning."

"Thank you." Aer stood to see him out. "As always, your help is appreciated."

He walked Florian to the door, then hesitated a moment after it closed, his hand flat against the wood, his back to Freya. She waited as patiently as she could, but it was a struggle not to go to him.

After a moment, he collected himself and walked to her.

He held her eyes and took a deep breath. "I think we should go back to Lindoroth."

"Aer…"

"We'll find another way, Freya."

She tried to ignore the way his voice nearly broke.

"There *is* no other way, Aer, and you know it. We don't have the numbers to defeat both Jotunheim and Dystone, regardless of how much magic we can muster. With the elvish army, we could potentially overwhelm them within a week, if not sooner." She laid a hand on his chest. "But we can't do this without additional forces."

"I can't lose you, Freya." He took her face in his hands. "I *cannot* lose you. Not after—" He closed his eyes and exhaled. "We've already lost so much."

Freya placed her hands over his and smiled, then tried hard to keep the sympathy from her voice. "I don't want to do this any more than you want me to. But we're losing this war. I have to try."

He shook his head. "No. No, there has to be another way."

"There isn't," she whispered. "You have to have faith that I'll get through this. That *we'll* get through this."

His eyes glistened as he stared down at her, twin knives that drove through her chest. The pain he'd been carrying these last few weeks, from the loss of his father and up until this moment, simmered there as each hurt he'd been dealt was on display. A lump rose in her throat, and she was overcome with the desire to soothe him.

He'd lost his father. He didn't know if he'd ever see his mother again. And now, here was his wife, preparing to walk away from him into one of the deadliest situations she'd ever face.

Gently, she leaned up on her toes and touched her lips to his. She waited, and a moment later, he reciprocated. He brushed his thumbs along her jaw, then ran his fingers through her hair as his mouth slowly moved over hers. Within seconds, his kiss was filled with an urgency that had Freya's heart quickening. Love poured from him and into her—a love tinged with fear for what tomorrow might bring.

She answered his kisses in kind, desperate to forget what she was about to face, what she—and he—could be about to lose. She believed in herself and knew, whatever the king and queen threw at her, she would stand against it.

But now, just for a moment, she let the weakness that lurked beneath that strength surface. Now, after he lay her on the bed and stripped her bare in every way, she let her husband, her mate, take his time memorizing every inch of her, revisiting places and feelings they hadn't taken the time to since their wedding night. Her instinct told her to rush so they could enjoy each other over and over, but she quieted that voice inside and gave herself over to him fully.

As they moved together, she drew strength from him, letting her own magic curl its fists around his as it washed over and through her. She gripped it tight, held it close to her heart, and knew, without question, she would take that piece of him with her into the forest the next day.

~

AFTER A LARGE BREAKFAST, Freya, Aer, and Florian met Nalaea, Ruehnar, and Fenian in the meeting room to draw up the agreements between their kingdoms.

The meeting room was an open, airy space surrounded by silencing spells that kept spoken words concealed while allowing the warm breeze to flow through. It was a far cry from the closed, marble rooms of Freya's own palace, and preferable, considering the sweltering temperatures outside.

Just thinking about the gleaming stone and echoing halls of her home had her heart twisting and her resolve strengthening.

"Ah, Your Majesties, come right in," Ruehnar said, gesturing toward the table in the center of the room. It was wide and oblong, carved of wood that was a deep red set with blue floral designs. A thick, leather-bound tome lay on the surface in front of him. Nalaea sat at his side, Fenian on the other.

Aer, Freya, and Florian took seats across from them.

"We'll write and sign our agreement in here," Ruehnar said, laying a dark hand on top. "It is our book of bargains, containing every deal we have ever made."

Arching a brow, Freya eyed the book's size. It was easily four inches thick.

"Only you, or all elves?" Aer asked.

Ruehnar chuckled. "Each monarch gets their own. Fortunately, your bargain is a simple one."

It took all Freya had not to scoff at that.

Ruehnar opened the book and flipped toward the back, spreading the book flat on the table once he'd reached a fresh page.

"Now," Fenian began, "we will go over the terms of our agreement in great detail, so this may take some time."

Indeed, it did. It took nearly an hour to close each loophole Nalaea, Ruehnar, and Fenian attempted to work into their terms, replacing vague language with painfully specific phrases, but once the four monarchs' names were signed in ink and blood, and Fenian and Florian had signed as witnesses, Freya felt a bit of a weight lift from her shoulders.

"I will take you to the weapons stores," Nalaea said. "You may choose one elvish weapon to bring with you into the forest. Your magic and venom are also permitted."

"You are also permitted to use anything the forest offers during this task," Fenian added. "A sharpened stick, a blunt rock..." He smirked. "You understand."

Freya swallowed. "Yes, I understand." Then, considering their words, she looked at them both. "I am allowed to wield all skills I have to offer as well, correct?"

Fenian chuckled. "Smart girl. Yes, Freya, anything you have access to in that forest is yours, including your own combat skills."

"The king and queen have allowed me to provide you with this," Florian said, handing Freya a pouch. "A few antidotes to poisons commonly found in the wild here and a salve, should you get injured."

Freya gave him a tight smile and took the pouch, then clipped it to her belt. "Thank you."

Nalaea looked at her, then Aer. "We will give you a few moments to say your goodbyes."

"Best of luck, Queen Freya," Fenian said. "I am eager to see what you can do."

You're doing this for your people, Freya reminded herself. *You're doing this for the future of Lindoroth.*

Freya repeated the words over and over as she turned to look at her husband, whose face was the picture of stoicism, slipping toward devastation the moment the room had been emptied of all but them.

He took her hands and rested his forehead against hers, and she closed her eyes, breathing him in, memorizing his scent.

"I love you," he whispered. "I'll be waiting with elvish wine and an army when you return."

Freya tightened her hands around his and ran her thumb over his ring. "There's no better gift I could ask for." She lifted her chin as he shifted to kiss her. It was a painful kiss, brutally so, and one she knew would not be their last.

She would come back to him. To do otherwise simply wasn't an option.

He hooked his thumb in the waistband of the leather pants Lyrei had brought her that morning and smiled against her lips. "Try not to ruin these. They look far better on you than anything the Allanorians could create."

She laughed, and the fist around her heart loosened a bit. "I'll keep that in mind."

"Queen Freya?" Florian called from the door. "It's time."

She loosed a breath, surprised and quite pleased at how steady it was.

Aer kissed her one last time. "I love you."

Freya framed his face with her hands and looked straight into his eyes. "I love you, too. I'll be back soon."

NALAEA WAS WAITING outside when Freya emerged into the courtyard from the meeting room. Her dark eyes ran over Freya's face, taking in her expression.

"Did your goodbyes go alright?" she asked.

Freya nodded, but cared little for making small talk with her. Maybe someday, when this was all over, a friendship could be fostered, but for now, all she felt toward the queen was indifference at best. "Yes. Where is the weapons room?"

Nalaea inclined her head toward the other side of the courtyard, where a set of steps descended into darkness. "Just over here. I think you will find it quite impressive."

Freya followed her across the sunny yard, then down the stairs into a cool, dry underground chamber lit by torchlight. When they reached the bottom of the stairs, Nalaea pulled out a key and unlocked a heavy wooden door, then stepped aside, gesturing for Freya to enter.

"Choose only one, and choose wisely," she said.

With a nod, Freya began scanning the room, taking in the various knives, swords, bows, arrows, and vials of odd, milky liquids that she knew better than to ask about.

After examining the stores, she settled on a cutlass. It was lightweight, easy to wield, not as cumbersome as a longsword or as limited as a dagger. She tested its weight, swinging it a few times to get the feel of it. The blade was sharpened to a paper-thin edge, and the grip was solid enough that she'd be able to use the pommel as a weapon, as well.

"Are you ready?" Nalaea asked from the doorway.

"Yes, I think so."

"Alright, then. Let us be on our way."

The queen held out a hand. Freya took it, and without warning, she was sucked into the frigid rush of the Between.

A moment later, she felt the damp warmth of the forest on her skin. She pressed her lips together to keep her nausea from becoming visible on her face and forced herself to focus on her surroundings.

"It's peaceful, isn't it?" Nalaea smiled softly. Her white hair and pale skin nearly glowed in the dim light. "I used to play here as a girl."

"It's unlike any forest I've ever seen, certainly," Freya said honestly. "It feels so... alive, yet..."

"Yet filled with death," Nalaea said with a nod. "A heavy feeling. Magic mixed with the memory of what came before."

Curious, Freya looked at the queen. "Do you know what took place here? What led to the forest's creation? Silmar said something about the magic here becoming... protective?"

Smiling, Nalaea faced her, then patted her cheek. "A very long story for another day, Freya. Give me your hand, please."

Obeying, Freya held out her palm. With a quick flick of one razor-sharp nail, Nalaea scored Freya's palm.

Freya hissed and jerked her hand back. The cut healed almost instantly, but the blood remained on her palm.

Nalaea inclined her head toward the forest. "You have one day to complete your task. You will emerge from the forest two miles due east of here. Succeed, and we will leave for Lindoroth the following morning."

"Why not immediately?" Freya asked as she shook the blood from her hand. She looked at Nalaea. "Why can't we leave right away?"

"Trust me when I say you will need your rest."

"Rest? Nalaea—"

But the queen had vanished, leaving Freya alone in the quiet, magical forest.

"Well then," Freya muttered. With a sigh, she wrapped her hand around the solid grip of her sword and slid the blade from its scabbard. Though it was larger than what she normally carried, as she looked around at the gnarled brush that carpeted the forest floor, she knew she'd been wise to choose it.

Her head whipped to the right when she heard something coming through the forest toward her. Whatever it was sounded big, bigger than any elf she'd seen since arriving in Avorell.

Then, her heart sinking, she let out a quiet groan.

Creatures.

Nalaea and Florian had both referred to the things hunting her as 'creatures,' not just 'elves.' She hadn't caught it at the time, but based on the sounds coming toward her, something told her she wouldn't just be facing a handful of Avorell's most vicious elf criminals.

When the scaled beast emerged from the trees, clearly having been drawn by the scent of her blood, she realized just how stupid she'd been to make that assumption. Its shoulders were hunched, and teeth the size of short swords protruded from its mouth, coated with green muck. Huge nostrils flared as it turned its massive head this way and that, seeking out its prey.

When it caught sight of her, it roared, spraying spittle and whatever the green substance on its teeth was.

She had a heartbeat to decide whether to fight or run.

You can do this.

Taking a deep breath, she tightened her grip on her sword, and charged.

35

LEA

After letting her discussion with Ettrian simmer in her mind for the rest of the day and stewing over Freya and Aer's predicament, Lea finally managed to convince herself to venture into the tunnels and test out Jonas' theory about her ability to navigate them using her connection to the earth. She hadn't dared attempt it before, knowing what she did of Willem snooping about, but now that she had been granted a bit more freedom, had the protection of her status as Jonas' wife, and seemingly had the ability to slip about unseen, she felt more confident in seeking out a solid means of escape.

After her conversation with Lessia, she was no longer afraid to wield her magic, should the human king attempt to confront her again. If it came down to it, she wouldn't hold back in protecting herself.

So, the following morning, and the next, after Jonas left to do whatever it was he did, she put on her darkest dress with a black wool cloak and slipped into the chilly tunnel that opened beside the fireplace. She didn't go far, only deep enough to expand her mental map of the tunnels. They wound through the walls and foundation of the ancient palace, and under the grounds outside, going quite a bit further into the mountain than she first thought. The more she explored with her magic, the more she could feel, and the sheer breadth of their reach was mind-boggling.

Over the course of two days she found more than a dozen passageways, although it would take her far longer to commit an extensive map to memory. Finding one tunnel, she would find three more, and she could only guess the months, if not years, it would take to properly map them out.

It was a start, though, which was more than she could've asked for.

She didn't tell Jonas.

She told herself it was for the best—the fewer people who knew she was exploring, the better. Currently that number was relegated to just one—her. She hadn't even brought it up with Tyna, although she suspected the pixie knew exactly what she was up to. It was hard not to feel a twinge of guilt over keeping her trips from Tyna and Jonas, but she'd come to realize in recent weeks that the only person she could really trust was herself.

So, she kept her secrets. When she overheard conversations, usually about the more mundane aspects of a takeover, treatment of prisoners, idle chatter of attacks spoken in the kitchens among guards, and the talk of the movement of troops in the training yards, she committed all she heard to memory. She didn't dare write it down but kept it all to herself until Tyna told her she was able to contact Rini. Then, and only then, would she tell her all she'd heard.

One of the biggest surprises she found when she finally ventured further in the tunnels was the lingering magic left behind by her aunt. She could only assume Freya and Aer hadn't noticed just how much the tunnels were doused in Ordona's earth magic, but Lea could feel it permeating the walls and floors, maintaining the integrity of the stone, keeping it from crumbling under the weight of a five-thousand-year-old palace. She could feel the echoes of the magic of earth witches who'd come before Ordona who'd done the same, and she realized there'd likely never been a king who allowed anyone into the tunnels to perform basic maintenance or inspect for damage aside from an earth witch who was connected to his family.

It was highly unlikely Lessia and Willem were being entirely forthright with Jonas—unless they stupidly thought he was too strong to succumb to the pull of a bond that would tie his allegiance to Lea—so she sought out more specific means of eavesdropping, hoping she could glean a bit more information than the things she heard by chance in the tunnels. While valuable, she knew those scraps were just the tip of the iceberg.

Which, Lea knew the moment the thought formed, was absolutely the case. It was the only reason they hadn't questioned Jonas' loyalty to Jotunheim yet assumed hers to Lindoroth had all but evaporated.

That arrogance was a weakness, one that could be exploited if circumstances allowed. So, Lea took each scrap she could get and tucked it away.

It was on her third day exploring the tunnels near Jonas' chambers that she sensed another person in there with her. She'd ventured down half a dozen tunnels that branched off the one that dead-ended at his room and had just turned down one that seemed a bit cooler than the rest, when she felt a disturbance touch the magic that she'd woven ahead of her.

Her magic rippled, as though Ordona and the witches before her had ensured magic-wielders would be just as adept as shifters to sense others nearby.

Despite that, her ability to sense others from far off was still somewhat limited, so she nearly missed her chance to slip into a small side tunnel to conceal her presence.

She drew in a breath at the scent, trying to channel her magic in a way that would allow her to separate the smell and feel of the earth from the living being moving in her direction.

Human.

Her heart stuttered when she smelled a second, unmistakably earthy scent of an elf.

She froze, not knowing whether to run for her life or stay put and hope that Ettrian's seeming-desire to keep her from death would continue once he caught her scent.

Making the choice to stay where she was, she prayed they didn't choose this tunnel to walk down. She closed her eyes and strained her ears to hear as much of their conversation as possible.

"...Lessia doesn't know," Willem was saying. "...could change the outcome of this war."

Ettrian chuckled quietly. "You put a lot of faith in a person you don't really know, wouldn't you say?"

"Considering the other areas I've placed my faith in of late, I'd say she's an improvement."

"If she's as amenable as you seem to believe," Ettrian countered. "I can't say I'm convinced of that."

"You'd be surprised at how much I've learned from her in my time here," Willem said.

Their voices got louder, no more than ten feet from where Lea stood in the shadows. She held her breath, not daring to make a sound as they walked past. There was no way Ettrian would miss her, but Willem was a simple human with human senses; as long as she was quiet, he wouldn't notice her presence.

"Even still, are you sure you can trust what she says?"

"With what I've promised her?" Willem scoffed. "Of course. She likes to think she's tricky, but she's in over her head with this."

"Are you certain of that?" Ettrian asked. "From what you've said, she's quite quick on her feet." Their voices slowly began to fade away as they moved further down the corridor.

"To an extent, perhaps," Willem allowed. "On another note, I've been told the Lindorothian king and queen vanished several days ago. I don't suppose you know anything regarding their whereabouts?"

Lea held her breath as Willem's words began to trail off.

But whatever Ettrian's response was, it became inaudible as they continued further down the passage. Lea waited a full minute before slipping from her hiding spot and making her way back.

She'd just rounded the corner to the tunnel to Jonas' room when a voice in the dark stopped her.

"Snooping?"

Lea yelped, the sound echoing off the stone walls, then spun, her magic pooling in her hands as she faced the intruder.

Ettrian stood a few feet away, a small light bobbing in the air beside him. A smirk rested on his lips, and in the dim light, the gold of his eyes seemed to burn.

"What are you doing here?" Lea hissed, taking a step back.

"I could ask you the same question, witch." He folded his arms and leaned against the wall. "It's impolite to eavesdrop, you know."

"I wasn't—"

"Liar."

She huffed. "If you found my behavior so improper, why didn't you announce my presence to King Willem?"

"Why haven't *you* told anyone I didn't properly bond you to Lord Edrin?"

"Stop answering questions with questions."

"Alright. I chose not to announce your presence because it was irrelevant. I know why you're here, Lady Calliwell, and I am quite certain Willem does as well."

"Quite certain?"

"He is... perceptive for a human. Smart. Smarter than his Jotnar counterpart, I might say."

Lea tightened her cloak. "Unlikely. If he knew why I was here, he would have sold me out to Lessia by now."

"Not without proof. She has her suspicions but finds herself above your level of scheming. Forcing you to marry her nephew is her way of ensuring your complacency." He frowned. "Surely you must know that."

"Obviously." Lea scowled. "Is that why new spy holes keep appearing in my room?"

Ettrian grinned. "Indeed, my lady. Among other reasons, I'm sure, at least on Willem's part."

Lea grimaced.

He looked down at his nails, then brushed them on his vest. "Care to tell me when you plan to free yourself from this place?"

She frowned at his conversational tone. "I have no plans to leave, Your Highness."

"Having no plan is not the same as lacking intent."

Lea looked past him to the darkened corridor, the depths of which were still daunting, despite the cheerful little light he'd conjured that had chased away some of the shadows.

"Speaking of intent, where has Willem gone? Or is he hiding just around the bend, waiting for me to spill some sordid secret?" Though she said it in jest, she couldn't help but cast another wary glance past the prince.

His lips twitched. "No, the king has been called away on other business. I had intended to go back to my chambers, but after catching your scent, I thought I'd see what you were doing skulking about."

She huffed indignantly. "No one is *skulking.*"

"Does Lord Edrin know what you're doing?" Frowning, he took a long sniff of the air. "Daily, based on the scent you've left behind."

Lea ground her teeth together in frustration.

"Exploring," she finally said. "My cousin was quite fond of these tunnels, but I never got the chance to see what all the fuss was about. I tend to have a lot of free time throughout the day, after all."

"Ah."

She narrowed her eyes and put her hands on her hips. "Why are you really here, Prince Ettrian?"

"Here in this tunnel? It's quite a useful means of traversing this palace."

"Here in *Lindoroth.*"

He quirked a brow. "One of our seers—"

"Informed you of a threat across the world." Lea shook her head in exasperation. "Yes, I was present for that conversation, although I question its validity a good deal. Why are *you* here?" She held out her hands, gesturing around her. "What does this world have to do with yours? Your kind lives so far from here we nearly forgot you exist, yet here you are, showing a sudden interest in the affairs of others. Why?"

Why are my king and queen in Avorell? What have your parents done to them?

His jaw tensed, giving Lea a momentary bit of glee that she was making him work so hard to give her an answer that would give her a truth without showing too much of his hand.

"What happens here can easily affect my lands, my people," he said. "If this is a war the elves should be involved in, I would like to make that determination first-hand, not through the eyes of emissaries."

"But you are involved, are you not?" She gave him a questioning look. "Here you are, in the palace that once belonged to Salazar Harridan, conversing with those who saw fit to murder him at his own son's wedding. It seems to me you've made your position known."

"Perhaps." Ettrian steepled his fingers in front of him and tapped one against his lip, then opened his hands in question. "And yet, where are my soldiers? My vast elvish army?"

"Likely invisible and waiting at the gates, if legend of your magic is anything to go on."

He gave her a withering look. "If my intentions are as you assume, would I not have thousands of *visible* swords and archers at my back? Wouldn't you say it's more likely I am here to make a choice, to decide whether or not to offer the support of Avorell?"

"No," she replied with a shake of her head. "If your kind are as smart as the stories say, you would never reveal your intentions in such a way. You wouldn't come here under the guise of decision-making, because that would mean you would also be considering siding with the Linds." She paused, watching for any sign of reaction to her statement, a flicker of recognition that his parents might be doing just that.

Infuriatingly, he smiled.

"Perhaps you are correct, Lady Calliwell. Or you could simply be too untrusting for your own good."

"Or you're too confident in your ability to bend the truth for *your* own good," she countered.

"You doubt my decades of experience doing so?"

"I question your decades of experience, assuming those decades led to great skill and not mere assumptions about said skills."

"In other words, you do not trust me."

"Not in the least."

He grinned. "Ask me anything, then. Something you know I cannot lie about."

"I know my king and queen are in Avorell," she began, searching his face for even a flicker of reaction. "You said you've come here to decide whether or not you want to join Lessia and Willem's cause. How am I to trust my own monarchs haven't walked right into a trap?"

"Ah." He nodded. "Well, I can assure you, Lady Calliwell, that a trap has most certainly been laid, although not in the way you're assuming."

"What does that mean?"

One corner of Ettrian's mouth tugged up in amusement. "You know very little about my land."

"I think I've made that quite clear. Answer the question."

"If you knew more, you would know that there's a certain tradition we elves adhere to. You might find it barbaric, but it's a custom that's quite important to our kind. It's how we choose our queens."

"Your queens?"

He nodded. "We don't abide by things like politics or a good family line. A prince chooses a female, and that female must complete a task in order to prove herself worthy. If she succeeds, she gets her crown."

The mischievous gleam in his eyes had dread pooling in her stomach. "Oh? What task might that be?"

His amused smirk turned into a grin. "Lady Calliwell... have you ever heard of the Wild Hunt?"

Her eyes widened. "No," she whispered, shaking her head

violently. "You can't possibly expect my queen to participate in a *soul reaping?*"

"To be clear, it's not a rule I came up with," he said, holding his hands up in defense. "But it does ensure a strong monarchy. And it's not exactly a 'soul reaping.' A queen who is unable to complete the Hunt—"

"Dies!" Lea shook her head and took several steps back. "She *dies,* Ettrian! I don't care what you call it! She's not even an elf! No. This— no. I need to—" She braced a hand on the rough stone wall and tried to catch her breath. All of it, all she'd come back to do, would be for naught if Freya couldn't complete the hunt. If the stories she'd heard of it—a savage chase of a female through the wilderness with the intention of slaughtering her in exchange for some reward—were true, Freya, strong as she was, would never come out alive. She looked at Ettrian, eyes wide. "Why haven't you forced Lessia to participate?"

"Only a true queen of a land can request assistance to defend that land. Lessia is not the Queen of Lindoroth, she is the Empress of Jotunheim. I assure you, Lady Calliwell, this is not something you need to worry about," Ettrian said.

She wanted to hit him.

"It's nothing I need to worry about?" She straightened up and met his eyes. "That is my *queen* you're talking about! The likelihood of her surviving that horrendous custom is practically nil and you damn well know it!"

"I do not," he countered. "And the only reason my parents would have allowed her and Aerelius to plead their case is if they thought her capable."

"And how would they know? How would they know any damn thing about her?"

Before he could respond, Ettrian stiffened, then sent a quick glance over his shoulder and held up a finger. A moment later, Lea felt the sting of magic settle over them.

"We have visitors," he said. "Shall I escort you back to your room?"

"That depends." She put her hands on her hips and tried to subtly inhale, hoping to catch a scent. "Who's coming?"

The prince cocked an ear. "Willem and a female companion, it seems." He gave her an expectant look. "Well?"

She was still unable to hear voices, but she could sense the change in pressure on her magic, so she knew better than to push her luck any further.

"I can see myself back, thank you. The tunnels dead-end at Jonas' room, so it would seem a bit odd if someone saw you *skulking* about that area, wouldn't you think?"

"Wise, indeed." Ettrian waved a hand and the light that had illuminated the corridor winked out, plunging them into darkness. "Have a good day, Lady Calliwell."

Ettrian's disembodied voice sounded uncomfortably close in the disorienting darkness, but when Lea reached out with her magic to feel the area around her, there was no trace of him at all.

Turning, she rushed back to her room to call for Tyna.

36

FREYA

The creature that charged Freya looked like a cross between a bear and a dragon, wide and cumbersome with a long snout and tail that ended in four long barbs. A troll of some sort, she assumed, although she would've expected them to be on two legs, not four. As it ran toward her, she considered letting out her wings, but knew they could hinder her just as likely as they were to help. One hit of the troll's barbs could easily shred them, and she didn't have the time it would take for them to heal without proper treatment.

So, steeling herself, Freya jumped, using her air magic to propel her over its wide body. It skidded to a halt in the middle of the small clearing, then roared when she landed on its back.

She brought her sword down straight into the nape of its neck. Its hide was thick, thicker than she'd anticipated, making her thankful she'd chosen the weapon she did. The beast screamed in fury and pain as it reared up on its hind legs as it tried to shake her off. She used the grip of her sword to keep her from tumbling to the ground when it dropped back on all fours with a shuddering thud. Putting all her force behind her sword, she set two long, magical daggers hovering in the air before them, then sent both directly at its eyes. It roared again, then began shaking its head violently. She pulled out the blade and drove it back in, hilt-deep. Blood spurted as she sliced through its neck, so she twisted the blade, widening the wound. Shifting her nails to long talons and forcing her venom into them, she dug them into its hide and clung to it as its life drained away.

It took several minutes for the troll to die, but Freya didn't dare let go until it had stilled entirely. She waited until she heard its heart stop beating before sliding to the ground and wrenching her sword from its flesh. Wrinkling her nose at the black sludge that now coated it, she looked around for something to use to clean it. Wary of touching any of the plant life with her bare hands, she settled for wiping off as much as she could on the thing's skin, using its tail to scrape most away.

"That wasn't so bad," she murmured, eying the destroyed beast. It was certainly the largest thing she'd ever fought, but it was fairly lacking in intelligence, from what she could tell. It relied on brute strength, although she wouldn't be surprised if, based on the greenish color, its saliva was pure poison.

Something told her none of the things Florian had packed for her included antidotes for that type of toxin.

She tucked all of that information away in case she came across another one and looked around as she tried to decide which direction to go.

She'd hardly made a choice to head east when she heard the pounding of feet and the thrashing of brush. With a groan, she turned toward the direction the sound was coming from and found another troll lumbering through the forest toward her.

"Gods above." She heaved a breath, then waited until the troll was nearly within striking distance. Jumping, she used her talons to latch onto its head and pulled herself onto its back. She narrowly missed its snapping jaws as it whipped its head around, roaring in pain, but she managed to get her sword into its side. The blade sliced through its flank, and she winced at the spray when she pulled it back out to slash across its throat.

As with the last, she waited until life had left it before jumping to the ground.

She stared in disgust at the two bodies, covered in blood and gore. The second had been mutilated worse than the first, but the stench coming off of them was reminiscent of the draugs she'd so often fought in Watoria.

"Maybe I'll get lucky and a few draugs will show up, too," she muttered as she wiped her sword clean again. Shaking her head, she laughed at the thought.

Squinting, she tried to gauge the position of the sun through the trees, then began to head east.

As she walked, she surveyed her surroundings. The forest was dense, the canopy so thick that very little sunlight filtered through, making her sharp eyes and sense of direction, two of her most important weapons, not nearly as useful as she'd hoped. Getting turned around in this place could land her here for days, especially once night fell. Casting her eyes into the trees, she considered how one of the wide branches on the massive oaks would work as a bed for the night.

She wrinkled her nose at the thought but knew it would be her best option.

The silence of the forest was unnerving, and the air was heavy with humidity, so it didn't take long for a thin sheen of sweat to glisten on her skin. When she'd passed this way before, the day they arrived in Avorell, the shade had been a welcome relief, albeit a bit humid. For the air to feel as uncomfortable as it did this time, Freya figured Nalaea must have dropped her in another part of the forest entirely,

She'd nearly reached a bright, open clearing when she heard something coming toward her. Whatever the thing was, it was smaller than the troll-like creatures she'd just fought, with lighter steps and near-silent breathing, but she didn't bother assuming it would be any less deadly.

Silently, Freya leapt onto the lowest branch of the tree she'd just stopped beside and slipped on an invisibility glamour. She waited, not daring to move as the elf, a creature far too large to have been able to move so silently in the dense brush, came to a stop beneath her. Letting out a slow, measured breath, she slipped a feather from under the vambrace on her wrist and contemplated her options. He was bare-chested, wearing only a pair of pants in a shade of russet that nearly matched his skin.

Her first choice was to wait him out and hope he didn't notice her presence. Her second option, and the one that seemed more likely, was to attack him before he caught wind of her scent.

The thought had hardly formed in her mind when his head jerked upward and his eyes met hers, confirming that the invisibility glamour she'd donned was useless. His eyes were solid orbs of black, his hair a reddish-brown. Though the light brown skin of his bare chest and face was smooth, something about him told her he was very, very old.

He spoke some words in elvish, and the sound was harsher, more guttural than when Nalaea and Ruehnar spoke the language.

When she didn't respond, he chuckled.

"They told me a queen was being hunted this day. I did not realize you would not speak my language."

"Forgive my ignorance," she called back. Slowly, she stood, then pulled herself up to a higher branch and lowered to a crouch.

In a single, rapid movement, he'd jumped the nearly thirty feet to the branch Freya was on. She bit back her startled cry at his sudden appearance and leapt to her feet, gripping her feather tighter.

"You survived the forest trolls, then?" he asked, folding his arms and looking her up and down.

She rested her other hand on the pommel of her sword and flicked a quick glance at his waist, surprised when she saw no weapons attached to the waist of pants. "If you're referring to the hideous creatures that welcomed me to this place, then yes."

He smirked, clearly amused. "You believe you killed them?"

"Their lack of blood and heartbeat indicate I succeeded quite well."

"Did you remove their heads?"

"Nearly."

He laughed, a low, dark chuckle. "Not nearly enough, I assure you."

"I'll keep that in mind if one comes looking for me again." Freya leaned against the wide trunk of the tree and tapped her feather against her palm. "So, are you here to help me or kill me?"

He took a step toward her, decreasing the space between them. "That will depend."

She arched a brow. "On?"

His head cocked curiously at the feather in her hand. "Is that a feather?"

Another step, then another. Only three feet of space separated them now.

"It is." She put up a barrier of air between them. "Now, answer the question."

He ran his hand over her magic, laughing softly at her scowl when his tan fingers brushed it aside with ease. "How would you feel about a partnership, Queen...?"

"Freya," she replied. "And you are?"

"Toskr," he replied with a sly smile. "If you swear not to kill me, I will help see you through this course in one piece."

She laughed at the ambiguity of his promise. "Alright, Toskr. As long as you swear not to kill or attempt to kill me, lead me into a trap or location where you know I'm likely to be killed, lead me to any sort of avoidable danger whatsoever, and ensure that I come through this course in one piece *and* with my life, I will consider a partnership with you."

He narrowed his eyes. "You do not trust me."

"I'd be a fool if I did, and I think you would agree."

He took a final step closer, nearly closing the distance between them, then stopped short when he found the tip of her sword at his throat. Slowly, he held up his hands and met her eyes.

"I would consider your next move carefully, Toskr," Freya said quietly.

His lips twitched into a smile. "What will it be, Queen Freya? Shall we make a bargain?"

"Perhaps. Once you've proven yourself, of course."

"And how might I do that?"

She shrugged. "You elves are a tricky sort, so I'll have to think that over. In the meantime, you may act as my guide."

He angled his head in question. "How will you know I am not leading you astray? You are being hunted, after all, and the reward for the one who catches you is quite large."

She eyed the distance between them, only a swords' length, and sighed. "If you were hunting me, you would've taken me by now. I'm in a tree and you've got the advantage of both elvish magic and familiarity with this land. If you were truly one of those things out here seeking my head, you would have sliced it off and delivered it to the king and queen by now."

"I suppose you make a fair point," he conceded with a slight bow of his head.

She ran her eyes over him again, taking in his russet hair and skin, black eyes, and pointed ears, then arched a brow. "When I was reading over past hunts last night, I came across a story about an elf who dwells in the forest, one who can transform into small things and thrives on mischief." She watched his expression for any hint of recognition but saw nothing.

"Oh?"

"If I'm not mistaken, *you* are that elf, and this hunt is likely the best fodder for mischief you've gotten in some time. Things are hunting me and I, them, and I'd wager *you* are not one of them. You might be leading this charade, but I don't believe you have a stake in it."

Toskr frowned. "You admit I would like to make this difficult for you?"

"Only inasmuch as you'll keep my enemies well-informed of my whereabouts, just as you will do the same for me."

His brow furrowed in confusion. "If you know I plan to help your hunters, why ask me to be your guide?"

"Having someone working with me half the time is better than having no assistance at all, wouldn't you agree?" She gave him an amused look. "And is that an admission that you're the elf I read about?"

"Perhaps."

A roar sounded in the direction Freya had come, causing her to wince.

Toskr smiled. "Permit me to say I told you so."

Freya rolled her eyes and huffed. "No, I don't think I will." Sheathing her sword, she leapt to the ground. She glanced up, then frowned when all she saw staring back at her was a small, red squirrel.

"Perhaps, indeed," she muttered. She started to walk away, and a moment later, heard the sound of tiny claws scraping across dead leaves.

"Watch where you step, Toskr," she muttered. "My boots don't take kindly to rodents underfoot."

⁓

"You know, it's strange," Freya said as she tossed aside the bodies of three small, fanged ravens that had just put up a noble attempt to shred her leathers to bits. "When I was told I'd be hunted, I expected a bit more than the local fauna attempting to destroy my clothing." After the two trolls, she had faced a handful of violent pixies, a serpent the size of a large dog, and now, ravens. None were the vicious creatures she'd been told to expect.

Toskr leapt down from a tree, shifting into his two-legged form in mid-air.

"What does that tell you, Queen Freya?"

Freya dusted her hands off and folded her arms. "That I'm either the subject of a joke, or these things—" she gestured around "—are little more than a distraction, maybe a way to deplete my strength before I reach my true opponents."

"What do you think they may be distracting you from?"

She gave him a speculative look. "You, perhaps? As much as I enjoy your company, I *do* find it convenient that you appeared when you did."

Toskr chuckled. "A fair assumption, but incorrect. I am—what is it your kind call it?—a gossip?"

Freya nodded slowly. "Yes. And while I'm fighting and you're... doing whatever it is you do, is it safe to assume you're off spreading your gossip to whoever else is out here? Herding me in a direction of your choosing?"

He held up his hands. "My offer for a bargain is still available."

"And if I had the time to sit down and pick apart each word you say to suss out your deceit, I might take you up on that." She took a swig from the skin of water that she'd attached to her chest with a leather strap, then began trudging through the trees again, keeping her eyes peeled for the attack she knew had to be moments off. Though her words to Toskr had been said lightly, they carried much more weight in her mind. They'd been trekking for hours through the forest, and she'd come under attack at multiple times, but each time was by a creature or creatures who she took down with relative ease. It made little sense that the king and queen would toss her into a forest such as this, one permeated with ancient power and nature spirits, only to kill a handful of wild animals, nor would they have been able to tell her she'd be fighting violent criminals unless that was truly the expectation.

She also held very little trust in her guide, but if the stories about him were true, he was a true mischief-maker. He would find fun in spreading the word of her and her hunters' whereabouts and was very likely leading her straight toward them. Under normal circumstances, she would avoid that at all costs, but she needed to be done with this game. The sooner she defeated her opponents, the sooner she could return to Lindoroth, whether that was with the elvish army or not.

"I would head west, if I were you," Toskr suggested, falling into step beside her. "I'm fairly certain that's where your opponents were deposited. Vicious creatures, too. Several of them led a genocide more than one thousand years ago." He spread his arms wide. "Part of this forest created itself to destroy the taint their deeds placed on the land."

"I'm to exit the forest due east of where I entered. Going west will take me off course." She slid him a wry look. "Perhaps you should scurry off and tell them to head in my direction, hmm?"

"It is just a suggestion, Queen Freya."

Rolling her eyes, Freya shifted direction slightly and began to head west. "Do forests create themselves often in Avorell?"

"Only when a grave offense is committed, which is rare."

"How does it work?" Freya let her eyes roam over the woods. "The way you speak—it's as though the magic here is sentient. It *feels* sentient."

"I suppose you could say it is. It gives us all life, after all." He brushed his tan fingers across a low-hanging branch with leaves thrice the width of his hand. "Trees, elves, forest trolls. It allows us to exist in this place."

A twig snapped to the left.

"I think we have been found out," Toskr whispered. "Best of luck, Queen Freya." Then he shifted into his squirrel form and scurried up a nearby tree.

Shaking her head, Freya turned to face her newest opponent.

When the tall, slender elf stepped from the trees, she couldn't help but smile.

Finally.

37

FREYA

The male looked just as Freya had expected when Nalaea and Ruehnar told her she'd be fighting some of Avorell's most vile prisoners. Though he carried the ethereal grace of his kind, his pants and shirt were dirt-brown and tattered, his hands were gnarled, his eyes a clouded gray. And where the other elves had two sharp fangs, when he flashed his teeth, Freya saw they each one ended in blunt edges, as though the points had been hacked off.

"Valkyrie," he hissed.

She sighed and drew her sword. "Yes, yes, let's get on with it."

He snarled. "You should fear me."

"I'm certain you're correct," she replied. "And yet, here we are." She pointed her sword at him. "What's your crime? Are you the 'genocidal maniac' or just a simple murderer? I was told I'd be facing a variety; yet so far, all I've seen are animals." She flicked her eyes up and down his body. "Although, I suppose you might fall into that category."

Still he didn't rise to the bait.

Come on, she thought. *Just fight me already!*

She gave him an expectant look. "Are you unaware of the terms of this hunt?"

He grinned, putting all of his jagged teeth on display as he slid a pair of long daggers from his hips. "No, Valkyrie, we are not."

"We?"

Instantly, she heard the rustle of brush, and she was torn between turning her back on the elf in front of her or letting another attack her from behind. She gritted her teeth and waited. Just as the elf behind her would've gained purchase, she dove to the side, and he went sailing over her, crashing into the first.

She jumped to her feet and stumbled back a few steps as her opponents stood. Her instinct was to run, but if she wanted to succeed, she would have to stay and fight.

The two elves were nearly identical in stature and speed as they charged her. She slashed out with her sword, catching the first's daggers on the edge with a force that set her teeth ringing. When the second took aim at her, she landed a boot to his chest that sent him flying back as she used her arms to send the first stumbling away. She conjured up four daggers, sending two into the chest of one elf, while the other two embedded themselves in the back of the other. She barely had time to take a breath before both elves shook off the daggers and stalked toward her.

"Well, that's unfortunate," she muttered dryly as she scanned her surroundings, taking note of a branch, wide as an oak, that hung about ten feet above the heads of the elves. She jumped, using her air magic to boost herself upward. As she went, she let out both wings and delivered a hard hit to the face of each elf as she rose past. She'd nearly made it to the branch when she felt one of the elves latch onto her wing and pull her back to the ground, where they both pinned her.

"You will not leave this forest, witch," one growled, his claws digging into her bicep.

Shoving the pain to the back of her mind, she released her magic with enough force to blow both elves backward several yards. She got to her feet and raised her sword as they both eyed her with a new wariness.

Slowly, she stalked toward them and let her magic gather in the air around her. When they squared off to come toward her, she threw the magic out in two long whips, capturing each elf around the throat. With a heavy pull and another burst of magic, she bound them together in the middle of the clearing.

Using a bit of flame to ensure the binds were secure, she walked forward, examining them.

"You know, I tend to avoid killing creatures that have already been trapped," she commented, stopping in front of the first who'd attacked her. "But for some reason, I doubt you would do the same."

The taller elf leered down at her. "If it meant freedom from that prison? No, we would not hesitate."

Freya nodded, and though she knew what she had to do, it went against her nature to kill a thing that wasn't actively attacking her. Her job in Watoria had been to deposit criminals to the marshals, killing only when draugs or huldra made their way into the city or when her own life was threatened. Ending the lives of creatures she'd trapped would have seemed excessive in any situation she'd been in before.

You've never been in a situation like this before.

She resigned herself to the truth of that as she met the tall elf's eyes. "Then I shall give you freedom of a different sort."

And with a single sweep of her sword, she removed their heads.

"I THINK THAT WENT WELL," Toskr commented after Freya had dragged the bodies of the two elves under the brush. "Your injuries are not so bad."

Freya rolled her shoulder and hissed at the stabbing pain there.

"Are elves venomous?" she asked.

"Some," Toskr replied, holding aside a branch for her to step past.

She let out an annoyed sigh. "Fine. Were *those* elves, the ones I just decapitated, venomous?"

"Now you are asking the right questions," he said with a nod. "And no, those two were not."

She gave him a deadpan look. "Were not what?"

His lips twitched. "The two elves you so neatly relieved of their heads were not venomous. The only risk to your injury is infection, which, considering our surroundings, is likely."

Freya squeezed her shoulder and grimaced. The bleeding had slowed significantly as the wound began to close, but the healing was slow, different than what she normally would've experienced.

"Why is it taking so long for my wounds to heal?"

Toskr made a clicking sound with his tongue. "Another good question, Queen Freya. The magic in this forest does not take kindly to intruders, especially those who spill blood. If I had to guess, as you have now killed more than a dozen creatures, I would say the forest is reluctant to allow you to continue your journey."

Freya stopped and gawked at him in disbelief, the pain in her shoulder forgotten. "Is *that* why Nalaea and Ruehnar sent me here instead of the moors? Because the *forest* would be fighting against me?"

He grinned. "As you said, we elves are a tricky sort."

She rubbed a hand across her face and groaned.

Pausing only long enough to rub on a bit of one of Florian's healing ointments, they continued on. They walked in silence for a few minutes as she mulled over what her options might be for getting through this relatively unscathed. If healing would be difficult, she had to take extra precautions to avoid even the smallest of injuries. Infection was something that could set in quickly, and without immediate care, she could find herself going back to Lindoroth completely useless. As they trudged through an increasingly muddier path, she gnawed at her lip. She'd never been a big hunter growing up, although she knew how to set traps well enough.

But traps always spilled blood.

She frowned at Toskr. "Is it just the spilled blood the forest doesn't like, or the death itself?"

"Both, and I assume that is yet another aspect of this task." He flashed her a smile. "Not to worry, Queen Freya. You are here with a purpose. The forest knows this." He hesitated a moment before continuing. "If I had to guess, I would not be surprised if I was also part of this test Nalaea and Ruehnar have set for you."

"How so?"

"You could have killed me the moment you saw me," he said. "Yet instead, you chose to use me as your guide. Why?"

"I've never been the type to kill first and ask questions later," Freya replied. "I assumed you might be hunting me—your words told me as much—but when you approached, you didn't attack. It piqued my curiosity enough to stay my hand."

"So I am a curiosity, then?"

Freya shrugged and scanned the woods ahead. "In a sense. I read about you in a book, then you appeared in front of me. It's not often one gets to meet fairytale creatures," she added with a grin.

"I believe I should be offended by that, but I will choose not to be," Toskr said after a moment.

"Why would they make you part of my test?" Freya asked. "Isn't this your home?"

"In a sense."

"What—dammit!" Freya threw out an arm to steady herself on a tree as her right foot slid nearly a foot into the ground. Toskr grabbed her and pulled her back, sending them both tumbling to the ground.

Blinking, she sat up and stared, bewildered, at the ground in front of them that had suddenly turned into water.

"I will assume the king and queen did not tell you of the bogs in this forest?" Toskr said as he helped her to her feet.

Scowling, Freya sat down on a fallen tree and began scraping peat and mud from the boot she'd nearly lost to the bog in front of her.

"No, they neglected to mention it." After tightening her boots, she stood and stamped off the last of the muck and stepped toward the bog. It was no wonder she hadn't noticed it before nearly falling in.

The meager sunlight that filtered through and the green moss that floated on top of the water made the bog indistinguishable from the forest floor around it. She inhaled deeply, focusing only on her sense of smell, and committed the scent to memory. It smelled of peat and water, a sweet scent with earthy undertones, nothing at all like the smells of the bogs she'd encountered before.

"Tell me about your home, Queen Freya," Toskr said, gesturing for them to continue. "What ails it of late?"

Freya gave one last scathing look at the bog, then fell into step beside him, making sure to keep a closer eye on where her feet landed.

"Foreign monarchs staged a coup on my wedding night three weeks ago." Her eyes burned as she thought back to the easy, carefree way her life had been up until that night. "They slaughtered my king, the governors of our lands, many of their children, and have been killing their way through my lands ever since. We've lost nearly a third of our own forces, and the casualties of the people of Lindoroth..." She shook her head. "I'm still not sure how high those numbers have risen. What I *do* know is that more forces will be coming into Lindoroth in just a few days and we need to stop them."

A small furrow formed on Toskr's brow. "And that is why you've come to Avorell?"

She nodded, then stepped aside, scowling when she caught sight of another bog. "We are one kingdom fighting against two. When the suggestion was made to contact the elves, my husband and I decided it was a chance worth taking." She carefully left out the fact that she knew Willem and Lessia had also considered contacting the elves.

"And what—ah." Toskr smiled and glanced over his shoulder. "I will leave you to it."

Confused, Freya watched as he shifted back into a squirrel and scurried up a nearby tree.

"Gods above," she muttered as her confusion turned to annoyance. Turning, she eyed the woods, searching for whatever was hunting her this time.

It didn't take long for the small female to find her. She came crawling through the woods, the only sign of her approach the shivering of the tall grasses as she passed through. Freya got a good look at her when she broke onto the path. She was tiny, crawled on all fours, and her skin was an odd shade of blue, as though a brighter shade had been left in the sun to fade.

When she saw Freya, she hissed, then wasted no time in her attack.

Freya raised her sword, but the female launched herself forward with such speed that Freya's own movements seemed sluggish. The sword was knocked away and the elf was on her, pinning Freya to the ground, jaws snapping only inches from her face.

The elf hissed, and green spittle dripped onto Freya's clothes, instantly sizzling, then burning through the thick leather.

With a growl, Freya flipped herself to her feet, causing the female to loosen her grip just enough for Freya to slip a feather from her waistband. In a swift movement, she'd embedded the feather in the elf's throat.

Seconds later, she was dead.

The smell of burning flesh hit Freya's nose just as the pain registered. The venom that had leaked from the elf's mouth had burned small holes through the leather and had continued on to burn her skin.

"Toskr!" Freya hastily began removing her jacket.

The small, red squirrel appeared in front of her, then shifted into the tan elf. "Yes, Your Majesty?"

"Will the water in that bog stop the burn of this venom?"

"Yes, Your Majesty."

"Will the water in that bog cause me any ill effects if I use it to wash my skin and clothing?"

"No, Your Majesty."

Freya hurried to the edge of the bog, then used her boot to shove aside some of the patchy moss that floated on top. Still unsure whether it was wise to fully trust Toskr, she dipped her jacket into the black water, gave it a quick shake, then pulled it back out. She cupped her hands and splashed a bit more onto her shoulder where the venom had burned through her tunic. When she felt only the soothing coolness of the water on her skin, she relaxed a bit before splashing a bit more on. Then, she reached for the pouch at her hip to see what ointments of Florian's might help the burn.

She froze when the water before her rippled, the patches of moss shifting as something cut through the water beneath.

Slowly, she stood, then took several steps back, quietly lifting her jacket as she went.

"Toskr?"

"Hmm?"

"When I asked if the water would cause me any ill effects, should I have clarified that I was referring to anything *in* the water, as well?"

"Oh, yes, Your Majesty, that would have been wise."

Cursing, Freya turned and ran just as the serpent slithered from the water.

38

FREYA

ll told, by the time the sun began to set, Freya had killed twenty-four creatures, only a handful of which were elves. The rest were vicious animals; strong, fanged, and venomous. Each left their mark on her clothes, her skin, their deaths causing her healing to slow just a bit more with every injury. The ointments Florian gave her helped some, but they mostly dulled the pain while doing little to promote actual healing. Spilling blood was unavoidable in most cases, but she managed to get around that by breaking a few necks.

"You are almost finished, Queen Freya," Toskr commented as she leaned against a tree and slumped to the ground. "Why not continue on?"

She stared down at her hands, covered in a mix of black, red, and green blood, then curled them into fists and looked up at him.

"I'm tired, Toskr. I'm not healing and I need a break."

"The sun has set and this place is not very hospitable after dark." He stared past her into the gloom. "There are not many left to fight, you know."

"Then they'll have to come to me, because I need to conserve my strength." She opened her canteen and took a long swallow.

He sat down in front of her, legs crossed, his elbows resting on his knees. "Do you think you will come through this with the reward you desire?"

She tilted her head back against the smooth bark and closed her eyes. "I don't know."

"You did not strike me as the type to give up, Queen Freya."

Freya opened one eye. "I never said I was giving up. I only need a rest."

He nodded slowly.

"Can I ask you a question, Toskr?"

"Of course."

"Why don't you leave this forest?"

A smile flickered across his lips. "My own punishment, Queen Freya. I told the wrong secrets to the wrong elf, and now this is where I reside."

"So you *are* a prisoner."

"In a sense, yes."

She was quiet for a moment, then asked, "If presenting my head to the king and queen would free you, would you do it?"

"I would," he said solemnly. "I hope that does not offend you."

Freya snorted. "But you aren't one of the creatures hunting me?"

"I am not."

She angled her head and looked at him. "Is there anything I could do to free you?"

He gave her a curious look. "You know so little of me. Why would you ask such a thing?"

"Perhaps I feel you've learned your lesson. And that doesn't answer my question."

There was a sound in the forest, a good distance away, and his eyes flicked past her again. "I believe your final opponents approach."

Freya's eyes fell shut and she sighed. "Go on, then. Let them know where I am."

"I told them long ago," Toskr admitted. "They have been tracking you for several hours."

Laughing, she shook her head. "Of course you did. Can you at least tell me what they are?"

"Elves." A pause. Then, "They are the reason this forest exists."

She was surprised at the heaviness of his words. "I thought the ones I killed earlier were responsible for it?"

Toskr shook his head. "No, they were simple murderers. Vile, to be sure, but genocide was not their crime."

"How many?"

"Three."

Freya's forehead fell to her knees and she let out a groan. Then, resolved to end this for good, she heaved herself to her feet.

"Alright, then." She held out a hand to Toskr and helped him up. "Regardless of your intentions, I appreciate your guidance today."

He grinned. "Perhaps one day you will learn the correct way to ask an elf questions."

Her lips formed a thin line of annoyance. "Yes, I'm beginning to realize a good number of things I should've been more clear on."

With a small salute, Toskr shifted back into his animal form and scrambled up a nearby tree.

Freya took several deep breaths and tried to rally her strength. She'd hoped to be free of this place before dark, but now, even if she defeated her final opponents in minutes, it seemed she would be spending the night here. Though her sense of direction was strong, she didn't trust herself not to get lost here in the dark, especially considering the type of creatures that she assumed would be lurking about once the moon rose.

Taking a few steps forward, she tilted her head back and looked to the sky, then smiled when she saw her namesake, the goddess Freyja, directly overhead. The wide constellation hovered above, as though the goddess herself was looking down. Silly as it might be, Freya allowed that to give her a bit of comfort.

Harsh, muttered words reached her ears. She recognized the language as elvish, but it sounded different than what she'd been hearing the last few days; older, somehow.

This forest was ancient, which meant the elves coming toward her were as well. Stronger. Primal.

And, after more than a thousand years stuck to rot in a hole in the ground, desperate.

She cursed Toskr for not sending them in her direction first, when she was still in possession of all of her strength. She had her magic, but she could feel it waning.

A feeling of dismay washed over her as she realized, for the first time in her life, she was entering into a fight all but certain she would lose.

The three elves slid out of the darkness before her, tall and languid, their eyes roving across her.

The tallest of the three muttered a few words at her.

Mustering as much of her strength as she could, she cocked a brow and stepped forward. "Come again?"

The two shorter ones growled, while the tallest—the leader, Freya guessed—sneered.

"I thought Nalaea would make this hard," the sneering one spat. His words were broken and guttural, like his voice hadn't been used in some time.

"That's quite an assumption to make without knowing me," Freya commented, resting her sword on her shoulder.

The one to his right hissed, and the sound sent a chill up her spine.

Then, with more speed than any living thing should have, the smallest of the three was on her.

He twisted her arm behind her back and flipped her to the ground. She had less than a breath to recover herself and throw her arms up before he lunged downward, teeth snapping. There was a flurry of movement to her right, another one coming to join, so she threw her knee up and caught the one on top of her in the groin. The pain stunned him for less than a moment, but it was enough for her to throw him off.

She'd barely freed herself from his grip and gotten to her feet when the second grabbed her by the hair and pulled her back down.

This time she was prepared, though, and ran ten air daggers through his back and head. When he released her and attempted to shake them off, she drew her sword and sliced his head clean from his body.

The other two converged.

Her magic shot forward, and she wrapped it tight around their necks. It worked, but with the way she could feel her magic weakening, it wouldn't last long.

The small one broke free first, and it was a struggle for Freya to keep her hold on the other, but she managed to angle her sword just in time for the elf coming at her to impale himself fully.

She turned to the third, but as she did, she felt her magic really begin to stutter. The rope she'd fastened so tightly around his neck vanished. As he was released from his bond, his smile grew, wide and horrifying.

"You are good at this," he commented. "I had hoped not to share this victory with them. I thank you for sparing me from that."

She tightened her grip on her sword. "Happy to be of help."

He snarled and lunged.

Freya had no choice. She ran.

Her legs burned with exertion as she tore through the forest, leaping over brush and fallen logs, and thanking the gods that her shifter senses hadn't failed her as horribly as her magic. The single remaining elf kept at her heels, mere steps behind her. Frantically, she looked for a way out, a way up, but the canopy was too heavily wooded for flight to be a means of escape.

Think, Freya!

A scent hit her nose, damp and sweet, and she nearly sobbed with relief.

She skidded to a halt and ducked, causing the elf chasing her to stumble. Not bothering to see how quickly he got to his feet, Freya took off toward the boglands, praying she didn't trip and fall into the murky water herself.

When the smell of the bog water became strongest, she rallied what little air magic she had left, bolstered it with her shreds of water magic, then used them to propel herself a few feet from the bank. Hovering over the surface of the bog, she doubled over and rested her hands on her knees, then held the leash on her remaining magic as tightly as she could while she waited for the elf to catch her.

I only need two seconds, she begged it. *Please don't fail me now.*

The elf reached the edge of the bog, and as she'd hoped, he didn't notice that her feet weren't touching the ground. When he continued to run toward her at full-speed, she propelled herself to the other side of the bog just as he fell face-first into the dark, moss-covered water.

His head shot above the surface and he let out an eardrum-shattering roar.

Then the sound cut off as he was pulled beneath the black water with a simple, quiet *plop.*

Freya fell to the ground, and the world around her went dark.

Freya came to with an odd whispering in her ear. A humming, soft and melodic, that slowly drew her back to consciousness. Pale blue light filtered through her eyelids.

Morning, she thought. *It must be morning.*

Wake now, a voice commanded.

The sound didn't register in her ears.

Who is in my head?

Wake now!

With a jolt, her eyes flew open.

She scrambled to a sitting position when she saw the vivid blue creature in the air before her. It was small and wispy, undulating as it jerked this way and that in a way that almost seemed... curious.

Slowly, she rose to her knees, wincing as pain lanced through her, then rested a hand on the tree she'd fallen beside and used it to help her draw herself to her feet.

There was a feathering on her arm where one of the elves had torn her tunic. She yelped, then froze when a second floating blue thing appeared at eye level.

She squinted at it, trying to make out some sort of facial features, but all she could see was vibrant blue with a blinding white center.

You should not be here.

Again, the words came to her like a thought.

It wasn't my choice, she replied back.

You have spilled blood.

More blood has been spilled on my land, Freya explained simply. *I need to help my people.*

The thing tilted one way, then another, before floating back to hover beside the one that had woken her.

Freya looked around the forest. It was full-dark, and any moon that may have risen was obscured by the dense tree-cover. She drew her shifter vision forward to get a better look at her surroundings, and immediately wished she hadn't.

All of the night creatures Silmar had warned them about when they came through the forest on their way to Andradath seemed to have congregated around her. Small things and large, some on two legs, others on four, and dozens that fluttered or floated in the magic-soaked air. Eyes of green, yellow, and red reflected back at her—some narrowed in suspicion, others wide with curiosity.

Swallowing hard, she looked back at the two blue lights.

And nearly screamed when she saw they'd been replaced by two elvish females who bore the same bluish glow, the air seeming to shimmer around them.

One of the females, a slight creature with wide black eyes, angled her head. "Do you know what it means to kill a thing in this forest, Valkyrie?"

"I was sent here by the king and queen," Freya said evenly. "To pass a test in order to gain their help in saving my lands."

"It is not their place to send outsiders here," the other one said. She was tall and narrow, with white hair that spilled across her shoulders and down her back, tumbling in a wave to her thighs. "Your problems are not ours."

Freya rubbed a hand across her brow and sighed. "Yes, I know.

Had I known my being here would cause such a fuss, I would've requested another task."

"And they would have denied you," the shorter one said. Her face turned curious. "What task did they give you?"

"To kill the creatures who they sent to hunt me before they killed me."

"With no help?"

"I'm to prove myself just as the queens do," Freya said. "Or so I was told."

"The queens never venture here when they perform their hunts," the tall one said. "They stay to the moors or the forests of their own courts."

"Yes, well, it seems they wanted to make things more difficult for me."

"Because you want their army," the short one stated.

"Which I'm beginning to think was a fool's errand," Freya muttered, casting her eyes skyward. She looked back at the two females, then to the creatures that were encroaching on the small bank. "I don't suppose you'd like to help me get through this forest tonight so I don't have to wait until morning?"

"It is not so far to your destination," the short one said. She raised a long, glowing arm and pointed past Freya. "The eastern edge of the forest is hardly an hour from here."

"You had a guide earlier," the tall one said. "Where did he go?"

Freya shook her head. "He left me just before the last few elves found me. I'm not sure where he went." Her head began to clear a bit more, and she narrowed her eyes at the two females. "What kind of beings are you?"

The tall one smiled. "We are the keepers of the forest."

Freya's blood went cold. "You're wights...aren't you?"

"Indeed," the short one said. "I am Thyxia."

"And I am Actaea," the other said.

There was a rustling of brush as the creatures around them moved closer.

"I mean this place no harm," Freya said, widening her stance a bit.

"We know," Thyxia said. "In fact, we feel you have done us a kindness."

"I—what?"

"The elves you just killed... they are the reason this forest exists," Actaea said. "The forest is thankful they have been punished. Their blood and bones will now offer sustenance to those who dwell here."

"We were prepared to offer you to the gods after the blood you spilled today," Thyxia continued. "But the blood you spilled last— that of the things that ruined this land so long ago—is what caused us to stay our hands."

Freya's thundering heart began to slow and she let out a quiet breath. "That's...very kind. And much appreciated."

"As it should be," Actaea said. "The forest does not grant clemency lightly."

Thyxia lifted a glowing white brow. "It would seem Nalaea and Ruehnar were not fully honest with you when they assigned your tasks."

That's an understatement.

"How so?"

"They did not tell you that the magic of this place would refuse your healing once you spilled blood," Actaea said. "They did not tell you that Toskr would spend the day herding you toward your opponents. Nor did they tell you what the punishment might be for taking life here. The hunters were not the only threats to your life."

"So I've noticed." Freya looked around, searching for a pathway out. When she saw none, she looked back to the wights. "Will I be free to go?"

"You will not fight your way out?"

Freya frowned. "I have no quarrel with you or any of the creatures here, but I will defend myself if it comes to it."

"Then we shall let you pass," Actaea said with a small nod.

Freya tilted her head toward the things around them. "Will they let me pass?"

A smile played on Thyxia's pale lips. "If we allow them to."

Freya nearly groaned in frustration. "Please, I'm begging you.

Allow me to pass. Tell the rest who live here to let me pass. All I want is to get back to my people to do what I can to save them." She felt as though she'd been stuck in this forest for weeks, and a pit of dread was beginning to settle in her stomach as she considered that she might be long-past the point of salvaging her kingdom.

The two females exchanged a long look. After a few moments, Actaea nodded slightly, then faced Freya.

"To show the forest's gratitude for ending the lives of those who defiled this ground so long ago, you will have safe passage to your destination."

Freya sagged with relief. "Thank you. Thank you so much."

Actaea held up a finger. "But you must never return. The forest has offered one kindness in exchange for another. It will not forget the blood you let spill here today. Do you understand?"

Freya nodded quickly. "Yes, I understand. I'll never come back, I promise."

Thyxia smirked. "Alright then." She tilted her head up, then waved a hand.

Freya let out a teary laugh when the trees directly above parted, exposing a wide expanse of starry sky, more than broad enough to fly through. Her wings burst from her back, and she sighed at the comforting feeling of their weight.

"Thank you," she whispered. "And I'm sorry for any distress I may have caused."

Actaea nodded. "Be well, young queen."

Freya nodded, then stretched out her wings and shot into the sky.

39

LEA

As the day wore on, Lea struggled to keep from slipping into the deep pit of fear and worry for those she loved.

The stress of secreting away information for her king and queen had quickly become compounded by her constant concern for their safety. Freya was one of the strongest females Lea had ever met. If anyone could get through something as vicious as the Wild Hunt, it would be her.

But it was still a big "if." Freya was strong, but what if whatever was hunting her was stronger? What if her magic couldn't hold up to whatever challenges the elves threw her way?

What if Aer came home a widower?

What if he didn't come home at all?

A small part of her hoped she would run into Ettrian again. She hoped he might get word from his king and queen and could tell her whether Freya was safe. But, though she wanted to speak with him, she didn't dare seek him out.

Another, larger, part of her wanted to talk to Jonas about her fears, but the last thing she wanted was for the wrong person to over-hear her speak of her king and queen currently in talks with the elves about an allegiance, or that they were absent from Lindoroth entirely.

Willem knew, but she had no idea who he'd shared that with, aside from Ettrian.

So, again, she resigned herself to being on her own.

As Lea pondered the bits of information she'd just sent with Tyna to Rini, she wondered how much longer she and Jonas would have to keep up their ruse. It was clear Willem didn't trust either of them an ounce and Lessia seemed poised to attack the moment Lea slipped up and said something to reveal her true intentions. The empress seemed to trust her nephew to some extent, though, which was a worthwhile thing, considering. She may not ever bring Willem around to trusting Lea, but she could potentially bring him around to trusting Jonas.

Hopefully.

Lea wasn't sure she could continue on indefinitely in a palace with Willem, enduring his leers, suspicious glares, and his sneaking about the passageways, and she was beginning to feel as though the other shoe was perilously close to dropping.

"I think I've convinced Lessia and Willem to retrieve your mother from the dungeons," Jonas said over lunch in their room the following day.

Lea lifted a brow. "Just like that?"

Jonas shook his head. "Of course not," he said with a sigh. "They expect you to convince her to change her views, or at least begin to. They believe she will be able to bolster your claim that Willem and Lessia are not the monsters they've made themselves out to be."

Lea laughed. "That will never happen. My mother is too proud to fake a relationship with them. Even if she saw the sense in pretending, she wouldn't do it."

"You did," he pointed out gently.

"She and I see pride in different things," Lea replied. "I am willing to go to different extremes to help my king and queen, even if those extremes involve debasing myself in some way or another in the process. It will all be for the good of my people in the end, and if I die with my name besmirched, so be it."

Jonas smiled. "Your mettle never ceases to amaze me."

"If only that were all it took to get us out of this mess," she said with a sigh. Her eyes flicked to the panel beside the fireplace. "What do we do next, Jonas?"

"Prince Ettrian doesn't seem apt to kill us any time soon or reveal our true motives to Lessia and Willem, but I would say we should aim to leave within the next few days."

"Do you think he knows what we've been up to?" Lea whispered, curious how much he knew of the elf.

"Oh, most certainly. At the very least, he knows we're not entirely on their side." Jonas frowned. "I hope that means he's biding his time while he determines what his best course of action will be, but I find it hard to believe he came here with no agenda."

"Perhaps he only wants to determine whether Lessia and Willem's cause is a worthwhile one?"

Jonas grimaced and shook his head. "No, I think that's a decision he would've made days ago. Are you sure he didn't indicate anything to you when you spoke in the library?"

"No, nothing," Lea replied. Jonas hadn't been overly thrilled that she'd had a second private visit with Ettrian, but when she quickly reminded him of their purpose there, he'd dropped the subject.

"For now, we'll assume the worst," he said with a sigh. "But do your best to steer clear of him. Willem, you can handle, I have no doubt, but elves are a different sort. Their magic is far stronger than what we're accustomed to."

"Yes, I'm aware." Lea couldn't help the irritation that flashed through her when she saw the wary look in Jonas' eye. He didn't trust Ettrian and she didn't blame him, but it bothered her a good deal that he seemed to think she wasn't as aware of the dangers the prince posed to them and their purpose.

"I know you wouldn't let your guard down, Lea, but just promise me you'll do your best to avoid time spent alone with him. Stay away entirely if you can." He set his napkin down and stood. "I have to go meet with Lessia. Hopefully I'll have more information when I return."

Lea gave him a tight smile. "Let's hope."

He patted her shoulder softly, then left.

WHEN THEY CLIMBED into bed later that evening, Jonas rolled to face her. "I have news," he whispered when she settled beside him. "Regarding the elf prince."

Her heart stuttered a bit. "Oh?"

Jonas slid closer and lowered his voice.

"I'm fairly certain I was followed when I came back earlier, so I had to wait to tell you. It seems he's made his choice—he's informed Lessia and Willem he is prepared to offer his kingdom's assistance to take control of Lindoroth."

A rock settled in her belly. There was only one reason he would have agreed to fight on Lessia and Willem's behalf, and that would be if Freya hadn't proven herself worthy in the Hunt.

And if she hadn't succeeded...

"That's quite unfortunate," she said, not bothering to hide her disappointment but trying very hard to keep the depth of her despair concealed. "Now what do we do?"

"Now that we know the arrival of an elvish army is imminent? We leave. Tomorrow." His tone brooked no argument. "We'll take the day to gather whatever other information we can and flee."

"And go where? Watoria? That's a week's journey at least!"

"Watoria is our best chance at safety. And it will just be the two of us, so concealment will be far simpler than Aerelius and Freya's group of nearly thirty."

"And if we don't make it there?"

"There are a thousand places between here and there we can hide. Edhil is in relatively good straits in the western regions, so we can move south if things in Allanor appear too bleak. Lessia and Willem will surely expect you to go straight to Errest if you flee, so I don't think that would be a safe option at all."

Frustrated, she stared at him, taking in his features as though they might offer some simple answer to the predicament they were now in. "And you expect Edhil to simply accept us with open arms? I wasn't lying when I said they'd never allow an enemy in simply because I encouraged them to. No Edhilian city or town will let you past the front gates. They may not let *me* past the front gates."

"I know this isn't ideal, Lea, but we have to try." He sighed and touched a hand to her cheek. "I know that you don't trust me." He touched a finger to her lips when she made to deny it. "I've seen the way you look at me and I don't fault you for it, but I swore with my own blood to protect you. This is the right path, Lea. Please, trust me not to lead you astray."

"You swore that you wouldn't hurt or betray me. That says nothing of the others in this palace, which, yes, we admittedly knew. And it's not that I don't trust you, Jonas. I just..." She closed her eyes and sighed. "This is far more difficult than I thought."

"Which aspect of 'this' did you expect to be simple? The part where you had to fake a marriage after sitting in the dungeons for a week? The part where I had to keep you under lock and key to prevent Willem and his men from coming after you? Or the part where, through all of that, we still need to be able to trust one another to make this work?"

She had no response to any of those questions, so instead she asked, "So we just leave, then?"

"It's the safest path for you. I will do what I can to get your mother out as well, but you must know I can't guarantee the safety of any of the prisoners."

"You can't expect me to leave them to rot!" she hissed. "Lazarus's mother is down there! Collin's, Myria's!"

"Then you have to make a choice," he said, the words ringing with finality. "If we stay, there is no guarantee any of us will get out alive. That includes the prisoners. So you need to decide which lives are of more value, which lives are more important to Lindoroth."

"You would place our lives above those of others?"

"Our lives are the only ones we know we can control," he said evenly. "We cannot say the same for injured, hungry prisoners."

"Not 'prisoners,' Jonas. My mother. Alyndra Cailen. Lucia Bryton.

Amelia Maddix. People with *names*. I would never forgive myself if I just left them behind!"

"Do you think your mother would forgive herself if you stayed because of her?" he snapped. "Do you think she could live with that? Do you think she would rather see her daughter, her only child, dead? Be reasonable, Lea!"

His words were like a slap, the harshest he'd ever spoken to her. She knew he was right, knew her mother would flog her bloody if she gave up any chance of escape, regardless of how honorable the reason may be.

"I'm tired," she said quietly. "I'll think on what you've said, but I'll make no promises."

With that, she rolled over and closed her eyes, ignoring his annoyed huff as he did the same.

THE FOLLOWING DAY, Lea had every intention of stewing over Jonas' words from the previous night. She knew she needed to make a decision about staying or leaving, and it should've been a simple one, but in reality, it was anything but.

Her plans were upended when one of Willem's guards came to retrieve her just after lunch, with orders from his king to take her to the throne room.

"Lord Edrin awaits with the king and empress," the guard said.

"Do you know what this is about?" she asked as she picked up a cloak. Winter had grown even colder, so much so that a simple fur stole was no longer sufficient to combat the chill. The cloak also made her feel a bit more secure because it kept her hidden from neck to foot.

"I'm not at liberty to say, Lady Edrin. Only that you are to proceed there immediately."

Recalling Jonas' news from yesterday, she paused just outside the door as he pulled it shut. "Is this about my mother? Have they brought her from the dungeons?"

"Again, I am not at liberty to say." The guard held out a hand, indicating for her to proceed, and he maintained a safe distance behind her.

Lea's fears were realized minutes later when she walked into the throne room and saw her mother standing beside Jonas, a guard on either side of her. She'd been cleaned again, dressed in a simple black dress that was nothing like the jewel tones she normally wore. Hope flashed across her mother's face when she saw her daughter, but it quickly diminished when Lessia stood from her throne and stepped off the dais toward Lea.

"Ah, Lady Edrin." She held out a hand for Lea. "Apologies for not retrieving your mother sooner. We had a few... disagreements about how she should be handled, you see." She shot a look at Willem.

"It's quite alright, Empress," Lea said, taking Lessia's hand and giving it a small squeeze. "She is here now, which is all that matters."

"Yes, well, about that," Willem said. "She is here under one condition and one condition only. If it is not met, she'll be tossed back in her cell, minus an appendage or two. Are we clear?"

Lea blinked up at him, surprised at his hostility. "Have I done something to make you think I won't cooperate, Your Majesty?"

Narrowed eyes met hers. "We'll see, won't we?"

"Ignore him, dear," Lessia said. "He's unhappy he didn't get his way, that's all."

Lea sent a look at Jonas, who was standing, stone-faced, at the foot of the dais, eyes furious.

"You do realize the futility of this, don't you?" he asked his aunt. "My wife has no control—"

"Your wife is loyal to her spouse, so she will do all in her power to convince her mother to relinquish all claim to the realm of Edhil *in writing*," Willem snapped.

Wrenching her arm from one of the guards, Perida spat at Willem's feet. "The only way you'll get me to give up my people is through death."

"That can be arranged, I assure you."

Lea sighed, bit back her revulsion, and stepped toward her

mother. She glanced at Lessia, who nodded at the guards, then took her mother's hands—hands that had grown bone-thin, the golden shade turned ashen. Smiling softly, she brushed her thumbs over Perida's knuckles.

"Mother, I truly think you should consider what they're offering," she whispered. "They will continue to attack Errest unless we do something to stop it."

"Errest will never fall to them," Perida hissed, her expression twisting in disgust. "That you have fallen so easily for their lies tells me you're more of an idiot than I thought. And the things you said about your *father*..." Perida blinked back tears and looked away from her daughter.

Lea clenched her teeth and attempted to force calming thoughts toward her mother, reassure her that this *wasn't* what she wanted, but in order for them to succeed in taking back their home, they needed to first put on a show.

"If we work with them," Lea said slowly, "we can bring Errest under control, along with the rest of Edhil. From there, we can begin the process of uniting our peoples."

Something flashed through Perida's eyes when she looked back to Lea.

"What of you, then, daughter? Are you to just be his wife and nothing more? A pretty mare for breeding?"

Lea shook her head. "No, I will help Edhil rebuild, help find a suitable leader to take over, one who will understand the needs of our people. I will not leave our lands unless I know they are safe." She took a deep breath. "And if along the way I am blessed with children, Lord Edrin and I have agreed they will be raised knowing their full history."

You know I wouldn't be that stupid, mother. Please, understand.

Perida's eyes narrowed, then darted to Lessia. "What guarantees can you offer that will let me reassure my people they will not be turned to chattel? That your people will not wipe them out, take their homes, their livelihoods?"

"The Jotnar love their lands, Lady Calliwell, so they will be in no rush to move south. For the most part," Lessia told her. "Your people will be under the joint rule of Dystone and Jotunheim, true, and we will require your realm continue to pay tithes to the capital as you have done for centuries. That amount will go up to account for the cost of rebuilding certain areas, of course, but the people of Edhil will remain under the control of a Lindorothian native of our choosing." She inclined her head toward Lea. "It's possible your daughter may even take up the role."

"Why?" Perida demanded. "If you're as stron—"

"Wouldn't a peaceful transfer of power be better than a violent one?" Lea said, cutting her mother off.

Perida's chin tilted up and she studied her daughter for a second. "I suppose it would. I would need more reassurances than mere words, as I'm sure you all can understand. And despite my ability to pass control to another in my husband's stead, I cannot guarantee I will be able to convince the Edhilians to agree to anything."

"Your status is most assuredly unchanged," Lessia said. "They will listen to you, hear your words, and take them to heart."

"And if I refuse?"

"Your people will be slaughtered and you will live out the rest of your days knowing it was your fault," Willem said dryly. "It's quite simple."

Lessia shot him a glare, then looked at Perida. "It does not have to be that way, though." She took a step closer and gave her a small smile. "Your family home still stands, Lady Calliwell," she crooned. "You can return to it and live out your days in freedom."

The room was silent as Perida looked at Lea and Lessia in turn. Finally, she dropped Lea's hands and stepped back, her face slipping into a mask of cold stone.

"My people would rather go down fighting than fall in line for a false ruler. Do what you want with me, but I will never encourage them to follow you." She sent Lea a level glare. "I would have thought the same of you."

Willem laughed darkly and Lessia's face turned furious. Before his empress could strike out, Jonas snapped his fingers and the guards that held Perida moments earlier grabbed her.

"Take her back to her cell," he ordered.

Lea let out a deep breath and cast her eyes toward the high ceiling, hoping Perida couldn't see just how relieved she was at her mother's response.

LEA'S JOY at Perida's refusal to concede to Lessia and Willem and their subsequent lack of execution reaffirmed the idea that had been forming for several days in Lea's mind.

Byrric was a strong commander and ensured all who led below him were as well. The only reason she could see that Lessia and Willem would be trying so hard to gain her or Perida's assistance would be because they couldn't get through the combined forces of the Edhilian army and the knights Byrric had left behind as support. She didn't believe for a single second that they were simply trying for the diplomatic approach—brute force would be far quicker *if* they were able to amass it.

Which, it seemed, they couldn't. After witnessing her mother's reaction in the throne room, she could only assume Perida had come to the same conclusion.

She voiced as much to Tyna, who fluttered about doing Lea's hair for dinner later that afternoon.

"If I had to guess, it's likely due to Errest's location," Tyna observed. "It's prime for defense."

"Because of the desert to the south," Lea murmured, nodding. She hadn't had much in the way of education on military strategy, but she knew a southern defense was all but unneeded in Edhil because of how vast the Edhilian Desert was. It stretched across the southern portion of the continent, from the Ellisonian Sea to the Brystone Sea, and was filled with nothing but sand, cacti, and, toward the north, beautiful canyons that would be of little use from a tactical standpoint. It was a beautiful region, but completely inhospitable, so travel that lasted more than a day or two would be nearly impossible, especially to those accustomed to a colder climate or weighed down by armor and weapons. The simplest way into Edhil would be either through the northern border or one of the coastlines, both of which were some of the most heavily guarded regions in Lindoroth.

"Exactly, my lady," Tyna said. "My guess is they've tried to get through, saw the impossibility of it, and are shifting their approach, hoping it can fall another way."

"And if a region as strong as Edhil can fall, so can all the rest." Lea rubbed a hand across her brow. "Especially considering how quickly Kildin and Watoria were taken."

"Edhil will be seen as the last stronghold, my lady."

"Then how do we make it stronger?" Lea gnawed her bottom lip. "It holds strong for now, but how do we ensure that doesn't change?"

"We pray that Their Majesties succeed in Avorell." Tyna sighed. "Unlikely as it seems."

40

FREYA

Exhaustion struck the moment Freya's feet touched down on the grassy, moonlit field that lay beyond the eastern edge of the forest. She fell to her knees, chest heaving at the exertion of flight, short as the trip had been. But despite the growing pain where her skin had been burned and sliced, she smiled.

She'd done it.

"Freya!"

Her head shot up at the sound of Aer's voice, and she let out a breath when she saw him running across the field, Florian beside him.

Nalaea and Ruehnar walked slowly after them.

She retracted her wings and struggled to get to her feet, but just as she got one foot under her, he was there, helping her stand, burying his face in her knotted hair. Her arms came around his waist as he held her tight. "Gods above, Freya," he murmured, his hold on her tightening.

"Your Majesty, we should tend to her injuries as soon as possible," Florian said when he approached.

"What?" Aer jerked back, his face filled with concern as he took in her appearance. "Why haven't you healed?"

"The forest," Freya replied tiredly, rubbing her face. "It wouldn't let me..."

His expression turned hard as he grabbed her hand. "Let's go."

Forcing a facade of strength, she retracted her wings and let him help her to her feet, her chin held high as she stood.

"Take us back to the palace," he demanded, looking at Ruehnar and Nalaea. "I know you can travel through the Between to Andra-dath, even if others can't."

Nalaea's brows shot up in amusement, but she held out a hand for his as Ruehnar put one on Florian's arm.

Freya twined her fingers around Aer's, and a moment later, they were all standing in their chambers.

"Get her healed and cleaned up," Nalaea said. "Then we will discuss our next steps."

"No," Freya protested. "I want to discuss this now."

"Once you are healed," Nalaea said. "It won't take long, now that you're out of the forest, but Florian's ointments and your mate's magic will surely speed the process."

"You're dead on your feet, Freya," Aer murmured. "Just let Florian treat you."

"No I am—*dammit!*" She growled when the king and queen vanished from before her. Pushing Aer off, she took a step toward the door. "I am not waiting—"

The floor tilted, and the room around her did a slow spin. Blindly, she reached out to steady herself.

"Sit her down," Florian instructed as Aer took her arm and guided her back down. "I just need to get my case."

Freya all but collapsed onto the sofa, sparing half a thought to the filthy state of her clothes against the silk brocade upholstery.

"Bastards," she muttered.

Aer crouched on the floor in front of her. "Tell me where it hurts."

Her head fell back against the couch. "Everywhere," she murmured. "There were so many..."

"I know," he whispered. "We received a lot of updates...they nearly had to bind my magic." He took her hands and his forehead came to rest on her knees.

She closed her eyes and tried to relax as his magic began to creep over her, seeking out her wounds. "I would've tossed you in a bog if you'd come after me," she murmured.

He let out a laugh and looked up at her, his eyes rimmed with red. "Do you think Nalaea and Ruehnar's threats were the only thing that kept me from breaking the rules?"

Florian came back from his adjoining room carrying a heavy black case. Aer shifted to sit beside Freya while Florian crouched in front of her to examine her injuries.

"Your Majesty, if you wouldn't mind releasing your magic?"

Aer gave the case a curious look as he pulled back his power so Florian could tend to the venoms that were still running through Freya's system. "How did you get that here? You came with no more than a satchel."

"Silmar retrieved it," Florian said. "I'll need you down to your undergarments, Your Majesty."

Freya nodded, then tried not to grimace too much as Aer helped her tenderly out of her pants and tunic.

She ignored his muttered curse when he saw just how extensive her injuries were. "How much were you told?" she asked.

Jaw tight, he looked back at her. "Only about your fights with the elves."

Freya gave him a surprised look, then obediently held out her arm when Florian started putting a salve on the cuts and burns from one elf's venom. "That's all? They didn't tell you about the rest?"

Aer shook his head. "No. They insinuated that there were other threats out there, but..."

"They wanted you to suffer, Your Majesty," Florian murmured, frowning at a particularly nasty slice on Freya's thigh.

"What next?" Freya asked. "I passed their test. Now what?"

"Now we pray we haven't missed any loopholes in their agreement," Florian said. "Which I can assure you, we have not."

Freya scoffed.

Aer let out a measured breath. "If she went through all of that just to be thwarted by a godsdamned *loophole*..."

"That's highly unlikely," Florian assured them both. "Despite their craftiness, Nalaea and Ruehnar are honorable people. You will get your army."

"And Fenian?" Freya asked. "I got the impression that he was the one who would make the final decision." It was a thought that had struck her halfway through her journey through the forest and had been nagging at her ever since.

"The king and queen have the final say," Florian replied. "He may disagree or try to challenge it, but ultimately, it is not his call."

Hardly reassured, Freya sat quietly, her hand in Aer's, as Florian finished tending to her wounds. After using his magic to clean up the dirt and blood, it took nearly an hour for him and Aer to seal the cuts and smooth away the burns. It would take several more for them to heal entirely as her body's magic regained its full strength.

When they were done, Florian began to replace his bottles and jars in his case. "You should rest, at least for a few hours, and have something to eat." When she opened her mouth to protest, he held up a hand. "We will leave as soon as is reasonable, but Your Majesty, your magic is nearly depleted and any that remains is currently working to make up for lost time to heal you. Even if we had an army at our heels this instant, you would be useless against any foes."

She snorted. "I would be able to handle myself fine."

"No, you would not." He shut his case with a snap. "Rest, perhaps eat something. A few hours won't make a difference at this point." He looked at Aer. "If you think you can manage it, try to use a bit more of your own magic to speed up the healing process."

"I can manage," Aer said, eying Freya's rapidly-healing injuries. Seeming to see her frustration, he sighed. "Silmar received word from Byrric. The Valkyrie from Iston were able to delay the Jotnar coming to Watoria by a day. They launched their own attack in central Caelora and took out a large portion of their camp, but it was a mission for distraction only. The Istonians don't have the numbers for a full-fledged attack on a squadron that large, so it didn't buy us much time. It gave us enough that you can spare some time to rest, though."

A small weight lifted from Freya's shoulders at that news. Even a day could prove invaluable at this point.

"Were many Istonians lost?"

"None, according to Ana," Aer said. "It was a surprise attack. They went in at night and set fire to as many camps as they could. There was hardly a fight to speak of, since they came in so swiftly, but they left enough Jotnar casualties that it would take easily half a day for the wounded to be treated and the dead to be disposed of."

"That's assuming they do either of those things," Freya countered. "What if—"

"Byrric already sent Zane out to ensure your aunt's report is accurate," Florian said. "It was. Now, please, get some rest."

There was a quiet knock at the door, then it opened and Lyrei and Ryul stepped inside. Lyrei held a large jug, and Ryul carried a tray of food.

"Their Majesties said you might need some sustenance," Lyrei said.

Ryul held up the tray. "It will help restore your magic more quickly."

Freya sighed, then gestured toward the table near the veranda. "You can set it all down over there." She smiled at them both. "Thank you."

Lyrei gave a small bob of her head, and Ryul frowned slightly as he examined Freya. "You encountered Ratatoskr."

He said it as a statement, not a question.

"I did," she replied, surprised. "How did you know?"

"I can scent him. Tricky creature, that one."

"Is that why you smell like a rodent?" Aer asked, his lips playing at a smile.

Freya shot him a warning look before replying to Ryul. "Yes, I'm still deciding if he was more helpful than troublesome, but I wasn't opposed to his company."

Lyrei clicked her tongue. "He is a troublemaker. There is a reason he was banished to that place."

"Trapped, more like," Ryul clarified. "Others were allowed to come and go, but he caused a great deal of trouble in his time that did not go unnoticed."

"I gathered trouble-making was one of his favorite pastimes," Freya replied.

"Who is this person?" Aer asked. He'd been silent as he watched the conversation between Freya and the two servants.

"He told me his name was Toskr," Freya explained. "A squirrel shifter. Keeper of the forest gossip, from what I could tell. He acted as a guide, of sorts."

"Did he lead you into harm?" Lyrei asked.

"No more than I was already in. He didn't strike me as malicious, though." Freya narrowed her eyes. "Why are you asking so many questions?"

Ryul's eyes flicked to the floor, then back to Freya. "We knew him... long ago. It has been some time since we last saw him."

Freya gave him a tight smile. "Well, hopefully after this he'll get a reprieve. As troublesome as he was, he still helped a good deal."

"That's something, at least," Aer said. Standing, he helped her to her feet, then smiled at Ryul and Lyrei. "Thank you for your help. Please tell the king and queen we would like to meet with them first thing tomorrow."

Each gave a nod, then left.

❧

DESPITE HOW BADLY SHE wanted to settle things with Nalaea and Ruehnar that night, once Freya had eaten and bathed, and Aer had used some of his power to heal her physical injuries more thoroughly, exhaustion hit. She'd hardly laid down on the thick mattress before her eyes fell closed and she was dragged into a deep, dreamless slumber.

She awoke the following morning just before sunrise feeling more rested than she had in a long time. Immediately, she reached out for her magic, and was thrilled to find it fully replenished, waiting.

Aer's arm snaked around her waist, and she couldn't help but smile as he pulled her closer.

"Does that smile mean you're feeling better?" he murmured.

"It does," she confirmed. She curled her fingers around his. "Well enough to go demand that army I earned us."

He chuckled sleepily and touched his lips to her shoulder. "Are you alright?"

"Physically? Yes, I'm fine." She put a hand over her eyes and sighed. "The rest, I just... I don't know."

"A lot was asked of you, Freya," he murmured. "None of it easy."

"I know. It's only... being asked to kill things like those elves has never been an issue for me. They were attacking me, hunting me. So, logically, I know I had every reason to defend myself. But the others... the animals..."

"You were on their land?" Aer finished. He propped himself up on his elbows and looked at her.

She nodded.

"I spoke with Florian after you fell asleep about the things you fought," he said. "He told me about the forest, about those creatures. The world will not miss any of them."

"I have no doubts. It doesn't change the fact that I took a lot of lives yesterday, very intentionally. This wasn't like in Watoria, where I'd patrol, come across some draugs, and make the city safer by killing them." She bit her lip and turned away, annoyed to feel her eyes burning.

"Don't do that," he whispered, touching her chin to turn her face back to his. "I'm allowed to see your tears."

"I know," she said quietly, her voice breaking slightly. "Those wights, though…they made it seem as though I'd committed some great wrong, that I'd tarnished the forest irrevocably."

"The king and queen explained that as well. The forest is supposed to be a place that quells violence, supplants it, even," Aer explained. "You spilled blood, which is an offense, but the forest has already retaken the creatures you killed."

"The wights said the last three elves I killed were the ones responsible for the forest's existence," Freya said quietly. "That I killed them was the only reason they let me leave. If I hadn't faced them last, I don't know that I would've been so fortunate. It was as if that made up for everything I'd done up until then." She gave him a curious look. "Actually…I guess I was so out of it last night, but I meant to ask… how were you getting updates about my progress?"

Aer shrugged. "Silmar would arrive now and then to inform us who or what you'd managed to defeat. There was no sadness for the forest monsters you killed, Freya, trust me. The wights may not have told you that, but the trolls and ravens had been tormenting the more peaceful creatures for ages."

"Silmar told you?" Freya frowned. "That doesn't make sense. How —" She groaned. "Toskr. It had to have been him."

"The squirrel?" Aer's lips tilted in amusement at her deadpan look. "I still find it amusing you had a squirrel, of all things, act as your guide for one of the most vicious missions of your life."

"Yes, well, that makes two of us." She sighed, then lowered her eyes to his chest. "Do you really think all those things I killed yesterday were bad for that place?"

"Based on what Nalaea and Ruehnar said? Yes." He touched her chin, bringing her eyes back to his. "The trolls? Their favorite thing to feed on is a rare plant that's used as an anesthetic for injuries. The fanged ravens gorge themselves on the fish in the nearby lakes, leaving very little for the more docile creatures. The serpent you fought from the bog routinely eats travelers, regardless of their intent. The rest have similar stories. Despite how cold they may seem, I don't think the king and queen would've sent you there to kill wholly innocent beings."

Freya nodded slowly. "I only wish I'd known that before I began yesterday. Maybe it would've helped stop this... feeling that's just sitting in my stomach."

Smiling softly, Aer brushed aside the strands of hair that had fallen across her cheek. "Their intent wasn't to make this easy, unfortunately. I wasn't exaggerating when I said they nearly had to bind my magic. Florian all but tied me to a chair."

"Did you doubt me?" she asked, mildly offended.

"No, of course not." He kissed her gently. "But every time you were afraid or in pain, I felt it. Your fear nearly broke me, Freya. It was all I could do not to go after you."

"I would've killed you," she said flatly. "Just so we're clear."

He laughed softly. "Yes, I'm aware."

There was a soft knock at the door, then it opened and Florian stepped inside.

"Good morning, Your Majesties," he said. "Breakfast is being prepared and will be served shortly in the dining room."

"We're dining with the king and queen?" Freya asked, sitting up.

Florian nodded. "And the princes. We should hurry."

Not needing to be told twice, Freya and Aer were out of bed. As if summoned, their attendants entered and began helping them dress.

Freya's heart leapt, then fell when Lyrei pulled out a fresh pair of leather pants, a beige tunic, and a thigh-length leather jacket that laced up the front.

"We're going home?" she asked.

Lyrei nodded. "Yes, Your Majesty. After you meet with the king and queen, you will return to Lindoroth."

"With them?"

Lyrei shrugged. "You have made your bargain with them. Assuming you have made it well, they will fulfill their terms."

Freya tugged her pants on under her nightgown. "That's hardly an answer."

"It is the only answer I can give you."

Trying not to show her annoyance, Freya lifted her arms so Lyrei could switch her nightgown for her tunic, then waited as she tucked it into her pants and fastened them up.

When Lyrei handed Freya her boots, she gave her a small smile. "However things unfold, Your Majesty, I am glad to have met you."

Freya smiled and began lacing up her boots. "I hope to see you again, Lyrei. Truly."

41

FREYA

The ballroom that had been so full of revelry a few nights before now sat echoing and empty, save for a table where Nalaea, Ruehnar, and their two sons were seated.

Fenian and Tavian rose when Freya, Aer, and Florian entered, and the mischievous glint in the eldest prince's eyes instantly put Freya on alert.

"Your Majesty," Fenian said with a deep bow. "May I be the first to congratulate you on a job well done."

"And I shall be the second," Tavian said, jumping from his seat to bow as well.

"Thank you," Freya said to the princes as she sat, not wanting to offend them. As soon as they were seated, servants began to set down covered dishes.

"Did you sleep well?" Tavian asked, his dark eyes darting between Freya and Aer.

"Very well, thank you," she replied.

"And now you're eager to go home?" Fenian asked.

"As lovely as your court is, yes, I'm anxious to return to my people." She looked at Aer. "We both are."

Fenian picked up a slice of toast and began smearing it with golden jam. "Do you feel you completed your task sufficiently?"

"Tasks," Freya corrected, flicking a glance at Nalaea, who sat across from her. "And, yes, I do."

"And you, King Aerelius?" Tavian asked. "You were a bit out of your skin yesterday, would you agree?"

"As anyone would be in my position," Aer replied. "I still fulfilled my terms."

Smirking, Fenian leaned back in his chair and chewed his food.

Refusing to let them see how much they were irking her, Freya picked up her fork and began eating her eggs. After a moment she said, "The creatures in your land are much different than I expected. I didn't see such large beasts when we traveled through the forest on our way here."

"Yes, those trolls are quite good at hiding," Tavian said. "Our scout said you did well against them."

"Toskr was your scout, correct?" she asked.

"Indeed," Nalaea said.

"We were surprised you accepted him as your... guide so quickly," Ruehnar commented. "What was your reasoning for that?"

Knowing full-well Toskr had already explained that to them, she sighed. "As I told him, I didn't believe he meant me harm, at least not at first. I was cornered in a tree. If he'd wanted me dead, I would've been."

"You admit a squirrel got the best of you?" Tavian asked, amused.

She gave him a level look. "Had a squirrel chased me up a tree, Prince Fenian, I would be ashamed to admit it. The only facts I had to base my assessment on were his size as an elvish male and the power I could feel coming from him. Neither of those things indicated 'rodent.'"

Fenian snickered and Ruehnar smiled.

"And when you saw the way he was herding you and your opponents?" Nalaea asked. "You didn't free yourself from him then, either."

"I wanted the task to be done as quickly as possible. Having to seek out my enemies on my own would've taken far longer."

"But you are a huntress," Fenian protested.

"Your word, not mine, and even still, hunting takes time, Prince Fenian. I did not feel I had the luxury of taking my time."

Nalaea looked at Aer, who was sitting perfectly at ease at Freya's side. "Aerelius, you've yet to say a word."

Aer inclined his head toward Freya. "She was in the forest, Your Majesty. I was not. What place do I have speaking for her?"

"You *are* her husband, after all," Tavian pointed out.

"And yet here we are, a day after I watched my wife walk into a forest to risk her own life for her people. If I had authority over her, I never would have allowed that to happen."

"So she holds authority over you?" Fenian asked.

"Gods above," Freya muttered as Aer chuckled.

"What my monarchs mean," Florian cut in, sending them each a silencing look, "is that their trust in one another is unwavering, and they demonstrated as much yesterday when King Aerelius chose not to fight Queen Freya's battle for her." He folded his long, dark hands and rested them on the table, then looked directly at the elf king. "Ruehnar, you and I both know she accomplished the tasks you set before her far better than even you would've expected. Give them their army and let them be on their way."

Freya saw Tavian lean back in his chair, eying his father as he locked stares with Florian.

"All we agreed to was to help Lindoroth once you completed your tasks," Fenian said. "We did not give a specific day or time."

Florian chuckled and Freya nearly rolled her eyes at Fenian's blatant attempt to talk his way out of their bargain.

Feeling Aer's temper rise, she laid a hand on his arm and looked at Fenian. "I would imagine, if I reread our bargain, that I could find a way to twist those words just as easily as you are. But if not—" she tilted her head toward the queen, "—Her Majesty stated a time, just before I went into the forest." She smiled. "I believe her exact words were, 'succeed and we will leave for Lindoroth the following morning.'"

Nalaea's lips quirked into a small, satisfied smirk when Tavian turned irritated eyes on his mother.

Freya had to hold back her answering grin as an uncomfortable silence settled over the table.

"I think we've reached a decision," Ruehnar finally said. "Fenian, ready your knights. You'll leave at dusk."

"I suppose I'm to go, too?" Tavian asked, then frowned when his father nodded.

"Look at the bright side, brother," Fenian said as he stood. He clapped a hand to Tavian's shoulder. "One of us could very well die in this war, and I, for one, would welcome the absence of another heir to fight with."

"WHAT ARE THE ODDS," Aer asked as he, Freya, and Florian stood at the palace entrance, waiting for Fenian, "that one of the Tordove princes kills the other two before this is over?"

Florian sent him a look, and Freya shook her head. "Slim," she said, then considered it a bit more. "Although, considering I haven't met the youngest, it's hard to say."

Aer frowned at Florian. "Speaking of... Has there been word on Lea's status yet?"

Florian shook his head. "No, Silmar has to wait until a predetermined meeting time with Ettrian in order to convey news to and from Iladel. Their next meeting will be tomorrow morning, and I believe Fenian will be joining them."

"And I can assure you, Your Majesties," Fenian said, coming up behind them, "I won't sully your war with family feuds. My brothers may be tiresome, but I do not *actually* hope for their deaths."

"It's good to know that distraction won't be weighing on your mind," Aer replied, seeming unruffled that the prince had overheard him.

Fenian flashed him a smile. "Shall we go?"

"Where are your knights?" Freya asked, not budging an inch.

"It will take a day for them to fully mobilize," Fenian replied, seeing her disappointment. "Not to worry, though. They will be there in time to save your kingdom."

Freya let out a quiet breath and smiled. Then, finally, she allowed herself the small bit of hope she'd denied herself for weeks.

THE FRIGID AIR of Allanor cut like a knife against the lingering warmth of the Summer Court, but the cold was instantly forgotten when she saw her grandparents' home rising up in front of her. It was only the presence of Fenian that stopped her from running across the lawn to the entrance.

As it was, they'd only taken a few steps when a golden lioness leapt from the trees and let out a loud, angry hiss.

"Myria," Freya greeted her.

Myria stalked toward them, shifting on to two legs as she moved. Her expression was furious. "How *dare you*—I don't give a single *damn* that you're my monarchs! How could you just *leave* us with no indication of where—" She came up short when she caught sight of Fenian and scowled. "Who is he?"

"Myria Bryton, this is Fenian Tordove," Freya said. "The eldest prince of Avorell."

Myria stood frozen for half a breath before her years of training took over and she dipped into a low curtsy. "Your Highness, it's lovely to meet you. Welcome to Her Majesty's family home. I'm sure you'll find it quite to your liking."

"Likewise, Lady Bryton." Fenian cocked his head. "You *are* a Lady, correct?"

Her eyes flared, then turned hard when she looked back at Aer and Freya. "You've come back with a single elf?"

Aer ran a hand over his jaw and averted his eyes.

"Might I suggest we bring this discussion inside?" Florian said.

"Where is my father?" Freya asked Myria as they began to walk across the lawn.

Myria gestured vaguely toward the house. "Poring over maps with Ashton, Collin, and Reginald, most likely."

Florian had just closed the door behind them when Laz started down the stairs. When he saw them, he paused in mid-step, then barreled toward them, not stopping until he'd dragged Freya and Aer into an awkward hug, effectively shoving Fenian, Florian, and Myria aside.

"I am so angry with you both," he mumbled against Freya's hair. "Byrric wouldn't tell us where you went." He pulled back but kept his hands on their arms. "Are you alright? Where were you?" His eyes drifted to the side, just noticing their company, then widened when he took in the prince's elvish features. "You went to Avorell? Without backup?" he exclaimed. He gripped Aer's chin. *Are you insane?*"

Fenian coughed.

"It was your idea," Aer said, gently brushing his cousin's hand away.

"I never meant—" Laz took a measured breath. "You know what?" He held up his hands. "Fine. It's fine. I'll just let Byrric know you've returned from the *foreign land* you traveled to with *no armed backup whatsoever*."

"Everyone seems quite angry here," Fenian remarked as Laz turned and stormed off in the direction of the study.

"That's what happens when you leave with no notice for five days in the middle of a damn war," Myria quipped.

Ignoring them both, Freya rushed after Laz to the study, where Byrric, Collin, Ashton, and Reginald were indeed hovering over a stack of maps.

She grinned at the sight.

"Byrric."

Her father's head flew up at the sound of Florian's voice. He froze, took in Freya and Aer standing beside the elvish prince, then straightened.

"Everyone out," he ordered. "Now." He paused. "And keep their presence to yourselves until I can fully debrief everyone on their return," he added. He looked at Reginald and Ashton. "Are we clear?"

"Of course, Commander," Reginald replied. "Let us know when you need us." He gave Freya and Aer a quick bow, then left the room.

Ashton and Collin each gave Freya a hug and Aer a pat on the shoulder as they moved past. Collin seemed to be fighting back a grin.

"You two have a *lot* of explaining to do," he whispered when he noticed Fenian hovering in the hall behind them.

"More than a lot," Ashton added with a shake of his head.

"You can say that again," Laz muttered.

Once they'd all filed out, Byrric exhaled.

"So you made it through alive."

Freya grinned. "You say that as if you doubted us." She gestured toward Fenian. "Fenian Tordove, this is my father, Byrric Balthana."

Stepping out from around the desk he'd been standing behind, Byrric bowed to the elvish prince. "Your Highness, it's an honor to meet you, despite the unfortunate circumstances. Your assistance here is greatly appreciated."

Fenian inclined his head in greeting. "Your monarchs have assured me they will return the favor in kind, if the need arises, so I feel we have struck a fair bargain."

Byrric arched a brow at Freya and Aer. "Yes, I'd like to see the text of that bargain as soon as possible, if that's alright."

"It's sound, I assure you," Florian said. "No matter how much some might try to convince you otherwise." He sent a look at Fenian.

Byrric made a small, noncommittal noise, then gestured for them to join him at the desk. "Come, let's go over how things are progressing, then we'll get everyone settled in." He glanced at Fenian. "Your Highness, when should we expect your knights?"

"Five hundred will be here with Tavian by tomorrow," Fenian replied. "Another two thousand will arrive with my father two days after that, once they finish preparations."

Byrric nodded. "Alright." He tapped a finger on the map, at a spot to the northeast of Watoria. "The Allanorians, just under four hundred, are currently camped here, along with about six hundred of my own knights. The human battalion that surrounds the city has nearly double that, in addition to the Jotnar in the city itself. We're unsure how many Jotnar are inside the city gates, but from what my scouts have been able to tell me, it looks like a few hundred more have set up residence."

"Where is the rest of your army?" Fenian asked.

"The Royal Army is divided up among the five capitals. All told, roughly one-third of Lindoroth knights were killed in the past two weeks."

Fenian nodded slowly. "And what is the state of your capitals?"

"The capitals of Saith and Edhil—Olthanas and Errest—are still under Lindorothian control, at least somewhat. Olthanas has been able to open to citizens who've fled from outer towns and villages, but Errest is at a stalemate. Jotnar and human forces are camped outside the gates, but the city is locked down from the inside by the Edhilian residents and knights. Two of my lieutenant commanders are acting as interim governors for the time being." He exhaled. "Kildin is lost, as is Iladel."

"Then we cannot focus on them now." Fenian gestured toward Watoria. "We will take back Watoria the day after tomorrow. Then, once the rest of my army arrives, we will plot our course of action for the remaining lands." He looked to the rest of them. "It is imperative that the amount of people who know we've arrived is kept at a minimum. Is that clear?"

"We need to let the capitals know help is imminent," Freya said with a frown.

Fenian flicked his eyes to the door, then Freya felt the heavy press of elvish magic settle over the room. She couldn't help but brush against it with her own magic, earning her a quirked brow from the prince.

"As you know, my brother is in Iladel," Fenian began. "Empress Lessia and King Willem believe they have a chance at gaining an ally in Avorell, and we need them to continue to believe that for as long as possible. My army needs time to prepare and our combined forces need time to coordinate our defenses, and we would also like to get more information from Lessia and Willem. A surprise attack will be far more effective at neutralizing the threats in the immediate area." He looked at Byrric. "Do you believe everyone here is to be trusted?"

Byrric exchanged a look with Freya before responding. "Unfortunately, it seems someone has been getting information to Willem somehow. So, no."

Fenian frowned. "How? The only way to get from here to your capital quickly is to travel through the Between."

"Yes, which is what makes this all the more concerning," Byrric said, glancing at Florian. "We're not sure how they're doing it, but based on the reports we've gotten from Iladel, Willem knows things that only someone who is here could tell him." He looked at Freya and Aer. "And he is aware you both left Lindoroth, so it's only a matter of time before he finds out where you went." He frowned. "What's interesting, though, is Lessia seems unaware of that fact."

Aer's brows rose. "That *is* interesting."

"I suppose it's safe to say Willem and Lessia are not as trusting of one another as they'd have you believe," Fenian commented.

"Indeed," Freya murmured.

"Has there been any word on my cousin?" Aer asked her father.

"As far as Lessia and Willem know, she is married and bound by blood to Lord Edrin."

Aer looked at him, surprised. "But Nalaea and Ruehnar said—"

"They said Lea consented and that Prince Ettrian could break the bond, if necessary," Florian interrupted, shooting an irritated look at Fenian. "They never said he actually bound them."

Freya's eyes fell closed as annoyance hit. She let out a measured breath, then looked at Fenian. "The marriage—do you know if it's something she wanted?"

"Again, she consented, but no, it was not something she would have chosen."

Aer narrowed his eyes. "Did he fake the ceremony as well, then?"

"An elf has no authority presiding over the marriage of people who are not his," Fenian replied.

"Yes or no?" Freya snapped.

"Yes, he faked the marriage, too, although your cousin is as-yet unaware of that. Based on what he's seen, Ettrian feels it is in her best interest to allow her to continue to believe she is bound to Lord Edrin in at least one way."

Freya forced down every curse that threatened to spew his away and instead, looked at her father.

"Why is he helping her?" Aer asked. "What kind of game is he playing?"

"My brother tends to take issue with others being forced into situations similar to what Lessia wanted to force your cousin into. And, from a more pragmatic perspective, it benefits us all if Lessia and Willem have more cause to believe your cousin is on their side. Let their focus stay with trying to get into Errest using her influence as the late-Governor's daughter instead of what might be happening out here."

Freya stared at Fenian, not sure whether to fully trust what he said about his brother's reasoning, and not quite caring to take the time to figure it out. "Alright," she said. "If that's the case, then that's one less thing we have to worry about. I'll tell Rini—"

"You called?" Rini exclaimed, appearing with a puff in front of Freya. "Oh, Your Majesty! You *did* call! I just *knew* you would come back! I—" She let out a surprised squeak when she saw Fenian, then darted behind Freya, taking refuge in her hair. "There is an elf here!" she hissed.

Fenian frowned. "You employ pixies?"

"Yes," Freya said. "But Rini is more of a friend. Her sister is the one reporting to us from Iladel."

He chuckled. "Not quite the same breed as ours."

"Yes, I noticed," Freya said dryly. "I ran into quite a few in the forest."

Fenian nodded, smirking at Rini. "We typically exterminate them on sight."

Rini squealed and ducked behind Freya's shoulders.

"We, however, do not," Aer said, his words ringing with authority.

"Please inform your knights and anyone else who travels to Lindoroth of that fact. Our pixies are peaceful."

"Consider it done," Fenian said, then huffed when Aer gave him a pointed look. "I will do all in my power to inform every elf who enters Lindoroth that the pixies are to remain untouched." He narrowed his eyes at Rini. "Unless they attack unprovoked, in which case I will not tell my people to stand down." His lips twitched. "I'm curious, though. Are you aware of where she meets her sister when she gives her reports? If your concern is someone traversing the Between to give Willem information—"

"How *dare* you!" Rini exclaimed, shooting up from behind Freya.

Aer held up a hand as Freya reached up to stop Rini from charging the elf.

"What are you talking about?" Aer demanded.

Fenian gestured toward Rini. "Pixies are the only other creatures who possess the type of magic that allows access to the Between."

Rini gasped in outrage. "If you're implying what I *think* you're implying, I will have you *know*—"

Freya grabbed Rini by the waist when she shot toward Fenian.

The prince gave her an amused look.

"Prince Fenian, I appreciate your concern, but the pixies have served the Harridan monarchy loyally for centuries," Florian said. "I brought them on board myself, more than six hundred years ago when your people drove the bulk of them from Avorell. Aside from me, the only others who knew of their ability to access the Between were my former monarchs. It was part of the agreement we made when they came to us."

Freya and Aer exchanged a surprised look. Having only the sitting monarchs know of the pixies' abilities made sense, but Freya had always assumed they had some other means of transporting themselves.

Fenian shrugged. "Then someone here is lying to you about their heritage."

"That's the conclusion we've come to as well," Byrric said, who had remained silent up until now. "But I can assure you, the pixies of Lindoroth are no threat."

Rini folded her arms and let out a quiet *harrumph*.

"Now, if we could get back to the matter at hand?" Byrric said.

"As I was saying," Freya said. "I'll have Rini check in with Tyna and relay your message to Lea," she told Fenian. "We would like to get them out of there as soon as we can, though."

"I think we should consider having Lady Calliwell stay," Florian said.

"No," Freya and Aer said in unison.

"She's nearly been forced into marriage *and* a mating bond," Aer said. "If Lessia or Willem gets a hint that either of those things has been faked, Lea will be executed."

"She has my brother's protection," Fenian argued. "And, if what you have told me is true, Lord Edrin has sworn a blood pact to keep her safe."

"Which will end quite swiftly if his deceit is discovered," Freya countered. "Lessia has no qualms about killing him."

"My suggestion would be to leave it up to Lea," Byrric said. He held his hands up at the sharp look Freya sent him. "You can order her to do whatever you want, but it's my opinion that it should be her choice, especially considering a rescue mission would alert Lessia and Willem to everything Lea and Jonas have been up to."

Rini cleared her throat and looked at Aer, pointedly avoiding Fenian's stare. "If I may?"

At Aer's nod, she drifted back a bit so she could easily address them all. "Tyna and Lea, and Lea and Jonas as well, have had a few conversations about leaving. Lea is reluctant to do so because she doesn't want to leave her mother, but she has been taking her newfound freedom to explore the palace's... lesser-known areas. I believe if she needed to flee on her own, she would be able to do so and quite quickly."

"You are referring to the tunnels?" Fenian asked with a frown.

Aer and Freya looked at him in surprise.

"Willem has shown them to Ettrian," he explained. "Willem has been attempting to map them ever since his knights chased you through the tunnels."

"We heard soldiers in the tunnels when we escaped," Freya asked. "Are you saying they weren't Lessia's?"

"As far as Ettrian can tell, she has only been made aware of those tunnels that go into the mountains, and that type of thing is not unusual for a palace situated as yours is. If you heard pursuit, they were likely human."

Freya turned to face Rini. "Go to Tyna. Tell her we've returned. Ask her to have another talk with Lea about leaving, and ask her if Lea and Jonas faced any soldiers or guards on their way back into the palace. If Willem is holding information like that back from Lessia, we need to know about it."

"Have Lea and Tyna come up with a solid escape plan as well," Aer said. "If it comes down to it, I don't want either of them floundering with uncertainty."

Rini gave a sharp nod. "I'll go now, Your Majesties, and will return as soon as possible." She bit her lip and paused, then launched herself at Freya, twining her spindly arms around Freya's neck. "I am *so* happy you've returned, Your Majesty. You gave me such a fright when you disappeared like you did!"

Freya patted the small pixie lightly on the back. "I'm sorry, Rini. I'll try not to scare you like that again."

Rini sniffed. "Perhaps next time, you could consider taking your attendant with you." Then, without waiting for an answer, she vanished.

42

———

FREYA

The last reported movements of the Jotnar battalion coming south had come a few hours before Freya and the others had returned home. Byrric had gotten word from Commander Alstad, who'd been relaying messages back and forth through Zane twice a day. According to him, the Jotnar would be crossing into Watorian territory by dusk the day after next. The following day would be spent coordinating with the Lindorothian forces that were camped to the northeast of Watoria.

Freya, Aer, and their friends took one final night to try and settle their nerves before going into what would likely be the first of many battles.

"I'm still confused," Myria stated as she poured herself a glass of wine. They'd just sat down in the drawing room—a soft, comfortable space filled with books, overstuffed leather furniture, dark wood, and a roaring fire—to hear Freya and Aer's story. "How did your request for an Avorellian army turn into Freya running the Wild Hunt?" She handed the jug to Laz.

"They wanted me to prove myself worthy of Avorell, just like any other queen," Freya explained, then looked to Laz. "I'm honestly a bit surprised you didn't prepare me a little better, what with your vast historical knowledge," she teased.

Laz paused, the jug of wine hovering above his glass as he sent her the most withering of looks. "Perhaps if I'd been informed you were *leaving* I would've been able to gather you some worthwhile information to go over there with." He resumed filling his glass before setting the jug on the table that sat between them. "Although, reports of the Hunt are pretty scarce. The books in the palace library likely have a lot more."

"Did you know it was how they chose their queens?" Aer asked. His arm slid around Freya's shoulders and she shifted closer to him.

Laz shook his head, then glanced at Collin, who sat beside him on the sofa. "No, I've never heard of such a thing. But again, my knowledge of elvish history doesn't include much about the Hunt." He stared down at his wine a moment, then looked up at Freya. "I'm sorry I didn't have more information for you when we gave you the idea of reaching out to the elves. If I'd known..."

Collin pulled Laz against him and brushed a small kiss to his temple. "You couldn't have known," he whispered.

"Couldn't have known that they'd be foolish enough to sneak out like disobedient children?" Myria asked sweetly.

"Have you forgotten who's King and Queen in this room?" Aer asked, amusement coloring his tone. "I sure feel like you've forgotten."

Myria scowled at him, then went back to her wine.

The ghost of a smile quirked on Laz's lips.

Freya gave him a sympathetic look. "You two gave us a solid idea and it worked. We knew it was a long shot, but Laz, it's unlikely we would've even considered going if you hadn't suggested it."

"And now we've got a real chance at turning this around," Aer added.

Laz sighed as he rested his head against Collin's shoulder, then smiled at Aer. "I suppose you should blame Collin, too. He *did* go along with it, after all."

"It was a good idea," Collin replied, not the least bit chagrined. "I'm no military expert, but I thought it was a good idea."

"As did we," Freya said. "Clearly."

"And how many additional knights will this give us?" Myria asked.

"Roughly half their army," Aer replied.

Myria nodded slowly, then shifted begrudging eyes at Freya. "I suppose you're more than just a smelly magical pigeon after all?"

Freya laughed as Myria repeated some of the first insults she'd thrown at her when they'd met. "Does this make us best friends?"

Myria narrowed her eyes, but a small smile tugged at her lips.

"So... can you tell us more about the hunt?" Laz asked cautiously. "How you went about getting through?"

Freya's lips parted to speak, then fell closed when there was a small scratching sound on the floor.

"What is that?" Myria asked, setting her goblet on the table as she leaned over to look over the arm of the chair. Her eyes widened. "Freya, do you have *mice?*"

The others sat forward, and Freya ducked her head to get a better look. She caught a flash of movement on the floor, then Myria screamed and scrambled to her feet in the chair.

"Rat! Rat!" She gripped the back of the chair and pointed down at the floor. Laz and Collin leapt to their feet. "Lazarus, kill it!"

"Calm down, Myria," Freya muttered, sliding to her hands and knees. She peered under Myria's chair, then yelped and scrabbled back when a small ball of russet fur lunged for her. Myria screamed again.

Aer shot out a hand and caught the squirrel just before it landed on Freya.

Then, Toskr shifted, and Aer fell back to the sofa under the sudden weight.

"Queen Freya!" he exclaimed with a grin, not seeming the least bit bothered that he was effectively sitting in Aer's lap. "How lovely to see you!"

Aer blinked, then shoved the elf to the floor, where he landed with a hard thud next to Freya.

"*Why is there a rodent in your house?*" Myria screeched, still half-perched on the back of the chair.

"Stop shouting and perhaps we'll find out!" Collin snapped, eying Toskr warily.

The door burst open and Byrric stormed in.

"I heard screams," Byrric said. "What—"

Fenian came up short beside him, then let out what sounded like a string of curses in elvish, causing Toskr to look sheepish.

Freya put a hand to her chest to slow her racing heart, then slowly looked at Toskr. The elf looked no different than he had in the forest —bare-chested, with brown pants and no shoes, completely contradicting the frigid temperatures of Allanor. "Please tell me you didn't catch a ride with me when I left the forest."

He pursed his lips. "Alright, I will not. Should I also not tell you how cozy that pouch your warlock gave you was?"

Fenian barked out some kind of command that Freya didn't understand.

"Well *that* was rude," Toskr admonished.

Fenian's face went positively venomous.

"What is going on?" Byrric demanded. "Who is this?"

Slowly, Freya stood, then pulled Toskr to his feet. "This is Ratatoskr. He was my guide in the forest."

"Rat—" Laz gawked, then turned wide eyes on Freya. "*He* was your guide?"

She grimaced. "I suppose I hadn't gotten to that part of the story yet."

"What are you doing here, Ratatoskr?" Fenian demanded. "The forest did not give you permission to leave!"

Toskr held up one finger. "See, that is where you are wrong, Prince Fenian." His expression turned smug. "*I* found a solution to my problem."

Fenian's golden eyes turned piercing. "What. Solution."

"The terms of my imprisonment were such that I was to stay in the Forest of Ages *until someone freed me of their own volition.*" He gave Freya another wide grin.

"Stowaways generally don't have permission to go anywhere," she argued. "Don't put this on me!"

"No one would be foolish enough to do such a thing," Fenian said.

Toskr cleared his throat. "Queen Freya asked, 'Is there anything I can do to free you?' When I asked why she would do such a thing, she said, 'Perhaps I feel you've learned your lesson.'" Another smug smile. "I took that to the wights, argued my case, and they agreed that a person *wanting* to free me was the same as said person *actually* freeing me, considering she was not aware she had that power. That I saved her from falling in a bog also helped my case." He frowned. "Although, it *is* possible they just wanted to be rid of me."

There was a stunned silence. Slowly, Myria slid back down to a sitting position, her mouth hanging open in shock.

Freya did everything she could to avoid the stares she felt coming from her father and Fenian.

"Freya."

Pursing her lips, she looked at Byrric. "Yes?"

"Did I or did I not tell you to watch every word you said while in Avorell?"

"To be fair, this was after she had killed—what was it?" Toskr began counting on his fingers. "I believe it was twenty-seven creatures at that point. Her mind was a bit addled."

"Addled," Freya scoffed.

"You took advantage of her," Fenian snapped.

Still on the floor, Toskr crossed his legs and rested his elbows on his knees. "Then you may want to have a talk with your land wights, if you believe that is the case."

"While I understand I may have... caused a problem," Freya began, looking at Fenian. "Can I ask *why* this is a problem?"

Fenian huffed out a small breath through his nose, then tilted his head toward Toskr. "He was tasked with guarding the area where the forest now sits. He failed in his duty when the final three elves you killed had their massacre. Two thousand elves were slaughtered on that land because *he* had gone off to tell secrets to a water wight half a day away."

Laz let out a low whistle.

Collin winced and scratched the side of his neck. "Can we, uh, I don't know, send him back?"

Toskr's mouth dropped open in outrage. "I am *not* going back, you smelly canine!"

Laz's brows shot up. "Says the squirrel who hasn't seen a bath in centuries."

"Enough!" Aer snapped, then ran a hand across his jaw. "Prince Fenian, this is a problem with one of your people. How would you like to proceed?"

Fenian barked out a dark laugh and shook his head. "Oh, he is your problem now, unless you want me to present him to my parents, who will not take kindly to his duplicitousness." He pointed a finger at Freya. "I thought you did quite well, sussing out our deceits while in Avorell. This is what happens when you fail."

Toskr leapt to his knees and gripped Freya's hands, his dark eyes pleading. "Please do not send me back, Queen Freya! Nalaea will turn me into a decorative pillow if you do!"

"Take your hands off my queen this instant!" Byrric ordered. He waited for Toskr to obey before giving Freya and Aer expectant looks. "Well?"

Aer gestured toward Freya. "I'm going to defer to my wife on this one." He shrugged when Freya gave him an incredulous look. "You spent an entire day with him. If it were up to me, I'd send him back to Avorell with a boot print on his ass."

Myria let out a short hysterical laugh.

"Gods above," Freya murmured, shaking her head. She cast her eyes skyward before looking back to Toskr. "You may stay," she said, then shushed him when he moved to speak. "*If* you fight with us. I will not have you lazing about here, soaking up your ill-gotten freedom while the rest of us are out risking our lives."

"I believe that is a fair bargain," Toskr said with a nod.

"In writing," Laz said around a cough, earning himself a glare from Toskr.

"*And* blood," Freya added. "Are we clear?"

Toskr wrinkled his nose. "Perhaps there is another, less violent option?"

"No, there is not." Then, considering, she looked at Fenian. "Is he a good fighter?"

The prince shrugged. "He was trapped long before I came into this world. Presumably, yes, as he has managed to survive in the forest for this long."

"Alright." Freya sighed, then addressed Byrric. "Go get—"

"I'm already here," came Florian's tired voice from the doorway. "Let's get on with it."

Freya gave him an apologetic look. "I'm sorry if we woke you."

His dark eyes homed in pointedly on Toskr. "It's quite alright, Your Majesty. I'm certain it wasn't your fault."

Toskr sniffed. "There is a good deal of hostility toward the one who helped Her Majesty get free of that forest alive."

"Perhaps if you'd announced yourself like a civil creature, we'd be a bit nicer," Myria grumbled.

He flashed her a wicked grin, then turned to Freya. "Alright, on with it. I would like some sleep sometime this year, if possible."

IT TOOK FAR LONGER than Freya liked to sort out their bargain with Toskr, especially since he seemed far more skilled at deceit than even Fenian or his parents. By the time they finished and Haegin had found a place for Toskr with the marshals and guards, as well as some more appropriate attire, it was well-past midnight.

Freya and Aer climbed, bleary-eyed, into bed, but despite her exhaustion, her mind remained on alert once they laid down. She curled into Aer's side, nestling into his warmth. Slowly, he began to stroke her hair.

"We need to sleep," he murmured.

"I'm having trouble turning my mind off," she admitted. "I'm thrilled we got what we wanted, what we went to Avorell for, but now all I can think about is having to wait even longer to fix things."

"It's only one day," he replied. "One day to lay out a strategy for taking back your city, then the rest of Lindoroth. Just be thankful we won't have to attempt to get to the Allanorian camp on foot. It's half a day's journey from here."

"Having elves here to transport us is certainly helpful," Freya agreed. She started tracing small circles on his chest. "Are you scared to fight?"

He huffed out a laugh. "Yes, and I have no trouble admitting that. What about you?"

"I'm terrified," she admitted. "After being in that forest and facing things that weren't simply trying to be irritating... Yes, I'm scared."

"Freya Balthana, admitting she's afraid of something," Aer murmured, his breath tickling her hair. "I never thought I'd see the day."

Smiling, she closed her eyes and snuggled closer. "Don't get used to it."

43

FREYA

When Freya opened her eyes the following morning and saw the blanket of gray across the sky, she instantly missed the balmy air of the Summer Court.

Even still, she was happy to be home.

She burrowed deep under the heavy down bedding, not ready to get up and face the day that loomed before them, a day that would be cold and filled with talk of battle strategy. There was no avoiding either the weather or discussions of war, but she, perhaps selfishly, wanted to take just a few more minutes where neither of those things mattered.

As she lay there in the silence of dawn, her mind ran over the events of the past few days. She'd hardly had even a moment to think of her time in the forest, of how much she'd accomplished in fulfilling her tasks there. In a way, she felt like she shouldn't be so surprised with herself. She'd been trained her whole life to defend herself and others, and while it had been extreme, that was what the Wild Hunt had required. A test, yes. But a test of skills she'd honed for years. And as horrifying and trying as it had been, she felt that the forest had strengthened her, even reassured her, in a way, that she could take on whatever was put in her path.

Quietly, she turned her head to look at Aer and smiled when she found sleep-clouded eyes looking back.

"You look rested," he murmured, sliding a hand across her stomach.

"I feel rested," she said. She bit her lip and smiled when his eyes drifted shut again. "You seem like you could use a bit of help waking up, though."

The corner of his mouth twitched up, but his eyes remained closed. "Perhaps you could help me with that."

Gently, she kissed his shoulder, then his chest. "I think I can do that."

LATER, once the sky had fully lightened and noises of the day began to filter through the house, they climbed from their cocoon of blankets and dressed. When they made their way down to the dining room to get breakfast, they found Byrric and Fenian already there.

"Prince Fenian," Aer greeted. "Did you sleep well?"

He nodded. "Yes, your guest quarters are quite comfortable."

Freya addressed Byrric as she and Aer took seats across from them. "Any news?"

He shook his head. "Zane should be along sometime this morning to give us his most recent report from Commander Alstad. Once we hear what he has to say, we can finalize our plans."

She looked at Fenian. "And your knights?"

"Five hundred are cloaked due south of your property, awaiting my command," Fenian replied, taking a sip of tea. "After we have news from your commander, I will direct them where to travel. They will join the Allanorian encampment from the southeast, away from Watoria."

Freya frowned.

"They need to keep their presence unknown for as long as they can," Byrric explained. "Until the last minute, if possible. Right now, we need Frederick Edrin to think sending the bulk of the humans north to back up the Jotnar coming south will be his best chance at eliminating the Lindorothian soldiers outside."

"Why not try to pull more away from Watoria by showing them our true numbers?" Freya asked as she began piling eggs onto her plate. "Wouldn't that make it easier to get into the city?"

"While the city is *a* priority, our first priority is decreasing the number of enemy knights on your land," Fenian replied. "A two-pronged attack—one on the Jotnar, another on the human encampments—will make that task easier."

When Freya still didn't look convinced, Byrric spoke. "We'll go over the details when we get to the Allanorian camp, but trust us, Freya."

Aer gripped her hand under the table when she tensed to press further. "Thank you, Byrric," he said. "Fenian, again, we can't thank you enough for all you're doing."

"We do not care much for greed, Your Majesty," Fenian said. "I know that may not seem to be true after seeing our lands, but conquest for the sake of conquest, taking for the sake of simply having more, goes against much of what the elvish people believe in."

"Is that why you never chose to take lands outside of Avorell?" Freya asked. She was a bit surprised to see his mischievous nature seemed to exist easily beside his more astute, princely self.

He nodded. "Our people are happy, and we want for nothing. More lands mean more work, more people to keep in line, and more resources diverted from Avorell to outside ventures."

"Keeping to yourselves also makes it easier to mount a counter-attack if your lands are ever threatened as well, correct?" Aer asked.

"Indeed." He gestured outside. "Look at Lessia Edrin's army. It is scattered across two lands, and as far as your commander can tell, may very well end up in Dystone as well. If Avorell wanted more lands, it would be a simple thing to walk in and take Jotunheim, eliminate the Jotnar guarding the capital there, and leave Lessia and her ilk for you to deal with."

When he noticed the awkward silence that hung in the air, he stopped eating his eggs and looked at Aer and Freya. "Which we will not do, of course."

"Good to know," Aer said.

Fenian flicked a glance toward the door, then gave them each a quick nod and set his fork down. "We can continue this conversation at another time."

An instant later, he'd vanished. Freya had barely had time to react to his sudden departure when there was a rustling at the door. Collecting herself, Freya smiled when she saw Isadora and Reginald walk in.

"Your Majesties!" Isadora exclaimed. "Reginald didn't tell me you'd returned! Are you well?"

"We are," Aer said with a smile.

"Are we allowed to ask where you ran off to?" Reginald asked with a grin as they took seats across from Freya and Aer.

Byrric chuckled. "Just a meeting with the Allanorian commander who's leading the encampment outside of Watoria."

"We wanted to get a bit more hands-on," Aer said. "See how Commander Alstad was planning things instead of hearing it second-hand through Officer Ristheld."

Reginald nodded. "Understandable, considering. My brother and Lessia have made quite the mess."

Isadora picked up a scone and began to spread butter on it. "I must say, the amount of direct interaction you two have with your knights is impressive."

"She's right," Reginald agreed. "It's unlikely Willem will ever set foot on the battlefield, yet here you both are, planning to join the fray."

"That's kind of you both to say," Freya said with a smile. "Although considering the circumstances, are you sure Willem won't actually join the fight?"

"Unlikely, Your Majesty," Isadora replied. "Too messy."

"She's not wrong," Reginald said, filling his own plate with eggs and sausage. "My brother is content to lead an army, but only from the comfort of his throne."

There was a quick rap at the doorjamb, then Zane walked in, looking a bit windblown.

"Commander, Your Majesties," he said. He nodded a quick greeting toward Reginald and Isadora before returning his attention to Byrric. "A word?"

"Of course." Byrric set down his fork and stood, gesturing for Freya and Aer to follow. They said their farewells to Reginald and Isadora, then followed Zane out of the house and to the bottom of the portico stairs, just as Florian and Fenian came across the lawn.

"Alstad's scouts estimate another day, at most, before the Jotnar forces are within striking range," Zane said once they'd stopped. "He's requesting a meeting with all of you. I would advise leaving as soon as possible for the Allanorian encampment."

Aer frowned. "Did you inform him that Prince Fenian has arrived?"

Zane sent a look at the elf, then he looked back at Aer. "No, Your Majesty. Only that you may have managed to acquire some allies. I thought he should know our knights were not the only ones he should factor into any plans he might be developing, but I also thought it best you deliver that news yourself."

Byrric was already nodding his agreement before Zane finished speaking. "Alright. Go back, tell Alstad we'll be there within the hour."

"Yes, sir," Zane said, then shifted into his hawk form and shot into the sky.

"What about the city?" Freya asked as soon as he was gone.

"Once we have a set plan, we'll determine our course of action as it relates to Watoria," Byrric told her. "For now, inform Lords Cailen and Maddix and Lady Bryton of our intentions and have them make excuses for our absence. Until we have something solid, the circle of those who know our plans must be kept as small as possible."

"What about Ashton and Reginald?" Freya asked. "Reginald knows more about Willem than any of us, and Ashton will need to brief the marshals on what's going on. We've already left once without warning. It would be a bit unfair to do it again."

"The last thing you should be worrying about right now is fairness," Byrric told her. "We'll speak with them after we meet with Alstad."

Freya nodded, although it didn't sit well with her to leave without letting the others know they would be back soon. But she knew her father was right. They still didn't know how Willem was getting information, and after learning that the pixies could traverse the Between, it widened their pool of suspects. She trusted Rini with her life, but that said nothing about the allegiance of the other palace pixies, who Lea hadn't seen since she'd returned to the palace. It was entirely possible one had been cajoled into working with Willem and Lessia.

She pushed the thought away. Likely as it was, she couldn't focus on that. Right now, she needed to prioritize what was in front of her: a city under siege and the potential to cull the largest portion of enemy forces in western Lindoroth.

Spies for the capital would have to wait.

FENIAN WHISKED them away to the Allanorian encampment a short while later, bringing them right into Commander Alstad's tent. Alstad, along with the two knights who surrounded the table with him, jumped at their sudden appearance, one toppling over backward into a chair.

"Apologies," Byrric said as the knight righted himself. "We thought it best to come straight to you."

Alstad, a tall, broad-shouldered bear shifter recovered himself immediately when he saw Freya and Aer.

"Your Majesties," he said with a bow. "Welcome to our camp."

"Commander Alstad, this is Prince Fenian Tordove of Avorell," Aer said. "He's here to help."

Alstad's eyes widened a fraction, then he bowed again. "Your Highness, welcome. Our camp is yours."

Fenian gave him a curt nod. "Thank you, Commander."

Alstad gestured for them to join him and his knights at the rear of his tent where a small table had been set up. On it was a map of Allanor, weighed down at each corner by a gray rock.

He picked up a narrow stick and tapped a spot on the map, northeast of their location. "As of right now, the Jotnar battalion is on course to cross the northern ridge by midday tomorrow," he began. "Whatever the Valkyrie from Iston did, hung them up a bit longer than we anticipated."

"What are their numbers now?" Aer asked.

"Our best estimate is that they're now just shy of five hundred," Alstad replied.

Freya couldn't help but smile as she and Byrric exchanged a look. Seven hundred knights down to five hundred was indeed something to be happy about, considering it had been only a handful of Valkyrie who'd done the job.

"What does their path appear to be?" Fenian asked, his eyes trailing over the various roads and waterways on the map.

Alstad dragged the stick along a straight path across the Allanorian countryside. "They don't seem to be following any roads. They've aimed for Watoria and haven't deviated."

"No wonder it's taking them so long," Freya murmured. "A good portion of that is forest."

"Dense forest," Byrric agreed.

"But it keeps them concealed," Aer said with a sigh. "Is it possible there are more than you've seen, considering they're staying to the forests?"

Alstad shook his head. "No, we've sent scouts out daily since we first received word of their approach. Their numbers haven't changed."

"Have you found any openings in the human encampments?" Fenian asked.

"None, Your Majesty," Alstad said. "We've been at a stalemate for nearly two weeks. They haven't so much as attempted to attack, and the barricade they've got in place is manned by dozens of archers."

"And your magic? Why have you not wielded that against them?" Fenian asked.

"We have, Your Highness," the knight to Alstad's left said. "But the bulk of our forces are shifters, and the enemy simply outnumber us by too many to allow our magic to work as well as we need it to in a timely manner."

Fenian nodded absently. "And what about the Jotnar? Have they been working with the humans?"

"All Jotnar who were mixing with them have gone back into the city," Alstad said. "That report came in just before you arrived."

"That's... odd," Freya said.

"They are divided, then," Fenian said with a nod. "Good. If they aren't coordinating thoroughly, that will work to our advantage."

"That's our hope as well," Alstad agreed. He looked at Aer and Freya. "Your Majesties, will you be joining the fight?"

"Without question," Aer said. "But as the leader of this battalion, you'll need to tell us where to be and when."

Alstad blinked. "That's... quite an honor, Your Majesty, but as our king, wouldn't you prefer to take that role?"

"Over someone who's been in the midst of it?" Aer chuckled. "I've never set foot on a battlefield. You and Commander Balthana have."

"We trust your judgment," Freya added.

Alstad considered them both for a moment. "Alright." He gestured back toward the map. "We should go over our formations, then."

44

LEA

Lea was beginning to hate knocks on her door.

They always came shortly after Jonas left and were rarely, if ever, a person she wanted to see. Most often, Rosie came to call so they could spend time together over tea or take a walk through the palace. Twice, Lessia had wanted to "bond," as she called it. Once, Willem stopped by to ask Lea to join him on a stroll.

They always wanted to walk.

So, of course, when she had just finished her second cup of tea for the morning and was picking up a book she'd gotten from the library, there was a knock at her door. Her eyes fell closed in resignation and annoyance.

When she opened the door to find Ettrian there, she wasn't sure whether to be relieved, annoyed, or suspicious.

Or hopeful. Briefly, she considered feeling hopeful, but she squashed the feeling almost as soon as it pushed into her mind.

"My lady," he greeted her. "I'm feeling a bit hemmed in. Would you like to walk with me?"

She nearly groaned, but instead forced a smile. If she was off with him, it was less likely she'd have to suffer through the company of one of the others.

"Of course. Let me just grab a cloak."

She took her time fastening her white wool cloak tightly around her shoulders, pondering what the prince might want. Tyna had come to her the night before, silently waking her from sleep to inform her that Freya and Aer had returned safely from Avorell. If they'd returned alive, that meant Freya had accomplished her task, which meant the elves would side with Lindoroth.

But had anyone told Ettrian?

She hadn't seen him since Jonas had told her he'd pledged his army to Lessia and Willem, but she'd hoped to be able to confront him soon.

Lea tossed a glance at him as she locked the door and slipped the key into her cloak pocket. "Shall we?"

"Lead the way," he replied with a quick smile.

They strolled through the halls at a leisurely pace, him asking questions about the palace as they went. It wasn't until they'd reached a rarely-used garden entrance at the rear of the palace that she realized he'd been attempting to make it look as though she was giving him a tour.

He immediately dropped a cloaking spell over them. Before she could speak, he placed a hand on her arm and started guiding her down a path.

"What in the gods' names are you doing?" she hissed, jerking her arm from his. "Someone could see—"

"No one in this palace is as powerful as I am, Lady Calliwell, so fret not."

"I'll *fret* if I want to fret! No one can see us *now*, but what about a few moments ago, when we happened to disappear into thin air?"

He chuckled, then sat down on a stone bench and patted the seat beside him. "You think so little of me, Lady Calliwell. You must broaden your mind if you ever hope to achieve anything in this life."

She scowled at him but sat, despite her annoyance.

"I thought you would like to know that your monarchs have returned from Avorell," he said. "Your queen is alive and well, and they are in the company of my eldest brother, Fenian." He gave her a knowing smile. "And I can see this is something you already knew."

Lea narrowed her eyes but chose not to answer. "When did you find out they returned?"

"I spoke with our emissary and my brother, Fenian, not one hour ago. Fenian seemed to think there was quite a fuss being made over *your* condition, so I thought it best I inform you myself."

Her expression shifted toward suspicion. "If you only just found out this morning, why did you pledge your army to Lessia and Willem last week?"

He gave her a knowing smile. "I did no such thing."

"You did, though. Jonas said—" She thought back to Jonas' words: *'He is prepared to offer his kingdom's assistance to take control of Lindoroth.'*

"Gods above," she murmured, shaking her head at such a simple twist of words. "Why mislead them?"

"So they would stop trying to entice me." His face twisted. "Do you know Lessia propositioned me? To *sleep* with her?"

Lea stared at him, dumbfounded. "She—she did *not!*"

"Well, to be fair, she said, 'I am willing to do all it takes to secure an alliance with Avorell.'" He gestured toward his eyes and grimaced. "It was in her eyes. I saw it. Odd thing, that one."

"Well... I'm, um, glad to see you've avoided that fate." Lea shuddered at the thought of Lessia attempting to seduce anyone. It was more likely she was willing to maim and torture Ettrian's worst enemies, free of charge, but Lea could understand why he might think otherwise.

"And I as well." Ettrian leaned back on his hands and tilted his pale face to the sky, his black hair gleaming in the morning sun. "So, am I to assume your pixie friend gave you the good news?"

Lea frowned. "Pixie friend?"

He opened one eye and looked at her. "Fenian mentioned something about 'the pixies we are categorically not allowed to exterminate' and that the sister of Queen Freya's attendant is with you."

Lea kept her mouth clamped shut.

When Ettrian saw she wasn't going to speak, a soft smile flickered on his lips. "Do you think my entire family was unaware of your placement here, Lady Calliwell? Or should I say, the reason for your placement here?" He snorted. "Did you *really* think I would've come just because a seer told us of a war in this country?"

"I don't... well, yes, I suppose I did."

Ettrian made an amused sound. "Avorell doesn't give two shits whether your kingdom is at war. Yes, we knew about it happening, but until your king and queen sent word, we had every intention of remaining content within our own borders."

"That still doesn't explain what *I* have to do with your deals with my king and queen," Lea pressed. "I'm no one, Ettrian. They're the ones you should be focused on."

"Ah, on the contrary," the prince countered. "You're quite important to Freya and Aerelius, a fact made quite clear when your king became incensed at the idea of me performing your mating bond."

"But you didn't." Lea shook her head. "You didn't perform the bond—" She scowled. "Aerelius doesn't know that, does he?"

Another sly smile.

"Ugh! You—you—"

"'Stupid bloody elf?' That's always one of my favorites. 'Deceitful bastard' is another I've grown quite fond of."

"If you weren't a prince, I would hit you," she snapped. "Quite forcefully, I might add."

He chuckled. "Settle yourself, Lady Calliwell. My parents simply explained to your king and queen how simple it would be for me to break a mating bond I had performed. They never once said 'they have been mated' or even 'they've been wed,' at least according to my mother."

"That doesn't make any sense," Lea argued. "Freya and Aer already had motive enough to go through with their plans."

"Aerelius had his own test, of sorts," Ettrian said. "He will have to explain it to you, though, because I believe we are about to have company."

"Wait!" Lea bit her lip as Ettrian raised a hand to drop his spell.

He arched a brow when she didn't speak.

"I—" She closed her mouth with a huff. "Never mind."

He gave her a curious look. "Alright. Well, if you care to continue this conversation, I will be in the library this evening before dinner."

He held her eyes for a moment. When she gave him a small nod, he dropped the spell just as Willem's voice floated around the corner only a few feet ahead.

"Your Highness," Ettrian exclaimed, just as Willem and Rosie came into view. "Fancy meeting you both here."

Willem's mouth snapped shut, and the only show of his surprise was a pause no longer than a breath. "I could say the same," he drawled as he took in Lea, Ettrian, and the few meager inches of space between them on the bench.

Lea gave him her sweetest smile, then looked to Rosie. "Princess Ristner, I was hoping I might run into you while I was on my walk! Would you like to take tea with me back in my chambers?"

Rosie beamed. "Oh, yes, Lady Edrin, that would be lovely." She rolled her eyes and lowered her voice to a stage whisper. "I'm so tired of hearing Willem babble on the complexities of running a kingdom."

With a small laugh, Lea stood, then held out an arm for Rosie. "Well, we can't have that, can we? Come, Dina has brought up a new blend of lindberry tea that I think you'll find lovely."

With a nod of farewell to the king and prince, Lea and Rosie strolled off down the garden path, arm-in-arm.

BACK IN LEA'S CHAMBERS, Rosie took a seat at the small, window-side table while Lea prepared two cups of lindberry tea and tried to keep her mind focused on entertaining the king's sister and *not* how much she wanted to throttle Ettrian for his tricks. She'd chastised herself repeatedly after they'd left the gardens, hardly hearing Rosie as she whined on about Willem's boring nature.

Rosie was a good distraction, though. She would prattle on about her annoyance of the day, sometimes giving Lea a bit of information that was worth squirreling away in the process. Though as the days passed, she couldn't help but feel a bit sorry for the girl. Yes, her brother was wretched, and she clearly had no qualms accepting what he was doing to Lea's kingdom. But Lea had slowly come to realize that what she once recognized as stupidity in Rosie seemed more to be a product of being sheltered her entire life. She was raised to be pretty and obedient, not stand up for the things she believed in, which had been a hallmark of Lea's own childhood.

"He wants me to be just like him, did you know?" Rosie asked as Lea set a cup in front of her. "Willem. He thinks I'll be able to bring Benjamin in hand once we're married! Me!" She snorted and took a small sip. "Me, a woman, bringing Benjamin Whitmore in hand."

Lea gave her a questioning look as she sat down across from her. "I take it you don't think Lord Whitmore is the type to be brought 'in hand'?"

Rosie giggled. "Oh, heavens no! Not by anyone, and *certainly* not by his wife. He's far more like Willem than either will admit." She clicked her tongue. "But I suppose Willem *does* have a lot on his mind."

"Yes, that's often the case during the takeover of a nation," Lea said dryly. "I'm sure he'll come around to logic soon enough." She picked up a biscuit and broke off a small piece. "Does Willem still plan to send you back to Dystone?"

"Yes," Rosie replied with a heavy sigh. "I was *so* hoping Benjamin could join us here, but Willem won't budge, no matter how much I beg."

Lea gave her a sympathetic smile. "Well, having a Ristner in Caldel *does* make sense."

"If only Reginald—" Rosie huffed. "He is *so* damn selfish! *He* should be the one going back to hold Caldel! Not me!"

"Well, I'm sure Benjamin will do a fine job of... helping you lead Dystone in Willem's absence."

Picking up her cup again, Rosie scowled over the edge at Lea. "I suppose. Ugh!" She thunked her cup down on the saucer with a rattle of porcelain, causing Lea to jump. "I just want to get married, be a good wife, and have children! Now my stupid brother has forced 'running a kingdom' onto that list."

Gently, Lea picked up Rosie's cup and set it beside her own, then used a napkin to sop up the few drops that had splashed onto the tabletop and saucer.

"I understand, Rosie, I do. These are just... complicated times, that's all. I'm sure King Willem is under a lot of stress. Once things smooth out a bit, he'll be eager to go back to Dystone. And to be fair, Benjamin will likely handle the bulk of Willem's duties. I'm sure you'll be free to do all of the wifely duties you hope for."

"Do you really think so?"

She reached across the table and patted Rosie's hand. "I'm sure of it."

Rosie gave her a small smile, then slid her cup back across the table. Taking another small sip, she said, "You're right, Lady Edrin. This tea is quite good."

LATER, after Rosie left and when there was still a bit of time before Jonas was expected to return, Lea slipped from her room and made her way toward the library. She'd given Ettrian's earlier admissions more thought throughout the afternoon and had decided she didn't quite care why or how he and his parents deceived Freya and Aer about her mating bond, only that her king and queen were safe and had, if the elves were to be trusted, acquired a coveted alliance.

An alliance Lessia and Willem knew nothing about.

That in itself was reason enough to continue her conversation with the prince. She needed to confirm that Lessia and Willem were still in the dark about the allies Aer and Freya had managed to gain and figure out how she could keep that from changing.

She was still deep in thought when she shoved open the library door, then came up short when she saw Ettrian reclined in one of the leather chairs with Tyna fluttering in the air beside him.

"What's going on?" Lea asked cautiously, taking a few slow steps toward them.

Tyna jerked back, her expression guilty when she whirled to face Lea.

"My lady! I, well, I was just discussing with the prince—"

"A plan to get you free of this place," Ettrian said. "And, before you argue, it's at the behest of your king and queen."

Lea folded her arms and tilted her chin defiantly. "They're on the other side of the kingdom. They can't force me to do anything."

Tyna bit her lip and deflated a bit, then cast a desperate look at Ettrian.

Ettrian smirked. "No, but they have asked for my assistance in the matter. And as I am here—" he gestured toward himself "—I am in a much better position than they are."

Ignoring him, she looked at Tyna. "Explain."

"It's for the best, my lady, truly," Tyna crooned. "I understand that you're hesitant to leave your mother behind, but we've discussed this."

"Tyna—"

"Please hear me out! You need to be away from this place. The longer you are here, the longer your people *know* you're here, the more likely they are to lose hope, either because they think you've defected—"

"They would never think that," Lea snapped.

"—or because they think you've been captured. If you flee now, they will know that you have not truly allied yourself with Lessia and Willem. That will bolster their hope and drive them not to give in."

"Do you think they believe that of me? That I would have turned my back on them?"

"It's unlikely, but not impossible." Tyna shot a look at Ettrian, then turned her gaze back to Lea. "Take the tunnels tonight, my lady. With or without Lord Edrin, that's your choice. I know you've spoken of a departure with Lord Edrin already, and now is the opportune time to do it. He was not wrong when he said your mother would never forgive you or herself if you stayed because of her," she added quickly when Lea went to protest.

Lea snapped her mouth shut and her eyes widened with incredulity. "You've been eavesdropping?"

Tyna gave a sharp nod. "Yes, my lady, on occasion."

Lea stared at her, surprised at her admission. "Why?"

Tyna sighed and took a seat on the table beside Ettrian's chair. "I needed to be certain Lord Edrin was not attempting to lead you astray. Now and then I listen in to ensure that is not the case."

"You could've just asked!"

"I know nothing of your mother," Ettrian interjected, "but mine would have me hanged if I were in your shoes and chose to stay. The point is, regardless of his intentions, Jonas is not wrong in—"

"Oh, I know he's not wrong!" Lea snapped. "I know precisely where my mother stands on the issue." Whether her mother knew Lea was not on their side didn't matter just now; what mattered was that Perida's refusal to cooperate had bought Lea precious time that, until her present discussion with Tyna, she hadn't realized she needed.

"And where should I go?" Lea asked. "There's no guarantee I'll be able to get into Errest—"

"Get to Their Majesties," Tyna said. "Regroup with them—"

"They're on the other side of the damned continent!"

Tyna pressed her lips together and coughed, then rolled her eyes when Ettrian didn't offer any assistance. "If you move quickly, sneak aboard a ship going west, perhaps you can be there in just a few days."

Lea thought for a moment, considered the plan Tyna was laying out. If she could get aboard a ship, which was highly unlikely, considering the current state of the kingdom, then she could be with Freya and Aer within just a few days. The more likely scenario was a trip on foot across the continent, a thing she relished little.

But... it would mean she'd be away from this place. If she couldn't get her mother out by staying behind, then she would find another way to do it from outside the palace.

"I'll think on it," Lea finally said. "But I can't promise anything. If I think the best thing for the Edhilian people would be to go to them *or* stay here, that's what I'll do. The same consideration will be given to the option of leaving to join Freya and Aer in Watoria."

Tyna's silvery eyes bored into Lea's for a moment before she nodded once. "Fair enough, my lady. Wherever you go, I will be at your side."

"Thank you, Tyna."

"Out of curiosity, what will you tell Lord Edrin?" Ettrian asked. "If you choose to leave, that is."

Lea bit the inside of her cheek and mulled over his question. "I don't know."

"*Will* you tell him?"

She blew a stray curl off her forehead and stared into the fire. "I don't know."

45

FREYA

Back at the manor, Byrric and Aer briefed everyone on their meeting with Alstad. Fenian had stayed behind so he and Alstad could coordinate more extensively now that the arrival of the elvish army was imminent.

Their plan was simple: the Lindorothians would face the Jotnar head-on, and when the humans moved to take them from the west, the elves would attack from the south.

Hopefully.

Freya couldn't help the nagging feeling that the elves might not follow through with their promises. She knew it was likely just her overly-suspicious nature, and she trusted that Florian had crafted a flawless bargain, but their reliance on the army from a land so far from their own, one she and her people could not command, concerned her.

So much so, she couldn't help but try to come up with her own backup plans should their alliance fail. As the day wore on, the necessity of that seemed to increase, especially now that Fenian wasn't there. The paranoia—she knew that's what it was—that he would leave, revealing a twist in words that they'd all missed, continued to tap at the back of her mind until finally, after having said hardly a word at lunch, her preoccupation became apparent to Aer.

"Walk with me?" he asked after they'd finished clearing their plates.

She nodded and took his outstretched hand, then they walked through the house in silence, not speaking until they reached the steps of the portico.

"What is it?" Aer demanded as soon as they were fully out of earshot. "You've been distracted since we returned from the camps."

Freya put her hands on her hips and frowned up at the cloud-strewn sky. "I'm not sure. I'm just a bit worried about... something."

"You don't trust the elves."

She smiled at the fact that he didn't even bother questioning it. "It's not that, exactly. I'd just feel a bit better if we had a backup plan?"

Aer folded his arms and gave her a curious look. "What did you have in mind?"

She drummed her fingers on her hip and thought. "I don't know, honestly. Planning has never been my strong suit."

"My wife, the one who surprised me with a spur-of-the-moment wedding and mating ceremony on the battlements, on the night *before* our wedding, doesn't know how to plan ahead?" He quirked a grin. "How shocking."

"I'm so happy you find this amusing," she deadpanned. Then, unable to help herself, she smiled and took his hand. "Come throw some knives with me. I find that always helps me think. Let's see if we can come up with something to ease my mind."

He nodded slowly. "I think I might have an idea, actually."

"No. Absolutely not."

"I wasn't actually asking for permission," Freya said, glaring at her father. "Whether or not I go into the city isn't up to you."

Byrric looked between her and Aer with irritation plain on his face. "Have you both forgotten what happened last time?"

Freya crossed her arms. "Are you forgetting that I just had to fight my way through a forest filled with creatures who were quite literally trying to tear me to bits? I think I can handle it."

"Because your confrontation with Traust went so well?"

"Last time, I had no plan and no backup," she pointed out.

"This time we do," Aer said. He looked at Ashton and Florian, who stood on either side of Byrric behind the desk in the study. "And we have no intention of running into him."

"Hear them out, Byrric," Florian said. "It won't hurt."

Byrric slid him an annoyed look, then nodded at Freya and Aer.

"We can't get reinforcements into the city without being seen," Freya said. "But if we can sneak a few in—five, at most—we might be able to prepare the citizens who weren't able to get out. If they know what's coming, they can be prepared to fight back."

"You think they haven't already been trying to fight back?" Ashton asked, affronted. "Freya, you know better."

"Of course we don't think that," she said. "But they also didn't know when or if reinforcements were coming. Anyone would be wary when they're at such a disadvantage."

"Telling them an exact time and place would be dangerous," Florian pointed out. "You don't know if any of them have been compromised, and even if you did, such a thing would be impossible because we don't even have those details yet."

"Which is why we don't tell them an exact time and place," Freya said.

Byrric rubbed a hand over his face and sat down, then looked at her expectantly. "You've lost me."

"All they'll have to know is that help is imminent, only a day or two off, and that, when the time comes, they need to be ready. If they're caught off-guard, they won't be able to fight, and we need every advantage we can get if we're to get Watoria dealt with quickly."

"And if you happen to come across Traust on this mission?" Byrric arched a brow. "Fighting forest creatures and elves was one thing,

Freya. They had no vendetta, no score to settle. Reykr Traust wants you dead, likely delivered in pieces at my feet." Freya didn't miss the small hitch in his voice as he said it, but his face let nothing on. "If you're caught, this will turn into a rescue mission—"

"So don't rescue me!"

"—which is not something we can afford right now," he finished. "And if you think that anyone on these grounds or in that army out there—" he pointed toward the door "—would leave their queen there, at the hands of our enemies, you're a fool. This isn't about trust, Freya. I know what you're capable of. But you're not infallible, and, despite what you saw in Avorell, Traust is quite likely the most vicious thing you'll ever meet in battle. And all of that doesn't even address the issue of the people of Watoria having no weapons to wield. No matter how well-prepared they are, it will do no good if they have nothing to fight with."

Suddenly, Toskr appeared beside her, causing her to jump and Aer to let out a loud curse.

"Dammit, Toskr!" she snapped. "A bit of warning next time?"

"Yes, Queen Freya, my apologies." He faced Byrric. "If I may, Commander?"

"This is a private meeting!" Aer snapped. "How long have you been here?"

Toskr frowned. "Ask your spymaster. He's been aware of my presence since I arrived."

Aer's eyes shot to Florian.

Florian shrugged. "He's quite harmless here, I assure you, and I believe he came to help." He lifted a white brow at Toskr. "Isn't that correct?"

"Indeed, it is, master-spying-warlock, sir." Toskr dusted a bit of dirt off Aer's jacket, then turned back to Byrric. "As I was saying... I think I may be of some use here."

Byrric had leaned back in his chair, his fingers pressed against his eyes, then muttered something under his breath, before dropping his hands and looking at Toskr. "Alright, go on."

"Well, as you know, I am very small when in my animal form,"

Toskr began. "Small enough to fit in a pocket and various other small spaces."

"Yes, we've noticed," Byrric replied.

Toskr flashed him a smile before continuing. "Well, I was thinking. Perhaps I could accompany Her Majesty into the city? I would be one less body that would need to be concealed, after all. No one questions the presence of a squirrel."

Freya gave him an incredulous look. "Just yesterday, you were ready to risk becoming a throw pillow if it meant you wouldn't have to stay and fight. Now you're offering to walk into battle? What are you playing at?"

"I am not playing at anything, Queen Freya. You have set me free twice, now—"

"Only one was intentional," she corrected.

"That does not change the fact of the matter. You have saved me twice. As frustrating a creature as I may be at times, I acknowledge that I... owe you."

Aer narrowed his eyes. "I don't buy it."

"Neither do I," Ashton added, shaking his head. "From what I've heard, you nearly got her killed in Avorell."

Toskr gasped in outrage. "I did no such thing! Just ask her!"

Freya held up her hands to silence them all. "Alright, that's enough. Toskr, while I *do* appreciate your assistance in the forest, you have to understand why this offer strikes us as a bit odd."

"It's clear you're attempting to strike some sort of bargain," Florian said. "State your terms."

Toskr folded his arms and looked at Freya and Aer. "I told you I would help you fight this war, and I intend to do that. But once it is done... I want my freedom."

Freya frowned. "You've already got that."

"No," he said with a shake of his head. "Here, in this place. I want to be able to move about Lindoroth freely."

"We never intended to keep you as prisoner," Freya said, a bit hurt he seemed to have thought so little of them. "But based on your history and the things you've told me about yourself, not to mention the things I've seen, it isn't such a simple matter as saying 'go on and do whatever you want.' You have to understand that."

"And what will you do once you have this freedom?" Aer asked. "You were trapped because you failed in your duties, which led to mass slaughter."

"I will have no such duties here," Toskr replied.

"And your penchant for gossip?" Aer lifted his brows. "What's to stop you from spreading secrets to the wrong person?"

He nodded slowly. "Alright. I shall prove myself to you, then, just as Her Majesty did in Avorell," he said firmly. He looked at Freya, Aer, then Byrric in turn. "In exchange, whichever of you is in charge at the end—I want a guarantee that we will revisit this discussion once this war is done."

Freya, her father, and Aer exchanged quick looks with each other, then Aer nodded. "Alright. That's fair. But we won't give any guarantees as to the outcome of said conversation. Is that clear?"

"As crystal, King Aerelius."

"Now, what are you suggesting?" Byrric asked.

Toskr's eyes darted to Freya's and he grinned wickedly. "How close can you get me to the man who's overtaken your city?"

"Do you really think this will work?" Ashton whispered as he, Freya, Aer, Florian, and Byrric stealthily made their way through the forest toward Watoria later that night. Toskr scurried along behind them, nearly invisible in his shifted form. "I'm worried Traust will see straight through these glamours."

"Florian's glamours are flawless," Aer replied. "As long as we stay together, we won't be seen, I assure you."

"Thank you, Your Majesty," Florian murmured. Freya could hear the irritation in his tone at Ashton's questioning.

Ashton didn't look entirely convinced, but a silencing look from Byrric kept him from asking any further questions.

They continued on the game trail that wound through the woods, lit only by the waning sliver of moon that hung high above. They were fortunate that it was such a dark night, as the woods were crawling with patrols. Freya didn't doubt the magic that protected them, but the darkness set her mind a bit more at ease.

Byrric halted, then held up his hand for the rest to follow suit. A moment later, three Jotnar patrols crossed their path, not ten steps from where they stood.

Even though Freya knew the wards and glamours that Florian and the others had woven into the woods were, in fact, flawless, she couldn't help holding her breath as the three knights continued past. Her confrontation with Traust had rattled her more than she cared to admit, she realized, and while she knew she could hold her own in the Forest of Ages, Byrric had been right about one thing—those creatures had been fighting for their lives, which, under normal circumstances, Freya would consider the ultimate reward. But Traust was fueled by vengeance, a centuries-old score that he was finally getting a chance to settle. Freya had a strong suspicion he didn't care whether or not he came out alive on the other side, as long as she and her father were crossing to the other side with him.

She exhaled silently when the knights continued past without even a faltered step or turn of the head to indicate they were aware of anyone nearby.

When they reached the southern wall of Watoria, they turned and continued west, making their way nearer the harbor, where Amara had informed them the patrols had lessened some. After a few minutes, they reached a small crevice in the wall. It was hardly wide enough to slide a hand in, and to the unassuming observer, it looked completely mundane.

Ashton stepped forward and reached his hand in, closing his eyes as he felt around the small opening. A moment later, there was a soft *click*. He stepped back and nodded at Freya. "It's open."

Before Freya lifted her hand to call forth her magic, Aer touched Freya's arm, looking concerned. "Are you sure about this? You've used this entrance before?"

"Yes," she confirmed as Florian tightened the glamour and silencing spell around them. "Trust me, this will be fine."

She sent a quiet stream of magic into the crevice, slipping it behind the door that sat nestled in the wall, nearly three feet thick and made of solid stone. Slowly, she funneled more magic behind it until, finally, it slid open, revealing a gaping chamber within.

Freya smirked up at Aer. "Welcome to Watoria, my love."

46

FREYA

The tunnel inside the city wall—a narrow corridor that ran parallel to the main one, invisible except for the occasional vent near the ceiling—looped the entire length of the border wall, from harbor to gate on either side. Freya and Ashton had never figured out what the second tunnel's purpose had been, because there was only one way to get from one side to the other that they could ever find, which was where, toward the end, the wall and the massive city gates met. They'd been hesitant to use it, considering the Jotnar had now had weeks to scour the city for things such as this, but the assumption they'd come to was that Traust would most likely be expecting them to come in through the sky, not on the ground.

They stopped when they neared the door that would let them into the adjacent tunnel that would allow them into the city.

"Amara said she found some of the citizens hiding in an old storage barn on the eastern edge of the city," Freya whispered. Her companions were almost impossible to see, even with her night vision. "Someone had cloaked it thoroughly, so it was by chance she and Naedan had even been able to make contact with them. I know exactly which place it was, and it's not far from our exit."

"We'll approach first," Ashton added. Freya saw his head shift in her direction. "I'll go in first. They may not recognize you on sight with that hair."

"Dammit," she murmured. "You're right." She'd completely forgotten about the glamour she'd so often worn when she was in Watoria to keep her obvious relation to Byrric concealed.

"Be quick," Byrric said. "I want to be back at the manor as soon as possible. Lord Florian and I will be behind you, out of sight."

Freya nodded, then turned to Toskr, who'd shifted into his elf form. "Do you have everything you need?"

He nodded, and Freya got the impression that this was the most important he'd felt in some time. "I will not fail you."

"Thank you, Toskr. You make me weary, but I'm happy to have met you."

He flashed her a smile. "And I, you, Queen Freya."

Within an instant, he'd shifted again and disappeared through the tunnel door.

"I certainly hope this doesn't come back to bite us," Aer said with a sigh. He glanced back in the direction they had arrived, then looked at Ashton. "Do the citizens know this passage exists?"

Ashton shook his head. "No. As far as I know, Freya was the first person to stumble across it in centuries. Otherwise, I'm sure we would've been told about it."

"It's a weakness in the wall that could easily be exploited," Byrric added. "I understand that you may want to spirit all who remain in the city out through here, Your Majesty, but—"

"I know," Aer said, holding up his hand. "Believe me, I understand the importance of keeping secret passages... secret."

"It was my first thought, too," Freya said quietly, taking his hand. "But my father is right."

Aer huffed with amusement. "Careful, Valkyrie. I think you may have just given our commander a heart attack."

Byrric chuckled. "It'll take much more than my daughter admitting I'm right to kill me. Let's go."

～

THEY MADE their way through the darkened streets and arrived a short while later at the barn Amara and Naedan had spoken of. Byrric and Florian had fallen back to act as lookouts, while Freya, Aer, and Ashton attempted to make contact with the citizens inside.

"Do you feel that?" Aer murmured as they stared up at the decrepit structure. It was old, moldering from years of disuse, and looked to be on the verge of toppling over.

"I do," Freya whispered. "They're still in there, but whoever is cloaking is doing a damn good job of it." She looked at Ashton. "Lead the way."

Ashton cast a quick glance around, then put a hand to his mouth. The sound that came out a second later was almost identical to that of a barn owl, but with a slightly different pitch. Anyone familiar with bird calls might hear it as false, but to the average ear, it would seem perfectly at place here in the darkest areas of the city.

They waited another moment, then he let out a second call. Just as he raised his hand a third time, there was a soft clicking sound, and the latch on the inside of the barn was lifted.

"Come on," Ashton whispered as he hurried toward the door. Freya and Aer followed close at his heels until they were inside the dimly lit space.

Freya sagged with relief when she saw how many people had managed to find their way to the barn. Dozens were scattered about —in the loft, the cattle stalls, on makeshift mattresses made of straw and burlap. Whispers ran throughout the building as they took in the newcomers, and mixtures of suspicion and hope flashed across their faces when they recognized them.

As Freya scanned the room, she saw a handful of people she knew, including the dark-haired female who stood before them now.

Nadya, a witch who had lived a few houses down from Freya, was a few years older than Ana and had been a bit of a busybody in the South Ward, but Freya and Ana had always gotten along with her well enough.

Nadya squinted, then shook her head. "I always wondered what you looked like under that glamour." Her eyes flickered with recognition when she took in Aer at Freya's side. "I hear congratulations are in order?"

"Later," Freya said, smiling. "We have to be quick. Ash? Everyone, listen up!"

"Alright, we have two options," Ashton said, raising his voice so everyone could hear him. "The first, for those who have someplace to go, is to attempt to secret you all out of here tonight. The other option is to prepare you to fight."

Nadya's husband, Finn, stepped forward. "To fight who? And when?"

"An attempt to take back the city is imminent," Ashton said. "I can't give you more than that because I don't know an exact time."

"What we can tell you," Freya said, "is that the number of knights patrolling the city streets will soon decrease. When that time comes, you and anyone else you know who might be hiding out will be in a strong position to fight back, take out some of the enemy before fleeing the city."

"This isn't all or nothing, however," Aer assured them. "Those who want to leave the city, may. We will make sure you're escorted safely out of the city and to safety. If any of you choose to stay, we will do our best to arm you."

"With what?" another female called out. "The Jotnar have managed to take everything!"

As if on cue, Toskr appeared beside Freya, causing Nadya and Finn to stumble back in shock.

"How did you get past the wards?" Finn demanded as he stepped protectively in front of his wife.

"Just a thought," Toskr said as he dropped two large duffels onto the straw-covered floor. "You may want to ward against those who can travel—"

"We can discuss that later," Freya said sharply. She looked at Toskr. "Well?"

"I was able to raid a good portion of their weapons stores." He gave one of the bags at his feet a light kick. "This may help solve your problem."

Ashton arched his brow at the heavy clink of metal. "How did you manage that unseen?"

Toskr's answering smile was smug. "I gave the guard on duty at the weapons storage shed a heavy dose of widow venom. He was only asleep for a few minutes, but it was long enough."

Crouching down, Ashton opened each of the bags, then looked up at Nadya and Finn, nodding. "Daggers mainly, and a few short swords. What are your numbers?"

"There are just over sixty here," Finn said. "We haven't been able to get out much, but I think there are roughly another one hundred scattered about nearby."

Nadya still hadn't taken her eyes off Toskr. "Who have you brought here, Freya?"

"Help. That's all you need to know." She gestured toward the bags. "Distribute these the best way you see fit. Stay here until it comes time to fight."

"When will we know the time has come?" Nadya asked.

"We'll do our best to signal you," Ashton said. "But if all goes as planned, you'll know."

"And those who want to leave?" Finn asked.

"The end of the southern wall will be the easiest route," Freya said. "The patrols on that side are a bit less than those near the northern wall, as far as we can tell." She looked around the room. "Who cast the wards?"

A short, broad-shouldered male lifted a hand from the back of the room. She smiled when she recognized him—a younger marshal named Quil who'd joined them a few years earlier.

"Can you make charms, Quil?"

"I can," he confirmed. "They won't last long, though."

"He's using most of his power on the barn," Nadya explained. "I worry if he diverts any of it, the protections on the building will fail."

Aer gestured at himself and Freya. "We can supplement the magic that surrounds this place with some of our own." He looked at Quil. "It will free up yours, and it's best if the one creating the charms is the one staying."

"May I help?" Toskr asked.

Aer gave him a surprised look. "How?"

"Can you cast wards?" Freya asked.

"Can we trust you?" Ashton asked at the same time.

Toskr scowled at Ashton. "Yes, you can trust me, and I cannot cast wards, per se, but I can use my own magic to... harden yours. Make it more of a shell than a cloak." Seeing Freya's hesitance, he added quietly, "I will do all in my power to help keep them safe."

Freya considered him for a moment, then shared a look with Aer and Ashton. When they nodded, she looked back at Toskr. "Alright. Thank you, Toskr.

While Nadya and Finn distributed the weapons to the people in the barn, Ashton conferred with the marshals who'd remained behind. Freya, Aer, and Toskr took over maintaining the wards around the building while Quil quickly made concealment charms for the people who were choosing to leave. All told, fewer than ten chose to leave. The rest were determined to stay behind and fight.

"Thank you, Freya," Nadya said as Finn helped distribute the charms. "Your Majesty, I mean."

Freya waved a hand. "There's no need to thank me. I only wish I could've gotten here sooner." She cast a glance at Toskr, then smiled at Nadya. "He's a bit of a nuisance at times, but most of this was actually his idea."

Toskr preened.

Nadya exhaled and gave Freya a look that clearly said she doubted that very much.

Once they were finished and Freya had ensured the wards Quil placed were sufficiently reinforced, Freya, Aer, Ashton, and Toskr went outside and signaled to Florian and Byrric, who'd been hiding a few hundred feet away in opposite directions. Once everyone was together, they all joined hands and Toskr whisked them back home.

"It certainly would have been easier to do that than trudge through those woods," Toskr complained once they were back in the safety of the study.

"And risk arriving in a strange place, unaware of who might be standing right in that very spot?" Byrric shook his head. "I think you're smarter than that, Toskr."

"I suppose you have a point," Toskr conceded.

"I need to go update the other marshals," Ashton said.

"Of course," Freya said.

"I'll be there shortly," Byrric told him.

"And now, what shall we do?" Toskr asked once Ashton had left. "I see you have accomplished a small portion of your goal. What comes next?"

"Now we prepare for our own battle," Byrric said. "I'll go speak with my knights and the palace guards. Toskr, we'll need you to transport us to the Allanorian encampment. Are you willing to do that?"

"Yes, Commander," he said with a nod. "Tell me when you are ready and I will take you there."

"Good." Byrric looked at Freya and Aer. "You two, go fill in the others, get something to eat, and pack whatever weapons and provisions you feel you'll need that won't encumber you. We leave in an hour."

"Will Collin, Laz, and Myria be coming with us?" Freya asked.

"That's up to them," Byrric replied. "A team will be staying here to protect the property and act as reinforcements if needed."

Freya tried to slow her pounding heart. "Alright. We'll be quick."

A SHORT WHILE LATER, she and Aer had called their friends to their room to discuss what steps they were planning to take. As much as she wanted Collin, Laz, and Myria to stay behind, she knew ordering them to do so would be unfair. And, despite what her father's beliefs were regarding fairness, she wouldn't take that choice away from them.

"Where do you both feel we'll be most useful?" Laz asked once they'd finished explaining their circumstances.

"I don't think there's one answer for all three of us," Collin said, looking at Laz. "And don't give me that look," he added when Laz scowled at him.

Freya winced. She knew exactly where Collin's mind was because it was in the same place as hers.

Laz wasn't a fighter. He was brilliant when it came to strategy, history, and politics, but, with the exception of archery, physical combat had never been his strong suit.

"Byrric is leaving about one hundred and fifty knights here, along with the marshals. Ashton will be in charge, with Reginald as second-in-command," she said, hoping that might give Laz an easy way out of joining them on the actual battlefield. "They'll be in the woods surrounding the property, and a large portion will be preparing to launch an attack on the harbor if the opportunity presents itself."

Laz met her eyes, and she could see the conflict there—understood it completely.

If he stayed, he risked looking weak. If he left with them, there was a true risk he might not make it back alive.

"Perhaps it would be easier if our monarchs gave us our orders?" Myria said, sending Freya and Aer a pointed look. "Personally, I'd prefer to just stay here and wait for you all to save the day."

Her tone was haughty, but Freya could see the path Myria had just laid at their feet.

With a nod, Aer looked at them each in turn. "Then, that being the case, you three will stay here."

When Collin opened his mouth to protest, Freya shook her head. "No. We understand why you want to come, but this isn't the only battle we'll be facing, I can assure you. We need to make sure this place is still open to us when it's over."

"We'll be leaving to head east as soon as we can, but until then, we need a base," Aer added. "This house has served us well until now. The only way it will continue to do so is if it remains protected while we're gone." He looked at Collin and Laz. "Everyone will be guarding, but I want you two working with Ashton and Prince Reginald on strategy. Heavier patrols, that sort of thing. If Traust and Edrin know we're out on the battlefield, they'll assume they'll be free to scour the woods, unhindered. We cannot let that happen."

Collin held his eyes for a moment, then nodded.

"And what happens after this?" Myria asked. "Once we save your city?"

Freya looked at Aer, then sighed. "One step at a time. Let's get through the next two days first."

47

FREYA

The tent that had been prepared for her and Aer at the Allanorian encampment had been warm, thanks to the wood stove placed in the center, so despite their circumstances, she'd managed to sleep surprisingly well on the soft bedrolls that had been provided. Despite that, the morning of Freya's first battle dawned cold and dreary. Fitting, she supposed, considering. Though she felt far better about their chances of saving Watoria now that some of the citizens inside had been prepared, she still couldn't bring herself to feel much hope.

That heavy sense of foreboding continued to hang over her as she dressed.

"We'll get through this," Aer murmured. He took her hands, which were in the middle of fastening the buckles on her vest, and kissed the back of each.

She closed her eyes and squeezed his hands, then looked at him. "I wish I had your optimism," she said quietly. "I truly do."

He grinned wryly. "It's not optimism. It's confidence."

"Call it what you will, it's still a better outlook than mine."

"You'll feel better once we go over the plan one more time," he said, dropping her hands so she could finish getting dressed. He frowned as he eyed her leather pants, vest, and jacket. "Are you certain you don't want armor?"

She shook her head. "The spells that are woven into the leather are just as strong and won't weigh me down. Now, where is—"

"Here, Your Majesty," Rini said, popping into the air beside them. "Come, let me take care of your hair."

Freya gave her a smile that she knew didn't reach her eyes. "Thank you, Rini." She was perfectly capable of tying her hair back on her own, but something told her she'd never hear the end of it if she didn't allow Rini to do it for her. As frustrating as Rini's fussiness had been, Freya understood the need for purpose.

When she touched the tight braid that sat firmly at the nape of her neck a short while later, she smiled. Pretty, yet perfectly functional—a theme Rini couldn't seem to stop herself from following.

As Freya and Aer walked hand-in-hand to Alstad's tent to go over strategy one last time, she tried to keep her thoughts from straying into dark territory. She forced herself to focus on the knights around them who were stepping from their tents and finding their breakfasts at the fires that had been set around camp. Some bowed, others nodded, but for the most part, they seemed focused solely on the task in front of them.

Her mood lifted some when she arrived in Alstad's tent and found her aunt there, waiting with Byrric.

"Oh, thank the gods," Freya said, opening her arms as Ana came toward her. She sighed as she buried her face in Ana's short blonde hair. "I know they told me you were alright after attacking the Jotnar, but it helps to see you here," she murmured.

Ana laughed, then stepped back and put her hands on Freya's shoulders. "It takes more than that to kill one of us, Freya. Once this is all over, we'll have to share our stories." She gave her niece a crooked smile. "I hear you had quite the adventure in Avorell."

"That's one way to put it," Freya said. She looked around the tent and saw that Byrric, Florian, and Fenian had already arrived. Prince

Tavian stood at Fenian's side, which brought Freya a little relief. If he was here, it meant their soldiers were, too.

"Ah, good, you're here," Byrric said. "Prince Tavian arrived last night with the first of Avorell's knights. Commander Alstad was just about to go over our plans."

Freya smiled at him. "It's good to see you again, Prince Tavian."

"We only wish it was under better circumstances," Aer added.

Tavian let out a small huff. "Yes, well, we'll see about that once this is all over."

Fenian sent his brother a warning look, then greeted Freya and Aer. "My knights are camped to the southeast of here, out of sight of the humans." He stepped aside and gestured toward the map that Alstad and Byrric were deeply contemplating. "We need to discuss our formations one last time before we set out."

As one, Freya, Ana, and Aer stepped forward and listened as the four commanding officers went over their plans one last time.

"The Jotnar will expect Lindorothian knights to meet them head-on," Alstad began in his gravelly voice. "It's the most logical assumption, especially since they know we're aware of their approach, and because they believe we have too-limited numbers to do anything else. We've been monitoring the skies and have seen no evidence of aerial patrols, and the scouts that I've sent out haven't reported any messengers, so it appears they've either planned this attack well-enough in advance that the Jotnar and humans at Watoria are already aware of their arrival, or they plan to surprise the human army as well."

"Regardless, it's safe to assume the humans don't suspect any subterfuge on the part of the Jotnar, which means we'll still be attacked from both the west and north. Whether the Jotnar will attempt to take on the humans is anyone's guess."

"A fair assumption, though," Fenian said.

"Is there any way we can use that to our advantage, if it is the case?" Freya asked.

Byrric shook his head. "There's no way to know for sure that's what they're planning without allowing them to pass through here without opposition, which isn't a risk either of us are willing to take," he said, gesturing toward Alstad.

"Which is where we will come in," Fenian said. He slid a handful of rocks that had been placed to the southeast of their encampment toward Watoria. "Combined, we have approximately fifteen hundred knights to the twenty-five hundred human and Jotnar. In order to get the upper hand, we need to corral the two enemy armies here," he said, setting two large rocks to the northeast of the city. "The Jotnar have magic, of course, but the humans don't, which puts them at a severe disadvantage, even with their numbers."

"It's unlikely the entire human encampment will attack, though," Aer pointed out. "There are nearly two thousand, at last count, between the ravine and the city gates. If more than half stay behind, or if they spread out too wide for your knights—"

"We don't intend to allow any of them to leave Allanor alive, Your Majesty," Tavian said. "I can assure you, that is not an option."

"Good." Aer nodded, and Freya felt somewhat mollified by his confidence. "That's good."

"The rest of our knights will arrive tomorrow," Fenian said.

Freya looked at her father. "Do you think we'll still be fighting by then?"

He shook his head. "It's unlikely, which is preferable, because I'd rather not reveal our full arsenal just yet."

"Alright, so if we aren't going head-on, what *is* our plan?" Freya asked her father.

Byrric set two stones representing the Allanorian and Royal armies on the map. "We will put our knights to the north and east of the Jotnar."

"And the Valkyrie will come in from the northwest," Ana said as Byrric set down a third stone.

"How many have you brought with you?" Aer asked her.

"Only thirty," Ana said. "Vara is insisting we keep a strong aerial assault intact when we move east to Iladel, so the bulk of the Valkyrie have remained behind in case the Jotnar launch a retaliatory attack on them ."

"And the marshals are prepared to enter Watoria from the harbor to support the citizens if they have an opening," Byrric finished.

Freya jumped when she felt something run over her foot, then yelped when Toskr, in squirrel form, darted up her leg and came to a stop on her shoulder.

Tavian gave her an amused look. "Ah, yes. I heard you've acquired a pet."

Freya tried to keep from turning scarlet.

Fenian's lips twitched. "And it appears he would like to accompany Her Majesty into battle."

Freya cast a pleading look at her father, who looked to be fighting back a grin.

"I'm not going into battle with a godsdamned squirrel—ow!" She flicked Toskr off her shoulder when he swiped at her neck with his claws.

He huffed with annoyance as he leapt to the ground and shifted to two legs. "I only want to be helpful! I think I did quite wonderfully last time."

"Then try asking!" Freya exclaimed. "Gods above, you can't just run up someone's—a *queen's*—leg like that and expect to be welcomed!"

He tilted his chin up indignantly. "I was simply indicating my transportability."

"Your status as a squirrel is indication enough, thank you." Freya narrowed her eyes. "But if you insist, then yes, you can accompany me."

"And answer only to her," Aer added.

Fenian and Tavian snickered.

FREYA WANTED to stop in Watoria before they left for the battlefield, but there simply hadn't been time. Though after their meeting with those who'd been left in the city the previous night, she was confident they'd be able to defend themselves, at least until the Linds could get into the city and take it back. So, not long after they finished going over their plans, she, Byrric, and Ana led the thirty Valkyrie who'd accompanied Ana to the crest of a hill that faced the forest the Jotnar were expected to come through. There was a ridge just in front of the tree line, blocking Freya's sight a bit, but it was the best vantage point they could get that didn't involve being in the air.

As she stood, waiting impatiently beside her father and aunt, her mind still struggled to catch up to her current circumstances. She'd been so focused on getting to this very point, yet now that she'd succeeded in acquiring more allies and speaking with the citizens of Watoria, she finally had time to comprehend just what lay before her. She was going into battle for the first time—a thing she'd honestly never thought would happen. Yes, she'd been trained to be a fighter, and a strong one, at that. But she was raised to be a queen, and in this age, queens didn't go to war.

Something lifted in her at that, and she couldn't help the small, satisfied smile that curved her lips.

Queens of millennia past had gone to war beside their husbands, but sometime between then and now, they'd begun to stay behind, to remain in the palace while the kings and princes and knights went off to fight. Freya knew in her bones that Ordona would ride off to battle if it was asked of her, but that was the thing; it never would've been asked of her.

With Freya, it wasn't even a question.

Still smiling at the thought, she looked up at her father. "You know, Commander, if you're to be our steward, we should probably look into finding you a female counterpart."

He cast her a sidelong look. "We're about to head into battle, and you think now is the time to suggest I remarry?"

She shrugged and looked out over the rolling fields before her. They were empty for now, but at last report, the Jotnar would be coming over the northern ridge within minutes. "It makes sense. If you expect your king *and* queen to go to war with you, it would only be reasonable to assume there should be someone capable of running the kingdom if we all end up smeared on a battlefield."

She scowled when Toskr swiped at her neck with his paw, then gave him a flick on the nose. Byrric had insisted she at least wear armor to protect her shoulders and chest, so Toskr had taken up residence between the crook of her neck and the edge of one of the steel pauldrons that now covered her shoulders. They were irritating, to say the least, but the Caelorian steel that they were crafted from was lightweight enough that she didn't think they would encumber her during flight.

"She's not wrong, Brother," Ana mused. "I know a fair few females back in Iston who would jump at the chance."

Byrric chuckled. "We'll discuss the order of succession once we oust the invaders from our lands." He clapped a hand on Freya's shoulder. "Once you and Aerelius have your thrones back, we'll talk about the future."

Freya looked to where Florian and Tavian were cloaking the rest of their army that spread nearly a mile to the east. Half were poised to encircle the Jotnar from the north once they got close, the rest stood ready to attack from the east. To the south, past the city, the elves stood hidden behind an even heavier cloak of magic, waiting for the humans to mobilize.

The Valkyrie, led by Freya, Ana, and Byrric, were to lead the charge, a thing that both terrified and thrilled her. The thirty leather and armor-clad females who stood behind them, wings tight to their backs, looked nothing short of fearsome.

When the call of a hawk sounded above her, she whipped her head toward the north. Her heart lurched when she saw the first of the Jotnar forces come over the ridge.

"Let's start by ensuring we have a future," she murmured. She tightened the glamour that she'd wound around their small company, then reached out with her magic through the mating bond, reassuring herself of Aer's presence. They'd said their goodbyes earlier, much as they had in Avorell before she had set off for her

Hunt, but after coming through that ordeal whole, neither chose to believe this battle would be their end.

"How close should we let them get?" Ana asked.

"Halfway," Byrric replied. "Take flight on my mark."

Freya thought back to Aer's memory of Salazar telling him that the worst part of war was waiting. She thought she understood it then, when they were sequestered in a house, unable to reach or help anyone. Now that impatience, coupled with the adrenaline and anticipation that were coursing through her, was nearly unbearable.

"Gods above, can't they ride any faster?" she said with a sigh.

"Just a bit further," Byrric murmured.

A moment later, he shot in the air. Freya and Ana followed suit, Toskr clinging tightly to the dip of Freya's shoulder as they ascended. There was a heavy flapping of wings as the Valkyrie rose up behind them.

One day, perhaps years from now, she would reflect on just how odd it felt to fly into battle with a squirrel resting on her shoulder, but not today.

The Valkyrie aimed straight for the Jotnar, who were only a few hundred yards away, a frontal assault that would likely look nothing short of desperate to the enemy. Freya hung back a bit, clinging tightly to the magic that kept them concealed. Then, just as she and the others reached the front line of knights, they dove as one.

Freya tucked her wings tight to her sides and aimed for a small space between two mounted knights, then spread her wings wide when she passed between them, knocking them from their horses and causing their mounts to rear or stumble. Her momentum carried her through three more before she had to pull up and take to the air again. Shouts rang out from below as the Valkyrie made for the cloud cover one of the water witches had conjured for them.

"Again!" Byrric ordered.

They pulled the maneuver two more times, unseating most of the front three lines and causing the riderless horses to scatter while the knights struggled to aim for their unseen attackers. Freya felt her magic strain against the movements of the Valkyrie flying around her.

"I'm releasing the glamour!" she called out. "Now!"

She let the glamour fall, then conjured a dozen blades and sent them all straight into the necks of the knights directly beneath her. Arrows flew into the sky toward the newly-revealed threat, but the Valkyrie dodged them with ease as they rose up above the mass of soldiers. She felt Toskr press her left shoulder with his paw, and she gritted her teeth with annoyance when she realized the damn squirrel was trying to *steer* her.

But when she glanced to the left, she saw a dozen Valkyrie bearing down on the army just beneath her. She banked hard in that direction, pulling herself out of the line of fire as they dove to the ground, pulled up, then dove again, leaving more and more horses without riders each time. They were blindingly fast and utterly beautiful.

Freya couldn't help but grin.

Toskr tapped again, and when she turned to see where his attention had been drawn, she saw that the Lindorothian army had just revealed itself and were coming in from the east. Magic and metal clashed as witches and warlocks charged behind a line of shifters. Now she just needed to help buy time until the rest of the Lindorothian knights could swing around from the north.

Toskr squeezed her shoulder, this time digging in with his left paw and tapping with his right. She looked below and saw an opening where two of the Valkyrie had just flown through. Half a dozen knights were dead or injured on the ground, and those around them had begun to regroup closer to the center of the melee. She glanced back to her own forces, saw they were only yards away, then nodded to let Toskr know she understood.

She aimed for the opening, wincing slightly when his sharp claws pierced her skin where he clung to her. When she was inches from crashing into three knights, she released her magic and Toskr leapt from her shoulder and shifted. Their sudden appearance startled the knights surrounding them long enough for Freya to summon her daggers once again. Toskr became a blur, shifting between squirrel and elf as he tore through three of them, snapping their necks. When two other knights tried to converge on her, one found a dagger in his throat; the other, a poisoned feather to the eye. She pulled her blade from the first, using her foot to kick him away as a third, then a fourth, came forward. She tried to see where Toskr was, but the Jotnar had realized the Valkyrie queen was in their midst, and Freya knew she had quickly become their top priority.

Sweat poured down her neck and back as she ducked and blocked against the bursts of magic the Jotnar knights sent her way. She punched and kicked, sliced and stabbed as bodies fell and blood spattered her leathers.

Five more Jotnar had fallen and she'd narrowly missed a hard blow to her chest when she spotted Toskr running through the knights at dizzying speeds.

"Come on!" Freya shouted. Toskr ran for her as she took flight, then shifted in midair. She plucked him from the air and took them skyward, just as several arrows and even more bolts of searing magic flew past them.

Toskr patted her shoulder twice once they pulled out of range, telling her he was ready to go a second time. They repeated the same maneuver four more times before Freya veered away to do a pass over the battle that was raging beneath them. The western line had been pushed back significantly, thanks to the Valkyrie. Florian and Tavian were attacking with a squadron of the Lindorothian knights from the east, brutally driving the Jotnar toward the center of the fight. She banked to the left, then aimed north to join the rest of her army.

She aimed for Aer's magic, landing beside him just as two knights were converging on him. She drew her dagger and drove it under the arm of one, sliding it neatly between his plates of armor as Aer took the second. "The enemy are down by a third!" she shouted. "I need to check on the southern forces!"

Aer nodded, then drew his own blade and thrust it forward, taking one knight and choking another with his magic—magic that had become far more useful now that he'd learned to weaponize it.

"Go get the status of the humans!" he yelled back, his focus unwavering as he continued to attack with his magic. "Report to Fenian, then get back here!"

No time for 'I love yous,' she thought to herself as she leapt into flight again.

"Come on Toskr," she muttered as she aimed for the southern defenses. "Let's go see what the humans are up to."

She cast a glamour as she approached the human encampment, and when they flew past, Freya saw the humans were doing just as she'd hoped. More than two-thirds appeared to be mobilizing to attack, while the rest were shoring up defenses around the city, mainly at the city gates. She breathed a sigh of relief when she saw far more were leaving than staying and prayed the Watorians who remained in the city would be able to hold their own until the Linds could get inside.

"Hold on, Toskr!" she called as she did an abrupt turn. His claws dug into her skin as she aimed for the elves who were hiding behind a glamour of their own. Recalling how Fenian's magic felt when he'd laid his silencing spell two days earlier, she reached out with her own until she found it. When she felt it, she broke clean through his shield, landing in a crouch beside him. She hardly had time to appreciate the beauty of the elvish army or its perfectly formed ranks, each knight glimmering in opalescent armor.

They could fight. That was all that mattered.

To his credit, Fenian only showed minimal surprise at her sudden appearance, even though it was clear he didn't care for the fact that she'd flown through his magic so easily.

"The humans are splitting," she told him, almost out of breath. "One-third are reinforcing the city, the others look to be moving to back-up the Jotnar who've come south. The Jotnar numbers have been decreased by about one-third as well. It's time to start moving."

He nodded, then shouted a sharp command to his knights before addressing her. "We will take the rear of the human forces and those left behind at their encampment. Go tell my brother that I am splitting our forces between the two human battalions and that we will have them handled within the hour. He will know what to do."

"Which is what?"

Fenian set his jaw at her clear distrust. "He will confer with Byrric and Florian to confirm the plans they have already made to drive the Jotnar south, toward us. We will force the human and Jotnar armies together and surround them." He shook his head and gave her an amused look. "You should work on your trust issues, Queen Freya."

She grinned. "I'll take that under consideration, Your Highness."

48

FREYA

When she and Toskr returned to the battlefield, Freya was pleased to see the Jotnar army had decreased in size significantly. She hardly spared the casualties a glance, though, as she sought out her own forces, needing to see that they hadn't been damaged as severely. Her stomach dropped when she saw how many lay dead in the trampled, muddy grass, nearly indistinguishable from the Jotnar who littered the ground beside them due to the blood and gore that coated their armor. Their casualties seemed fewer than the Jotnar, but it didn't make it any easier to stomach.

Instantly, she shifted her attention away from the ground and to the energy she could feel pulsing toward her through her mating bond. She only sensed adrenaline and anger coming from Aer, but she went to him regardless. She scanned the sky as she flew toward him, taking note of her father, Ana, and the rest of the Valkyrie soaring and diving, and deftly dodging arrows over what remained of their enemy.

Relief flashed across Aer's face when she landed at his side, lasting only a moment before they both dove back into fighting.

"Where is Prince Tavian?" she yelled.

"Ten steps to your right!" Aer replied.

Spinning, Freya ran toward the elf, who was fighting beside Florian.

"You've spoken to my brother?" he called.

Freya nodded, then quickly filled him in on her conversation with Fenian. He looked at Florian, clamped a hand on the warlock's arm, and they both vanished. Toskr jumped from her shoulder and shifted, then wordlessly, as if the two had the same mind, they ran back to Aer and fell into a rhythm at his side.

They continued to fight, ducking, stabbing, and expending their magic until no more came at them. The sun had nearly set by the time the sounds of battle, the cries and shouts of the injured and dying, the thud of hooves and boots, had all lowered to a din.

Freya and Aer had just pulled back their combined magic from a persistent Jotnar when Byrric landed beside them. He was a mess, covered in blood and dirt, with sweat streaming down his face. He was limping a bit and his armor was dented in several spots, but he was alive, which was all that mattered.

"What are our numbers?" Aer demanded breathlessly, shucking off his helmet and sheathing his blade.

"It's too soon to say, Your Majesty, but there are more of our own left than Jotnar or human," Byrric said. "Only a handful remain, and they've been taken as prisoners."

Aer nodded, then wordlessly reached out toward Freya. She took his hand, squeezed, and exhaled a heavy breath.

"We need to check on the city," she said.

Byrric wiped a hand across his brow, his fingers leaving clean streaks through the grime. "Go. Take Toskr with you, see how the citizens are faring."

Toskr, who was doubled over, his hands braced on his knees, winced. "Ah. Lovely. More fighting." With a deep breath, he straightened, grimacing a bit as he did. "Right, then. We should be on our way."

"I'd wait if I were you," Prince Fenian said, drawing Freya's attention behind them. Florian walked beside him, grim-faced, dragging a thin, dark-haired Jotnar. The prisoner's hands were bound behind him and he was filthy, but Freya could tell by the sheen of his leather and the sneer that twisted his handsome face that he was high-ranking.

Freya looked at Florian then, and the expression of hatred he wore was unlike anything Freya had ever seen on the warlock.

"Who is this?" Aer angled his head, looking down at the male.

"Frederick Edrin, Your Majesties," Florian said as he tightened his grip on Frederick's binds. "The city is nearly retaken, but Prince Tavian and I thought you might want to decide how to handle him."

"Get your hands off of me!" Frederick hissed, struggling against Florian's hold. "Lessia will kill you for this!"

Freya gave him an appraising look. "So you're the bastard who's been terrorizing my city."

"It's not your city anymore," he spat.

"We'll see about that," Aer murmured. The uncharacteristic rage in his eyes nearly had Freya reaching out to take his hand.

Frowning, Byrric scanned the skies around them. "Where did your winged dog fly off to?"

Frederick's answering, bloody smile was grotesque. "Reykr knew his chance to rid the world of you was lost the moment those blasted elves showed up. You'll find him soon enough, though."

"That's unfortunate," Freya said with a sigh. "I was hoping we might be able to rid the world of *him* tonight." Smirking, she looked up at Aer. "Well? What shall we do with him?"

"Bring him back with us," Aer replied, not taking his eyes off of Frederick. "It shouldn't take long to get something useful from him."

"Believe me, I have plenty of *useful* tidbits to share," Frederick sneered.

"Go back to the house," Byrric told them. "Tavian and I will give out orders and be there to handle this with you shortly."

Shouts rang out a short distance away where a small skirmish seemed to be continuing.

"Go," Freya told her father. "But hurry."

Nodding, Byrric took flight and headed toward where the cluster of fighting had resumed.

"Prince Fenian, would you mind taking us back?" Aer asked.

Fenian eyed Frederick curiously, then nodded.

Turning, Freya looked at Toskr to ask him to help with transporting them back, then stopped short when she saw that he was still holding his side. When she looked closer, she saw that blood was beginning to seep through his fingers.

"Gods above, Toskr!" She rushed toward him, replacing his hand with hers over the wound. "Why didn't you say you were injured?"

He hissed at the press of her fingers. "You were, ah, occupied."

"Stupid, idiot squirrel," she muttered. She shrugged out of her jacket and pressed it to the wound. "I thought you had a cramp. Here. Put pressure on it until we can have you treated."

"Please, Your Majesty, that isn't—"

"Tell me it isn't necessary and I'll give your left side a wound to match your right." Freya sent a look at Fenian, who shook his head and sighed, then transported all of them back to the estate.

"Get Edrin to the cellar," Aer said to Florian, then addressed two marshals who'd been assigned to the portico. "I want all of you watching him until we come down. Is that clear?"

"Yes, Your Majesty," they replied in unison.

"Haegin!" Freya shouted, wincing as she looked at Toskr again.

Haegin appeared in the doorway a moment later, then frowned when he took in the amount of blood on her and Toskr's hands.

"Give him to me, Your Majesty," he said quietly. "I'll get him fixed up for you."

Toskr, whose skin had gone a bit gray, smiled wanly. "Yes, please do, sir, before your queen follows through on her threats."

Freya gave him a warning look. "Behave. We'll speak when Haegin is done patching you up."

She watched in silence as Haegin helped Toskr down the hall toward the infirmary.

"And Toskr?" she called before they could get too far.

He and Haegin paused, and Toskr glanced over his shoulder. "Yes, Your Majesty?"

She smiled. "You did well today."

FREYA WANTED TO FIND LAZ, Collin, and Myria to fill them in on all that had happened, but her most pressing concern was what to do with Frederick Edrin. Or, more importantly, what information to try and get out of him before they carved him up and left him out as carrion. She'd been itching to lay eyes on him since they'd arrived in Watoria, and the thought of actually having him in the house, being able to extract information from him, had anticipation quickening her heart.

So, once Haegin had taken Toskr off to dress his wounds—she wouldn't spare a thought on the damn elf not being alright—she and Aer made their way down to the cellar, where someone had chained him to the wall through hooks Freya wasn't quite sure she wanted to know the origin of. His face was the picture of petulance, which was surprising, considering he was likely going to die quite soon.

"Where is Prince Fenian?" Freya asked.

"He went back to help his brother deal with the last of the humans," Florian murmured. "I told him we would handle any... problems here."

Aer crouched down in front of Frederick. Freya stood quietly at his side, arms folded as she stared down at Frederick in contempt.

"What should we do with you, Lord Edrin?" Aer grabbed a fistful of Frederick's hair and yanked his head back. "You're responsible for the deaths of most of Watoria. So what would be a proper punishment in your opinion?"

Frederick laughed, his teeth still bloody from whatever beating Florian and Ashton had doled out before Freya and Aer had arrived. "I did what I came here to do. Your city is destroyed. Your people are dead."

"Not all of them," Aer said quietly. "Many, but not all."

Frederick shot him a derisive look and laughed. "But enough."

"Enough for what?" Freya asked.

"Enough to break you, for one," he said, then winced when Aer tugged harder on his hair. "Enough to keep you occupied and away from my sister-in-law."

Freya wanted to snap that they weren't as far separated from Lessia as he thought, but she bit her tongue.

"Perhaps," Aer said. "It's unlikely you'll ever know the true outcome of this war, isn't it?" He released his hold on Frederick's hair, then kicked the man's legs out from under him, causing him to cry out when the chains pulled on his shoulders.

"Now," Aer said, taking a step back. "Let's see how much you actually know about Lessia's plans."

Frederick sneered at Aer, his face furious through his pain, but when he opened his mouth to speak, his eyes shifted focus for a moment. He grinned, then laughed outright—a hysterical, high-pitched sound that had Freya questioning his sanity.

Before she could speak a word, however, the air whistled quietly at her ear and a dagger lodged itself in his chest.

49

LEA

Someone, likely Willem or one of his idiot spies who liked to follow Lea around, had told Jonas of Lea's stroll through the gardens with Ettrian. It could've been Rosie, Lea assumed, but she had a strong suspicion that hadn't been the case.

"I told you to stay away from him," Jonas said the moment he walked in the door of their room. "He's dangerous, Lea!"

Lea set down the book she'd been reading and leveled him a look. "Everyone in this palace is dangerous, Jonas."

"You know what I mean."

She angled her head and eyed him curiously. "Alright, fine. But just so we're clear on the matter, what exactly should I do when a prince arrives at my door and requests my company? If I refuse him, Lessia will think I'm being rude," she said with a calm that unnerved even her. "*He* will think I'm being rude, and if the wife of Lord Jonas Edrin is rude to the elvish prince, what might that do to the alliance your aunt managed to secure?"

She let the question hang in the air, hoping he would offer something, *anything,* that indicated he knew the elves were not the allies Lessia and Willem thought they were.

A muscle feathered in his jaw as his pale eyes held hers.

"Fine. But—"

"But nothing. If the prince asks me to take him on a tour of the palace or the gardens or the gallery, I will take him. He's been nothing but proper toward me and I see no reason to think he has any ill intent."

Jonas sat down in the chair beside her and rested his arms on his knees, steepling his fingers in front of his lips. He stared at the floor for several moments before finally looking at her.

"Your distrust of me has gotten worse."

She quirked a brow. "I trust you."

"No, you don't, and you must think very little of me if you think I haven't noticed."

"Jonas—"

"You've been keeping things from me this past week," he pressed. "Big things, from the look of distraction that's on your face half the time." He paused, studying her, before continuing. "*Does* this have to do with Ettrian?"

She rolled her eyes. "Ettrian has nothing to do with anything, and it's not about trust, Jonas. It's about who might have their ear to the wall at this very moment." She bit her bottom lip. "Actually, speaking of that..."

"What is it?"

Lea's eyes darted toward the panel beside the fireplace that led to the tunnels. "There was something I've been meaning to ask you. Does Lessia know...? "

He followed her gaze, then shrugged. "I certainly haven't spoken to her about them, and I honestly can't recall her mentioning them, but yes, I would assume she knows. Willem does, and I can't imagine he hasn't told her."

I could.

"What about the spy holes?" Lea continued. "It seemed she knew about those when you retrieved me from the dungeons."

He nodded. "Yes, I told her about those. She didn't confirm or deny that she'd placed them there, but I know Willem complained to her when I sealed them up." He frowned. "Why are you asking?"

She shrugged. "For some reason, I just recalled the fact that we only encountered humans in the tunnels on the way back to the palace the night of the wedding. I hadn't considered it then, but now I'm wondering if we should worry about facing Jotnar and the humans, or only humans, if I—or we—attempt to flee. If it's both, that could be problematic. If it's only the latter, it could be quite simple."

"You've given more thought to leaving, then?" Relief flooded his face. "Gods above, Lea, that's so good to hear."

"I have," she admitted. "You were right when you said my mother would never forgive me. Guilt is the only thing motivating me to stay, but I know leaving is the better choice."

"Let's plan for tomorrow," Jonas said. "After dinner."

She nodded slowly. "Tomorrow it is."

THE FOLLOWING MORNING, Tyna secreted away two packs; one for Lea, one for Jonas. Each held two sets of clothes, some dried meat, a few rolls, and a canteen of water, along with two heavy canvas tarps that could be used for shelter. The food wouldn't last long, even if they rationed it, and the tent would just barely shelter them both, but they would be enough to hold them over until they got far enough from Iladel to safely sneak into a village to replenish their supplies.

The hours crawled by as Lea waited for dinner to come. She read through two books while she waited, then spent half the afternoon fiddling with her magic, making sure it was there, ready to be wielded.

Finally, as the sky began to dim, Tyna arrived to help Lea dress for dinner. They considered putting pants under her skirts, but decided it wasn't worth the risk of flashing an ankle and potentially alerting Willem or Lessia to their intentions.

"I will be waiting for you when dinner ends," Tyna said quietly as she fussed over Lea's hair in the bathing room. She'd twisted it into a tight braid that fell over Lea's shoulder, with just a few curls framing her face. It was as pretty as it was practical, and the last thing Lea wanted was to have to worry about her hair while trekking through the woods.

"Do you really think this will work?" Lea asked. "This plan... it just seems so... simple."

Too simple.

"If you use your power as you've been practicing—don't give me that look, I know what you've been up to—then yes, I think this will work." Tyna paused to smile at Lea in the mirror. "You can do this, my lady."

Lea gave her a half-smile in return. "Thank you, Tyna." Her grin widened a bit. "And I think it's time you start calling me Lea."

Tyna beamed.

LEA'S HEART pounded as she and Jonas sat down for dinner. She'd been so hesitant to leave, but now that her departure was only a few hours off, anticipation had snuck its way in, mixing with the guilt that continued to hound her.

She wanted to leave. She knew it was the best choice.

She also knew it could very likely lead to the death of the only parent she had left.

Her mother. Ordona's sister and Aerelius' aunt.

Aer might never forgive her. Nor would Lazarus, for leaving his own mother behind, especially when Lea had no concrete information to give him regarding her condition.

That thought speared straight through her heart.

But Perida would forgive her. Even if this all ended with her death. Her mother wouldn't step into the afterworld with anger because Lea knew, unequivocally, that she would make the same choice.

Aer and Laz, however, her two closest friends, her *family*, might never forgive her.

"Why so glum, Lady Edrin?" Willem asked as he carefully buttered a roll. "You look as though your mother just lost her head."

"Willem!" Rosie hissed, her cheeks going scarlet with embarrassment.

Effina swatted her husband with the back of her hand. "Oh, be nice, darling!"

"You do seem a bit preoccupied this evening," Lessia remarked.

"We had a bit of an argument before we left," Jonas said. "A lover's quarrel, that's all."

"Oh, you poor thing," Rosie said with a small pout, touching her hand to Lea's.

Ettrian's eyes found hers as he picked up his wine and took a sip. "So soon?"

"I don't think there's a proper timeframe for when a married couple should have their first argument, Your Highness," Jonas said dryly. He gave Lea a pointed look. "We can make it up to one another later."

"Ah." Lessia set down her glass. "Speaking of that. We need to have a discussion about heirs."

Lea nearly spit out her wine, and Ettrian outright laughed.

"Oh, how exciting!" Rosie said, sitting up a bit taller. "Lady Edrin and I were *just* talking about this very topic not too long ago, weren't we?"

Willem's brows winged up at Rosie's revelation. "Is that so?"

Jonas sighed. "We're in the middle of a war, and we've only been mated one week. I think that discussion can wait."

Lessia waved him off. "No, it should be now. As it stands, you are my only heir. Seeing as it can take such a long time to produce children, and I am not exactly *young*, I'd like you two to get started on that quickly."

"Gods above," Jonas muttered. "I am not discussing the *production* of heirs at the dinner table, Empress. Toss me in the dungeons if you must, but this is a conversation to be had in private between me and my wife."

"Oh, by all means, carry on," Ettrian said, smirking. "I'm quite curious about your line of succession myself."

"We need to be sure she can produce heirs," Lessia insisted. "Her fert—"

"Enough!" Jonas snapped.

Lea frowned at him, then at Lessia, confused at the turn the conversation had taken. Lessia was a bit odd at times, but this topic was a bit much, even for her.

Lessia and Jonas held each other's eyes for a heavy moment, then Lessia huffed. "Fine. Tomorrow, then."

"It's alright," Lea said when Jonas went to argue. She laid a hand over his and tried to look reassuring. "I'd like to be sure as well." She looked at Lessia, then back at Jonas. "We can discuss it later, though."

His mouth snapped shut, then he looked at her and gave her a sharp nod.

For the remainder of the meal, Effina simpered at Willem's side; Willem, Jonas, and Ettrian discussed the most efficient methods of attacking a city held as firmly as Errest; Rosie attempted to pull Lea into the same idle chatter as always; and Lessia brooded at the head of the table, her eyes drifting from Willem, to Ettrian, to Lea, and back again. Aside from their initial conversation, she'd barely spoken a word throughout dinner and was silent through most of dessert.

It was Lessia's last look that set Lea at unease. She knew both rulers had been suspicious of her from the start, and she hoped her mother's refusal would only lead them to think her mother was too stubborn for her own good, not that Lea hadn't tried hard enough to change her mind. Lessia's expression, though, told Lea she was leaning more toward the latter.

Jonas must have noticed the attention his aunt was giving Lea, because he leaned in and brushed his nose against Lea's ear. She put on a small smile and shifted closer, then bit her lip when he wound a finger through one of her curls.

"You look bored, darling," he commented quietly.

"Apologies, my lord," she whispered. "This week…" She set down her napkin and sighed, then looked at Lessia. "Empress, I know I've said it before, but I must apologize about my mother. I was so sure..." She shook her head. "No, I think I must've fooled myself into thinking her thoughts would align with mine. I *so* hoped she would see how important ensuring our peoples' safety would be." Eyes beseeching, she looked at Lessia, then Willem. "I'm so sorry to you both. If you would like me to try again, I'm more than willing. Please know that. If not, I will do all I can in her stead to rally the citizens of Errest to your cause."

"That seems a silly promise to make," Ettrian said, eyebrows raised. "If you couldn't convince your mother, what makes you so sure you can convince an entire city?"

Lea glared at him. "My mother is a proud woman, Your Highness. I am as well, but I am also pragmatic, as King Willem so kindly pointed out to me not so long ago." She gave Willem a tight smile. "Perhaps my mother has been around too long to change her perspective on things such as this. I simply don't know. But I know what's in my own mind, and that includes not only a new version of Lindoroth, but a good life for the family I hope to build, as well."

Ettrian's eyes sparked gold, and she knew instantly he'd seen her twist on words for exactly that.

The mischievous look in his gaze shifted to humor. "Noble as those sentiments are, it still gives no guarantee," he said.

"It certainly doesn't," Lessia mused.

Lea frowned. "You expect me to predict how an entire city will react to my words? I've never said I could guarantee anything, but I will do my damnedest."

"She's not wrong," Willem said with a sigh. He drummed his fingers on his goblet, his heavy ring tapping against the pewter. "We'll give her a chance, of course, and if you prove less-than useful, we'll decide what to do with you after."

Jonas sent the king a glare. "That's my wife you're threatening, Willem. I'd think carefully how you proceed."

"Yes, Willem, please. Let's refrain from threatening our own at the dinner table," Lessia said tiredly. "My nephew is more than capable of punishing his wife should she fail us."

"Indeed, Empress, although I think I must request he perform the punishment in present company." Willem leered at Lea as Effina snickered. "A punishment is always so much more effective when humiliation accompanies it, don't you agree?"

"Don't forget the utter disappointment of your spouse," Effina added with a nod. "That adds an extra layer, too."

Rosie, to her credit, looked slightly horrified that Willem was speaking so casually about Jonas harming Lea, but she kept her words to herself.

Lea exhaled softly through her nose. "Yes, of course. The last thing I want is to disappoint any of you, but to disappoint my husband, my mate, would be a thing I'd never hope to feel." She wrapped her hand around Jonas'. "I promise to do all I can to live up to your expectations of me, my love."

"And let us also not forget the strength of the mating bond," Ettrian pointed out. "Disappointing one's mate would equal the pinnacle of misery in a marriage. Jonas' disappointment would become Lea's as well." He smirked at Lea. "It would almost be like she was punishing herself."

"Well I, for one, am sick of hearing about all of this," Effina said, setting her napkin down and picking up her goblet. "The elder lady Calliwell's refusal to help is unfortunate, but surely there must be *something* we can celebrate?" She looked at Willem. "Darling, you're always so good at finding a silver lining."

Willem smiled softly at his wife. "You know me so well, darling."

He stood from his seat and held up his goblet. "My lovely wife is correct. As loathe as I am to admit that our plans do not seem to be panning out in the direction we'd hoped, there is still cause to celebrate." He lifted his cup toward Ettrian. "To new alliances. With Lord Edrin mated to a lady of Lindoroth, and now a partnership with Avorell, our position here will be that much more secure. To three kingdoms, united as one."

"Oh, what a lovely toast, Willem!" Rosie said, clasping her hands. She smiled at Lea. "My brother has such a way with words, doesn't he?"

"He certainly does," Lea murmured, then took a large sip of wine.

Willem's face softened as he looked down at Effina. "And you, my dear Effina. Had I know I could have had a Jotnar bride such as you, I would have cast Isadora and the human realm aside long ago. The children you would grant me would be a boon to Dystone, but the love you share is worth more than all the gems in Edhil."

Effina preened at him, and Lea didn't miss the self-satisfied smirk that twisted Lessia's lips.

Willem cupped Effina's chin in his hand, then leaned down and touched his lips to hers in a surprisingly tender gesture. "You're just so lovely," he murmured.

Lea couldn't help but grimace at their display. Whether Effina found him genuine, or if she herself was even genuine, Lea wasn't sure, but the entire situation just reeked of... something.

Her initial disgust shifted to confusion when a small click sounded from the direction of Willem's hand. Half a moment later, a wide-eyed look of shock twisted Effina's pretty face.

"And so much stupider than I gave you credit for." Willem pulled his hand away from his wife, and Lea saw blood dripping from her chin.

A short, sharp blade now protruded from Willem's ring.

No, not a blade.

A needle.

Effina made a hiss, then a choking noise.

"Willem—" she gasped, reaching for his arm.

He stepped back, then smiled when blood began to foam on her lips.

50

LEA

The room was silent for a single, heavy moment as Effina Veldin slid from her chair and to the ground as she continued to choke on her own blood.

"Willem!" Rosie squealed, staring in utter shock.

Lessia and Jonas leapt from their seats, sending the chairs toppling to the floor as Lessia stared, aghast, at her cousin. Slowly, as to not draw Willem's attention, Lea slid her chair back and tugged on Rosie's hand, pulling her from her seat. The human girl's grip on her fingers was almost painfully tight.

Lessia swallowed hard, and the pain that was beginning to reveal itself in her expression vanished as she turned venomous eyes on Willem. "What have you done?"

"Ore serum," Willem explained. He picked up his napkin and wiped off the few drops of blood left on his hand, then dropped the napkin and faced her, not sparing Effina a glance as she twitched on the floor, still clawing at her throat. "Crafted from the very ore powder you used to kill Salazar. It's much more effective when it's delivered directly into the bloodstream." With a thoughtful look, he slid his hand into his pocket.

Lea followed the movement carefully.

Willem smiled. "Do you think I was ignorant of your plans, Lessia? Do you think I was unaware that you planned to double-cross me once we had the Linds in line? That I didn't know you have two battalions bearing down on them from the north, aiming to take out my armies in Watoria and Kildin?" He shook his head and tsked. "For such a smart person, you've been quite stupid."

Shocked at this turn of events, Lea looked at the Empress. Lessia's jaw was clenched, and she seemed to be forcing herself not to look at Effina.

"The knights from Jotunheim were marching to handle the Lindorothian armies, you stupid, *idiot* human!" the empress spat.

The look Willem sent Lessia's way said exactly how much he believed that, and Ettrian chuckled quietly.

"Even I find that hard to believe, Empress," the prince said, smirking.

Movement to Willem's side caught Lea's attention, and she stared, frozen, as Effina tried to stand. When Effina gripped the arm of her chair, Willem kicked it out from under her, causing her to stumble, her head cracking hard against the edge of the table before she crumpled to the ground again. Lea jerked, feeling the blow, and had the sudden urge to help her. Rosie, her face still slack with shock, clutched Lea's hand.

Lessia screamed in rage and reared back her arm to throw her magic.

But she faltered. Pain flashed across her face.

The hand she'd been about to use to destroy Willem moved to her throat instead. Her sharp nails scratched against some unseen irritant there and her face purpled as she began to gag.

Taking advantage of her lapse, Willem put his hand to his mouth and blew a fine, green powder in her face. It shimmered in the air as it drifted from his hand to Lessia's skin, a telltale gleam that Lea recognized instantly.

Lessia screamed in pain when the *eitr*, the most deadly poison known to exist for their kind, hit her, singeing her skin and eyes. Jonas pulled Lea back, causing her to stumble away from the table as they watched Lessia fall to her knees. Rosie's hand still clung to Lea's hand, and Lea found the princess getting dragged back as well.

"Stay back," Jonas murmured to them both.

"No," Rosie whimpered. "What is he *doing*?"

Lea couldn't help but feel sorry for the girl, so she linked their fingers together and wrapped an arm around her shoulders.

"Shh," she breathed. "It's alright."

Perhaps this night will end well, after all, she thought.

"You vile mongrels don't deserve to exist," Willem hissed down at Lessia, his terrified sister seemingly forgotten.

Blood from whatever poison Lessia had ingested trickled from her nose and mouth as she gripped the edge of the table, struggling to stay on her feet.

Suddenly, Willem's men poured in, and within seconds the ten guards Lessia had stationed within the room joined with the humans and surrounded the table, their spears aimed inward.

"You see, Lessia," Willem began, "your soldiers don't particularly care for your method of ruling. It was quite easy to get them to join me in ousting you. Even easier to get one to poison your food."

Instantly, Lea's eyes shot to her own half-eaten plate of food, terrified that the same had been done to hers. She sent a panicked look toward Ettrian, who had remained seated this whole time at the opposite end of the table and was now calmly tearing off a piece of bread from his roll. He arched a brow at her, his lips tilting into a crooked smile.

'*Was there something you needed, my lady?*'

Lea jumped at the sound of his voice in her head.

"Stop them!" she begged him. She didn't dare call forward her magic, not when she knew Willem held such a deadly poison at the ready.

Willem flicked the last of the powder onto Lessia's body, which had ceased almost all movement, save for a small twitching in her blistered, blood-streaked cheek. He cast a glance at Jonas, who'd gone still at Lea's side, then stared down at Lea, his face considering.

"You think he'll help you?" Willem grinned at the elf, then at Lea as he came to a stop in front of her. "He hates them just as much as I. Just as much as *you* do."

Jonas moved forward but was stopped when Ettrian held up a hand, throwing up an invisible wall that prevented him from going further. "Not so fast, Lord Edrin."

Ettrian set his roll down, then leaned back, folding his arms, and eyed Willem. "I have to admit, Willem. The thought of destroying the Jotnar scum who've so greatly perverted the magic the elves bestowed upon them is quite appealing. I'm curious, though. How do you plan to defeat the armies that are currently marching south toward Kildin and Watoria? You have Lessia's knights here in your corner, but the others are days away."

"The army marching on Kildin has been handled, and I have enough of my own stationed in Watoria to hold defenses there, despite what Lessia thought."

He doesn't know, Lea realized, her heart thundering. Willem had no idea that Freya and Aer were meeting that army in battle this very moment. Ignorance was the only explanation for Willem's confidence, because she was certain that his measly army had no chance against such a surprise attack.

Willem approached Lea, then gently brushed a finger along her cheek. "Now, what about you, pretty girl? I think we got off on the wrong foot, you and I. We both find the Jotnar equally as vile, wouldn't you agree?"

"Perhaps before you joined with them in overtaking my kingdom and killing my family," she hissed. "Now I see you as no better than the empress you just killed."

Willem laughed. "See, I knew it was only a matter of time before you revealed your true colors! You never had any intention of joining us, did you?"

Lea sneered. "Only a fool would've believed such a thing. And if you think this—" she gestured toward the bodies of Lessia and Effina, "—changes that, you're even more of an imbecile than I thought."

Ettrian laughed. "Oh, she *is* a smart one, Willem! And you can't truly blame her, can you?"

"Not to worry," Willem said. "Minds can be changed."

Lea cast a panicked look at Jonas, who stood stock-still beside her and the terrified princess.

"Let her go, Willem," Jonas said quietly. "You've dealt with Lessia and Effina. Let Lea go."

Willem's gaze swept over Lea, appraising her as he'd done so many times before. "Oh, I don't know, Jonas. I may want to... keep her."

"That was not what we agreed to," Jonas growled. "Leave her alone."

Lea's head turned slowly toward him. "What are you talking about? Jonas!" she snapped when he didn't so much as look at her.

"Relax, Lord Edrin," Willem said with a sigh. "Your female will be kept perfectly safe, not to worry."

Ettrian walked forward then, coming to a stop beside Willem.

His lips twitched when Lea sent him a poisoned look. "She's a fighter. She might make a good wife."

Lea's heart stuttered with betrayal when Ettrian's golden eyes met hers.

No. There was no way he could've been so... duplicitous. And Jonas...

Willem's lip curled. "Perhaps if you hadn't already performed their mating bond, that would be an option."

"Who better to break a mating bond than the elf who cast it?" Ettrian replied, pulling his eyes from Lea and looking at Jonas.

"Willem!" Rosie exclaimed. "You can't *force* her!"

Willem sent his sister a disparaging look, and Lea shifted so Rosie was completely behind her.

Jonas continued to struggle against the wall that Ettrian had constructed in between them. "Lea, run!"

Willem laughed and glanced pointedly at the guards that still surrounded the table. "Noble suggestion, Jonas. Although, I'm not quite sure how you expect her to carry that out. I'll follow through on our agreement, though."

Revulsion roiled in Lea's gut at the twisted leer that accompanied those words. She looked at Jonas as betrayal struck hard. "What have you done?"

He closed his eyes, his chest heaving. "It's—I can explain." He opened his eyes and looked at her. "Willem and I—we made a deal."

"It's simple," Willem said. "Jonas will lead the Jotnar, and I will lead the humans. He gets the throne he so desperately desired, and we'll all be rid of the filth that Lessia brought into this world." His face filled with pity as he looked at Lea. "Sadly, I can't say the Linds will fare any better than they are at present."

"But—but—you *killed* them!" Rosie exclaimed, her eyes still frozen on Effina and Lessia's bodies.

Willem sighed. "Yes, Sister, I did. Now, do shut up before I have you tossed in the dungeons." He nodded at Ettrian as Rosie let out a squeal of outrage. "Go on, do it."

"Willem, you can't just take her from me," Jonas said. His voice was even but Lea could hear the desperation in his words. "She's my wife. You said she wouldn't come to any harm."

Willem smirked. "She won't. I promise."

Ettrian frowned but didn't make a move to do Willem's bidding. "Now that I think of it... do you truly believe a Lind bride will better your position with the Lindorothian people?"

"Once she tells everyone of the wicked spell Lessia put me under to convince my army to serve her? Once we tell everyone how desperately I wanted to free my people from Jotnar control? Once they realize their own monarchs have fled, leaving them behind? Yes, I think this Lindorothian bride will do exactly that." Willem nodded, his eyes hungry now as he gazed at Lea. "Yes, she'll do quite nicely."

"They'll believe it just as easily if she's married to me," Jonas said desperately.

"He's right," Lea said. "They'll never believe me if I'm at your side."

"They will, because *you* will convince them of it," Willem said.

Lea shook her head rapidly. "No. I won't do it. Do what you want to me, but I will never tell my people to follow the likes of you!" She gazed pleadingly at Ettrian. "Please don't do this!"

The prince slowly walked toward Lea.

"Willem," he began, not taking his eyes from hers. "I had a thought."

"What thought is that?" Willem snapped, eyes turning slightly wary.

Something flickered in Ettrian's eyes.

The prince faced the human king, his lips curved into a sly smile. "Seeing as Lord Edrin intended to oust Lessia before all this nonsense began, perhaps that can be used to your advantage here."

Lea held her breath, not daring to breathe.

"How?"

Ettrian arched a brow at Jonas. "Lord Edrin? Care to elaborate?"

Jonas swallowed, then nodded. "Lessia was hated by most of our people," he told Willem. "But I was not. I can wrest her armies under control—"

"I can do that for myself," Willem snarled.

Ettrian laughed. "You think they'll listen to you, a human? Come, Willem. Even you can't be that stupid."

Willem jutted his chin out defiantly.

"It will be in your best interest," Jonas said evenly. "I wanted to take Jotunheim for myself. That was my intention long before now. And that will be easier for me to do with Lea at my side. You can have your pick of brides, but if you take my wife for yourself, my people will see that for precisely what it is."

The room was silent for a long moment while Willem stared at them each in turn. Finally, he turned cold eyes on the elf.

"Fine."

"Wonderful!" Ettrian exclaimed. "Now, as dreadful as this dinner has been, considering the circumstances, I think we have a bit to celebrate."

"Indeed," Willem murmured, looking bored. He gestured toward Lessia and Effina's bodies. "Someone get this cleaned up."

Jonas stumbled as Ettrian dropped the magic that had been barricading him, and the guards lowered their spears.

Smiling broadly down at Lea, Ettrian held out a hand to help her up.

She sent a hateful glare at Willem, then reached out to take his hand, pulling Rosie off the floor along with her.

The moment Lea touched his skin, there was a flash of cold, then heat, then the world spun and something squeezed Lea's hand. As she felt her body come back to itself, cold air bit against her face and her breaths came out in harsh, frosted pants.

She squeezed her eyes shut and dug her fingers into cold soil as the nausea of passing through what had to have been the Between hit, wave after wave that made her entire body heave. Hands hooked under her arms and dragged her to her feet, and when she stumbled, Ettrian's arm caught her by the waist.

"What did you do?" she whispered. She pressed a hand to her forehead in an attempt to ease away the headache that was forming there.

"I saved you, Lady Calliwell. What did you expect?"

After ensuring she was steady, Ettrian removed his arm from her waist and stepped back.

The ground they were on sloped sharply upward, making it that much harder to regain her footing, but she finally righted herself and looked around. They were in a forest. In the distance, not too far off, she thought she could make out the familiar walls that encircled the palace.

She faced Ettrian and rubbed her forehead. "What are you playing at?"

"I'm not playing at anything. I simply want the best possible outcome for this fiasco those people call a coup. In your case, I believe your best outcome does not involve being stuck in that dining room with that wretched human." Disgust twisted his features. "Foul creature, that man."

"And my husband? You've just left him there!"

"Yes... about that. I may have embellished my ability to perform a wedding ceremony for a kingdom that is not my own."

Lea went still. "Excuse me?"

His answering smirk sent waves of fury up her spine.

Her eyes widened and she stepped toward him. "All this time, I've been torn between breaking my vows when this is all over or forcing myself to try and love him, and now you're telling me we're *not even married?*" She shoved his chest hard. "You stupid elvish bastard!"

"Now, that's no way to speak to a prince."

She shoved him again.

Ettrian's eyes widened, but he didn't budge an inch. "I thought you would be happy!"

"Of course I'm happy!" She scowled and took several angry steps back. "Why would you let me think—nevermind. Nevermind!" Folding her arms, she turned away, not wanting him to see the mix of emotions she was sure were clear in her expression.

Not married. She was not married. She'd never *been* married.

Slowly, she took a deep breath, then turned to face him again. "And what about you? What is your 'desired outcome'?"

"Ah, that. Yes, that involves replacing Willem Ristner with someone far more deserving of the title of King. Possibly his brother, but I suppose that's yet to be seen." He wrinkled his nose and glanced around the forest. "What is that horrid smell?"

"Goddess help me," Lea muttered, pressing a hand to her stomach and bracing against a tree. "*What* is going on?"

"Consider it a rescue mission. I've spirited you away, so to speak. You and an interloper, it seems." He angled his head. "I've forgotten what a hard time humans have when they're taken through the Between."

"What are you talking about?" Lea spun, then her eyes fell shut and she groaned when she saw Rosie Ristner's unconscious form on the forest floor. "She was holding my hand. Gods above, she was holding my *fucking* hand and you *let her come with us!*"

Ettrian threw his arms up. "I took your hand, Lady Calliwell. It's not my fault—"

"Ugh, just shut up!"

Lea covered her face with her hands and shook her head, struggling to wrap her mind around all that had just happened. Slowly, she dropped her arms and looked at him.

"I was supposed to leave tonight," she said quietly.

"Jonas seems to have felt otherwise."

Lea froze as she realized the truth of his words. Jonas had made a deal with Willem. Yes, it benefited him—and her, in a sense—in that Lessia was now dead. Lea couldn't help but feel relieved at that, and thankful for whatever role Jonas had played in expediting that outcome.

But that he had the gall to question her trust in him just the night before...

"The palace is just through there," she said, pushing aside the anger that accompanied those thoughts. "Why not *spirit* us someplace further out of harm's way?"

"Good manners?" When she gawked at him, he laughed. "I will only take you away of your own volition, Lady Calliwell. If you refuse me, I will happily send you back to that room, but I will not be returning with you."

"No!" She shook her head. "No. I just...don't understand."

"Lord Edrin plans to stay behind and handle Lessia's armies now that she is dead. Willem was aware of what little respect her knights had for her and sees the benefit to an alliance with her nephew, instead."

"Jonas would never agree to send me off with you," she whispered.

"Jonas is aware of the beneficial position he is now in. He is in control of Jotunheim, just as he desired. He holds control of the Jotnar armies, just as he desired. He knows you are with me and safe."

"You planned this. The two of you."

"Had you not been so stubborn, we would've included you."

She opened her mouth to ask the question she was most afraid to know the answer to, then stopped.

Ettrian read the intent on her face. "He is loyal to you. Willem believes he has done Lord Edrin a service in killing his aunt and that vapid thing he called a wife. From what I can tell, Willem still intends to take Jotunheim for himself, but—"

Her eyes widened. "And you just left Jonas there?" Shoving past him, she started stalking through the forest toward the castle. Ettrian quickly fell into step beside her, then grabbed her arm and pulled her to a stop.

"Lord Edrin and I are in agreement that staying here is no longer wise nor safe for you," he said.

"What do you care?" she snapped, jerking from his grip. "You've already made your choice."

"Have I? Do you see an elvish army at my back?" He arched a brow and cast a glance over his shoulder. "Because I certainly don't."

Lea sent him a scathing look. "So now what? You've just chopped off the head of an army. You plan to, what, leave them be and hope they'll follow Jonas? He may find that to be a simple task, but I certainly don't!"

Ettrian frowned as though insulted. "There's a far better chance of them retreating under his command than Lessia's, seeing as he may actually *command* it."

Her lip curled in aggravation. "And what shall I do in the meantime?"

"I will take you to your king and queen," he replied.

"And the prisoners?" She gave him an expectant look. "What will happen to them?"

"The prisoners have already been taken away." Ettrian's face soured once again at the scent that was beginning to prick Lea's nostrils as well. "They are perfectly safe, I assure you. You will see your mother soon."

"What do you mean?" she asked. "How?"

Ettrian gave her a curious look. "Did you neglect to notice the method of your most recent trip, my lady?"

"But you've been in front of us this whole time!"

"Have I?"

"Enough!" she snapped. "You can assure me that the prisoners are safe?"

"I can. Now, shall we go?"

"Go—" Her words cut off when she noticed a handful of carrion birds landing at the edge of a depression in the earth. "What is that?"

Ettrian frowned and turned in the direction she was facing, then his face went grim. "No place we need to be at present." He sent a look at her, his smile a bit too wide to be genuine. "I believe it's time to depart."

"No, wait." Lea moved toward where the ground dropped off, wincing as the smell increased.

"Lea—"

She froze when she reached the edge, holding up a hand when Ettrian tried to stop her, then let her arm fall weakly to her side.

Bodies, all in varying states of decay, were piled beneath her. Some had been picked nearly clean, others held the bloat of recent death. The smell, viscous and cloying, assaulted her senses, causing her to cover her mouth with her hand.

The winter chill that had come in recent weeks had preserved some of them, enough that, as her eyes ran over the mess, it was inevitable that she saw some of their faces through the rot. Blessedly, those of her father and the other governors who'd died the night of the wedding weren't present, or were likely buried deep.

Others, palace servants and guards she'd known for years, stared back at her, their faces frozen in death, their flesh puffed and full of violent gashes where they'd fed the local fauna.

She tensed when she felt a hand on her arm, then jerked her head to the side when she heard Ettrian's whispered encouragement to step away. But as she turned, a sight caught her eye.

She shoved the prince away and stumbled toward the end of the depression to get a closer look.

"No," she whispered when she was directly above the body.

He was at her side immediately, a hand on her elbow. "Lea, we must go."

She covered her mouth with a shaking hand as she stared in horror at the lovely pile of blonde curls, still attached to pretty porcelain skin. The flesh was marred from exposure to the elements and predators, but what remained of the face, the lovely gown, were unmistakable.

"Dare I ask?" Ettrian whispered. "It's a wonder you can even recognize her."

Lea took a stumbling step backward. "No, it can't be."

"What is it?" Ettrian's brow furrowed.

Lea's eyes remained frozen on the corpse beneath her.

"Ettrian, take me to my king and queen. *Now!*"

51

FREYA

Freya and Aer turned as one, then froze when they saw Isadora standing in the doorway to the cellar, her chest heaving, face red with anger.

"I appreciate you bringing him right to me," she said quietly, angling her head to look down at Frederick's still form. "It was getting a bit tiresome, waiting all this time. I was actually just about to go out searching for him myself."

"We needed him for questioning!" Freya exclaimed as she stormed forward, coming within inches of Isadora's face. "You stupid, *stupid* woman!"

Isadora shook with rage as she stared past Freya at Frederick's body. "This world is better without him in it, Queen Freya. You must know that."

"What were you thinking?" Aer hissed as he took a slow step toward her.

Isadora threw up her hand, and suddenly, Aer and Florian found themselves on the other side of an immovable barrier of magic.

Shocked, Freya took a step toward them, trying to wrap her mind around Isadora's sudden use of magic.

"There," Isadora said quietly as she let her hand drop to her side.

She smiled at Freya and stepped closer to her. Frantically, Florian and Aer started to attempt to unwind her magic. "Now it's just us girls."

"What are you doing?" Freya asked. She wanted desperately to attack, but curiosity and wariness gave her pause, especially once she saw Isadora's attire.

She'd divested herself of the pretty dresses she'd worn the past few weeks, so like the others she'd donned since Freya had known her. Now she was clad in head-to-toe leather, with two sheaths strapped to her hips. One was now empty, while the black handle of a blade stuck out of the other. Her hair hung in a tight braid down her back, and the loveliness of her face had been replaced by unnerving malice.

She smiled sweetly at Freya. "I'm doing my part to rid the world of Jotnar stench, of course. Isn't that part of our master plan?" Suddenly, the point of her second dagger was pressing against Freya's throat as her lips curled with hate. "Or perhaps I should just put an end to all of you magic-wielding freaks right now."

Freya froze, holding Isadora's wide, blue eyes as she considered her options. Her magic was beginning to wane after so much fighting. If she attacked, she risked using up the last of her power, and as she didn't know exactly what power Isadora had, that didn't seem the best choice to make.

Her other option was to gut her, but that also didn't seem prudent, considering they'd undoubtedly need to question her.

"Isadora, let's talk about this," she said gently. "We're on the same side here. We both want—"

"There was a time, Freya Harridan, that I dreamt of being in your position," Isadora said with a sneer. "Of being queen, ruling over an entire land." Isadora sent twin bursts of magic, one toward Freya as she tried to advance again and the other at the stairwell, putting up another barrier between them and whoever they'd just heard enter the house. "I would have subjects who worshiped me, little girls who wanted to *be* me, but no. That was all taken away by that filthy, rotten bitch."

"And how is that our fault?" Freya asked, keeping her words even.

She tightened the grip on her power, testing its strength. "We've done nothing to you."

"You all think you're so superior. And I suppose it makes sense. Why wouldn't you be? You've got the power of the gods, of the elements at your fingertips! You may think you're different than Lessia, but you're all the same." Isadora shook her head.

Florian and Aer broke through the barrier Isadora had put up, then Aer sent a sharp sword of spirit that made Isadora falter. Freya took the opening and plowed into her, slamming her against the wall. Florian's power wrapped around Isadora's wrists, pinning them to the rough stone.

Freya unsheathed her own dagger and pressed it to Isadora's throat. "We aren't the same as the Jotnar," she said quietly. "Not even close."

Isadora barked out a laugh but didn't bother fighting against Freya's hold. "Oh, but you are! See, you assume we're weak. That *we* could never subdue *you*. Only the other way around, am I right?"

"We?" Aer arched a brow. "As in 'humans'?"

A flicker in Isadora's eyes was the only confirmation Freya needed.

Freya nodded slowly. "So you *are* the original Isadora, then. The one Lessia replaced with her niece."

"Reginald didn't even realize when I made the switch, the fool."

"At the palace," Florian said quietly. "Am I correct?"

"Yes, spymaster, at the palace." Isadora glanced down at his feet, and Freya felt small tendrils of his magic snaking toward them. "I caught Dania Edrin—" she sneered as she said the name of Jonas' sister, "—when you were in the tunnels." She smirked. "She's dead now, in case you were curious. I snapped her pretty little neck."

Freya's heart dropped.

"How are you able to wield magic?" Aer asked.

"Willem made a deal with some elvish witch he met in Jotunheim." She laughed. "Five years ago, she helped us fake my death, gave me my own magic..." Isadora twisted her hand against the restraint of Florian's power, showing them the magic that crackled there, flowing between her fingers. She hissed when Florian used his own power to stamp out hers. She scowled. "I disguised myself as a seamstress in Madrya so I could keep an eye on things there. When Willem and *Dania* set sail for Lindoroth, I left Jotunheim to meet him."

"You've been conversing with Willem this whole time?" Freya asked.

She smirked. "I have."

Freya and Aer exchanged a glance, then looked back to Isadora.

"Then I suppose it's a good thing we didn't give you any valid information to feed him," Aer said quietly.

Isadora's smug smile froze. She scowled at Florian and Aer, and Freya knew it was idiotic pride that had Isadora's curiosity piqued. "What—"

Freya scratched her chin, then smiled at Isadora. "We've been on to you for a while now, Isadora. You're not terribly discreet."

"This witch... she gave you the ability to traverse the Between, correct?" Aer asked. "That's how you've been giving Willem information?"

Isadora's mouth formed an O of shock, then her face twisted with fury. "On occasion, and you have no idea how much information I've gotten to him."

"Nothing we didn't want you to," Freya said, stepping aside as Florian stepped closer, tapping his onyx blade against his palm.

"The resemblance truly is uncanny," Florian said quietly. "Lessia did well with her glamours. But this witch you speak of... her magic is strong, but sloppy. It took a bit of time, but I could see it..." Softly, he touched a finger to Isadora's forehead. "All I had to do is find the chink in your armor..."

Isadora screamed at some invisible assault, the sound causing Freya to wince.

Florian chuckled. "When a witch casts a sloppy spell, it leaves a very clear mark to those of us who are more... knowledgeable."

"There's no way you could've known," she hissed, then flinched when he hit her with his magic again. "She was too powerful."

"Oh, but I did. And when I informed my king and queen of your deceit, they chose to see how far you would take it."

"It was quite entertaining, really," Aer said.

"The wide eyes, the blushing, the feigned surprise when I announced someone was giving Willem information," Freya said, shaking her head. "A bit of a travesty. It's a pity Reginald never figured it out."

Sweat began to bead on Isadora's brow as she continued to fight against Florian's magic.

Aer folded his arms and looked at Freya. "What shall her punishment be, my love?"

"Hmm." Freya touched a finger to her lips and narrowed her eyes. "Lord Florian, it's been some time since you've had a proper interrogation, hasn't it?"

Florian bared his teeth at Isadora. "Indeed, Your Majesty."

"Do as you wish, then."

Isadora's eyes widened in fear.

Suddenly, the air crackled beside them. Lea stumbled forward, then a male, tall and thin and very clearly an elf, with a curious look on his face, appeared at her side. In his arms was an unconscious Rosie Ristner.

"What the—" Freya stared at them all, wide-eyed.

"Aer!" Lea cried, making a beeline for him. She latched onto his arms, then turned and glared at Isadora. "She's—"

She took in Isadora's current state of confinement, the expressions on their faces, and deflated. "I see you've already figured it out."

"Is this the creature you were so concerned about?" the stranger asked, eyeing Isadora in confusion. Gently, he laid Rosie on the floor, then frowned at Florian. "Andreus? Care to weigh in?"

"Ettrian," Florian said in greeting. "Their Majesties just gave me leave to interrogate this one, if you'd like to join."

The elf chuckled. "That *does* sound entertaining." He turned to Freya and Aer. "Your Majesties, my apologies. I am Prince Ettrian Tordove. I believe my two brothers are around here somewhere?"

"Yes, they're finishing off the human battalion that was

surrounding Watoria," Freya murmured. She looked at Lea, who was standing, full of indignation, beside Aer. "Are you alright?"

Lea scowled at Isadora. "Peachy."

Shifting his focus back to Isadora, Ettrian studied her carefully. "It's a shame," he whispered to her. "For a human to wield magic the likes of which you have in you, well, that's a feat, to say the least." He stepped closer, then brushed a finger along her jaw. "Tell me, who made the deal for you?"

Freya felt his magic ripple through the room as he worked to force the truth out of her.

Isadora's lips snapped together. Ettrian waited patiently for a few moments, then smiled indulgently when the air in her lungs let out with a gasp. "Her name was Kosandra!"

Ettrian's eyes went cold.

"When was the last time you met with Willem?" Florian demanded.

Again, she struggled against the strength of his and Ettrian's power. "One week ago." She let out a pained cry.

"I suspected it not long after we left the palace," Florian murmured to Ettrian. "Just a feeling, really. But something about her didn't ring true."

"Well, based on my conversations with Willem, it didn't seem she gave him anything too damning," Ettrian said. "Considering Willem seemed unaware of my brothers' presence here, my assumption is she can only access the Between sparingly. Even the strongest of elves wouldn't be unable to grant that power indefinitely."

Isadora glared at all of them. "I've given Willem plenty. He knows your plans."

Ettrian gave her an amused look. "Does he?"

Isadora nodded sharply.

"Out of curiosity," Freya began, "did you tell him my family's home is to the south or north of Watoria?"

Confusion filled Isadora's face. "To the north."

Freya smirked. "And did he tell you what he did with that information?"

"His knights have been scouring the woods for this place."

"To the north?" Freya bit back a smile and shook her head, then grinned at Aer. "You were right."

"Right about *what?*" Isadora demanded.

Freya looked at her. "Did you know that, with the right combination of magic, it's possible to alter one's senses? What you hear, what you see, even your sense of direction?"

Aer's face turned hard. "Especially when that person does little more than laze about the house while everyone else is working to end a war."

"But—but I know—I saw maps!"

"Did you?" Freya lifted her brows. "Did you also know that this estate sits due *south* of Watoria, not the north?"

Isadora's mouth fell open in shock, and whatever words she'd had prepared died on her lips.

Florian chuckled.

"Bind her magic," Aer snapped. "Now."

"Might I recommend an execution, instead?" Ettrian asked. "I could make it quite thorough." His voice carried the same level of concern he might have when ordering a side of toast with his eggs.

"Not just yet," Aer told him.

"We need to find out what else she knows," Byrric said, stepping into the room. Freya breathed a quiet sigh of relief at the sight of him, Ashton, and the knights that followed them. "I want to know every word she and Willem shared."

The elf sighed. "Very well. Andreus?"

Florian nodded, then the two joined hands and focused on Isadora. Her eyes widened and her struggles began anew as shimmering chains formed around her, tightening as the moments passed until they disappeared inside her. On a sigh, she slumped to the ground. Byrric barked out an order for his knights to take her. When she was gone, Freya was left with Aer, Lea, Florian, her father, Rosie, Ashton, and the elf prince.

Aer looked at Lea and Ettrian expectantly, then down at the still-unconscious Rosie. "Care to explain?"

52

FREYA

"How could you not inform us of this?" Ashton demanded, glaring at Florian, Freya, and Aer. "She's been among us this whole time!"

"Ash," Freya admonished. They'd gathered in the study that Byrric had taken to using for his planning sessions to discuss what they'd just learned from Isadora and the outcome of the day's battle. "You have to understand that we needed to keep the amount of people who knew at a minimum."

He shook his head, the hurt clear on his face. "What if one of us had given her information she shouldn't have had?"

"That wouldn't have happened," Aer said. "We were very careful in what information we gave the knights and the marshals, and you were under explicit orders not to divulge information you were given in private meetings unless we allowed it." He arched a brow. "Freya assumed we could trust you."

"Of course you could trust me!" Ashton exclaimed.

"Ashton," Byrric said quietly. "You haven't been betrayed. Set aside your offense for a moment and see logic."

Ashton huffed out a long breath and shook his head, then looked at Freya. "You could've told me."

"I know," she said quietly. "But I didn't. We kept the information within a small circle because that's what we felt was best."

His jaw tensed, then he ran his fingers through his hair, stiff with the grime of the battle he'd just fought in the city. "Can you explain it all now, then?" He frowned down at Rosie, who they'd laid down on a sofa. "And why is there a human princess unconscious on your sofa?"

"That was... unintentional," Lea said. "The princess was holding my hand and *he*—" she sent a withering look at Ettrian "—transported me out of the palace with no warning. Our options were to either leave her in the forest—"

"Which I still stand firmly behind," Ettrian cut in.

"—or take her back to the palace, which wasn't an option." Lea sighed. "Or bring her with us."

Ettrian gave them a smooth smile. "Unintentional, as she said."

Ashton shook his head and sighed. "I'm sorry I asked." He looked at Freya and Aer. "Well?"

"Lord Florian grew suspicious of Isadora a few days after our trip west began," Aer began. "So, he warned us to watch what we disclosed in front of her until he determined if his suspicions held weight."

"Which they did," Byrric explained. "He sent word to me a few days after they arrived here explaining that she'd made a switch somehow."

"If she thought for a moment that any of us were suspicious of her or her intentions, she would've ceased all contact with Willem," Florian added. "Letting her ploy run its course was the only way to ensure we had not one but two open lines of communication with Iladel. We needed to know what information Willem was delivering to Lessia; this was the best way to do that."

"At the cost of our people?" Ashton asked.

"You know we wouldn't have allowed anything to happen to them," Freya said. "Allowing her to maintain her ignorance made it far easier to kill two birds with one stone and potentially lessen just how many of those sacrifices we had to make."

"Lessia is dead now," Ettrian interjected. "In case you were wondering."

Freya's eyes widened in shock. "How?"

"Willem," Lea said. "Somehow, he managed to turn her own army against her."

Aer exhaled and shared a look with Freya. "Likely due to the information Isadora sent back to him. We let her know there was an army marching south from Jotunheim and let her believe we'd gotten word they were marching on the humans, not the city."

Ashton's eyes widened a fraction, but it was Lea who spoke.

"Is there a reason you couldn't have informed me of all of this?" she asked. "It would've been useful to know—" Her eyes grew round, and she looked accusingly at Ettrian. "Gods above, *that's* who Willem was with in the tunnels! 'A female companion?' Really?"

Ettrian grinned. "Are you going to call me a 'stupid elvish bastard' again?"

"Worse," she snarled. "Did you know?"

"To be fair, I only knew he had a human woman spying for him. He never disclosed who she was."

Ashton rubbed a hand over his face and sighed. "Okay, so what did all of that get us?"

"Her plans with Willem were coordinated quite perfectly," Florian said. "As far as we could tell, at least."

"Yes, Lessia was holding back a good deal of information from Willem, and he, her," Ettrian said. "The movement of troops, the status of certain cities, plans for once this war was done."

"Exactly," Freya said. "If he thought Isadora was in danger or compromised in any way..."

"He would have continued to play the submissive co-conspirator with Lessia," Aer finished. "Biding his time until he could implement a backup plan, if he had one. The information Isadora handed him gave him what he saw as a valid reason to enact his plans to end his alliance with Jotunheim sooner rather than later."

"And we'd still have two usurpers to deal with instead of just one," Ashton said with a nod. "It was a risk, but I suppose I see the sense."

"Where is Jonas?" Freya asked, suddenly taking note of his absence. "He should be with you."

Lea's face turned furious, but it was Ettrian who spoke.

"As Jonas was... unaware of Willem's relations with Isadora or Dania's status as deceased, he made a deal with Willem in exchange for his aunt's swift death. Lord Edrin is now at the head of Jotunheim's army."

"Wait." Byrric held up a hand. "Are you saying one of our own allies has taken hold of Lessia Edrin's knights?"

"The Jotnar will surely follow Jonas, but it will be tenuous at first, especially as he has not been officially crowned," Ettrian said.

"Are there any who could question his right to it?" Freya asked.

"No, but that doesn't mean there aren't any who won't try to take it. Willem, for instance." Ettrian folded his arms. "There's something else you should know, though. As king, Willem is now in control of Iladel and he claims the army marching south from Jotunheim—a second one that Lessia had aimed for Kildin—is 'handled.' He's not wrong. His forces from eastern Dystone have been sailing toward Lindoroth and will make landing on the shores of Caelora within just a few days—a force that numbers thrice that of the Jotunheim army. Then, they'll begin their march to quell the Jotnar and any other Lindorothian resistance they come in contact with."

The room was silent for a moment as everyone digested that news.

Lea's eyes widened. "How—how did Lessia miss that?"

"How did *we* miss that?" Freya asked her father.

Ettrian answered instead. "According to Willem, they sailed across the north of Dystone with the intention of traveling down the coast from northern Jotunheim. If it helps, Avorell missed that bit, too."

Byrric dragged a hand across his face. "Prince Ettrian, how do you know this?"

The prince blinked. "You doubt me?"

"Only the accuracy of your statements and how much you think you know," Byrric replied.

"I met with Willem just yesterday to discuss where it would be best to land Avorell's knights when the time came to attack," Ettrian said. "I asked him where his ships were coming in, he told me, and now I have told you."

"What exactly do you suggest we do about this?" Aer asked. "Our armies are divided among five capitals and there is no guarantee any will stand if we pull our soldiers away. Even if Jonas is at the head of the Jotnar army, a regime change in the middle of the war doesn't guarantee the army will follow him, especially not when they're so far removed from him and have already gotten a head for battle."

"Have you forgotten Avorell?" Ettrian asked.

"Your parents have committed just over two thousand knights," Freya said. "But the Lindorothian army is spread throughout the kingdom; Willem's is now largely in one place. Even if you bring all of your knights to Iladel today, and even with your magic, he's got overwhelming numbers on his side."

"Yes, I see your point." Ettrian drummed his fingers thoughtfully on his arm. "I suppose we've found ourselves in a bit of a predicament, haven't we?"

"Wait." Lea turned to Ettrian, her eyes narrowed. "Where have you taken the prisoners?"

"We'd like to know the answer to that as well."

Freya turned at the sound of Laz's voice. Collin and Myria stood beside him, just inside the door.

Ettrian cleared his throat. "They are safe, as I said."

"That's not an answer," Lea replied.

"They are in Iston," Ettrian said with a sigh. "Safe."

Collin frowned at Ettrian. "Who are you?"

"Prince Ettrian Tordove, at your service, Lord...?"

"Maddix," Collin said, continuing to eye the elf suspiciously.

"Our families are safe?" Laz asked.

Ettrian looked affronted. "Of course they are."

"We'll be leaving for Iston as soon as possible," Byrric said before any of them could question. "The marshals have retaken the governor's residence, so they will remain here with Officer Carinald in charge," he said with a nod to Ashton. "Along with five hundred knights to help quell any enemy that might still be in the area. Everyone else, go pack your things. One bag apiece. Anything you aren't able to carry, we will get in Iston."

Freya took a deep breath and looked at Ettrian. "Go find your brothers, tell them what's happened." She cast a glance at the door that led upstairs. "I've got one more traveler to grab."

IT TOOK two trips for Ettrian to carry all of them through the Between to Iston. Fenian and Tavian had remained behind to settle things with Commander Alstad and the knights of the Royal Army Byrric had left behind as support, but they planned to join them the following day. Reginald, who'd taken a dagger to the thigh during battle, but was recovering, would travel with them, assuming Florian's treatments had healed him well enough for the trip. Rosie, who'd awoken terrified not an hour before they left, insisted on staying behind with Reginald. Neither were looking forward to another trip through the Between, but Florian instructed Prince Tavian to find a way to make the trip a bit easier on them, if he could.

Freya and Aer's personal guards, along with Naedan and Amara, traveled with them.

And, as he'd grown on her significantly, Freya had insisted on bringing Toskr. Haegin assured her as they said their goodbyes that Toskr was patched up enough to travel and would be fine by morning. So, grudgingly, she let him curl up in the same pouch he'd snuck out of the forest in for the trip.

Isadora, her magic bound, had also come with them so they could adequately question her about all she knew of Willem and Lessia's plans.

Byrric and Ana went with Ettrian first so they could go right to their mother, Vara, and fill her in on everything. Freya, Aer, and their friends packed up a few of their belongings, mostly weapons and some clothes. Then, with one final, somewhat teary goodbye to

Haegin and Ashton, with a promise that she'd return soon, Freya traveled back to Iston for the first time since she'd been a child.

When they arrived at the gates to the city, tall, wooden, and worn gray with age, Freya sighed, then smiled up at Aer when he squeezed her hand. "This isn't the way I'd hoped to come for a visit," she said. "It's my first time here in so long, and my sole purpose is to discuss war."

"We'll come back, once this is all over, for a real visit," Aer promised. "And you know your grandmother. I'm sure she's eager for a fight, especially now that she's heard what a turncoat Traust has become."

Freya nodded and looked over at the others, about thirty in total, who were standing quietly, most looking a bit green around the edges, waiting for the gates to open.

Moments later, Byrric flew over the gates and landed beside Freya, his face looking much calmer than it had a few minutes earlier. Ana landed beside him right as the gates slowly began to open, and the tall, lanky form of Vara Balthana strode through the gates, her white wings high at her shoulders. She looked taller than Freya remembered, more lean, but just as terrifying as she'd been when Freya was a girl.

Freya was surprised to see Lord Silmar at her side.

"Your Majesties!" Vara called as they approached. "Welcome to Iston." Warmth flashed across her face when she looked at her granddaughter, almost too brief for Freya to catch, but it comforted her to see it, nonetheless.

"Grandmother," Freya said. "I'd like you to meet my husband, King Aerelius Harridan." She gestured toward her friends. "These are Lazarus Cailen, Collin Maddix, Grevillea Calliwell, and Myria Bryton."

Vara shook her head and clicked her tongue. "Such a pity to hear what happened to your parents." She looked at Collin. "You're Gunnar's nephew, yes?"

Collin nodded. "I am, my lady."

"Yes, you have that look about you. The prisoners from Iladel have been fed and are being treated for any injuries at my home," she said, then inclined her head toward Ettrian before looking at Freya and Aer. "I suppose you have that one to thank for saving them, even if he did leave them in my sitting room without so much as a word of explanation before he vanished."

Though her words were harsh, Freya was surprised to see a bit of that earlier warmth return to Vara's eyes.

Vara peered behind Ettrian and a slow smile spread across her face. "And I see Andreus has finally made the trip with you!"

Freya exchanged a sharp look with Aer.

Florian cleared his throat, then gave Vara a tight smile. "It's good to see you, Vara."

As one, Freya and Aer turned to face them. "You two know each other?" Aer asked.

Florian, for once, in all the months Freya had known him, had the grace to look slightly abashed when he looked at his king and queen.

"I suppose there is a discussion to be had," Ettrian mused. "As long as my uncle is up for it, that is."

Freya's eyes widened, and she didn't have to see Aer's face to feel the shock that mirrored hers at Ettrian's revelation.

"Your unc—"

Before she could finish, though, Silmar stepped forward and cut off her response.

"That will have to wait," he said.

Freya blinked, turning shocked eyes on the emissary. "Wait?"

"I've just arrived from a scouting mission on the eastern coast of Caelora," he said grimly. "There's news of the humans who were supposed to land three days from now."

"What about them?" Aer demanded.

"They've just crossed into Lindorothian waters. They'll be docking tomorrow."

Continue reading for a preview of *The Valkyrie's Triumph*, the thrilling conclusion to the *Half-Blood Rising trilogy…*

1

———

FREYA

When the queen of Lindoroth was a girl, she hoarded secrets. Discovering a secret was akin to finding a bit of treasure she could keep in a box under her bed, far from her father's prying eyes.

This was something she and the crown prince both shared, so much so, that, one summer, they held a competition to see who could collect the most secrets.

That summer, there had been no shortage of gossip and tidbits from the occupants at the palace. From royal guests consorting with courtesans, to which squires would make the most promising knights.

In the end, the prince had won. The revelation that his chambers once belonged to a king's paramour had beat all of Freya's handful of collected secrets. To eleven-year-olds, that kind of news was scandalous, salacious, something they'd not bat an eye at now at nearly twenty.

As she grew, Freya Harridan continued to gather secrets, surrounding herself with them until they became a part of her. The result was that trust never came easy. It had to be earned. Even Aerelius hadn't been an exception, not until he had deemed himself worth keeping in Freya's eyes.

The hidden truths of childhood didn't hold a candle to the revelations she and her husband, now the king, had faced since taking their thrones. Secrets that held more weight, that tested her loyalty, her intelligence, her trust in those closest to her.

And now she was second guessing everything she'd heard.

The most recent revelation was one she took more personally than the rest. Andreus Florian, royal spymaster, deliverer of justice, was elvish royalty. And no one, not even her father, had thought to inform the king and queen, who currently held his employ. Perhaps it wasn't something Freya needed to be concerned about. Indeed, it likely wasn't. But this brief moment was causing her to question her closest advisors, which was something her overburdened mind was struggling to take on. And the fact that thousands of human knights were preparing to dock on the eastern shores only compounded the issue.

Today, as she stood at the gates of Iston, home of the Valkyrie, surrounded by her most trusted advisors and confidants, she wondered just how much more she could take.

"I think we should bring this inside," Byrric stated, eyeing his daughter warily. She could only imagine how she must've looked to him in that moment.

Anger, annoyance, frustration, and the knowledge that it simply shouldn't *matter* warred inside her, making her full to bursting with the need to fly.

"Yes, these are topics better discussed in private," Vara Balthana added. Freya's grandmother had opened her home in the city of Iston, home of the Valkyrie of Lindoroth, to the soldiers and people that Freya and Aerelius now carried with them.

Despite the truth in her grandmother's words, Freya needed a breath before discussing how to handle the humans who'd just crossed into Lindorothian waters or the topic of Florian's elvish heritage.

"I need a few moments to myself," Freya murmured to Aer. "Get

Toskr settled. I'll be there soon." She unclipped the pouch from her belt that held the injured squirrel shifter and handed it to her husband. Brief concern flashed in his eyes, but he took the pouch with a short nod, clipping it gently to the empty sword belt at his waist. Then, not waiting for a response, she turned and spread her wings, taking to the skies for passage to her grandmother's home.

Thankfully, Aer didn't try to stop her. He knew when she needed to take a moment to breathe, and he especially knew when she needed to take that moment in private.

She needed to fly, needed to see the city below, that it was safe, just as Watoria was now. Her city had fallen to the Jotnar and humans, but she, Aerelius, and three armies had taken it, wresting it from her enemy's hands and giving it back to the people.

A moment later, she heard the familiar flap of her father's wings behind her. She knew better than to think he'd let her fly off on her own, but when he didn't rush to keep up, she realized he was giving her what she needed. It warmed her heart to be reminded of just how well he knew her.

As Freya soared over the city, she shoved all thoughts of war aside and took in the home of her ancestors. The last time she had visited, she'd been in her early teens. It had been only a year or two after her mother's death, and not long before her father decided she would stay in Watoria for good, at least until it was time to return to the capital to marry her prince.

The sprawling lands below made Freya's breath catch. The land had been built for Valkyrie eons ago, built with wings in mind: Training fields, courtyards, and rooftop gardens made the area perfect for those who enjoyed feeling the wind in their feathers.

Freya shifted her sharp eyes toward the north, past the remaining stretch of Allanorian countryside to the Caeloran border, which lay only a few miles away. Another two day's journey beyond that sat Jotunheim. A flare of anger lanced through her at the thought of the enemy lands so close to her own. Now wasn't the time for anger, though. Right now, she needed draw in the cold air and settle her nerves. So, as was her habit, she soared, taking solace in the face that, thus far, war had yet to spoil this place.

Slowly, Freya circled the city, finally allowing Byrric to catch up. For the moment, the people she loved were safe, although she couldn't say the same for the rest of her kingdom.

"It's beautiful," she said to her father once he was soaring beside her. The snapping wind nearly drowned out her words, but he smiled.

"I should've brought you here more often." He gestured toward Vara's estate. "This is your ancestors' home. You should be more familiar with it."

"Perhaps you should've sent me here instead of Watoria," she told him, sending him a smirk. Without another word, she tucked her wings to her sides and plummeted in a wordless challenge, making a straight line for Vara's gated estate.

She touched down moments before Byrric, but she had the sneaking suspicion her father had given her this win. When he landed with a soft thump beside her, she turned and looked at the main house.

The Balthana family was old and well-established, so Vara's home was one of the more posher ones in Iston—posh by Valkyrie standards, anyway. There was no ostentatious décor or rising turrets. Instead, the Balthana estate was a sprawling one-story masterpiece of stone, glass, and wrought iron, one that had stood at the center of Iston for centuries. Gardens bursting with winter-blooming and cold-hardy flora dotted the rooftops. She could picture herself there, basking in the sun, surrounded by lush foliage.

Today, however, the clouds obscured the sun, and the chill in the air that promised frost made being indoors much more favorable.

"It's going to snow soon," Byrric murmured, as if reading Freya's mind. "Travel east will be difficult if we wait too long."

"Agreed." Turning to him, she asked, "Why didn't you tell us? You had to know we wouldn't have taken issue with Florian being elvish royalty, but why keep it from us?"

He tilted his head back, gray eyes scanning the skies, his

cinnabar-streaked hair brushing his ears. "Because it didn't matter, as I'm sure you know. We're in the middle of a war, Freya. What would it have accomplished?"

"I—" Her shoulders slumped in a very un-queenly movement. "I don't know. I'm just tired of having things sprung on me." She rubbed a hand across her forehead. "I'm so, *so* tired."

Byrric turned to face her. "Florian's heritage is his to disclose. You know that as well as anyone." He placed his hands on her shoulders, then waited until her gray eyes met his before continuing. "There will be far more confidential information to come to light now that you're queen, Freya. What's important is that you understand *timing*. When this is all over, Ordona and I will sit down with you and Aerelius and discuss everything we should've the moment you were coronated. Until then, please trust that we are solely focused on getting that bastard on your throne out of this kingdom."

Her eyes closed as his words sunk in. Hadn't she spent years hiding who she was? Hiding under glamours and secrets, sharing information only when necessary? Hadn't she tried to *continue* that once she'd gotten to Aldridge?

"You're right," she finally said. "I know you're right. And I know I'm probably being a brat right now, but Father, I need you to promise there will be no more surprises. Can you do that for me?"

He smiled softly, then cupped her chin in his hand and met her eyes. "Yes, I can do that. If not because you're my queen, then because you're my daughter." He dropped his hand to her shoulder. "Now, let's get inside. They'll be waiting for us."

The rest of their group had just arrived when she and Byrric stepped up to the portico, her two guards, Rissen and Cecilia, shoving open the heavy double doors that led into the foyer. Lea, Lazarus, Collin, and Myria hurried off to find their remaining family members who were recovering in the guest quarters after having been deposited there by Prince Ettrian two days earlier.

Byrric followed Vara as she led him, Prince Ettrian, and Florian into the sitting room, her standard place for welcoming guests. Aer hung back and held out his hand, wordlessly inviting Freya to walk with him. She squared her shoulders, then gave him a small smile and slid her hand into his, thankful for his comforting touch. Together, they went into the sitting room, where their guards, Florian, and Ettrian were waiting.

Feeling a bit steadier now that she'd spread her wings and spoke with her father, she looked at Andreus Florian, their most trusted advisor.

"Explain," Aer demanded. "And I don't mean explain why you lied, Lord Florian. I understand that, to some extent. Your heritage is yours to disclose, of course, but Freya and I need to know how deep your connection with the elves goes in order to make the best decisions going forward."

"I've always trusted you and your judgement, Lord Florian," Freya added. "But I'm sure you can understand why my husband and I need more than you've given us."

Ettrian, the youngest of the elf princes who'd accompanied Freya and Aer to Lindoroth, snickered.

Aer shot him a sharp look. "Something funny, Your Highness?"

Ettrian shrugged, then leaned back against the wall, one black-booted foot propped behind him, his golden eyes dancing. "There's always something funny with you lot. But since you asked, I'm simply wondering why this matters to you. Personally, I'd be more concerned with the fifteen-thousand human soldiers who just docked in your harbors." Infuriatingly, he examined his nails, rubbing them against the pale blue velvet of his jacket. "Perhaps on that we differ."

Freya felt her cheeks pink with annoyance. Aer, seeming to see her anger rise, put a hand on her back.

"My queen and I need to be able to trust the people around us," Aer said, looking first at Byrric, then at Florian. "As I'm sure you can understand, the news of your true identity brings with it a number of questions." His eyes shifted to Ettrian. "The topic of the human incursion can wait a few more minutes."

Again, Freya's frustration rose. Ettrian was right; they needed to get on with reclaiming their land. But if Florian was elvish royalty, his connections went much further than a simple friendship with Lord Silmar, their guide in Avorell.

"If I may?" Vara asked.

Freya shifted her eyes to the aged woman before her. Vara was somewhere in the vicinity of seven hundred years old, yet her short chestnut hair had barely begun turning gray.

"Yes, Grandmother?"

Vara retracted her wide white wings and folded her arms, gray eyes stern on each of them, her stare brooking no argument. "Perhaps you should let Andreus tell you his story before unleashing that anger of yours."

"We're not *angry*, Grandmother," Freya said wearily. "Just tired of being the last to know. Especially considering he was hesitant to reach out to the elves when we first discussed it." As the royal spymaster, he'd kept things from them before. Secrets Freya knew, at least in hindsight, were necessary. But when she looked at her father, she sighed. "I know there's a lot about the monarchy we simply haven't had time to learn. We just need to know there are no other major secrets lurking about."

"My hesitance was not because I didn't want their help," Florian explained. He held his tall, wiry frame stock-still, showing no signs of chagrin, remorse, or humility. Not that Freya necessarily expected him to, knowing the spymaster as she did, but on the same token, his apathetic expression nearly set her hackles rising. "It was because I knew what they would ask of you in return."

"The Wild Hunt," Aer said.

"We do enjoy our games," Ettrian murmured.

Freya rolled her eyes, then looked at Florian in question. "You didn't think I could win?"

Florian shook his head, his dark expression never leaving his king and queen. "Oh, I had no doubt you would. But welcoming the elves back into our world could cause more problems, which I didn't want you to have to deal with so early in your reign."

Aer looked at Ettrian. "Such as?"

Ettrian lifted his brows. "Let's be honest, Your Majesty. What do you think your citizens will do once they know their dreams can be realized with a simple elvish bargain?"

Outraged, Freya took a step toward the prince, stopping when Aer grabbed her arm.

Florian held up a hand and sent Ettrian a warning look. "I did all in my power to ensure that eventuality was written out of the bargain we made with King Ruehnar and Queen Nalaea."

"And how do you think your people will like it if they find out your refuse to let them make elvish bargains?" Ettrian quipped. "I'd be quite upset if I were them."

Gritting her teeth, Freya let out a breath. "Lea was right about you, Prince Ettrian."

"That I'm a 'stupid elvish bastard'?" He grinned, his sharp incisors flashing against his lips. "Yes, I'm quite aware. Although, to be fair, my parents and brothers were the ones who made those bargains."

"When we wrote the bargains, we included limits on elvish involvement in Lindoroth." Florian shot a look at Ettrian. "Limits that allowed *only* military bargains and can only be made by the king and queen."

Ettrian shrugged. "There are always loopholes."

Aer rubbed a hand against his forehead and sighed. "Prince Ettrian, if you could refrain from attempting to make trouble, we would greatly appreciate it."

"Ah, of course." Ettrian gestured a long, pale hand toward the spymaster. "Carry on."

"Then I'll be brief." Florian met each of their eyes in turn. "My father was Devdan Tordove, the former king of Avorell. Approximately eight hundred years ago, we had a falling out because I refused to marry the female he and my stepmother chose for me. Instead, I took on mercenary work." Each word was clipped, intentional, and devoid of emotion. "It's how I became so skilled with toxins and eliminating threats."

"You mean killing people?" Freya asked drily.

He nodded curtly. "As the second of four sons and only half-elf, I didn't see the need, nor did I have any desire, to adhere to their wishes. When it became clear my father wouldn't stand for my disobedience, I chose to leave my homeland. My father and his wife found me when I attempted to leave, punished me, then exiled me to the Forest of Ages."

A chill ran down Freya's spine at the memory of her time in the living forest of Avorell.

"King Salazar's grandfather, Avinald, knew me by reputation," Florian continued. "When word got to him that I'd had a falling out with my parents, he sent for me, taking care to avoid raising my parents' suspicions."

"He snuck into Avorell undetected?" Aer asked sharply. "How?"

"Relations with Avorell were much better back then, at least for the Linds. Avorell had closed its shores to humans after their war, but the Linds still had trade access."

"Your great-grandfather took him in," Vara said to Aer. "Took him out of that gods-forsaken place and brought him here."

"Ruehnar knew, of course," Florian continued. "We were close growing up, and he never cared for the way our father handled certain aspects of our upbringing."

"It should go without saying that Lord Florian's placement in Lindoroth needed to be kept quiet to avoid the ire of King Devdan," Byrric told them.

"Not to mention, your people likely would not have been thrilled at the idea of an elf in the royal court," Ettrian added with a smirk. "Our reclusive nature has garnered us an...unsavory reputation, as you know."

"Half elf," Florian corrected. "Devdan was my father, but my birth mother was human. She died in childbirth, as is common for elf-human pairings. Queen Mariona was presented to my father by her parents two years later. She was kind enough and raised me as her own, even though she didn't wholly agree with allowing a half-elf to be in line for the throne. Nor did she care for rebellious children, so she stood by my father when he tried to force the betrothal and when he ultimately decided to disown me."

"We planned to tell you," a soft voice said from the door. "When the time was right."

Aer's hand jerked in Freya's, and her own heart stuttered at the sight of Ordona Harridan standing framed in the arched doorway.

"Mother," Aer rasped, his voice filled with a broken relief that Freya had seen only rarely these past weeks. Dropping Freya's hand, he rushed toward Ordona, sweeping her off her feet in a huge hug.

Tears pricked at Freya's eyes as she watched Aer greet the former queen. Aer hadn't seen his mother in more than a month, not since she'd fled the besieged palace after watching her husband die.

And just like that, Florian's identity didn't seem quite so important.

Ordona gripped her son tightly, the sight so moving Freya had to look away. Something told her if she started crying right then, she might not be able to stop. Now was not the time for that—she needed to be strong for her people, for her husband, and for the rest of the travelers they'd brought with them to Iston.

After a moment, Aer set Ordona down and took a step back. "Are you alright?"

"Yes, I'm fine. Lady Balthana has been taking good care of me." Despite the circumstances, she still looked just as regal as the day they'd left the palace. Someone, likely a palace pixie, had ensured she still looked every part the queen, even in hiding. Her dark hair back was pulled back into a low chignon with soft curls drifting loose along her cheeks. She wore a soft pink dress that belied her dire circumstances. Instead, it cast a beautiful contrast against her deep tan skin.

She caught sight of Freya, and her eyes watered. "Freya, dear."

No longer able to hold back her tears, Freya rushed forward to accept Ordona's embrace, squeezing her eyes shut as she buried her face in the former queen's silk-covered shoulder. Even in exile, Ordona carried the regal air only a queen could possess.

"Your Majesty," Freya breathed, her voice cracking. "I'm so happy to see you."

Ordona pulled back and knuckled away a tear from her cheek.

"Yes, well, I'm just glad we're all under one roof now." She looked around the room. "I know we've much to discuss, but I'd like some time with my son and daughter-in-law, please."

Vara stood. "Of course." She shot a look at Byrric. "Come on, son. We have our own matters to discuss."

With one last look at Freya, Byrric left the room, Florian, Ettrian, and Vara following behind.

2

LEA

Once she'd arrived at Vara Balthana's home, Lea barely spared herself a thought as she, Laz, Collin, Myria, and the others rushed off to find their families. Instead, her first order of business was to find her mother. She and Perida suffered several painful weeks with minimal interactions, not counting their brief conversations in the dungeons, as those had most certainly been overheard. Lea knew her mother was as eager to catch up on recent events as Lea was.

Most importantly, Lea hated that her mother had watched as her only daughter was married off to a Jotnar lord while spewing lies about her father. She needed Perida to know it had all been an act.

Her skin crawled at the at the memory of being in such a debasing position and she knew without question she'd die before letting herself end up there again.

An act. Perida had to have known that it had *all* been an act and that the lies Lea had told about Orin Calliwell being a horrid person were just that—lies told in order to gain the trust of their enemies.

She had to know.

The halls were crowded as Lea made a beeline toward the western end of the estate that housed the guest chambers. Pixies flitted about, carrying bedding, medicines, and food. It was a wonder Vara wasn't losing her mind with the influx of people in her home, considering she spent so much of her time here alone.

The door to Perida's room opened on Lea's first knock. Before Lea could speak, Perida's shoulders slumped as relief filled her features, and she pulled her daughter into an embrace so tight, Lea felt her ribs flex. Perida held her for a few moments, her face buried in her daughter's shoulder. At that moment, Lea knew her mother had done just as good a job as she had at acting her part in the palace.

"Thank god," Perida breathed, pulling Lea inside.

"Mother—" Lea stepped back, then opened her mouth to spill her apologies, not quite ready to trust the relief creeping into her heart.

"Darling, before you say anything, I know what you were doing at the palace all along." Perida gripped Lea's biceps and met her eyes. "I hoped I was able to hide that knowledge well, but I worry I managed to hide it *too* well."

Lea was already shaking her head before her mother finished speaking. "Mother, you have nothing to apologize for. I worked very hard to make it seem I'd turned on our family, knowing full well you might believe my ruse. I'd hoped you'd see through it, but I've spent weeks preparing for the opposite."

"Oh, Lea... of course I saw through it!" Perida cupped Lea's cheek and smiled softly, her eyes sparking with dread. "My only concern now is—"

"Jonas and I are not married, nor are we mated." Lea rested her hands on her mother's shoulders, gaunt after weeks of malnutrition. Her soft black hair and honey gold skin still carried a dullness left from her time in the dungeon, although the spark that had always lived in her dark eyes had returned in full. "It was all part of the ruse. Ettrian never performed the mating bond and has no authority to perform Lindorothian marriages."

Small furrows formed between Perida's brows, telling Lea that her mother wasn't quite convinced of the elf prince's allegiance. She contemplated bringing Ettrian in to explain, but found it unlikely Perida would believe him. Not yet, at least.

"I know you might not believe me or trust Jonas or Ettrian," Lea said. "I don't fault you for that. But... well, we can discuss that later. Right now, we need to focus on getting back to Errest. Prince Ettrian can help us get home to ensure the city remains in our hands."

Perida shook her head. "How can you trust them? After everything Jonas allowed to happen to you—"

"Jonas didn't allow anything to happen to me that I hadn't agreed to." Frustration creeped into Lea's tone, but she forced it down. "We carefully orchestrated everything with guidance from Byrric, Freya, and Aer. My attendant, Tyna, ensured everything appeared as real as possible." She curled her fingers around her mother's hands and gave her a beseeching look. "I know some things might've looked terrible, but I assure you, Jonas never touched me improperly or in a way that I didn't approve of." She thought back to their one and only kiss in the hall after their fake marriage ceremony. "Or wasn't out of desperation."

Perida raised her chin a fraction of an inch. "And the elvish prince?"

"Ettrian was there as a spy for the elvish throne." Then, with a frown, Lea shook her head. "No, 'spy' doesn't seem quite the right word. Scout, perhaps. After Freya and Aer left for Avorell seeking allies, Ettrian arrived at the palace. I assure you; you have nothing to worry about with him. The elves hate the Jotnar nearly as much as we do." A fact that still surprised Lea.

Ettrian had given Lea an abbreviated version of the elves' relationship with Jotunheim and how they believed the Jotnar had taken the gift of elvish magic and used it for evil and greed, doing nothing to help the rest of the world. Although the elves were a capricious people, even they seemed to have their limits. Lea hadn't interacted with the elvish monarchs yet, but Ettrian's disdain for the Jotnar had been clear in his tone, his words, and his golden eyes.

Perida still looked doubtful, but she huffed out a breath, then nodded. "As you were in close contact with them all, I'll trust your judgment. If the Commander and the king and queen gave their approval, this whole charade must be far bigger than I thought."

For the first time in weeks, Lea's heart flooded with relief. She and her mother needed to retake their home, something that would take far longer if Lea had to spend excessive time convincing her mother they finally had allies.

"We need to get back to Errest," Lea repeated. "Commander Balthana will help ensure we're well supported, and Prince Ettrian can transport us inside the capital gates. But we must go quickly."

Tyna appeared beside them. Her soft glow shone brighter now than Lea had seen in weeks. "My ladies," the pixie said with a nod. "As much as I'd like to encourage rest, I understand you must be eager to return home."

"A bath and some food are all we have time for," Lea replied. Knowing Byrric, he and the others were already plotting their next steps. "Tyna, will you please see to lunch? I'd like to go find Prince Ettrian."

"Of course, my lady," Tyna replied, pearlescent wings fluttering madly behind her.

"Thank you." Lea gestured to Perida, waving a hand toward the bathroom. "Mother, I'll be back shortly." She softened her tone as she touched the soft sleeve of her mother's wool dress, so unlike the gown she'd worn every day since the wedding.

When Lea had last seen the ball gown, its ice blue silk had been stained brown with her father's dried blood. If she knew her mother at all, the dress had likely ended up in a fireplace somewhere, any hint of its beauty destroyed.

Another reason for Lea to see to it Willem met the same fate as his former ally.

Exhaustion tugged at Perida's eyes, slicing through Lea like an ax. Not only had her husband been murdered and her magic dampened, but she'd also had to watch as her daughter lived among their enemies. Regardless of what Perida knew of their ploy, Lea couldn't imagine the strain it had all put on her mother's psyche.

Whatever shone on Lea's face must've betrayed her thoughts, because Perida's eyes softened with sympathy. She wrapped her arms around Lea, exhaling a long, shaking breath.

"Oh, Lea," she murmured, pressing her cheek to her daughter's. It took all of Lea's strength not to let her emotions flow freely, but now wasn't the time.

"It will be alright, Mother." She took a step back. "Trust me."

With a quick kiss to her mother's cheek, Lea hurried from the room in search of the youngest Tordove prince. She found Ettrian on the portico, his glinting gold eyes watching the road that led to Vara's home. The tenuous nature of their relationship and the fact that he was a bit terrifying had led Lea to avoid seeking him out on most occasions. Unfortunately, if she wanted to return to her home quickly, she would need him to assist her.

"Your Highness?" Lea said, coming to a stop in the doorway behind him.

"Hmm?" Ettrian's gaze shifted slowly to her. "Ah, Lady Calliwell. How are you faring now that you're so far from your tormentors?" His elvish accent added a rolling lilt to his words that Lea might've considered soothing during normal conversation. As it was, despite the lovely softness his language added to hers, she couldn't focus on more than simply getting home.

"Just lovely." She took a small step forward. "When can we leave?"

"Tomorrow." Ettrian quirked a brow, challenging the retort her saw on her lips. "Perhaps the day after."

Wisps of annoyance pricked at her patience. "My mother and I want to leave today."

"As my brothers have yet to arrive, that would be unwise, considering we need their knights to accompany us."

Lea ground her teeth, seeking an alternative option, but coming up empty. "When will they be here?"

"Soon."

"*When* is soon?" She was so close. *So* close to being home, back with her people.

"You know, Lady Calliwell, for someone who needs my help so desperately, you might consider being a bit less demanding." Eyes flashing, Ettrian faced the road once more. "I'd expect you to be more grateful, considering."

"Considering what?"

He slid her a sly look, one corner of his mouth sliding up. "Considering there's an entire continent between you and your home, and you need *me* to get you there."

Stupid elvish bastard, Lea thought, although she couldn't refute his claim *or* the chill that skittered down her spine. The only way to get to Errest in a timely manner was through the Between, and the only way to access the Between was with an elf. *This* elf, apparently, as his brothers, soldiers, and the rest of the monarchy were currently absent or otherwise assigned.

"Fine." If she wanted his help, she'd need to play this game his way. With a frown, Lea followed his gaze back to the road. "What are you doing?"

"Watching," he murmured, his brows drawing together. "Listening. There is much going on in your lands, as I'm sure you know. It feels...prickly."

"Prickly?"

"Yes, my lady. Prickly. Among our other skills, we elves have strong spirit magic." His eyes continued to drift over the landscape. "Your peoples' suffering is like a scythe. A dull one, at that."

Lea's tongue turned to cotton in her mouth as she took in his words. She had no doubt her people were suffering. But here in Iston, at the furthest reaches of Lindoroth, she'd never expect anyone, including an elf, to be so affected by a continent's worth of pain.

But then again, what did she really know of the elves? Perhaps they were the cold, calculating creatures she'd assumed on meeting Ettrian. On the other hand, maybe she hadn't given him enough of a chance to shake the mask her wore whenever they were around other people. Which seemed to be nearly always.

"Can you...turn it off?" A stupid question, maybe, but still worth asking to her mind. She couldn't imagine holding onto that feeling indefinitely.

"Of course," Ettrian replied. "If I couldn't I would've gone insane long ago. It simply helps to get a feel for the state of the world, especially when I've been summoned here to *help* said world."

"And what does this prickly feeling tell you about the state of my world?"

"That your people suffer, but they still have hope." Impatience flicked across his face when he looked down at her and noticed her doubtful expression. "I cannot *lie,* Lady Calliwell, and I believe my statement was quite clear."

Cheeks aflame, Lea nodded. "Yes, of course." She raked a hand through her dark curls, wincing when her fingers caught almost instantly in the tangles.

Ettrian smirked, running his eyes across her face and hair. "Perhaps you should go bathe before a bird attempts to nest in your hair."

Indignation flared. "You—"

"Yes, yes, all the bad names you can think of." A smile played at his lips as he jerked his chin toward the house. "Go, bathe, have some tea and eat something. If not because you smell, then because you *should.*"

"I don't *smell,*" Lea snapped. Out of everything, she knew that to be true.

"Indeed, but you look as though you might pass out any moment." With a frown, he gave her body an appraising look, but then his eyes softened with something akin to concern. "When was the last time you had a good night's sleep, my lady?"

Lea lips parted, the argument on the tip of her tongue. But the words froze as she considered his question. She had slept well enough every night in the palace, but upon recollection, Jonas' presence beside her and the lack of weaponry in her bedside table had prevented any *true* sleep. Then, once they'd arrived at Watoria, everyone had been so focused on recovering from battle and preparing for Iston that there'd been no time for proper rest or bathing.

As though her body realized that, a wave of exhaustion hit, causing her to wrap her fingers around the iron railing in front of her.

"You've never been in war, my lady, or even war adjacent. You should rest while you can." Ettrian looked around, taking in the gray Allanorian skies and sprawling expanse of Iston, which straddled the two northern territories. "Especially in a place so peaceful."

"And if our enemies decide to attack Iston?"

"The Istonians have powerful defensive magic protecting their borders, thanks to your queen's mother's family. Your enemies may know where Iston sits, but they do not have the tools to break through its magic."

"Cina Enrieth placed protective spells here?" Freya's mother had been dead for nearly seven years, but if there was one thing Lea had learned in her time as Freya's friend, it was that the Enrieth magic was strong and enduring.

Ettrian shook his head. "Her coven, but that was centuries before she came to be."

Lea frowned, casting her eyes outward, as if she might see wisps of Enrieth magic floating about. "How do you know this?"

"All magic tells a story, my lady. Lady Enrieth's mother, Selinda Cantor, had magic that was no exception." He waved a pale hand toward the area around the estate. "The Cantor Coven's magic is old and particularly dense. Nearly impenetrable."

"Can elves break through the magic?"

He gave her the same sly look he'd shown her moments ago. "Of course. Now, go get some rest. *Proper* rest."

She wanted to argue, but the desire to return home warred with the sudden need for rest and a hot meal. With a nod, Lea rubbed a hand across her brow, knowing he was right and hating it all the same. "Yes, I suppose you're not wrong. I'll go tell my mother we're not leaving just yet." Perida wouldn't be happy, of course. Everyone needed rest, *adequate* rest, but her mother and the other prisoners more so. They were malnourished, weak, and in some cases, injured. In her rush to leave, Lea hadn't considered her mother might not be physically up to the task.

She hadn't even considered whether *she* was up to the task, whether Tyna would be willing to leave her sister so soon, and whether any of them were mentally prepared for what they'd find when they reached home.

With a faint smile goodbye, she turned and walked back into the house, aiming directly for her chambers. With the uproar caused after Isadora killed Frederick Edrin, sleep had been impossible for everyone. Lea had no doubts Freya, Aer, and her other friends were realizing the same.

Lea's temper flared at the thought of the false human queen who'd spent so long with her own monarchs. She'd spent weeks thinking Dania Edrin, Jonas's sister, was disguised as the human queen in exile with Freya and Aerelius. Instead, the true Isadora had murdered Dania and carried out a different type of ruse.

She hated Isadora for it all, but most of all, her heart ached for Jonas at the loss of his sister, knowing he wouldn't be able to properly grieve until this battle was over. She knew what it was like to have to hide your grief, and it wasn't a fate she'd wish on anyone.

But Jonas was a kingdom away. There was nothing Lea could do to help him from Iston. She could only hope Willem hadn't told him of Dania's death or Isadora's duplicitousness. Ignorance would be best in Jonas' situation. Lea was certain of that.

When she turned down the hall toward her room, she smiled at the sight of Iska, the guard who'd been with her since childhood, standing sentry at her door. He'd traveled to Watoria with the other palace guards and they'd been happily reunited when she arrived with Ettrian. Having him back at her side was a little shred of normalcy that gave her an added layer of relief when she shut the door behind her.

Hopefully his presence would give her enough peace of mind to sleep peacefully for the first time in weeks.

THANK YOU!

Thank you so much for taking the time to read *The Valkyrie's Calling!* If you enjoyed it, I'd love it if you could take a minute to leave a quick review on any of the following sites:

Goodreads

Amazon

BookBub

Barnes & Noble

ABOUT THE AUTHOR

Lucy grew up "down the shore" in New Jersey, where her love of the mythological was born when her middle school English teacher introduced her to the Odyssey. After high school, she received Bachelor's degrees in Psychology and English Literature before continuing on to her Master's degree in Library and Information Science. In her spare time, Lucy loves to read, cook, and go hiking with her husband and two daughters. Chaos is her debut novel.

Stay up to date! Hop over to www.lucyroyauthor.com to sign up for Lucy's newsletter, follow her on social media, and read up on news and other bookish things!

ACKNOWLEDGMENTS

To my daughters. You're my constant source of inspiration, and I hope we can always have our little brainstorming sessions.

To my husband for supporting this dream of mine.

To my dad for his kick-ass map-making skills.

To my friends and family for their unwavering support. Every time I get the "when's the next book coming?" text (MOM), it pushes me to write just a bit more.

To Eric. You were pivotal in helping me make Tessa who she was, and your advice and guidance carried over into Freya's story. "What would Eric say?" will always be one of the first things I ask myself when I'm unsure of something, and for that, I'll be forever grateful.

To my betas, Shay, Katy, Kelly, and all of my ARC readers. None of you told me what you thought I wanted to hear, and my work is better for it.

To Theresa for letting me ask the tough questions.

To the readers who took the time to message me to tell me their thoughts. Hearing from readers is one of my favorite parts of this job.

To Denise Worisch for my gorgeous cover—thank you for putting up with my pickiness.

To Jenifer, my amazing editor, for putting up with my inability to write short books.

To the authors I re-read over and over that inspire me to keep going.

Finally, to all of the readers who took a chance on Tessa and have followed along to meet Freya. Writing started as a fun hobby but has become so much more. I'm so thankful for all of you who've taken the time to read my work and hope you'll all continue on this journey with me.